Praise for *On T*

'Jesmond explores the adrenaline ru... original mystery… A promising de... ...y *Times*
(A Best Crime Novel of the Month)

'Intriguing… The landscape of Cornwall, with its history of smuggling, makes a suitably mysterious backdrop' – *Herald*

'Evocative, compelling and pulse-pounding, with cliff-edge suspense, riveting action and a plot as tricksy as a dare-devil free-climb' – **Philippa East, author of CWA Dagger-shortlisted *Little White Lies***

'With complex characters battling their demons in the bleakest circumstances, *On The Edge* brings the dark side of Cornwall to life in this atmospheric thriller. A true page turner with unexpected twists' – **Sophie Flynn, author of *All My Lies***

'*On The Edge* is an outstanding debut. With distinctive characters, an intriguing plot and an enticing blend of action and atmosphere, it is a truly gripping read' – **Sarah Clarke, author of *A Mother Never Lies***

'Jenifry Shaw is smart, impulsive, bull-headed, and too daring for her own good. She might be a bit of a mess, but she never, ever backs down from a fight. In short, she's the girl you want at your side when stuff hits the fan and a fantastic character to anchor a new mystery series' – **Heather Young, author of *The Lost Girls***

'Thoroughly original – hooks you in from the start and keeps you guessing' – **Frances Quinn, author of *The Smallest Man***

Also by Jane Jesmond
On The Edge

CUT ADRIFT

JANE JESMOND

VERVE·BOOKS

First published in 2023 by VERVE Books,
an imprint of The Crime and Mystery Club Ltd.
Harpenden, UK

vervebooks.co.uk
@VERVE_Books

ISBN
978-0-85730-837-5 (Paperback)
978-0-85730-838-2 (Ebook)

2 4 6 8 10 9 7 5 3 1

Typeset in 11.4 on 14.6pt Garamond MT Pro
by Avocet Typeset, Bideford, Devon, EX39 2BP
Printed and bound by CPI Group (UK) Ltd, Croydon, CR0 4YY

For Nikki
With all my love

Prologue

A Beach in Northern Libya

Rania pushed a corner of the rug hiding her aside so she could watch the streetlights flash past through the car window above her. Uncle Eso drove faster now they'd left the stretch of road between Tripoli and Sabratha behind and were heading to Zuwara. She'd pull it back over her head if Uncle slowed down.

Aya, her younger sister, curled up in the other footwell, whined a complaint and wriggled until their mother stretched round from the passenger seat to pat the little girl and tell her to hush.

Rania felt a moment of irritation. Aya should be used to travelling like this by now. They moved every week or so from one of Mama's friends' homes to another and every time they were crammed into a footwell or squashed in the boot. Anyway, Aya, at six years old, was half Rania's size so she had nothing to complain about. Rania's legs and body had suddenly elongated over the last few months and, although Uncle Eso had done his best, cutting away the underneath of the rear seat to make more room for them both, Rania was cramped and hot. Her legs ached from keeping still and her skin was scratchy with the ever-present sand on the rubber mat that crept into every fold of her body. She shifted. The comfort of a change of position was good even if it never lasted for long. Except now her phone, shoved in her pocket, dug into her narrow hips.

For a moment she considered pulling it out, then stopped herself. What would be the point? Her mother had removed the sim card the night everything changed. She couldn't message her friends or play Fortnite or do anything except listen to the music she'd already downloaded.

Maybe she should do that. Because she could feel tears prickling behind her eyes as sharp as the sand that had worked its way up the cuffs of her blouse and into the crease of her elbow. When you couldn't move or make a noise, crying was tricky. She hated it when her nose ran over her face and onto whichever part of her body she was lying on. Thinking about the night everything changed always made her cry but she couldn't stop the memory unrolling.

She and Aya had been staying with her grandparents, while her parents were away on one of their trips. Mama had returned early and unexpectedly – and alone – with her arm in plaster and a look Rania had never seen before. Empty and distant, as though someone had peeled the skin off her face and stuck it on a robot.

Rania's nose filled and her mouth trembled. She'd have to listen to music and let the beat clean everything out of her head. But Uncle Eso barked as soon as she twisted round to get her phone, so she had no choice but to lie there and remember.

'We're leaving,' Mama had said, when Rania and Aya hurtled out of Jidda's kitchen at the sound of her voice. 'No! Don't hug me. My arm is broken. Rania, go to your bedroom and take Aya. You must pack a few things together. Just clothes. Only as much as you can fit in your backpacks. And quickly.'

'Nahla –' Jidda protested.

'Go, Rania.'

Something about Mama's tone made her do exactly as she was told.

When she started back downstairs, Mama and Jidda were talking in urgent whispers in the kitchen. She stopped to listen.

'Leave the girls here,' Jidda was saying. 'Your father and I will look after them. You know that.'

'No. They must come with me.'

'But their schooling, Nahla? Their friends?'

'No. They're not safe. They will be pawns in a game you don't understand.' Her mother's frantic tone frightened Rania. Mama's voice was normally soft and gentle even when her actual words were tough and uncompromising.

'This will pass,' her grandmother went on. 'If you lie low, people will forget.'

'They are not going to forget.'

'I told you no good would come of messing with politics. But you would only listen to Ibrahim. See where it has brought you. You are a woman on her own. Rania is twelve and Aya is six. What kind of life are you taking them into? They will be safer with us. Your father is not without influence here in Tripoli.'

'I say again, Umi, you don't understand. They aren't safe.'

Rania's brain tried to make sense of what she'd heard.

'Umi.' Mama's voice again. 'I wish you'd leave too. You could still get out of Libya. Take a plane. I have friends who'd help you once you were away. Morwenna would welcome you and she knows many people who –'

'Leave! You want us to leave our home? Your father's job at the university? Our friends? You don't know what you're saying.'

'Mama,' Aya called from the top of the stairs. 'Can I bring one doll? Rania said I couldn't.'

Mama and Jidda came out of the kitchen and looked at them.

'Why can't you shut up for once?' Rania hissed at Aya, then picked up her bag and walked down the rest of the stairs, trying not to wonder what Jidda had meant by Mama being a woman on her own.

Maybe she'd known then her father was dead. Or maybe the

knowledge was forced into her mind over the following days, weeks and months, by the sheer weight of hints in Mama's words, of her expression when Aya asked when Babba was coming, of his name murmured by the weeping hosts who greeted Mama each time the family moved, and by the way they stroked Rania's face, with the bony nose and deep-set eyes she'd inherited from her father. She was certain Mama hadn't told her Babba was dead. Surely she'd remember that? Except her memories of the last months were rocky and vague. She'd lost track of the order of events and without a timeline to tie them together they were loose in her head.

The one constant of these months was Aya's endless chatter. There was no escape from it in the cramped rooms they hid in. It stressed Mama, who hated noise. It was one of her things. Even the jangle of Rania's bracelets was too much. So Rania tried to keep Aya amused, to play her stupid games and tell her to hush every time she laughed too loudly. That was Rania's overriding memory. That and the fear in those dark rooms with closed shutters pressing down on them like stones pressed white grubs into the earth.

Last night, it had changed. Someone had arrived unexpectedly, during the curfew, knocking quietly on the door of Uncle Eso's apartment. Uncle Eso came and fetched Mama, and for a wild moment Rania thought it might be Babba. She tried to listen, easing the bedroom door ajar, but Aya, woken by her mother's sudden departure from the bed they shared, had started to cry and Rania had to go and calm her. She heard her mother's sharp wail of 'No', and afterwards the broken breaths of her weeping. They'd talked for hours and, in the morning, Uncle Eso told her they were going to Zuwara.

In the car, Rania let herself remember the holidays they'd spent at Zuwara. The sand, too soft for sandcastles but gentle beneath her toes. An endless strip of it, dotted by palm trees and beach huts selling pastries, sinking into the turquoise sea. She'd like to swim in the sea again and sit on the beach afterwards and sift the sand between her fingers and dream of her future. The sort of dreams she would never tell anyone. About when she would be a famous singer touring her first album of songs with the reviews calling her the spokesperson of her generation, a poet for everybody, like her mother. About the houses she would buy in far-flung places and stay in quietly until someone recognised her quite by chance in a local shop and she'd have to smile and say, yes, she was Rania Shebani.

Uncle Eso, in the seat in front of Rania, shifted suddenly and his weight pressed into Rania's knees. The car swung right and raced across bumpy ground.

'Road block,' Uncle said. 'I don't think they saw us. We're close now.'

They continued on little roads and the streetlights stopped appearing in the dark sky. Uncle rolled down the window and Rania heard the sound of the sea. The contrast between her recollections of Zuwara and their fear-filled mode of travel began to worry her.

Mama had said they were going to Zuwara to take a boat. Memories of golden days on the water had slipped into her mind but now she realised she should have asked Mama what she meant.

Not that Mama would have told her.

The thought took her by surprise. As did the feeling of resentment it provoked. She loved Mama but she couldn't shake off the feeling she should share more with her. Actually Mama didn't share anything with Rania, except the kind of soothing answers she gave Aya that meant nothing. It was all very well to be *still waters running deep* as Babba called Mama but… Babba. Oh, Babba.

She gave up the fight not to cry.

The car stopped and they eased themselves out. They were on a beach. It was night but they were not alone. Rania stared at the crowd sitting on the sand as Uncle took their bags out of the boot. Aya moaned about the dark and Mama, a stranger in the black abaya and niqab she'd worn for the journey, whispered to her. A couple of men detached themselves from the group and came up to Uncle, sticking their faces into his. Angry words Rania couldn't hear passed between them and the men shook threatening fingers, but Uncle stood his ground. Afterwards he spoke to Mama.

'They say I must go. But everything is fine. The boat will be here soon.'

'The boat. Where is the boat?' Aya's voice cut through the silence. Faces turned to stare. There must, Rania thought, be a hundred pairs of eyes looking at them. Prickles of fear traced paths up and down her arms.

'Nahla, you must keep the child quiet.' Uncle's voice was panicky.

He embraced them one by one. Whispering messages in their ears. He told Aya to stay silent. Rania knew because the little girl put her finger to her lips as he spoke. He asked Rania to look after her mother and her sister. 'You are a big girl now, *habibti*. And I couldn't be prouder of you if I was really your uncle. When I look at you, I see your father. Your mother needs you to be strong like he was. You understand?'

She nodded because she thought she did. It was true Uncle Eso wasn't really a relative but if Rania had had an uncle she would have liked it to be him. As he strode away into the dark, she wanted to run after him. Back to the car, back to the footwell. She wanted to leave this beach of unnaturally still people behind. Go to Jidda's. And to school. And her friends. But before she could move, Mama pushed her down to sit on the sand with all the others and the sound of Uncle's car creeping over the stones and away told her she'd left it too late.

A stir among the men encircling the crouching and sitting people. In the distance, the noise of splashing. A few flashes of torchlight revealed a large inflatable boat coming towards them. It bucked and rolled on the choppy sea, so unlike the rippling blue-green waters of Rania's memories.

The crowd stood as one. Rania realised they were all waiting for this boat. The boat for her family must be coming later. A proper boat like she remembered, with neat bunks that doubled as seats and a table that folded away, a little kitchen with a fridge where Babba kept his squirming bait despite Mama's laughing complaints.

She looked up at Mama ready to ask, but Mama had stripped off her niqab. Her eyes and mouth gaped holes in her face.

'Mama.'

'Hush.'

Mama put Aya down, dragged the abaya off and picked up their bags, heading with the crowd into the water and pushing Aya before her.

'Quick,' she said to Rania.

A man seized the bags from her and threw them back on the sand, gesturing at Aya with what Rania realised was a gun. It was black and metallic, and she didn't think it was a toy. Mama hesitated then picked up Aya and plunged into the water, leaving the bags behind.

Something split inside Rania as she ran after her, only vaguely aware of the tears running down her face. The beach shelved steeply and the water reached Rania's waist quickly. Ahead of her, the first of the crowd were at the boat and hauling themselves aboard as it tilted from side to side under their weight. How would they all get on? There wasn't enough room.

The sea was up to Rania's neck by the time she got near. Her feet slipped away as she stretched up to grab the boat's side but a man leant down and seized her, lifted her up and inside where the rocking knocked her off her feet. She crawled out of the way. Mama held Aya up to the same man but her sister, shocked into silence up to now, panicked and started to scream. The man swung his arm back, the movement casual then sharply forward until it connected with Aya's head in a resounding slap and knocked her head sideways. Before the little girl could react, he slapped her again.

'Be quiet,' he said.

And she was.

Mama dragged herself in and the three of them squashed together. Mama gathered Aya to her, burying her in her body briefly then holding her away to examine her face. In the dark it was difficult to see the damage. Aya's lip was cut and one eye was closed. The bruising would show later. But it was her other eye, unfocussed and wide, like the eyes of the butchers' dead and bloody sheep's heads at the Friday market near Jidda's, and the complete stillness of her face that shocked Rania. She wrapped her arms around her sister, whispering comforting words and hoping Aya would answer in her too shrill voice so Rania could tell her gently to hush while she hugged her tighter and promised nothing bad would happen again. But Aya was limp and motionless in her arms as the boat set off.

At first Rania was sick. A lot. And glad to be near the side. Later, the second night, she thought, she was less happy there. The boat had softened, its edges no longer rigid, and waves broke over the top and swilled round her feet. She was afraid of tumbling out until exhaustion took over from fear and she slipped into a peaceful state, unaware of even the wilder splashes. She dreamed of her songs. Of Babba and Jidda. She chatted to her friends. She wandered as far into her head as she could, away from the growing panic around her as the boat sank deeper and deeper into the sea.

So, when the ship appeared in the distance, the shouts didn't wake her. Nor did the orange lifejackets hurled down to them from above. It was only when Mama shook her and thrust her head and arms into the rough plastic vest that she came to and saw, towering above, the dark blue hull with white writing emblazoned on the side. *Sea-Watch*, she read. And then a little further along, *Amsterdam*. She knew Amsterdam from a jigsaw of Europe Jidda had. Amsterdam was in the Netherlands, with a picture of a girl in wooden shoes and a hat with curly horns.

'Are we going to Amsterdam, Mama?' she asked.

Mama didn't answer but the woman in front turned.

'Malta,' she said. 'I think we're going to Malta. Here, take this.' She passed Rania two of the silver blankets that were dropping from the boat above.

Rania didn't think Malta was on Jidda's jigsaw and Mama's face, locked with numbness, revealed nothing. She wrapped a blanket round herself and one round Mama and Aya. Something her father said came back to her. *You must always thank a stranger for their kindness, habibti. Otherwise they might choose not to help the next person who needs them.* She waited for her mother to thank the woman and, when she didn't, Rania smiled back.

'Thank you,' she said.

Aya clung to Mama like a limpet but she was quiet. Not that it mattered anymore because all around them there was noise. Sailors called from above and answers were shouted back.

'We're going to Malta,' Rania told Aya, because no one else was going to. The little girl didn't seem to hear her.

'Mama,' Rania repeated. 'We're going to Malta.'

But her mother seemed to be unaware of Rania's existence. Her gaze was focussed on something far, far away.

An acid flame of anger flickered in Rania's stomach.

PART ONE

Spain

One

I fled Cornwall in the quiet season. The overwintering curlews were still pincering the mud flats in the estuary for worms and shellfish with no thought of heading off to their breeding grounds in Scandinavia and Russia, while the skies were empty of swallows still sunning themselves in Africa. In a few weeks the changing seasons would drive the birds to migrate along the tried and trusted routes to their summer homes but I could wait no longer. My body twitched with unspent energy.

My hands, badly lacerated when someone tried to kill me at the end of last year, had healed and hours in the gym had restored me to peak fitness. I'd even been parkouring in Plymouth. Sensible parkouring with a club dedicated to 'developing the strength and balance that would enable practitioners to interact with their environment safely', to quote their website. This was code for *Strictly no nutters allowed.*

So I'd kept quiet about my history.

But now, it was time to go climbing again like I'd promised myself. Except not in Cornwall. It had witnessed too many of the crazy escapades I'd turned my back on. Plus I was staying at Tregonna, my childhood home, with my brother Kit and his wife and small daughter. I didn't want Kit to know what I was doing or, worse, to offer to come along. This was between the rock and me.

So I went to Spain. It was cheap and warm. It had plenty of mountains and it was nearby. My choice had nothing to do with a postcard I'd been sent. A postcard of a bar with a cork ceiling in Alájar, a little village nestling in the lower slopes of the Sierra Morena. That was pure coincidence.

I picked up a battered campervan from a second-hand dealership in Malaga and headed northwest through flat fields of olive trees, grey-green and dusty under a milky-blue sky. The austere beauty of the high sierras called me and when the mountains appeared between gaps in the softer hills, my blood sang in my ears and I knew I'd done the right thing.

My days were spent on the rock. Climbing. Safely. All kit checked and backed up and I used a top rope or fixed anchors as I went, even if it meant a long hike at the beginning and end of each day. Not that I use the ropes to climb. They're only there to save me if I fall. It's called free climbing but there's nothing free about it, really. You're trussed up like a chicken ready for roasting.

The individual climbs have blurred into a single memory that's purely physical: the roughness of the stone against my fingers and its coolness; its shape against the sky, curved here and jagged there; and my muscles tightening and loosening as I climbed. Over the days the itchiness seeped out of me and left calm behind.

Most evenings I was too tired to do more than snatch a meal at a local café and use their internet to decide where to go next. At night I parked the van on the side of roads that clung to the mountains so that when I opened the door in the morning the view rushed in to fill the space. It was as beautiful as I'd hoped it would be.

And in the quiet I thought about the recent past.

My love of climbing had been overwhelmed by the urge for thrill, for those magic moments when adrenalin sparkled through my veins and caressed my skin. I'd never felt so alive as I did then. However, other people had got hurt in my chase after excitement so I'd made myself give up climbing completely, until a mad race across the moors in Cornwall, fleeing for my life, had left me with no alternative but to escape by climbing. The other magic had returned then. Not the wild thrill of danger but the quieter happiness of moving in tune with the cliff face, the intertwining of fingers and limbs and body with the rock in a dance of equals. I'd known then I needed climbing back in my life. I'd sworn to climb alone, though. No one else would ever get hurt because of me. These days in the mountains in Spain had shown I could succeed. I realised I'd made my peace with the rock.

But as always when I remembered the night on the moors, Nick came into my thoughts. Nick Crawford, the undercover policeman, who'd escaped with me and disappeared straight afterwards, whisked away by his bosses and never heard from since.

Apart from the postcard he'd sent.

I hadn't thought of him for days. No, that was a lie. He'd been in my head like the constant hum of traffic in London you learned to ignore. Unanswered questions, I told myself. You can't get him out of your mind because he arrived in mysterious circumstances and left as suddenly and secretively. That's all. But part of me knew I'd travelled hundreds of miles to Spain on the whisper of a promise. A shared moment on a dark hillside, full of possibilities, when Nick had said he'd drink to me in a bar with a ceiling carved from cork. Wet and exhausted from our flight across the moors, we'd said goodbye then and I'd watched him walk away to the waiting police car and disappear into the night.

I pulled the postcard out of my jeans pocket. It had reached me weeks later, when Gregory, my hometown's retired lighthouse keeper who Nick had trusted, gave it to me although there was no address and no Jen Shaw written anywhere. Nor was it signed. It could have been from anyone to anyone but Gregory knew it was for me and I knew it was from Nick because the picture showed the inside of a typical Spanish bar. Nothing special except for the intricate and fabulous cork ceiling, carved like brown lace shaped into flowers. There might be a few bars in Alájar but there'd only be one with such a ceiling. Four words were written on the postcard. *Wish you were here.*

And when I first read the words, I knew I'd been waiting for this. That, in my heart of hearts, I hadn't thought our goodbyes were forever. The postcard was an invitation but one that was whispered so no one else could hear.

And I hadn't known what to do. I knew nothing about Nick really. It might be fun to find out, it might be exciting, but it might turn out to be a big mistake. So I'd waited.

But now it was time to decide. Alájar was only a day's drive away and my return flight was fast approaching. I took a deep breath and tore the postcard in half. Nick Crawford – if that was his name – was probably trouble. I didn't need any more trouble. Not now I'd conquered so many of my demons. He was best relegated to the pile of might-have-beens.

I was happy as I was.

The next day I climbed a great granite face overlooking a forested valley. The view was magnificent and distracting. I kept on stopping to gaze at the distant peaks crowned with late snow that poured dark green trees down their slopes, the flow only broken by spurs of rock like the one I was edging up. It was a straightforward climb. Dull, really. To my side I noticed another way up via a long thin fracture leading to an overhanging cliff, easily reached with a series of finger locks and foot smears, but getting over the jutting rock at the top of the overhang would be a serious move. I'd have to leap for the next hold. For a moment my body wouldn't touch the rock and I'd fly through the air. The old sense of boredom curled an arm round me and whispered in my ear that it might be fun.

Except I was clipped into a top rope and it wouldn't reach. I'd have to climb down, walk up the path at the side of the face and move it, then climb the tedious pitch again.

The urge faded.

Until my hands brushed the clasp of my harness and the image of them undoing it slipped into my brain.

I didn't, although the effort of denial shocked me. It coated my skin with a film of sweat as I made myself chalk up and move on.

At the top I sat on the grass and stared out at the rows of mountains descending towards the coast to the south and Portugal to the west. The sun was still high in the sky and its warmth licked my skin. Eagles circled far above, as silent as was everything else. No buzz of insects. No goats' bells jangled. I was too high for them.

I thought about what had just happened. I'd nearly blown it, nearly let the adrenalin junkie out of the bag I'd put her in after all the grief she'd caused last year. And, for the life of me, I couldn't work out why it had happened now. Now that my life was as ordered as it could be.

And Nick came into my thoughts again, dragging with him the cloud of unanswered questions. Maybe I was unsettled because of that. Maybe I needed to find some answers.

I didn't trust myself to climb any more so I headed south but, before I reached the main roads to Malaga and the airport, I turned west into gentler countryside where soft hills were lined with pastures of oak – cork oaks, stripped of their bark below head height, and bare holm oaks whose acorns carpeted the ground beneath where a few wild flowers braved the mists lying in the hollows. The acorns were for the pigs, I was told by the owner of a bar where I stopped for lunch. The pig was king here – coddled, acorn-fed money on legs – and he carved me a plate of their ham, deep red and shiny but so thin I could see the sharp outline of the village chapel through it.

I reached Alájar late that evening. A little village strung out along a river. Its name meant 'stone' in Arabic and a rocky cliff, pockmarked with caves, shot up from the forest at its edge. I parked the van on its outskirts and slept.

The owners of the small café I chose for breakfast spoke English well. They knew a lot about the tourist sites in Alájar but they didn't know of any British people. Not ones who lived here. There were lots of British tourists, most of the year, although the summer months could be quiet. It was very hot then and people preferred the coast, but they hadn't been here long themselves, only a couple of years, so they didn't know everybody. They came from the city. From Malaga. And it took time to fit into a village like this. Did I realise? I nodded and said that I did.

After breakfast, I took the road that wound up the side of the cliff above Alájar and looked down at the village. It was the shape of a lizard basking in the sun. Not that the sun was shining. Today was wintry and damp. The white-painted houses with their red roofs nestled in a forest of bare-branched trees. I wondered again at the strangeness of Nick being here, in the middle of deepest, rural Andalusia, where properties outside the villages and towns rarely had mains electricity and people could remember the time before the roads were built. A flicker of doubt tainted my excitement.

In the centre of Alájar, the main bar overlooked a square lined with plane trees for shade in summer. No need for that this evening. It had drizzled all afternoon. Water still dripped from the branches and mist rolled down the hills towards us. A few hardy tourists sat outside. Walkers, I thought, judging from their waterproof trousers and thick boots. They had the smug look of people who'd hiked long miles during the day.

The bar was called El Corcho. It took me a while to realise this because the other signs that plastered its front, advertising Spanish beer and local fiestas, crowded out the simple writing above the door. It took even longer for my brain to work out Corcho might mean cork.

Inside, the ceiling was everything I'd expected and the bar was quiet. Too early for locals, I thought. The barman, a fearsome man with a shaved head, earrings and arms covered with tattoos as intricate as the bar's ceiling, glanced up. His name was Angel according to the only other person sitting inside, an elderly man watching a football match on the TV.

'Good evening.' His English accent was good and his voice much gentler than his appearance. I realised he wasn't much older than me.

'Coffee, please. With milk.'

I steer clear of alcohol because I don't like the places it takes me to.

'Bad weather for walking.' He gestured at the sky. 'You are hiking?'

'No. Climbing.'

His eyes stopped flicking round the bar and the tables outside and focussed on me.

'On your own?'

'Yes.'

I picked up my coffee and prepared to move away. The last thing I needed was someone hitting on me.

I chose a seat right at the front by the glass windows and began to wish I hadn't come here. I'd give Nick a couple of hours. No more. If he didn't turn up by then, I'd leave. And tomorrow I'd go home. Forget about him and his stupid postcard because he needed to play his part too. He'd sent an invitation and he should be here every night on the off chance I might accept.

Angel, now on the phone, gave me a quick, hard look as I sat and I glared back at him. He could get lost too. He turned his back on me.

Ten minutes later, the church bell rang nine o'clock, the lights outside the bar came on, reflecting in the puddles on the square, and the locals emerged. Old men shuffled out of their tall houses and farmers in muddy cars emerged from narrow, cobbled streets built with donkeys in mind. A trickle of professionals who must have jobs in the nearest city arrived, the men slick in designer jeans and sweaters and the women with their endlessly long legs clattering over the cobbles in vertiginous heels. They gathered outside the bar, kissed each other or shook hands, spilled into the road and forced the cars to swerve round them.

Something familiar about the back of a driver's head, sticking out of a car window as he reversed into a narrow space in the square, jolted the pit of my stomach. I thought it was Nick and, when he got out of the car, I saw I was right. His dark curly hair was long and a coating of not-quite-beard darkened his jaw making him look untidier but more relaxed and open than when I last saw him.

I thought I liked it.

His car was similar to the battered thing he'd driven in Cornwall apart from the clutch of ornaments hanging from the rear-view mirror. Every Spanish car had them. Be careful, I warned myself. He was a chameleon, changing his colour and ways to fit in wherever he went. I thought I'd had a glimpse of the man underneath in Cornwall.

At least I hoped so.

He leaped the low wall separating the square from the road without looking and went straight to Angel at the bar. Their heads bent forward as they spoke and someone jostled my table. I turned away and reached out to grab my drink. When I looked back, Nick was already walking towards me through the crowd of people inside, his expression politely blank, which was annoying because now I'd never know what his first reaction on seeing me was. I'd never know if he'd hoped I'd be here.

He came over to my table and I felt the heat rise in my face as embarrassed thoughts raced through my mind.

He smiled. A smile with a hint of amusement. Like all the times he'd smiled before.

I smiled back.

'Is this seat free?' he asked, pulling the chair from the table.

I looked him up and down, taking in the stained jeans, the crumpled shirt sleeves, rolled up to show tanned forearms overlaid with dark hair, and the blunt fingers. A shadow of uncertainty flitted across his face when I didn't reply. I was pleased about that.

'Hello, Jenifry Shaw,' he said. 'And welcome to Alájar. What brings you here?'

Good question, I thought.

'Curiosity,' I said and nodded for him to sit. 'Simple curiosity.' And in case he hadn't got my meaning. 'Nothing except that.'

He bowed his head in an oddly formal manner.

'Then I hope you'll stay for a while. Let me show you around. It would be my pleasure and the least I can do. After all, you did save my life.'

Two

Nick did show me around. It was a whirlwind of sightseeing, every day crammed with visits to castles and churches and mosques. We went to museums, where I learned the region's history, and down caves of weird crystal formations. We walked for miles along the walled dirt tracks, only wide enough for two donkeys to pass, that had connected the villages and towns for centuries, and through the oak and sweet chestnut woods lining the slopes Alájar nestled in. We wandered round the market in the nearest town buying enormous juicy olives and fingering the gaudy, joyous pottery.

One day we drove to Seville and visited the Alcázar Palace with its myriad of gardens and afterward ate sweet, crispy *torta de aceite* on the steps of the Spanish pavilion while we cheered students from the local flamenco school as they danced for the tourists.

Once we spent the evening sitting in the square at Alájar, watching the bats swoop in and out of the caves in the vast cliff towering over the village and listening to the animals in the forest. But mainly we went to the bar or one of the little restaurants, where everyone called Nick 'Nico' and chatted to him while I smiled and wished I'd paid more attention to Spanish lessons at school.

For all intents and purposes, I discovered, Nick was Spanish. His grandparents came from Alájar, along with their parents and their parents' parents. His family, the Carrascos, had roots in the area that had been unbroken for centuries until Nick's mother, an only child, married a Scot and left. However, Nick had spent every holiday in this remote corner of Andalusia as well as his last two years of school. And his grandparents had left him their house when they died. He was related to a great number of people here; Angel from the bar turned out to be a second cousin.

He was a wonderful companion, knowledgeable and amusing, brimming with little stories about his childhood and the places we visited and the people we met. However, after a week or so, I began to wonder if he was playing yet another role – the perfect and charming host enjoying himself as he showed a friend around his beloved home. Not that I'd been to his actual home. He picked me up and dropped me back at my campervan, parked now in an old farm where a group of hippies lived off-grid. There was water from an old well and enough electricity from their windmill to keep my phone and laptop charged. Hot showers were out unless I went down the hillside and used the ones in the bar.

Some subjects, I realised, were forbidden. He never talked about his work. Nor his family in Scotland. I didn't even know if his real name was Crawford – I suspected not. He was known locally as Señor Carrasco, his grandparents' name.

'Do you feel Spanish or English?' I asked him one afternoon as we were driving back from the market at Aracena. Today the skies were clear and piano music filled the car. It was one of the few things I'd discovered about Nick. He loved music and it accompanied him everywhere. Sometimes it was classical; sometimes ballads and rock anthems from the past fifty years. He adored the music of Andalusia but also had a strange liking for punk music from the late seventies and early eighties.

'Don't you mean Spanish or Scottish?' he replied.

'You don't have a Scottish accent.'

'I can.'

'Yes, but you don't.'

'Not when I'm talking to you. But I do when I talk to my... to Scots.'

I half thought he'd been going to say his family but before I could ask him about them, he began an amusing anecdote about an elderly farmer who'd lived in Linares de la Sierra, the little village of white houses we were passing, and how he'd lost his pigs in a storm.

I laughed when Nick finished but my heart wasn't in it. I was sure he'd diverted me from asking about his family. It wasn't the first time either.

I cast a look at his face but it was a blank and his eyes were fixed on the road ahead. His hands moved smoothly over the steering wheel, gripping and relaxing as he guided the car round the twists of this serpentine road.

Shit! Why did I find him so attractive? There was no point denying I did. No point denying that I wanted him to be more than a charming tour guide. That my body felt his nearness like it felt the heat of sun-warmed granite without touching it. I wondered how his skin would feel against mine. Would its touch ripple a shock along my nerves? Would it be warm and smooth over muscle and bone? Would it...

'How's Morwenna?' he asked suddenly and when I didn't reply straightaway, added, 'Your mother, I mean.'

I took my eyes off his hands and saw he was looking at me. Suddenly breathless and wondering if I was blushing, I gathered my thoughts together fast, glad he couldn't read them.

'She's fine.'

'Good.' He cast me another look. 'I like your mother. She reminds me of one of my aunts.'

An aunt, I thought. She might not be his immediate family but it was the closest he'd come to talking about them. I opened my mouth to ask about her but he got in first.

'What's Morwenna up to?'

'I wish I knew.'

'You don't?' He laughed. 'How very typical!'

'What, of me or of her?'

'Both of you.'

'My mother's crazy. You know that.'

'And you're not?'

'No. Well, I'm not crazy like her. Anyway I don't know what she's up to. She's gone off and we don't know where.'

'She's left Tregonna?'

Nick sounded startled and I wasn't surprised. Tregonna was Ma's beloved family home in Cornwall and her refuge against a world she claimed had lost its way. It was hard to imagine her leaving but it had come at the end of a long and stressful time, culminating in a terrible row with Kit when he'd discovered our father still owned Tregonna although Ma and Pa had split up years ago. After the row, Ma had stormed out and not come back.

'Kit's trying to find her,' I said. 'He needs her to sign a few things but we've heard nothing from her except a postcard.'

'Nothing but a postcard?'

His surprise annoyed me. Or maybe it was talking about Ma that irritated me.

'Yes, a postcard. People in my life seem to think it's an acceptable way to communicate.'

He didn't react. He seemed lost in his thoughts. I wished I knew what they were but he was so difficult to read.

'Gregory might know where she is,' he said, breaking the silence that had crept between us. 'I bet she's been in touch with him.'

Why hadn't we thought of that? Ma was very close to Gregory, the ancient and retired lighthouse keeper who'd given me Nick's postcard. He lived down the road from Tregonna in a tiny cottage at the base of our local lighthouse. She'd have been unlikely to go off without a word to him although she might do that to her children.

'How is Gregory anyway?' Nick asked.

'The same really. Social services tried to persuade him to go into sheltered housing in St Austell recently but he refused. He'd be lost away from the lighthouse. It reminds him who he is.'

The lighthouse might be an anchor for his identity but I wasn't sure Gregory knew *when* he was any more. He confused the present and the past although he lived in both with equal determination. A couple of times he'd mistaken me for Ma, and Kit said he often called him Charlie, our father's name.

'I hope your brother's keeping an eye on him.'

Nick had liked Gregory, I remembered, and even more strangely, Gregory had liked Nick.

'Everybody is,' I said shortly, knowing Nick's concern hadn't stretched to keeping in touch with Gregory himself.

Forming fleeting relationships then disappearing was part of his job. He must be used to it. Maybe too used to it. Too used to playing a part and too used to keeping his barriers in place. For the millionth time, I wondered what I was doing here.

'I'll be flying home soon,' I said.

I hadn't meant to say it but as soon as I did, I knew it was the right thing. I needed to know whether or not Nick wanted me to stay. Nothing more.

He was silent for a long few minutes during which I felt stupidly sad and confused, then he pulled into a small lane off the main road and turned the car round.

'What are you doing?'

'If you're going back soon, there's one thing we haven't done and tonight's the perfect night. We're going up into the mountains. Are you ready for an adventure?'

He smiled at me with eyes that held a thousand questions and my heartbeat quickened in response.

'No,' I said and straight afterwards I wasn't sure if the *No* was for him or for the flicker of excitement inside me. 'I don't do adventure anymore,' I added.

'Seriously?'

'Yup.'

His smile faded.

'What's happened? The Jenifry Shaw I met in Cornwall, she was up for anything.'

'Well, this one isn't. She's learned her lesson. She doesn't do adventure.'

'That's a pity.'

'I thought you didn't like climbing anyway,' I said. 'You told me you hated heights.'

He laughed. 'I should have guessed mountains and adventure meant climbing to you. I want to take you stargazing. Not climbing. And not dangerous.'

'Stargazing?'

'Yes. It's going to be a clear night and the mountains above us, the Sierra Morena, are part of one of the largest natural starlight reserves in Europe. There's no light pollution so the skies are beautiful. You must have noticed when you were climbing up there.'

I hadn't. But then I'd been tired in the evenings and preoccupied with planning the next day's climb. I'd never thought to look up because you can't see the rock in the dark.

Stargazing. Why not?

'OK,' I said. 'Let's go.'

He drove up into the mountains and into the fading light with music crooning in the background. Neither of us spoke as the setting sun flamed orange and sank behind the sharp black silhouettes of mountain ridges, and night surrounded us. We stopped by a little cabin in the middle of nowhere and got out of the car.

'Don't look up,' Nick said as he turned on a torch. 'I want you to see the stars when there's absolutely no light.' He rolled a rock over and picked up a key from under it. 'This place belongs to a friend who lets me use it. I often stay here for a couple of weeks when I come back from...'

I wondered if he was going to mention his work.

'When I come back from a job,' he said. 'I need a bit of time to... It's hard to explain but being up here rinses the person I've been living out of me.'

The torchlight flickered over his face and I realised he was staring intently at me. Once again my breath vanished and my blood thinned until it felt as though my heart was beating water through my veins.

Who, I wondered, was left when the character he'd been living had drained away?

He unlocked the cabin door and we went into a dark room. Torchlight picked out bunk beds and an iron stove.

'Close your eyes,' Nick said.

I obeyed and he put his hands on my shoulders and guided me across the room and through a door. I felt the chill of a breeze on my skin and knew I was outside.

'Count to fifty, then open them.'

His hands lingered on my shoulders and their warmth was the only thing I felt.

When I opened my eyes, a rush of glory made me gasp. No need to look up because we were already standing high on a wooden deck built into the mountainside. The sky wrapped the night all around us. It wasn't the dark emptiness seen in the city. Instead it glimmered with millions of stars. Some were distinct and bright but most clustered together to create great washes of light sweeping through the air. It was a universe of beauty and the sheer vastness of it disorientated me. I felt as though I was falling through space and I staggered.

Nick's hands tightened on my shoulders. 'You understand why you couldn't go home without seeing this.'

'I do.'

He talked about the stars as we gazed. Names of constellations and how far away they were. How long the light had taken to reach us and how the earth moved through the cosmos like a giant ship, dragged this way and that as though by invisible currents and winds, so that the view changed with the hours and the seasons and the years. I listened but his words flowed through me so I remembered little of what he said. Only the tone of his voice, soft and quiet and so right in the face of such magnificence, stayed with me.

We watched for a long time until the chill reached my bones.

'You're shaking.'

'I'm shivering. It's freezing.'

'Wait.'

He came back with a blanket and wrapped it round us both, gripping me tightly to his warmth. The trembling wouldn't stop. So, in the end, I turned my back on the stars and wriggled round to face him. The starlight reflected in his eyes as his fingers traced the outline of my face.

I'd guessed right. His touch sent quivers along my skin.

'Jenifry Shaw,' he said.

I stretched up and kissed him.

I woke slowly. Clear, fresh morning light came through the open door leading onto the deck. The stove we'd lit at some point during the night had gone out but I was cocooned in the mess of bunk bed mattresses and blankets we'd pulled onto the floor. Memories of last night wafted through my thoughts and I smiled.

I was alone, though. Where was Nick? Definitely not in this one-roomed cabin.

His voice, impatient and almost angry, cut through my drowsiness. He was arguing with someone outside on the deck. On his phone, I realised as he strode past the door, dressed only in a pair of jeans. A faint sense of disappointment clouded my comfort. I should get up but I couldn't be bothered to move. I caught glimpses of Nick as he walked up and down outside. He stopped eventually in the doorway and muttered explosive OKs down the phone as the skin on his back shifted with each breath and gleamed in the cold sunlight.

Tension seeped back into my muscles and tightened them. The tangle of rugs and mattresses looked tawdry in the cool morning light. The cabin's wooden rafters dripped with cobwebs. I felt a sudden urge to go for a run then a long shower.

Nick came in.

'We have to leave.' His voice was impatient with barely controlled frustration.

'Now?'

'Yes.' He made a big effort to speak calmly. 'I'm sorry. But I have to go to London and fast. There's a plane I must catch later today.'

'Work?' I asked but all I got in reply was a terse nod.

We flung our clothes on and tidied the cabin without speaking. We didn't speak during the journey either but he was concentrating on driving as fast as he could, flinging the car round the bends we'd driven up so hopefully the night before. His phone automatically started playing music. Some playlist of great film themes. But he swore and switched it over to a Spanish talk radio station.

I felt a bit blank really.

'I'm sorry,' he said again as he pulled into the old farm where I parked my campervan. 'If I had a choice, I wouldn't go.'

A sneaky little voice murmured that there was always a choice.

'No problem,' I said.

'You don't mind then?'

'Of course not.'

I suspected I was lying.

'It should only be for a couple of days. Maybe three?'

It sounded like a question but I wasn't sure. Go on, I thought, ask me if I'll still be here. And, above all, tell me you hope I will be.

He didn't but looked at me as though waiting for me to respond.

So far, I'd done all the running in this relationship – if you could call it that. I sodding well trekked all the way to Spain and came looking for him. I was even the one who made the first move last night. Well, I wasn't going to hang around any longer unless he made an effort.

'I might be gone when you get back,' I said.

He muttered something under his breath.

'What?'

'You've satisfied your curiosity then,' he said with an edge to his voice.

'What do you mean?'

'It doesn't matter.'

'Fine.'

I got out of the car and went to slam the door behind me but he reached out an arm and held it open.

'Jen,' he called.

I waited while he got out.

He pulled a hand through his hair. 'I'm sorry,' he said. 'I don't know what else to say. I'll be back as soon as I can. I hate leaving things like this but I have to go *now*.'

'Sure,' I said and strode off into the hippies' farm.

I might have cried if I hadn't been so angry. With myself as much as with Nick.

I made tea, a fragrant brew of Indian spice-infused black tea, and sipped it. I should probably sleep but I didn't think the emotions in my gut would let me. I was upset and I was angry about being upset because I had no reason to be. Nick had a job and he'd had to go do it. The timing was unfortunate, but last night had probably only been about sex. Nice but not important. Very nice… but still unimportant. It had been fun and the stargazing had been splendid but nothing more.

I should go home.

Except going home meant tackling all the things I'd put off to come here. I needed to find a job as my money wasn't going to last forever. I needed to do something about my flat. I'd been going to sell it to get Kit out of a financial hole but Pa had come to the rescue instead. However, preparing to sell it had made me realise how little I wanted to stay in London. There were so many decisions I needed to make. So many dreary, life-sucking decisions.

And then I had a much better idea.

Three

I didn't go home and I didn't hang around for Nick. Instead I went back up into the sierras, to the crag I'd been climbing when I frightened myself. I parked on the road beneath, lugged my kit up the footpath through the pine forest to the top and set up anchors.

I spent a week preparing. First I explored the face, trying all the possible ways up until I was sure I'd found the best one. And then I climbed it, rapped down and climbed it again. And again and again. I refined every move, paring each one back until it was pure. I practised and practised until each sequence was imprinted on my brain and body. My life shrank down to the rock. I thought of nothing else. Not Nick. Not Ma. Not the future. I knew every fold and ripple of the rock, where it was rough and where it was smooth. I knew how it changed during the day. The chill of the edges in the morning when the sun threw oblique shadows and made every crack seem vast. In the evening the stone's surface, warmed by the spring sun, caressed my skin as I moved up it. And when it got too dark to climb, I shut the door on the outside and lay on the bed and visualised each square foot of granite face and let my body curl and stretch in response.

I never looked at the night sky.

Nick called me in the café one evening. It was a dingy little place except for the colourful tiles on the floor. Empty apart from a cluster of old men at the bar, reading their newspapers and exchanging the occasional comment. It reminded me of the pub in Craighston, the village near my childhood home in Cornwall. That too had the same taciturn old men except their faces were whiter than the sun-dried faces of the men here.

'I'm back,' Nick said. 'Are you still here? Angel told me he hadn't seen you. If you've –'

'I'm not in Alájar.'

'Oh.'

'But I'm not far. I've gone climbing.'

'Of course.'

He paused as though waiting for me to say something.

'How was your work trip?' I asked.

'Tricky.'

Silence.

'You know I can't talk much about it.'

I did but I didn't like it.

More silence.

'Are you coming back then?'

My turn to be quiet. Was I coming back? I still wasn't sure. My head was full of the climb.

'I could,' I said.

'I'd like that.'

'I'll text you.'

We tried to chat for a few minutes after that. A few details of where I was. How the chestnut trees were budding and the pigs getting fat. It's tough to chat when neither of you can explain what you've been doing because one of you is forbidden from talking about it and the other is too scared of what she's planning to give it words and both of you are wary of each other.

I ended the call, walked to the van and lay on the bed, but not even visualising the climb could completely banish Nick from my thoughts. In the end I took my sleeping bag and settled outside at the base of the crag with my back pressed against the rock. Sleep came. In the morning I knew it was now or never.

I tied the rope off out of the way and climbed without it.

It wasn't difficult. I'd learned the moves so well they flowed through my body without my consciousness guiding them. There was no heart-stopping thrill, no wave of adrenalin racing through my blood but I felt alive in a way I never had before. The physicality overwhelmed me. I had no emotions. Not fear. Not excitement. Not even pride at each perfect placement of hand and foot. My head was empty except for the concentration on making each move as stark and simple as it could be and all I felt was my limbs moving with the stone as if we were dancers performing a perfect pas de deux.

When I got to the top, I sat and dug my fingers into the long grass. I didn't need to rest. I wasn't at all tired but I wanted time to let the pleasure rise from my bones and seep into my mind. I could have stayed there forever, held in a moment of deep contentment.

And then it was broken.

'Man! That was fantastic!' A voice with a hint of an American accent smashed the silence. 'I was watching you.'

A youngster, blonde and tanned, with the kind of skin only the lucky have, came over from the top of the footpath. 'Weren't you scared?'

'No.'

It was the truth. Climbing without a rope left no room for fear. No room for anything except an intense focus on living in the present. A complete commitment of body and mind to each move. Because you cannot fail. You cannot even think of failing. You have to trust yourself completely. That's the key.

His eyes glinted with the fear and excitement he thought I'd felt. He'd never understand. No one would understand.

'No,' I said to the youngster, as I stripped my climbing shoes off my feet and slipped on the old trainers I'd left at the top, wincing as the damp accumulated during the night met my skin. 'No, it wasn't a bit frightening.'

Back at the van, Nick came into my mind. The climb had clarified my thoughts in a way I couldn't explain because I didn't understand it myself but I knew I didn't want to leave things as they were between us. I had no idea if Nick and I had a future. I wasn't sure if I wanted one. And I certainly had no idea what he wanted. However, something he'd said to me that morning when we'd parted at the hippie farm, after our night at the cabin, had come back.

You've satisfied your curiosity then, he'd said.

I hadn't understood what he meant but now I thought I did. When we'd met in the bar, our first conversation, he'd asked what had brought me to Alájar, and I, searching for an answer that would commit me to nothing, had replied it was curiosity. Nothing except curiosity. It had been true but also a warning to him to read nothing into my arrival. I'd thought he understood when he bowed in that oddly formal way and asked permission to show me round.

So maybe he'd taken that warning to heart. Perhaps he was as unsure as I was…

I knew I was going back to Alájar.

He picked me up from the bottom of the footpath that led up through the woods to the farm. The face he turned to me was wary rather than welcoming.

'You're back,' he said.

'So I am,' I said and I couldn't help smiling. 'Who'd have thought it!'

A flicker of laughter rippled across his face.

'I'm glad,' he said.

'I am too.'

'I need to talk to you.'

'Go on then.'

'Well, not here.'

He looked around as though hoping somewhere suitable to talk might appear.

'Let's go back to my house,' he said. 'You haven't seen it, have you?'

There were about a million answers I could have given but in the end I said, 'No, I haven't. But I'd like to.'

We drove in silence. A nice silence. It was a beautiful day. The sky was cloudless while the air felt crisp and dry. The chestnut trees lining the road were dusted with the green of tight bundles of leaves sprouting along the branches.

'Here we are,' he said as we turned into an entrance and took a track through yet another part of the forest.

The car jolted along for a short while then Nick stopped, got out, walked round to the front and stared at the ground, where a line of twigs lay vertically across the road. He kicked them to one side.

'I like to know if anyone has driven up to the house while I'm away,' he said as he clambered back in.

'Have they?'

'No.'

The car moved off, rattling and bumping over the track.

'Nearly there,' he shouted over the noise.

A house appeared in the distance. Square and low, built out of stone the same colour as the grey-yellow of the track, it was almost invisible among the trees. A low roof cast the terrace into shade.

As we neared, he swore under his breath and tapped the brakes, turned off the track and came to a halt behind a barrier of bushes. He switched the engine off and the music died away.

'What is it?' I asked.

He jerked a finger to his lips and shot me a quick, tough look. 'Someone's here.'

I looked around, trying to work out how he knew.

'Someone on foot. I'd have seen the signs if it was a car. They're on the terrace.'

He pointed through a gap in the foliage to a rope hanging between the steps leading to the terrace. A hand-painted sign on it said *Casa Privada* in big red writing.

'I twist the rope so the sign hangs off-centre; it's straight now.'

It was silent in the forest apart from the occasional rustle as the last of the winter leaves fell to the ground. Nick was strung tight. Like a leopard in a tree readying for a group of unwary antelopes to approach, or like a fox trapped by a pair of jackals, its eyes flicking as it searched for an escape. Was he hunter or prey? I couldn't tell.

A sudden flicker in the dark shadows under the overhanging roof of the terrace caught my eye. Someone waiting there had moved.

Quick and lithe, Nick reached under his seat and pulled out a knife. A hunting knife, its rubber handle black and scratched, but its blade glinted as he slid it out of its sheath.

'Nick,' I whispered.

'Go to the bar. Take the car and drive to the bar. Keep off the track until you're away from the house. Don't stop for anything.'

His hand went to the door handle.

'Do it, Jen. You're in my way here.'

'But the knife? What are you going to do with the knife? Come with me.'

'I'm a sitting duck in the car. Don't argue. Go. It's probably nothing. But if it isn't they want me not you.'

He eased the door open, slipped out in one swift, quiet movement, and into the trees.

I slid into the driver seat. I'd go to the bar then call the police. Or get Angel, the bar owner and Nick's cousin, to do it. He spoke English. I'd explain to him. My feeble Spanish wasn't up to the job.

Yet I couldn't bring myself to leave.

Nothing moved except Nick gliding from tree to tree as he approached the house. It seemed unreal as if I was watching an action sequence being filmed. Any minute now the director would shout *cut* and the crew would emerge from the bushes.

I wrenched my eyes from Nick to the terrace. Someone was hiding there, lurking in the shadows. A sickening thought came to me. They must know we were here. The noise of the car on the track would have told them. They'd have a gun. Of course they would. Why didn't Nick have one? Or maybe he did, but in the house.

We needed help. I reached forward to turn the engine on and another flare of movement from the terrace caught my eye. At the edge of my vision I saw Nick flick the knife through his fingers and grip it. The smooth, automatic movement spoke of years of practice and the sureness of a professional.

A man stepped out of the darkness under the low roof. Tall. Brutally short hair. White shirt, bright in the sunlight. Jacket slung over his shoulder. Shading his eyes as he looked down the track. Nothing in his hand. No gun.

'Why are you here?' Nick's voice broke the quiet as he stepped out from behind a tree.

What was he doing? There might be other men. On the terrace. In the trees. Waiting. My eyes raked the bushes and shrubs around my hiding place.

'I told you *never* to come here.' Nick spat the words out. He sounded furious but without the slightest hint of fear. He stood in the open, his hands stuck in the pockets of his jeans. There was no sign of the knife.

'He's dead.'

My brain whirled with a million thoughts. Who was this man? Who was dead?

'Wait.'

Nick shoved the bushes apart and came the shortest way back to me.

'Who is he? And who's –'

'He's my boss.' Nick's eyes were steel doors, shut against me. 'Nothing to worry about. You'll have to go. Take the car. I'll call you.'

And with that, he left and pushed his way past the man on the terrace, unlocked the door and disappeared inside the house. The man, Nick's boss, lingered, looking in my direction. I knew he couldn't see me. The thicket was impenetrable from the terrace. Some anger rose in my throat. I wasn't going to give him the pleasure of showing my face, so I waited until he'd gone into the house before I drove away.

Four

I went to the bar and drank little hot, bitter cups of coffee until I could think about what had just happened without feeling sick and shaky. Angel was busy in the far corner of the bar, wiping glasses and discussing football with the men from the ham factory opposite. At least I thought it was football. The word was practically the same in Spanish and I'd heard enough talk to recognise the names of a couple of players. I caught his eye and asked him for a tapa of *patatas bravas* and a glass of the sweet lemonade that came in thick glass bottles with a stopper.

'Where is Nico?' he asked.

I shrugged and he raised one eyebrow.

'You OK?'

I nodded.

I wasn't, though. I felt as if I'd tumbled off a wall in the gym and been winded by the rope as it broke my fall. My mind kept on returning to the knife. So brutal. So functional. And clearly Nick wouldn't have thought twice about using it if he'd had to. This was the reality of his job. I shuddered and sipped at the lemonade. And the way he'd told me to leave. Equally brutal. He hadn't wanted me there, so he'd got rid of me.

I nibbled at a potato and let the spicy tomato sauce warm my mouth. Chips and tomato ketchup, really. But with a fancy name. A sudden longing to be home overwhelmed me. To be down the chippy in Fowey, queuing outside on a Friday night, peering through the steamed-up windows as the salty, vinegary smell wafted out into the street.

Or to go to the Saturday market in St Austell and wander around the stalls selling Cornish clotted cream and cheeses, and vegetables, common, unexotic vegetables like potatoes and carrots. Not that there was anything dull about Cornish potatoes. Especially the new ones that would be filling the stalls now. Lightly boiled, salted and with a knob of butter. Nothing could beat them.

I pushed the *patatas bravas* away.

What was I doing here? Living in a battered campervan without running water and electricity, hanging around for a man who, after what had just happened, I wasn't sure I particularly liked.

A phone call interrupted my thoughts.

Kit.

I answered it.

'Hi.'

'You OK?'

'Yes. Why?'

'Nothing. Just thought you sounded a bit off.'

'And you could tell that from one little word? From the way I said "Hi"?'

'Jen!'

'Sorry. Bad moment.' I cast around for a reason. 'Flat tyre on the van,' I said vaguely. I'd told Kit I'd bought one. 'Just waiting for it to be mended.'

And a momentary flush of annoyance heated my face. I'd had enough of this. Having to lie to my own brother about where I was and what I was doing.

'Why have you rung anyway?'

'I know where Ma is. Or at least I'm pretty sure.'

'Where?'

'Malta.'

'You mean the island in the Mediterranean?'

'Well, of course I do. What other Malta do you know?'

'I don't, Kit. I was just checking. It seems a very strange place for Ma to be.'

I dragged my mind away from Nick and tried to think what I knew about Malta. Not much. I thought it might have been part of the British Empire once, but I wasn't at all sure.

'I went and asked Gregory, like you said. He'd had a postcard from her from Malta. Of a lighthouse. A squat, little one in the middle of a harbour wall. Although it was difficult to tell from the angle. It could have been bigger —'

'Shut up about the lighthouse. What did she say?'

'Nothing, I mean apart from information about the lighthouse. Its range. Its power.'

I let Kit meander on about the lighthouse and then about how impossible Ma was while I stared through the window to the square outside, willing Nick to appear like he had the first time I'd been here. To leap over the low wall and smile when he approached me. Anything to smother the memory of the grim sureness with which he'd tossed the knife in his hand.

Forget about Nick. Think about Ma.

But that wasn't much better. Something about Ma being in Malta made me uneasy.

'When did the postcard arrive?'

'Difficult to say. The postmark was blurred. Gregory kept it above the sink and it's pretty damp there. But weeks and weeks ago.'

'She's probably back in the UK then.'

'I don't think so. Apparently she sends Gregory postcards wherever she goes, mainly of lighthouses or something nautical. She's been doing it for years. He had a postcard of the lighthouse in Plymouth from when she did a yoga course there and one of a canal boat in Birmingham when she gave a talk at a book festival. But none since Malta. So she must still be there.'

What had Ma been doing for months in Malta? Something stirred in the depths of my brain.

'Does she know anyone in Malta?' Kit asked.

'I don't know. Where is it exactly?'

'The southern part of the Med. In between Italy and Africa.'

Africa. Shit. North Africa. I had an awful feeling I knew what she was up to and, if I was right, Kit would think it was my fault.

'I've never heard her even mention Malta.'

Kit was getting himself worked up. Why was it so important to him to find Ma? This was more than needing a few things signed.

'What's going on?'

He hesitated.

'There's been a bit of a development since we spoke last.'

'And what might that be, Kit?'

Kit muttered something about things changing.

'What's changed?'

He sighed.

'Pa's moving lock, stock and barrel to the States.'

'Well, that's not going to change anything much. He's always away anyway. When did you last see him face to face?'

Kit ignored my comment. 'He's setting up an agency with a couple of other people, but, the thing is, he wants to be finished with Tregonna. He wants to sell it, pay off the mortgage and split the rest of the money between us and Ma in some way or other.'

'And?'

'He wants it done fast.'

'Fuck him.'

'If he doesn't do it fast, he'll have to pay a lot of tax.'

'Still fuck him.'

Kit was silent.

'Doesn't Ma have some rights over it? He agreed she could stay there if she paid for its upkeep.' I didn't mention how Ma had let the house gradually fall apart over the years.

'If she was still living there, she would,' Kit replied. 'But she left months ago and told everybody, including mutual friends, that she would never come back.'

I didn't believe Ma had really said goodbye to Tregonna forever. Despite storming out! The house was everything to her. What a mess.

'Look, if he's going to give us the money anyway, why can't he just give us Tregonna instead? Or give it to Ma?'

'I suggested that but he won't. Told him I'd borrow the money to pay off his mortgage but he still won't.'

'Why not?'

'I don't really know. He wasn't very clear. Just said we'd all be better off without the house.'

He had a point but I didn't think Ma would see it like that. Whatever the truth was, it lay between the two of them and their complicated relationship.

'I can't stop Pa putting it on the market,' Kit said. 'But he's living in cloud cuckoo land if he thinks it will sell quickly. So we've got a bit of time. I spoke to Ma's solicitor and he thinks he can prevent Pa selling it but he needs Ma to instruct him.'

'We'll have to get hold of her.'

'What do you think I've been trying to do? I've rung all her old friends. I just rang Miranda.'

'Miranda?'

'The woman who runs the charity for refugees in the camps at Calais.'

I remembered. She was a buddy of Ma's from when Ma had flirted with being a political activist. Miranda was extremely forthright.

'What did Miranda say?'

'What *didn't* she say? She told me exactly what she thought of my behaviour. Didn't give me a chance to explain.'

'Ma must have been in touch with her then. Did you ask where she was?'

'She wouldn't tell me but I think she knew.'

Maybe I should try Miranda. Surely Ma wouldn't have blackened my name to her. Not if the subject of their conversation was what I suspected.

'Look, Jen. Could you go to Malta?'

'You're joking, aren't you?'

'Why not? You said you're just mooching around. Go and mooch in Malta.'

'Without any clue as to where Ma is or what she's doing? Hang around and see if I bump into her?'

'I don't think it's very big.'

'Kit!'

'Well, have you got a better idea?'

'Look, let me think. Give me a day or so. Like you say we've got a bit of time.'

I rang off. Angel and the regulars had stopped chatting and were staring at me. Our conversation had probably been a bit heated. I wondered how much Angel had followed.

Shit. I could really do without worrying about Ma on top of feeling sick about Nick. How much longer was he going to be?

I looked up Malta on my phone. Two little islands in the midst of an expanse of sea. No three islands. There was a tiny one between the two others. The nearest mainland was Italy. But as I zoomed further out, more land appeared to the west. It was Africa. The top of Tunisia rose above Malta. My sense of the Mediterranean as a wide band separating Europe to its north and Africa to its south was wrong. The coastline of each continent was jagged and Italy and Tunisia were great tongues of land that almost grazed each other.

Africa was very close to Malta. To the west, Tunisia was less than 200 miles away and to the south Tripoli was 221. Tripoli, Libya. Libya was closer to Malta than Cornwall was to London. Libya. Malta. It all made a kind of sense I didn't much like. I googled a few things to check I wasn't being stupid. And I wasn't. Pages of news and information confirmed it.

Migrants Adrift Off Malta Call for Help.

Third Boatload of Migrants from Libya arrives in Malta in 24 Hours.

Hundreds of articles. Hundreds of pictures showing too many people crammed into drifting inflatables, or lying on the decks of the rescue ships or on the sand and pebble shores of Malta. Along with stories of the terrible conditions in Libya, the horror of the crossings and, even worse, the migrants forced to turn back.

Ma was in Malta. I was sure of it.

Last year, when we were together at Tregonna, she'd talked about a friend of hers called Nahla, a Libyan writer who she'd known for years. They'd met when Nahla was guest lecturer for a while at the School of Oriental and African Studies and we were all still living in London, before Pa bought Tregonna.

Nahla Shebani. That was her name.

She and her husband had been outspoken critics of the regime in Libya until they'd fallen foul of one of the warlords. Her husband had been killed and Nahla and her two daughters had gone into hiding. Ma had been desperate for money to pay for them to get from Calais to the UK illegally and when Pa had suddenly given me money, I'd sent some to Ma.

But now I wondered if Nahla had ever reached Calais. Perhaps she was still in Libya and Ma had gone to Malta to help her. Malta was the nearest place to Libya. Was Ma trying to organise a crossing? Or, even worse, trying to charter a boat to sail across and get her?

Shit.

And I'd given her the money to do it.

Double, triple shit.

Angel came over and asked me if I wanted anything. I ordered another lemonade and told him I hadn't fancied the *patatas bravas* after all, then buried my head back in my phone to avoid everyone's curious glances.

Where was Nick? How long did he expect me to wait here?

I googled Nahla Shebani for want of anything better to do. A few things came up, mainly poetry she'd written, which is not really my thing and wasn't going to tell me much about where she was.

I found a short article from ten months ago about her husband's killing in a small village in the east of Libya. Apparently the two of them had been on a fact-finding mission for a blog they wrote called *Libyan Spring* when an unnamed faction ambushed them. They'd both been attacked and Ibrahim had died instantly. Ma had told me he was dead and Nahla in danger but reading it in black and white made it seem more real especially as I could find no record of their blog. Someone had taken it down.

I carried on scrolling and came across a piece about female Libyan journalists, written three years ago, with a short section on Nahla.

… Nahla Shebani spoke to me from the relative peace of the university campus in Tripoli where her father still teaches. A quietly spoken woman in her late thirties, she was best known as a poet and academic until the violence that followed the overthrow of Gaddafi compelled her to use her international profile and popularity within Libya itself to speak out. Her reporting has largely been restricted to writing features and more reflective pieces for the international press rather than the 'on the ground' live reporting for TV that most of the other female journalists we interview are involved with. Nevertheless she too has received threats. She refused to say from whom they had come, commenting

that Western media was too quick to reduce the violence in Libya to a struggle between Islamist and secular factions when the reality was far more nuanced and complex.

I asked her about the wildly popular blog she and her husband, Ibrahim, an outspoken critic of the current situation in Libya, had just started and whether she thought the exposure would lead to more danger for them both.

'Whatever happens Ibrahim and I will never leave Libya,' she told me. 'I believe that we will come through this and a new Libya will be born. Besides, even though I do not always like the things that happen here, Libya is my country, my home; its people are my family. I am Libyan. If I desert my land, I will no longer be Libyan and then what will I be?'

A small photograph accompanied the article. A head-and-shoulders shot of Nahla in what looked like a blue jacket with a wide floral scarf wrapped round her neck. Her soft oval face was pleasant but unremarkable except for the hint of wary concentration in her eyes that gave her the look of an observer, someone who had seen a lot and learned to wait before she spoke.

I wondered if she looked as composed now.

There was every chance Ma had gone to Malta to help Nahla and I'd given her the means. I didn't know what I was going to do but I'd have to do something. And, of course, the first person who came into my mind was Nick. Nick the policeman. Nick who'd gone undercover with the people-traffickers in Cornwall. Surely Nick might be able to help me. Or might know someone who could.

Five

By the time Nick arrived, my head was killing me. I don't get headaches normally. They're for people who sit hunched over computers and never walk anywhere. However, the combination of too many shots of coffee, the encounter at Nick's and the latest news about Ma had been too much.

The bar was closing. Only a group of youngsters remained but, as they regularly stayed until Angel kicked them out, I knew I was on borrowed time. Angel shot thoughtful looks at me as he wiped down the tables and collected stray glasses perched on window sills, mantelpieces and the narrow shelf that ran at eye-level round the bar. I guessed he was still open because he didn't like to ask me to leave. And just when I was thinking I'd have to take pity on him, a taxi drew up in the square. Nick got out and slammed the door behind him. The taxi stayed, its engine running.

Angel glanced at him as he pushed the door open and Nick shrugged his shoulders. He looked wrung out, like a T-shirt worn and washed too many times and ready for the rag basket. Whatever had gone on between him and his boss hadn't been fun. Angel poured Nick a small glass of something red, held up the bottle and raised his eyebrows at me. It was Pacharán – a sort of sloe liqueur a bit like sloe gin but sweetish and intense. I don't drink much but I'd tasted it in the market.

The taxi still waited outside. Nick's face was blank and I

hated the way he'd gone straight to the bar without looking at me.

I nodded and Angel poured a glass and gave it to Nick before retreating to the stragglers at the other end of the bar.

Nick came over and put the drinks on the table.

'Is this seat free?' he asked but I didn't feel like smiling. His own smile didn't reach his eyes.

'Hell,' he sighed as he sat down. 'I've got five minutes before I have to go.'

'Where?' I asked stupidly.

'You know I can't tell you that. Another job. And it'll be for a long time.'

All thought of Ma and her predicament faded from my mind.

His hands fiddled with the glass, swirling the liquid round one way and then the other. I took a sip of mine. It tasted both bitter and too sweet.

'Jen,' he said. 'You know what this means.'

His eyes were steel-grey and his lips pressed in a thin line. His expression told me rather than his words.

'This is goodbye,' I said. Because, of course it was. He just couldn't bring himself to say it.

Outside someone sounded the horn of the waiting taxi. Nick ignored it but he pinched the bridge of his nose.

'I don't want it to –'

'End like this?' I interrupted him. 'Well, it has.'

'No. There are so many things I want to say but I haven't got the time.'

'You've got five minutes.'

He took a deep breath and opened his mouth, glanced at me then let the air slowly drain out of him.

'Time's ticking away,' I said.

'This is impossible.' His voice was tight.

I looked at the clock above the bar.

'One minute gone.'

'OK.'

He put his head into his hands.

'Two minutes.'

'Enough. Please, Jen. That's enough.'

Enough? I didn't believe I was hearing him right.

'You're telling me you've had enough? No problem!'

I thrust the chair away and stood, dragged his car keys from my pocket and flung them on the table before marching out of the bar.

Outside the dark of the night was shot through with the warm gleam from windows high up in the stone houses lining the square. People were going to bed. I stopped and stared up through the plane trees' budding branches. In summer, Nick had told me, their shade created a dark green oasis away from the white heat of the sun.

I realised I'd never see it.

Nick called my name from the bar doorway. The taxi door opened and the man I'd seen at Nick's got out.

'We have to go,' he called.

He had razor-cut hair and a little moustache. A stupid moustache, like a smudge of hot chocolate on a child's upper lip.

'Don't wait for me,' I yelled at them both.

I ran along the road out of the village to the path leading up to the hippies' farm. Part of me hoped I'd hear footsteps running after me, but all was silent. The night wasn't old enough for the owls and little nocturnal creatures to have ventured out. I swung into the path and was sick behind a tree. The mixture of Pacharán with coffee and lemonade had been too much.

The clouds were thin so the faint radiance of the moon helped me find my way now the lights of Alájar were far behind me.

Nevertheless I tripped over roots as I walked through the parts where the trees were thickest. The thin branches of a broom bush whipped me in the face and brought tears to my eyes. In the distance a dog howled and I sat with a thump on the path and felt like joining him.

Memories of the things Nick and I had done together flooded back as I snivelled. Driving round the countryside while Nick played me his favourite pieces of music. Listening to the triumphant noise of Zadok the Priest while racing along high-up roads and staring at the unfolding view, and to the quiet melancholy of some piano pieces by a French composer I'd never heard of while watching the sunlight flicker through willows onto the water of the stream that ran through Alájar.

I remembered the haunting Spanish music he'd played on our way back from Seville when the flamenco dancers' powerful and proud struts and swirls were still echoing in my body. And, of course, I thought of the night, up in the sierras, stargazing. No need for music then. The vastness of the light-filled sky and Nick's warmth around me had been enough.

Yeah, I thought. So romantic, wasn't it? But it had meant nothing. It was a fantasy, played out in beautiful surroundings. And desperate for a break from everything else in my life, I'd fallen for it hook, line and sinker.

I found a tissue in my coat pocket and scrubbed my face dry. It was time to be serious. Time to get back to reality. The last weeks with Nick had been fun, I told myself fiercely. That was all. Nothing to do with the real world. The real world for Nick was full of deception and violence.

And Ma, who'd been hovering at the back of my mind since the call from Kit, strode into my thoughts. She must have felt lost and bereft like this when she stormed out of Tregonna, her home for years and years. I'd only spent a few weeks in Spain. Things had been much worse for her. I had a flat in London and money in the bank. She had nothing. And though I had to get a job, I knew it wouldn't be difficult. For Ma, after fifteen or so years of surviving on selling odd crafty stuff she made, giving classes in various New Agey things and having the occasional paying guest at Tregonna, finding a job would be tricky to say the least. Impossible to imagine her filling shelves in Lidl.

Shit. I'd always thought of her as a survivor but now I saw her as someone who barely managed to hang on by the tips of her fingers while chasms of uncertainty opened beneath her.

I was really worried about her. She'd lost her beloved home. Her life. She'd been reeling from a dreadful row with Kit. She'd been in exactly the sort of state that makes people do stupid things. But surely she wouldn't sail across to Libya herself. Surely, even anchorless and unhappy as she must be, she'd know it was a reckless and risky endeavour.

Of course she would.

Wouldn't she?

I'd have to find her. No doubt about that. And with that decided, I stood up and stumbled back to the van.

PART TWO

England and Malta

Six

I didn't go straight to Malta, though. In the morning, I realised I'd be much better checking Ma was actually there first and, if so, exactly where, before I went to find her. Making rash decisions had been my downfall so many times.

I felt deeply mature and sensible as I walked down the footpath to the bar, and very grim. I'd organised a taxi to pick me up at the farm early afternoon and take me to the airport for a flight to London. The hippies had said I could leave the van with them although I'd told them they could get rid of it if it became a nuisance. Now I was going to have a final hot shower at the bar so I could wash every trace of the last twenty-four hours off me.

Afterwards I had a coffee with Angel. Well, I had a tea. I didn't think I'd be drinking coffee or lemonade or Pacharán for a long time after last night.

'So Nico's gone again.' Angel sat down on a stool the other side of the bar with a pile of card receipts and matched them against a list.

'He told you then.'

'Of course. I look after his house and his car while he is away. He leaves his phone with me too.'

'So you know what he…'

'I know enough.'

I'd always been aware of an undercurrent of trust linking him and Nick in the understated way it often did between men.

As if in answer to my unvoiced question Angel spoke.

'Nico and I played together as children when he visited during the holidays and went to school together as teenagers when he lived here. We've always looked out for each other.' He put his pencil down and looked at me over the half-moon glasses I'd never seen him wear before. 'He is one of my closest friends. Of course I know what he does.'

It must have been mid-morning break time because a wave of children's shouting and footsteps from the nearby primary school broke the quiet. Angel got up and closed the door. I wondered what it had been like for Nick as a child, splitting his life, splitting himself, between his Scottish and Spanish identities. Had his Scottish life fitted him as tightly as his Spanish one?

'I know a lot about Nico,' Angel said when he came back and sat down, resting his tattooed arms flat on the counter. 'But then, I know a lot about many people. Normally I keep their confidences to myself but today I think I am going to tell you something. More tea?'

'No. I'm fine. In fact I need to go. I've got a taxi coming to take me to the airport.'

'You are leaving. I don't suppose you plan to come back?'

'No.'

'Then I will be quick. When Nico returned from his last job, he came here first. Normally he goes straight into the mountains.'

I nodded.

'He bought a postcard, one showing the bar ceiling and sent it. He said it was a shot in the dark but he hoped it would reach the right person. Then he told me he was going up to the cabin but he asked me to look out for a young woman. A climber, he said she was, with long, curly hair and hands that were never still. Her name was Jenifry Shaw but she called herself Jen. If she arrived, I was to call him straightaway. That's all. I thought you should know he hoped you'd turn up.'

He gathered up the receipts, shoved them back into an envelope and left me to finish my tea.

Thoughts and questions buzzed in my head and for a few moments I felt sad. It didn't matter, though. Maybe Nick had come back from Cornwall with the same sense of something unfinished between us. But it was finished now. He'd chosen to leave and I'd learned that I didn't like what he was and I didn't trust him. So that was that.

I went back to London and forgot Spain, cleaned my flat and failed to decide what to do with it, hooked up with old colleagues in the event and film industry and spread the word I was looking for work. As a jobbing rigger, of course, hanging the structures to support scenic elements and technical equipment and checking everything was safe. I didn't expect any of the specialist design work Kit and I used to do. Not after my fall from grace last year.

A couple of weeks later, an offer of a last-minute job came in – rigging for a party in a badly equipped venue down by the Thames. It was a shit job with neither the time nor the budget to do the work properly. Moreover, the production company were notoriously bad payers. Normally I wouldn't even have answered the phone to them. But this time I said yes, did my best to find ways round the worst of the problems, smiled through gritted teeth when things went wrong and was thankful I spent most of my time in the roof and could avoid the questioning looks from old colleagues. I knew I had a lot of ground to make up after my behaviour last year and I needed word to get round that I was back to my normal, efficient self.

Work trickled in over the next few weeks. Always last-minute stuff but I knew people were starting to think about me for bigger and better jobs. I just needed to be patient.

Kit called and texted more and more frequently. Prospective buyers had come to look round Tregonna although he didn't think any of them were seriously interested. So in between jobs I did my best to track Ma down. I got sick of being stonewalled by Ma's friends. Most of them didn't know where she was but they'd heard about the great row on the grapevine so they'd plenty to say about Kit and, by extension, me. It was grossly unfair but I stopped trying to defend myself. *Ma would let me know where she was when she was good and ready* was the most common response to my questions.

I suspected some of them knew more than they let on so I tried a different tack with Miranda. I called her on the pretext of some advice for a friend who wanted to donate to one of the Calais charities, and asked her casually if Ma had been in touch since she went to Malta.

'No,' she said. 'Apart from a postcard saying she'd arrived.'

And then I blew it.

'So she is on Malta,' I said. 'Why? What is she doing there?'

There was silence and when Miranda spoke again her voice had taken on a frosty edge.

'You'll have to ask her that yourself, Jenifry.'

'I would but I've no way of getting hold of her.'

'That's your problem. Yours and Kit's.'

She rang off and I was left staring at a blank screen. At least, I thought, she'd confirmed Ma was in Malta.

I slammed the front door of the flat shut and went off to meet an old friend, Barb, who wanted to talk to me about a job later in the year. It involved working with a small production company making a film about climbing. They needed someone to work with their camera crew to get the best shots and maybe do some camerawork themselves. It was the first sniff I'd had of interesting work.

I wished meetings like this didn't always take place in pubs. The Spanish bars had been OK but in London they reminded me of the madness of last summer when, full of cocaine and alcohol, I'd lurched from one crazy night to the next. Not that I was tempted to fall. Far from it. But I could feel again the emptiness the drugs had been trying to fill. Maybe London wasn't for me. Maybe I needed to move.

I pushed the thoughts away and concentrated on what Barb was telling me, wondering why I'd ever thought her a laugh. She reminded me of a rat with her pointy features and flat front teeth and I had to hide my smile in my orange juice when she wrinkled her nose as she recounted a piece of gossip I'd heard ten times before.

The job sounded great. They'd be shooting all over the world and, although she wouldn't give me any names, I got the impression some of my climbing heroes might be involved. It was exactly what I needed. Time out of London and work that required all my skills. A tinge of excitement fizzed along my nerves.

'So,' Barb said. 'As soon as they asked me if I could recommend someone, I told them I absolutely knew the perfect person but I wasn't sure if I could persuade them to do it because they'd been out of the industry for a while. What do you think, Jen?'

I started to tell her that I'd love to do it but she interrupted me.

'Will you help me persuade Kit to take it on?'

Kit?

I stared at her with my mouth open, then pulled myself together.

'I doubt he'd do it, Barb. And I doubt even more that he'd listen to me. You'll have to ring him yourself.'

And because I knew it had to be done, I swallowed my angry feelings and spoke again.

'I'm a pretty good climber myself, you know, and I'd be interested in the job if Kit turns it down.'

I wondered if she'd teased me with the job deliberately. Had I pissed her off somewhere in the past? Or was she just stupid?

My phone buzzed with a message. Next week's job was cancelled. Very sorry, etc. Invoice fifty per cent cancellation and so on.

'I'll have to go, Barb. I need to deal with this. See you around.'

Once outside I turned into Green Park rather than heading back to the flat. With the job cancelled I'd no work lined up now although something last minute was bound to come in if I hung around. Except I was sick of London and sick of being given the runaround by Ma's friends. Miranda had been my last hope. Going to Malta suddenly felt like the right thing to do. I knew it might look like a typically ill-thought-out and impulsive move. But, hey, I'd done them in the past and they'd worked out. Fuck it! I should have gone weeks ago, as soon as I left Spain.

Seven

Malta was a disappointment. I'd imagined a mountainous outcrop rearing out of the sea with perilous cliffs guarding a barely inhabited wilderness. Instead the landscape was gentle and the island bursting with people. Sure, I'd known it was a holiday destination and probably built-up, but I hadn't realised it was so tiny that all the villages and towns had long since sprawled into each other under the weight of its permanent and visiting population.

In the past, its position, halfway between Europe and Africa, had made it a prize fought over by a stream of conquerors who'd left the island with a rich legacy of buildings and monuments according to the guidebook I'd bought at the airport. Not that I intended to visit any of them. I was going to find Ma and leave.

But my search wasn't going well. In fact, I'd failed completely, I thought, as I sat in a small café down by the sea's edge, near my hotel in the fishing village of Marsaxlokk and took stock.

Marsaxlokk was nice. Very picturesque, with gaily coloured fishing boats bobbing in the bay and the sun flashing the rippling water with streaks of light. Smells of fish and garlic wafted out of the restaurants lining the quay whose old stone walls bathed in the warmth.

Didn't make me feel any better, though.

I'd arrived five days ago and spent every minute looking for Ma. My search was as hopeless as I'd told Kit it would be. I'd been to every part of this tiny island and it had been a total waste of time. No sign of Ma at any of the boat-hire places and marinas. And when I'd asked if anyone like her had been around, everyone had shaken their heads.

I waved at the waiter and ordered another tea, then changed my mind. I'd have one of the only good things I'd found in Malta – a slightly bitter orange soft drink.

'No, a Kinnie, please. A really cold one.'

The last couple of days had seen a wave of heat settle on the island although it was only spring. My jeans were already sticking to the backs of my knees.

There was nothing else for it but to try Miranda again. At least she'd admitted she knew Ma was here. I dialled her number, crossing my fingers that she wouldn't be too annoyed with me to answer and, when she did, I spoke immediately.

'Miranda. It's Jen again, Morwenna's daughter. Look, I don't know what Ma told you but things are OK between us. We haven't been in touch much but we've always been like that with each other and I don't believe she's told you differently.'

Miranda grunted. I ploughed on.

'I need to speak to her. I really do. It's about Tregonna. Pa owns Tregonna. You know that, don't you?'

I waited for Miranda to speak and smiled at the waiter as he placed my Kinnie on the table.

'Yes,' she said eventually. 'I told her to get it sorted but your father was always so difficult to contact and, when he was around, so hard to pin down.'

A quality he and Ma both shared. No wonder the stupid situation between them had dragged on.

'Well, he wants it sorted now. He's moving to the US and he's selling Tregonna.'

She made a little sound like a cross between a snort and laugh.

'Ma's the only person who might be able to stop him and whether she wants to or not, she needs to know what's going on. You must see that.'

Silence.

I took a sip of my drink and considered telling her about my fears Ma was doing something breathtakingly illegal and dangerous but decided Miranda was quite capable of approving.

Still silence.

'If you're in touch with her, will you at least tell her I need to speak to her? And that it's about Tregonna,' I said in the end.

Miranda said nothing for a few seconds and then she rang off.

'Thank you, Miranda!' I said to the phone. 'Thank you for nothing!'

It was hopeless. Maybe I should go back home. I drank my Kinnie and googled flights but I couldn't quite bring myself to book one. And, as they often did in moments when I had nothing to do, my thoughts drifted to Nick, wondering where he was and what he was doing. The papers had snippets of stories about people traffickers in Manchester running cannabis factories or supplying labour for farms in Norfolk and, of course, there were always tales of sex-trafficking women and children in all the large cities. Nick must be quietly digging his way into one of these operations. Maybe among the back streets of some northern town or a part of London where the shifting population masked the presence of the sex industry. I wondered whose life he was living now.

And then I made myself stop. Whatever he was doing, there was no part in it for me. I needed to focus on whether Ma was also skirting the edges of danger. She might well be mixing with the kind of lowlife Nick hid himself among. I shuddered at the thought of it again. With her stupidly trusting beliefs in the power of positive energy and cosmic unity, she'd be easy meat for them.

Or had she already left for Libya? The one useful thing I'd gleaned from the guidebook was that it was only a few days' sail away. I imagined her picked up by the authorities. Maybe stuck in some hellhole of a Libyan prison.

My phone rang. It was Miranda.

She cut straight through the normal pleasantries.

'Have you got something to write on? I'm going to give you a number you can call. Your mother said she'd be there at five o'clock if you want to speak to her.'

I grabbed a napkin and scribbled down the number she gave me.

'What is it? Where is this?' I started to throw questions at her.

'You'll have to ask your mother. I've done what you asked.' And with that she ended the call.

It was a Maltese number. Thank God. She was here. Clearly Miranda assumed I was still in London because she'd given me the full international prefix. I looked the number up and found it belonged to an organisation called Musaeada that provided assistance to refugees. I went to their website and learned that Musaeada meant 'help' in Arabic. They had a clinic in one of the refugee camps in the south of the island and provided English lessons and legal advice in their main office.

What was Ma doing with them?

I thought for a bit. I wouldn't call. Of course not. I'd go there and speak to her face to face.

Musaeada's offices were one room on a dusty street. An old shop, judging from the big window at the front, now covered by locally woven rugs to give some privacy, so I couldn't see if Ma was inside. I pushed the door open. The small space was lined with filing cabinets, cupboards and shelves of books and paperwork, while posters of what I thought was information (but couldn't tell because the writing was Arabic) covered every still-visible square foot of the walls. It smelt of dust and coffee.

An assortment of chairs circled a desk, its surface as cluttered as the walls, where two women sat, one facing me but staring at a computer and the other reading a letter with her back to me so I saw nothing except the rust brown and black cloth round her head.

Neither of them were Ma. Although if the woman at the computer had been older, I might have mistaken her for Ma. She looked up at me and smiled brightly. She had a pencil stuck behind one ear and through her long, lightly curling hair. She wore the same floral prints Ma liked and her arms jingled with silver bracelets as she moved paper around the desk. She said something to me in Maltese and when I shook my head she spoke in perfect English with a trace of a Scottish accent.

'Hi, how can we help you?'

'I can wait until you've finished.' I nodded my head towards the woman sitting in front of her who turned to look at me. She must be a refugee. From Sub-Saharan Africa, I thought. I'd read that a lot of migrants came to Malta via Libya from there. It occurred to me their conversation might be private.

'I'll wait outside. I'm a bit early anyway.'

'Early? For what?' the woman who looked like Ma asked.

'My mother.'

She looked blank but the other woman stood and gave me a curious look.

'Are you Morwenna's daughter?'

She had a distinctly Birmingham accent, I realised, and now she was standing I saw she wore high-end jeans and a beautifully ironed blouse.

'I didn't tell you.' She turned to the other woman. 'Morwenna asked if her daughter could call her here this evening.' She turned back to me. 'I must have misunderstood. I thought you were phoning. I'm Amalia and this is Shona.'

'Jen,' I said. 'But Ma probably called me Jenifry.'

I kicked myself inside and prayed the self-possessed Amalia hadn't guessed I'd mistaken her for a refugee. Dark skin plus headscarf equals Muslim equals refugee. The unavoidable deduction. Even for someone who thought of herself as fairly aware.

'Morwenna's daughter!' Shona stood and held her arms out wide, reaching over the table to me. She looked as though she wanted us to embrace but contented herself with seizing the hand I stretched out with both of hers. 'I should have known when you walked in. You bring the same life force with you. It is unmistakeable. Don't you think, Amalia?'

Amalia smiled and I tried to remove my hand from Shona's grasp.

'Morwenna – your mother – she is doing wonderful work here.'

I couldn't quite see it myself although I was sure Ma must get on like a house on fire with Shona.

Amalia spoke with that unmistakeable nasal Midlands twang.

'Unfortunately though Morwenna's not back until six.'

'Six?'

Too late I realised Miranda's instruction to call at five had been based on the assumption I was in the UK.

Amalia picked up a bag from the desk. 'I'm waiting for a taxi to take me and our nurse to the camp. We've a clinic this evening and I'm going to pick up my car from the garage nearby, then go and get Morwenna. You can come with us if you like.'

Shona interrupted. 'You're going to tell Yasmiin, aren't you? She'll be with Morwenna.'

'Of course.' Amalia sighed. 'She'll know soon enough anyway. Better hearing it from me.'

An elderly Ford Zephyr drew up outside.

'Mohammed's here,' Shona said. She stacked the paperwork on the desk into an unwieldy pile and waved at the driver who peered in at us with a big grin on his face. He opened the door. He was a cheerful-looking, rotund man with tightly curled short hair who bounced up and down on his toes as he spoke, making me think of a rubber ball.

'I cannot wait long,' he said. 'You know what the cops are like. Come on, ladies. Anything to carry?'

'Follow us in your car,' Amalia said to me. 'Or come with us if you like. I can drop you back here afterwards.'

'I'll come with you.'

The taxi, although old, was immaculately clean. Upholstery cleaner, air freshener and Mohammed's aftershave all fought together and I opened the window as soon as I got in.

'Are you OK with the window open?' I asked Amalia who followed me into the back. In the front a woman who I assumed was the nurse turned round and smiled.

'Fine. Mohammed's car doesn't have air-conditioning unless he's managed to magic it up from somewhere. Have you, Mohammed?'

'No, no. Not yet. But you never know!' he said, tapping his nose with a toothy grin. He was one of those people whose age it was difficult to guess. His unlined skin and dark hair gave nothing away.

'Paulina,' Amalia said to the nurse. 'This is Jen. She's Morwenna's daughter.'

Paulina looked at me with mild interest. She was a bit older than I was although it was difficult to tell because she was immaculately made up. I wondered how long it took her every morning to paint and blend all the different shades of foundation onto her face and put her blonde hair into its intricate bun of interlacing strands. More time than I was prepared to spend.

'Hi,' I said.

She smiled again and went back to listening to Mohammed's relentless chatter. Clearly they knew each other well. And just as clearly she was used to his forthright opinions on everybody else's driving.

I learned a bit about Amalia as we drove through the traffic-clogged roads towards the south. She was a lawyer in the UK and a pretty radical one. Her family did come from Birmingham although she lived in London and we knew a lot of the same clubs and bars. She'd set Musaeada up ten years ago with a lawyer friend whose family came from Gozo, the other large island of the Maltese archipelago. They'd both been on holiday when they'd witnessed a boatload of migrants arrive and be seized by local police. Curious, they'd investigated and been horrified by the lack of help available.

At first, she told me, they'd thought they were achieving a great deal, using their legal knowledge to help migrants obtain refugee status but in recent years they had felt more and more hopeless, faced with the sheer numbers of people crossing the Mediterranean.

'Burnout,' she said. 'And despair at the impossible size of the task. I know now that's what happened. But we pulled ourselves together. Set Musaeada up so it could function without us. Shona joined us as a volunteer and stayed on to run it. We pay her a pittance but I think her family have money. Otherwise it's all volunteers, like Paulina.'

She nodded to the nurse in the front seat, who gave a thin smile as though fearful of disturbing her make-up.

'Shona found Paulina and she's been an absolute godsend. She speaks good Arabic. She gives us a quite a few hours of her time each week. So now I come over several times a year but devote myself to fundraising. Mainly making other lawyers feel guilty about how much they earn,' she finished with a laugh.

I wanted to ask Amalia how she knew Ma and what Ma was doing and all the other questions that had been crowding in my head since I arrived in Malta but I didn't know where to start.

'How is Ma?' I asked finally.

'She's good, I think. She'll be even better when I give her the news.'

The car stopped. I looked round. We were in the midst of an industrial area far from the touristy part of the island. A battered wall, topped with spirals of barbed wire, ran along the road and came to an end by the rolling steel gate in front of us. Ahead the wall had been replaced with a high metal fence and more barbed wire, through which rows of stacked containers gleamed white in the spring sun.

'Where is this?' I asked as Paulina got out of the car.

'One of the camps. We have a clinic here.'

I noticed the containers had windows cut in them and spiral steps led up to the ones piled on top. Shit.

'Not great, is it?' Amalia said in response to my silence and I saw Mohammed looking at me curiously in the rear-view mirror.

'No. Not great.'

Mohammed dropped us at a small garage to collect Amalia's car and we drove away through swathes of wasteland interspersed with ugly industrial yards: crane and equipment hire companies, cement factories, dumps piled high with old cars and washing machines, shipping companies whose yards were full of rusty and battered containers. I saw no one apart from guards by gates and the occasional group of dusty and shabby men waiting at roundabouts.

Amalia, who up till then had appeared to be brooding over something, saw me staring.

'Yes,' she said. 'They're refugees. They get picked up here for work on the rest of the island. Although these men are waiting for the drop-offs in the hope of a lead on some work tomorrow.'

'What sort of work is there?'

'Mainly labouring. Not great. Some of them do better. Mohammed, for example, the taxi driver, he's one of our success stories. He arrived with nothing but was always prepared to turn his hand to anything. Somehow he scraped together enough money to buy his first car. It was in a shocking state but he said its engine was sound. He had his own garage in Syria so he knew what he was talking about. Anyway he fought his way through the paperwork to become an accredited taxi and he's doing very well. He took a holiday a few weeks ago and we were the ones who were lost without him. Whenever I'm feeling down about everything, I think of him and it cheers me up.'

We left the industrial area behind and drove through empty fields hemmed in by squat stone walls and tired-looking bushes, finally pulling over onto a patch of earth by the side of the road.

'Where are we going?'

'You'll see,' Amalia said and headed down a barely visible path. I heard the slap of waves against stone and felt the hint of a breeze. The path rose then fell as the ever-present Mediterranean filled my eyes.

Below us, a short clamber down, a flat horseshoe-shaped stone shelf curved round an inlet of turquoise sea, which looked like a jewel cut into the creamy-coloured rock. A group of women sat there with their backs to us. Many of them wore long, shapeless garments in a myriad of faded prints and colours and the sort of head coverings that Ma's radical feminist friends hated.

The seated women all watched someone demonstrate 'The Tree', a yoga pose I knew well. I'd had it shown to me countless times by the same person who was now explaining in serene tones what it meant.

It was Ma. Dressed in a floaty, floral top and loose trousers, both adorned with silver beads that glinted as she moved. Her long, curly hair sprang away from her head, its white threads gleaming in the sun.

Ma.

The relief that she was safe smoothed away the stress I hadn't known was there but it was tinged with the familiar flickers of exasperation Ma provoked in me. I pulled out my phone and took a quick photo then sent it to Kit with the caption 'Found!' He would understand how I felt.

Eight

'Yoga?' I said to Amalia. 'She's teaching yoga to refugees?'

'And practice for English. And doing it here means they get away from the camp. Away from being refugees all the time. Your mother understands how important that is.'

A teenager sat on a convenient rock near us on the edge of the low cliffs and also watched the scene below, but without much interest, fiddling with the elastic band on her long plaited hair and listening to music on a phone with a cracked screen. The tinny sound leaked out of old-fashioned earphones with coloured sponge over the ends. Hers had lost one of its sponges.

'Hello, Rania.' Amalia waved a hand in front of the girl's face.

She looked up and nodded, letting her hair drop and fiddling with the frayed edges of the holes in her jeans instead.

Below us the class stood and tried 'The Tree' themselves. Ma darted between them, adjusting their bodies, encouraging them and laughing with the ones who collapsed in a heap. Amalia went down to join them but I sat on the other end of the rock next to Rania. She'd removed her earphones and was gazing at the now blank phone.

'Out of battery?' I said.

She looked startled.

'I think it's broken.' She spoke English with a faint American accent.

'It doesn't look as though it's in great shape.'

80

She narrowed her eyes as she tried to work out what I'd said.

'It looks very battered,' I explained.

'It got wet. So it doesn't work all the time. Nothing does.' She muttered the last words under her breath but I caught them, along with the sense that she wasn't in the mood to chat. I'm not stupid. The screen flickered back into life as she shook it. She shoved the earphones back in and continued fiddling with her hair and gazing moodily at the women below.

I wondered if her mother was one of them and she'd been forced to accompany her. You and me both, I thought. Dragged where we don't want to go by our mothers. And then all the differences between us struck me and I stopped the thought dead.

Ma's class finished. Women stood. Some climbed up the path and walked past us. Most of them ignored me but a couple of the younger ones glanced over. The stragglers below chatted in little groups. Amalia said a few words to Ma, pointing up at me. Ma laughed, held her arms up and beckoned me with both hands. I couldn't help smiling back as I went down to meet her. We hugged and her familiar smell washed over me. Patchouli, because she was an old hippy at heart, along with salt from the sea air. She held onto my hand as we let go of each other.

'I'm glad you're here.' She sounded faintly surprised.

I shook my head at her and opened my mouth to ask her a million questions but she turned to the woman with her.

'This is Jenifry, my daughter.' Ma said. 'And this is Yasmiin.'

Yasmiin was a few years older than me and taller, dressed in the loose drawstring pants Ma wore and the Muslim headscarf I thought was called a hijab. Hers was loose and her short, curly hair sprang out from underneath. She must be the person Amalia had been talking about in the office with Shona.

'Pleased to meet you,' I said, holding out my hand and wanting to get the pleasantries over as quickly as possible. My phone

buzzed in my pocket. Probably Kit reacting to the photo of Ma
I'd sent him. I wondered how much longer before I could get Ma
away from here and talk to her.

Yasmiin threw me a sardonic look.

'Pleased to meet me? Really,' she said, her intonation conveying
a degree of disbelief that marked her out as a fluent English
speaker.

'Yasmiin,' Ma said. 'Of course Jenifry is pleased to meet you.
Remember. Positive thinking. It puts us in resonance with the
positive energy around us.'

Yasmiin was clearly as unimpressed by Ma's crap as I was. Her
mouth settled into a sour shape. 'No one is pleased to meet a
refugee,' she said to Ma. 'Nothing positive about that.'

I kept my eyes steady and hoped I wasn't flushing red.

'Yasmiin.' Amalia joined us. 'I need a word.'

The two of them moved away but Amalia turned back briefly
and shook her head at Ma.

'Shit,' Ma said.

I didn't think I'd ever heard her swear before.

'What is it?' I asked.

'News for Yasmiin. Not good, I think.' She shook her hands
as though scattering water off them. Her heavy rings glinted and
the jangle of her bracelets mingled with the splutter of tiny waves
breaking a few yards away.

'What are you doing on Malta, Jenifry?'

'Trying to find you.' I heard the note of exasperation in my
voice. 'Why else would I be here? Kit and I need to talk to you but
none of your friends would tell us where you were.'

Ma's reply was drowned out as Yasmiin's voice pierced the
soft air. We turned as one. Even the teenager, Rania, broke out
of her moody trance on the clifftop and looked interested. Words
poured from Yasmiin's mouth. I understood none of them but

their focus was clearly the letter her hands tore into shreds and hurled into the light breeze. The wind lifted the scraps in a whirling dance against the turquoise and gold backdrop of sea and stone, while Yasmiin's voice hurled its anger to the sky. Her fury was terrifying in its lack of restraint but Amalia seemed unfazed. She tried to interrupt occasionally but mostly stood and let her rave.

Eventually Yasmiin calmed. Her hands sank back to her sides and her fury settled into a sullen brood. She walked away from Amalia and headed for the cliff, passing Ma, who reached out to touch her. Yasmiin shook her off.

'Don't.' Her voice still vibrated with anger. She caught sight of me staring. 'I was wrong. After all, I am not a refugee. No. My story is not good enough. It did not please some white official in an air-conditioned room, digesting his lunch. My application is refused.' She spat each syllable of the last phrase out.

No helpful words came to mind.

'What do they know about my life? Nothing. None of you do. You know nothing. You have never had to climb a tree and hide while armed men pass underneath. No one has held a knife to your throat. Have they?'

She waited until I shook my head.

'Yasmiin, we can appeal.' Amalia joined us.

'But I have nothing more to tell them. Nothing more to give them. I have emptied myself to them. Told them things I hoped to forget. There is no point. No, I will spend the rest of my life here. On this island crammed full of refugees and people who hate refugees. One day it will crumble into the sea with the weight of us all.'

She turned and stalked away, climbing the path with loping steps and breaking into a run when she reached the top.

My phone rang. It was Kit. I rejected the call.

Ma's fingers fiddled with the silver beads on the front of her top.

'You've heard about Yasmiin,' she said to Amalia. 'Have you heard about Nahla? Has she been granted refugee status?'

Nahla? That was Ma's Libyan friend.

'Yes,' Amalia passed Ma an envelope. 'Nahla has received full refugee status. I told you not to worry. She's known because of her poetry and with her blogging and her newspaper articles, her story is well documented.'

Ma shut her eyes and breathed deeply. 'Thank the Gods.' She walked a little way from us and leaned her head against the cliff.

So Nahla was already on Malta; I hadn't needed to worry what Ma was up to.

'Your mother's friend,' Amalia explained. 'She's one of the lucky ten per cent who get full refugee status. Most of the rest get something called subsidiary protection – like Yasmiin – which means they can stay in Malta but that's all.'

I nodded my head as she carried on explaining that Nahla could now apply for resettlement off Malta. My phone rang again. Kit, of course. He'd have to wait.

'Resettlement is the Holy Grail for them all,' Amalia said. 'They are so happy when they arrive on Malta but, after a few weeks of detention and seeing what life is like here, most want nothing more than to get off the island.'

My phone rang again. 'Sorry,' I said to Amalia and quickly texted *Not now* to Kit.

Ma walked over to us.

'Does Nahla know?' she asked.

'Not yet.'

'Then we must go to the camp now.' She clapped her hands. 'Jen, I can't wait for you to meet Nahla. You'll love her. She's so very…' She hesitated and a look of doubt, rare to see in Ma, scudded across her face.

'So very what, Ma?'

'So… Never mind. Let's go.'

She headed towards the path before I could say anything. I really didn't want to go to the camp but I wasn't sure I had a choice.

'Ma's not telling me everything, is she?' I said to Amalia.

'No. Nahla's not in a great way. No one is, particularly after weeks in detention, and Nahla only came out a few days ago.'

A text arrived from Kit.

It's urgent.

Ma waved at us from halfway up the cliff. I'd have to go with her. I turned to Amalia.

'Tell me what to expect. Please.'

'Nahla and her daughters arrived a couple of months ago, rescued from a sinking boat. Everybody spends the first weeks in detention being processed and, believe me, it's not great in there. It makes the camp look like paradise. I met Nahla and she asked me to contact Morwenna.'

'And Ma came straightaway.'

Amalia nodded. 'Not that Morwenna could do much while the family were in detention. She couldn't even visit so it was a bit of a shock when she saw Nahla for the first time a few days ago. It dimmed even your mother's perpetual positivity.'

I thought I detected a sardonic note in her last comment but her face showed only sadness.

'No one comes out of this unscarred,' she said. 'Come on. Morwenna's right. We shouldn't make Nahla wait for the good news.'

I followed her up the path. I really didn't want to visit the refugee camp but Kit had texted it was urgent and unless he was being overly dramatic, which was unlike him, I needed to speak to Ma fast. Going with her would be the best way. And after we'd spoken, I'd be free to get off this claustrophobic little island, which I was starting to dislike intensely.

At the top Rania still listened to her phone while moving her feet in some complicated sequence of dance steps she clearly knew very well. Her gaze was far away.

'Rania,' Ma waved her hands in the girl's face until she pulled an earphone out. 'We're going back to see your mother but wasn't it lovely to come here and see the sea and feel the air on your face? Tell your mother all about it and maybe next time –'

Rania nodded, shoved the earphone back in her ear and stomped after Amalia. Ma's voice trailed away.

Rania was Nahla's daughter. The sullen teenager was not what I'd expected from Ma's descriptions of Nahla and her family. I wondered what waited for us at the camp.

Nine

No one felt like talking in the car and I took advantage of the silence to text Kit.

Why so urgent?

He replied immediately. *Call me. I'll explain.*

OK but not possible now.

Then soon.

Ma twisted round and spoke to us.

'I've brought Aya some fruit, Rania.'

'She can't hear you, Ma. She's listening to music.'

'Oh.'

'So, what have you been up to?'

Ma smiled.

'I've been exploring my new self,' she said. 'Finding out about her.'

I tried not to roll my eyes. Ma was always becoming a new person.

'I found her as soon as I set foot on Malta and realised this is where I am meant to be. You see, I have become a person on the move, a nomad, and Malta has always been a place for migrants.'

Amalia's shoulders stiffened at the word *migrants* and I wondered if Ma realised quite how insensitive she was being. Probably not because she waffled on about the countless civilisations that had conquered Malta, left their mark and moved on. The Phoenicians, the Byzantines, the Romans.

I interrupted her. I'd read the guidebooks too.

'Yasmiin doesn't seem too thrilled about staying on Malta.'

'Yasmiin is a spiky creature. Like a chestnut still in its prickly coat, she antagonises the people trying to help her.'

'Ma!'

'There's some truth in that,' Amalia said. 'It'll be one of the reasons her asylum was refused. She finds it difficult to hide her anger and it showed through at the interview. They don't want angry people.'

'Anger makes people uncomfortable,' Ma said in a chanting tone as though it was one of her mantras. Possibly it was.

And besides,' she added in a far more matter-of-fact voice, 'Amalia says there are holes in her story, didn't you, Amalia?'

Amalia tightened her lips but nodded.

'Her family left Somalia because of the fighting when she was a child,' Ma went on, 'and Yasmiin grew up in a refugee camp in Kenya. But she went back to Somalia a couple of years ago and can't really explain why.'

'Does it matter?'

'Oh yes. They're terrified of letting terrorists in and Somalia is rife with training camps.'

I caught sight of Amalia's furious glance in the rear-view mirror.

'It's ridiculous,' she said, her voice brimming with anger. 'Everybody has holes in their stories. Fear and distress destroy memories. You ask your friend Nahla to give you an account of the months she spent in hiding in Tripoli and I guarantee she won't be able to. But the European press paints asylum seekers as either terrorist masterminds or poor, brainwashed fools who've been radicalised into mindlessly following orders.'

I remembered the attacks a couple of years ago in Paris and Brussels. I was sure I'd read the terrorists had arrived in Europe pretending to be asylum seekers.

'But it does happen, doesn't it?'

'The vast majority of terrorist attacks – and I mean *vast* – have been carried out by EU citizens and residents, not asylum seekers. But yes, IS, Islamic State, has exploited the migrant flows to send or return fighters to Europe. But their numbers are tiny. It's blown out of all proportion by the media. The average Westerner looks at someone dressed in Muslim clothes and their first thought is *terrorist.*'

She ground to a halt and I couldn't think of anything useful to say.

The tinny sound of Rania's music filled the silence. I cast a quick glance at her. She was totally oblivious to Amalia's rant and staring out of the window.

'Is that the sign to the airport?' Her voice was loud. She pulled her earphones out as she repeated her question more quietly.

'Yes,' I said.

'Could we go there, Morwenna?'

'Not now, darling. I need to see your mother.'

Rania's face lost its animation.

'Why do you want to go?' I asked quickly before she went back to her music. 'It isn't very interesting.'

'Yasmiin told me the Wi-Fi is free there. I want to call my grandmother and message my friends.'

'Your friends?'

'At home. I have so much to tell them.' Her voice was soft with longing. 'They will be so surprised to hear from me. Is the airport near the camp?'

'Very.'

'I could walk?'

'Yes. But –'

Amalia's voice interrupted me. 'Rania, you mustn't leave the camp on your own.'

'Why not?'

89

Amalia paused and I wondered if she was unsure whether to tell Rania the unvarnished truth. I should have known better.

'Because thousands of youngsters like you go missing every year. There are no exact figures but many of them are trafficked for sex. Do you know what that means?'

Rania shook her head.

'It means men imprison you and sell you to other men for sex. Do you understand me now?'

Rania muttered *yes* and went back to her music, although her eyes blinked rapidly as she took in what Amalia had said.

Ma looked shocked too.

We stopped briefly at the entrance to the refugee camp while a guard looked us over. Amalia flashed a plastic badge on a lanyard but he recognised her, lifted a hand in greeting and raised the barrier. We drove between the rows of containers with small windows cut into their fronts and sides. They were stacked two high with narrow metal staircases leading up to the top level. Close to, they weren't as white as I'd thought. Sand and wind had battered the paint, leaving streaks of rust and dirt behind.

There was rubbish everywhere. Shreds of blue plastic sheeting and bottles, dirty rags and discarded packaging provided the only colour. Nothing grew here, not even weeds. Nothing was alive except the flies and the people sitting on the concrete in front of the containers, swatting them away from their faces. No wonder Ma made her yoga group take the long, dusty walk to the coast where there was beauty and a cleansing breeze off the sea.

Amalia stopped the car by one of the containers.

'Here you are,' she said.

Rania, Ma and I got out. I didn't think any of us wanted to be here.

'Will you ask your mother to come down?' Ma asked Rania. 'I've got some good news for her.'

Rania plodded up the steps and into the top container.

I had Ma on my own. Finally. Well, almost. A group of women sat opposite on the concrete blocks beneath the containers, knitting squares of brightly coloured wool. They glanced over and a couple of them laughed. Whether it was directed at us or at one of the people slouching past, I couldn't tell. Whatever. I didn't think they could hear us.

Ma was standing with her face turned up to the sun, her eyes closed and her arms stretched out like she was happy to be here.

'I thought you didn't like the heat.'

'I've learned to accept it,' she said with an irritating smile. 'The women here love it. It drives the cold from their bones after a night spent in one of these.' She gestured towards the container. 'Yasmiin said, during winter, the cold never leaves you for one minute.'

'Why didn't you tell me where you were?'

Ma considered my question for a few seconds.

'Did it matter to you? I didn't think it did much.'

This wasn't an unfair comment. I'd spent years not bothering about what Ma was up to.

'I was worried. I thought you might have gone to fetch Nahla.'

'Fetch her? From Libya?'

'Yes, Ma. Where do you think I meant? I thought you might have sailed over to get her.'

She laughed and I remembered why I was here.

'Ma. I need to talk to you. About Tregonna –'

'Morwenna.'

Rania stood at the top of the staircase. No longer mired in apathy, she trembled with panic.

'Tregonna?' Ma said. A question flared in her face then she turned to Rania. 'What is it?'

'It's Mama. She's talking all the time but in a strange way and she doesn't hear me.'

Ma raced up the staircase and I followed but she stopped me at the top. 'Eight women and children live in here. They have little privacy. Plus Nahla's younger daughter is terrified of anything or anyone new. Let me go on my own.'

I nodded and waited by the open door. The smell of sweaty bodies and vomit from inside was overpowering. I cast a quick glance at the ceiling. It was bare metal without any insulation. On a day like today, it must be sweltering inside.

The door opened straight into someone's living space: two beds close together, both piled high with torn carrier bags of possessions. An old sheet hung from the ceiling so that it masked the rest of the container and gave the illusion of privacy.

I understood what Ma meant and went down the stairs. I'd call Kit while I waited for her.

'What's up?' I said when he answered.

'Have you told her?'

'I haven't had a chance.'

'You've got to. Right now.'

'I can't and don't ask me to explain why. Just tell me why it's so urgent and I'll talk to her as soon as I can.'

One of the women opposite laughed but when I looked round sharply she was holding a green square of knitting up to the sun and pointing through a hole in it.

'Please, Kit.'

'Pa's sold Tregonna. Or he will have in the next few days.'

'What? You said it would take ages.'

'Some people made a silly offer and he's accepted. He said he's sick of waiting. He wants it sorted.'

Of course! The money didn't matter to him. He was going to give it to us anyway.

92

'Ma needs to talk to her solicitor now,' he went on. 'The buyers want a quick sale and they're going to exchange contracts asap.'

'Text me the solicitor's number.'

'She should have it.'

'Kit. We're talking about our mother.'

'Fair enough. I'll send it. Just make sure she calls.'

I wiped the damp marks left by my sweaty skin from the phone as Kit's text arrived. How much longer was Ma going to be?

'Jen.' Her voice called me from the stairs. She and Rania stood there. Between them they supported a woman whose head lolled back to reveal a sunken face with traces of dried vomit over her chin and in her hair.

'Jen will help me. You fetch Aya.' Ma said to Rania and beckoned me with a jerk of her head. 'We need to get Nahla to the shower block and cooled down.'

I tore up the stairs and grabbed Nahla's other arm. Tregonna would have to wait a little longer. Beneath the loose clothing Nahla wore, I could feel her feverish skin. She was light but floppy and difficult to manoeuvre down the narrow staircase.

She started muttering and crying out as we half-dragged, half-carried her along and I thought she needed more than cooling down in the shower. She spoke in Arabic with only the occasional English phrase, but there was no mistaking the crazed pattern of her speech. Lilting, dreamy passages would be suddenly broken by a torrent of machine-gun-rapid fury. The women knitting fell silent as we passed them. We reached a hut made from chipboard at the end of the line of stacked containers. Ma called out to warn any occupants that we were coming in, then pushed the door open. A blast of foul-smelling air hit me along with the buzz of flies. I gagged.

'Too many people for too few toilets,' Ma said through clenched teeth. 'This part of the camp is for women and children only. They make an effort to keep it clean. Amalia says the ones in the male areas of the camp are unbearable.'

We rinsed Nahla with the only shower that produced a steady flow of water, leaning her against the plastic sheeting on the wooden walls and ignoring her protestations. When she felt the water on her face she opened her mouth to drink it.

'No,' Ma said. 'Don't drink it, Nahla. It's not clean. We'll get you some water.'

I found a bottle of water in my bag and she drank it thirstily in great gulps. Ma winced and, sure enough, Nahla thrust the bottle back to Ma, bent over and vomited. It was mostly water and easy enough to clear away but Nahla wouldn't stop weeping.

Ma leant over her, took Nahla's face and turned it towards her.

'It's all right. It's going to be all right. Listen to me. We heard today. You've been granted asylum. Do you hear me, Nahla? We can start to think about the future.'

Both of them were drenched from the shower and I wasn't much better. I tried to stop the water but the tap turned round and round in my hand. Probably only a failed washer. I could mend it myself if I had a screwdriver and a spanner. Although, with its rickety pipes falling off the wall, the whole plumbing system looked as though it was about to fail.

Nahla slithered to the ground, her wet clothes clinging to her body. At first she only wept but soon the angry muttering started up again and she thrust her arms in front of her as though pushing away something we couldn't see. The cool water had brought back some colour to her skin but she was still out of it. I wondered if she'd even heard Ma's news.

Ma bit her lip and wiped the water from her face.

'Mama is here.' Rania's voice came in from outside. 'Look, Aya, she is here.' She appeared in the doorway with a much younger child in her arms. Bareheaded and dressed in a T-shirt with a picture of Peppa Pig that had faded until it was only a dark pink patch, and a grubby skirt held up by an old belt, she was as rigid as a stick in Rania's grasp. Not a flicker of emotion passed over her face.

Rania pointed towards Nahla but the little girl's eyes were wide open and fixed on me.

'Jen,' Ma said. 'You'll have to leave. Aya is terrified of strangers. In fact, it's probably better if I go too. Rania, move back and let us out.'

The note of defeat was back in Ma's voice. The child's impassive face followed us and once we were clear of the door, she let Rania take her into the block. Ma bent her head into her hands and took a few deep breaths.

I felt pretty shaken up myself.

'What is going on?' I asked.

And when Ma said nothing.

'With the little girl. Aya, did you say her name was?'

'Aya won't speak. She hasn't said a word since they arrived. And she won't be separated from her mother, except for very, very short times with Rania.'

Ma scrubbed the loose, sandy dirt with her foot.

'Look at Nahla. Look what this place has done to her. You wouldn't believe this is the woman whose poem "My People" inspired so many women to fight in the 2011 rebellion, who helped draft the Libyan Women's Agenda for Peace but who also found the time to write to me every day when your father left. I barely recognised her when she came out of detention. She cried when she saw me and, as soon as the children were asleep, she told me everything that had happened. It all came out like water gushing from a burst pipe. I thought sharing it with me would help, but since then, Rania says she has refused to leave her bed. It's as though the telling of it has emptied her and she has nothing left. Nothing.'

I couldn't bear to hear Ma sound so hopeless. It was so out of character.

'She's ill right now, Ma, she needs a doctor. And for the rest, she needs time. Time to recover. You need to be patient.'

'No.' Ma's voice rang out. 'I have been patient. For too long. You thought I'd sailed to Libya to fetch her. That's what I should have done. I should have helped her months ago instead of being patient.'

She spat the last *patient* out as though it tasted bad.

This was unlike Ma, who normally held that people had to find their own way to truth, love and fulfilment and all the other things she thought we should be striving for.

'I have had to accept help.' She gave me a defiant look as though she guessed what I was thinking. 'And maybe that is why I was brought to Malta. To learn to accept help and to give it.'

Actually, Ma's speech made me feel a bit emotional. As did the clenched fists she tapped together as though preparing to go several rounds with Anthony Joshua.

'The family need time to heal,' she said. 'But they won't find it here.'

Time. We had no time. And now was definitely not the time. Nevertheless I needed to talk to Ma about Tregonna.

'Ma. There's something you need to know.'

'What?'

'Tregonna —'

'Later, Jen.'

She whirled around, her feet swirling little explosions of dust, and headed back to the shower block.

'Pa's going to sell Tregonna,' I said sharply.

That stopped her.

'Pa's selling Tregonna,' I said again but in a calmer voice. 'There's nothing Kit and I can do to stop him. Only you can do that. Or your solicitor can, but he needs you to instruct him.'

Ma waved my words away with a swift jerk of her arm and peered through the hut door.

'Nahla,' she called. 'Jen and I are coming in. We're going to take you to the Musaeada clinic and ask Paulina – she's the nurse – to examine you. Can we come in?'

'Ma, didn't you hear what I said?'

'Not now.'

'But I'm not sure there'll be a later.'

'There's always a later.'

True enough. Although I didn't think Ma would like this particular later. But talking to her now was pointless.

'What are you going to do?'

'Get them out of here, of course.'

'Are they allowed to leave the camp?'

'Of course. People live here because they have no other option.'

'But where? How?'

Rania appeared at the door with Aya in her arms. Both dripped water.

'Sshh.' Ma's hiss cut me off. 'Don't say anything until I've had a chance to discuss it with Peter.'

'Peter? Who's Peter?'

But she disappeared into the shower block.

Peter?

Too many new people in one day: fierce and angry Yasmiin; Amalia, equally angry but keeping a lid on it; the hippyish Shona, who reminded me so much of Ma; the nurse, Paulina, with her mask-like make-up; and, of course, Rania, shifting between caring for her mother and sister and removing herself via her music from the surroundings she hated.

And now there was Peter.

I gave up and followed Ma into the hut to fetch Nahla. I was sure I'd find out who Peter was when Ma was good and ready. I was equally sure I didn't have a chance of persuading Ma to call her solicitor until she'd seen through whatever crazy idea she was chasing.

Ten

I was hot and sticky by the time we reached the clinic. My clothes clung to me and my skin was coated with gritty dust. Ma wasn't much better. The walk had finished Nahla and she sagged against us both, eyes closed, stumbling as she tried to put one foot in front of the other. Rania trailed behind, clutching Aya in her arms, and occasionally staggering under her weight.

The clinic stood hard up against the high perimeter fence, with an expanse of stony ground in front. A temporary building made from chipboard already crumbling on the outside, it was low and mean and windowless, dominated by the tower of massive concrete tubes stacked on the other side of the fence. The waste ground in front served as a car park and a dumping place for overflowing rubbish bins, stacks of pockmarked plastic chairs and a few old bikes chained to the fence. A locked cage in one corner was piled full of pallet trucks, ladders, and barbed wire.

Just as Ma and I were readying ourselves to drag Nahla up the steps, Mohammed, the taxi driver who'd dropped Amalia and me at the garage near the camp, rushed in front of us, clutching cardboard boxes of medical supplies.

'Mohammed,' Ma called out.

He turned, a frown of irritation quickly smoothed into a smile when he saw Ma.

'Could you help us?'

We'd faltered at the steps and the sudden lack of motion stirred

Nahla into life. A stream of invective and spittle bubbled from her lips.

Mohammed, ever courteous, placed the boxes on the ground and took Ma's place by Nahla's side. He smiled at me. 'Shall we get this poor lady inside?'

It was dim in the clinic and warm with a trickle of draught from a window somewhere. Two doors led off the waiting room. One was open revealing a tiny washroom with a sink. The other was closed and, I guessed, led to the surgery itself. An assortment of chairs lined the sides and Mohammed and I placed Nahla in one. She slumped back with her eyes closed, finally silent.

'Thank you,' I said.

He creased his face into its perpetual smile and nodded but, as he turned to fetch the boxes, a look of distaste wrinkled his nose and he pulled his shirt, grubby and damp from contact with Nahla, away from his body. Despite our rinsing in the shower a faint odour of vomit still rose from her clothes and I supposed he wasn't too happy about it.

Rania gazed at Nahla expressionlessly then put Aya onto her mother's unresisting lap and sat beside her, sticking her earphones back in and shutting her eyes as the music took her away. A couple of other women, one with her arm in a sling, looked over briefly, then ignored us. Amalia sat at a table and patted her damp face.

'Could Paulina see Nahla next?' Ma went straight up to her. 'She's delirious and sick. She can't keep anything down.'

As if on cue, Nahla opened her eyes, called out and started retching. Amalia grabbed a bowl and passed it to Rania, who held it for her mother while Aya clung to her lap. Amalia spoke a few words to the waiting women, both of whom nodded quietly.

'That's fine, Morwenna,' Amalia said. 'Paulina will see Nahla next. Luckily the clinic isn't overwhelmed today.' She handed

Rania a cloth to wipe her mother's face and disposed of the bowl's contents in the little washroom off the back.

We waited. In silence. I tried to think a bit but my head was all over the place. I still needed to get Ma away so I could talk to her. Preferably as far away as possible from this awful place with its dirt and dust, its smell of heat and sewers, and its lost and exhausted inhabitants. No one could think clearly here. Was it really possible that the lovely fishing port of Marsaxlokk with its brightly coloured boats bobbing in the bay was only a couple of miles away?

The door into the surgery swung open and banged against the wall. Paulina, her make-up and blonde hair still immaculate, ushered out a heavily pregnant young woman, helped by a man and an older woman.

'Nahla,' Amalia called. 'You're next.'

The call jerked Nahla out of her daze and she looked around her with focussed eyes. For a brief moment I caught a glimpse of the intelligent woman Ma had talked about. She looked towards Paulina and stood up suddenly. Aya rolled off her lap. The child made no attempt to save herself but fell onto the floor with a thud and lay there unmoving and noiseless. Everyone stared.

'Aya,' Nahla's voice was shocked. 'What are you doing?'

It was the first time she'd seemed properly aware of her surroundings and the first time she'd shown any reaction to her daughters. I wondered if she'd even known Aya was on her lap.

'Come on, Nahla,' Ma said and she and Paulina helped her into the surgery, leaving Rania to pick up her unresisting sister. She struggled a little but I knew better than to offer help. My last glimpse of her as she shut the door behind them showed tears streaking through the grime and damp on her cheeks.

The couple who'd been in the surgery sat down and started talking, while the older woman with them picked up a pencil from the table. I fled outside and sat on the step and felt like crying myself. The look of utter despair on Rania's face had cut me.

My phone buzzed. Kit, of course.

Has she called?

There was nothing for it but to ring him.

'Has she spoken to her solicitor?' he said straightaway.

'Not yet. I have explained, though, and tried to get her to call him.'

'Well, you'll have to try again.'

'There's no point, Kit. There are things happening here… It's too hard to explain. But she's on one of her missions.'

We both fell silent and I knew he, like me, was remembering the times spent trailing after Ma when she'd been consumed by some idea and was hell-bent on following it through immediately. How often had she thrown things in the car and headed off with neither of us quite sure what was happening? Maybe a visit to Glastonbury to hunt for King Arthur's tomb or a trip to a shaman visiting Truro to have our dreams interpreted.

'But this time,' I added, remembering Rania's face, 'it's something serious. Can't you have another go at persuading Pa to sign Tregonna over to us? You said you'd pay off the mortgage and he's giving us the rest of the money anyway.'

'He won't. He's got some sort of thing about it. About Tregonna.'

About Tregonna and Ma, I thought. About her love for the place. Had he felt shut out by it? I'd thought it was the other way round. That Pa's feelings for Ma had always come second to his love of the mountains so he'd bought Tregonna for her as compensation. Maybe it had rankled when Tregonna became every bit as important to her as climbing was to him.

'*You'll* have to speak to Pa,' Kit said. 'Persuade him not to sell.'

'No way.'

The words were out of my mouth before I could stop them.

'He'd listen to you.'

'Really?'

I hadn't seen Pa for years. Not since Ma had put me on a train to London for a visit when he was there for a few days. We'd spent an uncomfortable afternoon together saying nothing and then I'd taken the train home. Something about Ma's shuttered face as she waited for me at the station and the way she stretched a smile across it when she caught sight of me made me decide there and then to avoid him. It hadn't been difficult as he was mainly away.

'He asks about you all the time.'

'So?'

'I think you could persuade him.'

'No, Kit.'

'Then Ma can wave goodbye to Tregonna. Think about it.'

I thought about it.

'All right. Maybe. Send me his phone number.'

I rang off and went back inside and walked straight to Amalia who was ticking off a delivery list while Mohammed smiled and waited by her. It was time to get some things sorted.

'Aya,' I said. 'Nahla's younger daughter. There's something very wrong with her. She made no effort to save herself from falling. She just let it happen. Surely that's not normal.'

'Of course it's not normal. Nothing here is normal like you know it. But —'

'Extreme dissociation.'

It was the older woman who interrupted Amalia, the one who'd come out of the surgery with the heavily pregnant woman.

'Pardon?'

She wasn't as old as I'd thought. The lines round her mouth weren't the sagging and wrinkling of tired, old skin but fine threads drawn by life and worry.

'Extreme dissociation,' she explained. 'A disorder when you disconnect from your surroundings and from yourself.'

She stood up and joined us, leaving the pregnant woman leaning against her husband and fanning herself with her hand.

'The child has shut down following some trauma.' Her English was faultless. 'She needs help.'

In a nutshell, I thought.

'As they all do,' Amalia said. Her voice was flat and empty. 'But there isn't any.'

The woman nodded.

'But surely there must –'

'Believe me, Jen, there isn't. And if there was, Aya is one of hundreds of children who need help dealing with trauma.'

She breathed in deeply through flared nostrils, then spoke in a softer voice.

'Mohammed is going back to the office if you want a lift, Jen. Morwenna may be a long time.'

I hesitated. Part of me longed to get back to my clean, light room with its hot water and white bed linen but Rania's expression as she'd followed her mother and mine into the surgery still clung to my thoughts. I wasn't quite ready to leave.

Paulina opened the clinic door and beckoned Amalia to join them. Ma's voice rang out in the background.

'I'll wait,' I said quickly as Amalia left.

'You are sure you want to stay? Really sure?' Mohammed's sheen of bouncy cheer had already worn thin and now it deserted him.

'I'll stay,' I said.

He shrugged and went.

'The little girl – her name is Aya?' The woman who'd talked about extreme dissociation leaned over to me.

'Yes.'

'And the mother?' She fingered the curling edges of children's drawings, the only decoration on the bare wooden walls and I noticed her hands shook. Under her serene surface she was as tense as the rest of us.

'Nahla, and the elder daughter is Rania. And I'm Jen,' I said quickly, wondering how to explain who I was. 'I'm not... I'm...'

'Not a refugee.' She raised an eyebrow. 'Of course you're not. You're white, for a start.'

'I...'

'And you still think help exists. So clearly you're not a volunteer unless you've just arrived.'

'I'm here with my mother, Morwenna.'

'I know Morwenna. She gives the yoga classes?'

'Yes. She and Nahla are old friends. From before. When Nahla was...'

'When Nahla was someone? Before she became a refugee?'

Her eyes held an unspoken challenge.

'When Nahla was teaching in London,' I said quietly. 'They met then. And when she went back to Libya, they stayed friends. Nahla helped my mother through difficult times. It's what friends do.'

I thought I'd passed some sort of test because her face relaxed.

'I'm Marwa,' she said. 'And I *am* a refugee. Or I hope to be one. I'm just waiting to be told if I am acceptable.'

A stray lock of hair fell out from under her headscarf and she pushed it back impatiently.

'But before I became a refugee,' she continued, 'when I was still Marwa Hakim, a woman of standing and ideas, and not merely a refugee, I studied psychology so I understand the theory of what trauma does to children and I have seen the process in many of them.'

Her eyes slipped out of focus for a few seconds, then she shook her head rapidly and looked at me again.

'Your friend, Nahla. Has she been here a long time?'

'She's been in detention on Malta for a while but only in the camp for a few days.'

'Like us. We left detention a couple of weeks ago.'

She pointed over to the heavily pregnant woman and the man beside her.

'Who are they?'

'They are all the family I have now. Zubaida is my niece. She is expecting her third child. The man with her is Yousef, her husband. Zubaida is not well at all. We are worried the baby will come too soon. This clinic is a blessing.'

I nodded, conscious how frail the threads holding Marwa, Nahla and their families to health and hope were.

A voice called Marwa's name and a man peered through the door. His nose had been broken at some time and badly set. Or not set at all. It twisted in a flattened curve to one side and skewed his mouth to a slant.

He opened the door and came in with a couple of children and a young woman.

'This is our friend, Khaled,' Marwa said. 'And his sister, Sarah. They are looking after Zubaida's children. Khaled, this is Jen. She is Morwenna's daughter.'

Something bright lay behind Khaled's eyes. Something alive, whereas so many of the others seemed weighed down by everything. Even Marwa's smiles papered over bitterness.

Through the open door, I saw the shadows cast by the clinic had lengthened. It was getting late.

Khaled spoke rapidly to Marwa while Sarah, his sister, watched him intently. Slightly plump and awkward, she wore a headscarf like most of the women. Metal-framed glasses beneath thick eyebrows cut deep into the sides of her nose. Her eyes were wary.

A van drew up outside. Doors slammed and the sounds of shouting broke the calm of the evening. Khaled said a few words in Arabic and shut the door to the clinic.

'Khaled came because he thinks there might be trouble.' Marwa shot me a quick glance as she explained. 'Sometimes the guards are too harsh and many of the men in the camp were delayed leaving this morning so they missed the vans and had to walk to their work. They are coming back now and they are drunk and angry. Do not go out.'

'No,' Khaled said. 'We must wait.'

The inner door to the surgery opened, revealing a glimpse of white walls. Amalia ushered Nahla out. Aya, walking on her own, clung to her and Ma pushed a drip on wheels by her side. Rania was the last out. She was no longer crying and her face had settled back into listless apathy.

'Severe dehydration,' Ma said in answer to my questioning glance. She fussed around, helping Nahla to sit, while Amalia told the two remaining patients to go in.

The noise outside grew louder. Khaled gestured for everyone to sit and spoke to Amalia. Zubaida, Marwa's niece, drew her children to her and signed them to keep quiet. Everybody sat where they could, their eyes flickering with each new shout.

Ma patted Nahla's arm. 'Nahla and the children are staying here tonight,' she whispered to me. 'Amalia has agreed. It's probably only dehydration making Nahla ill and there is a chemical toilet here and plenty of water.'

Nahla looked less grey and her eyes were open. Her gaze circled the waiting people, resting on each face in turn but I thought she was far away, her vision disconnected from her brain. And when she started crying and ranting once more I knew I was right.

'Paulina,' Ma flung the surgery door open ignoring Amalia's protest. 'It's begun again.'

'She's delirious,' I said to the watching faces wondering if they understood Nahla's ragged phrases. They went back to talking quietly to each other. Only Sarah still stared at her while Marwa patted her hand.

Paulina emerged, followed by the last two patients, and knelt beside Nahla, checking her pulse.

'She'll be fine, Morwenna. It takes time for the drip to rehydrate.' She stood up. 'That's me finished,' she said to Amalia. 'I'm ready to leave whenever you are.'

A body slammed into one of the outside walls, reverberating through the structure, making us all flinch and one of the children whimper. The women edged away from the door.

'I don't think we'll be leaving quite yet.'

A sudden feeling of claustrophobia overwhelmed me. I didn't like confined spaces at the best of time so being stuck in this small room with the heat of nearby bodies thickening the fear in the air made me edgy. Beside me, Rania buried her face in her knees. She was trembling and the sight of it pierced me again. I thought my teenage years had been difficult, rattling round Tregonna with only Ma at her battiest for company, but they bore no comparison to Rania's. I wished I could magic us both away.

'I need to go soon, Amalia. I'm working at the hospital tonight.' Paulina shot a quick glance around and headed into the washroom.

'I'll call the guards,' Amalia said. 'I don't like to do it because they'll throw the men out for the night but it's getting dark and we all need to go home.'

There was no reply from the washroom but a sharp smell of citrus and the sound of a bottle being unscrewed cut through the background miasma of hot bodies and fear. I suspected Paulina was redoing her face.

The shouting increased when the guards arrived and for a few seconds the clinic was encircled by yells and the sound of running feet. Aya's face was blank as granite with the effort of blocking it all out and Rania shrank into an ever-tighter ball. Even Nahla was quieter, only muttering now. I hoped the drip was taking effect. In the washroom, Paulina slammed the window shut, cutting out the worst of the din.

Finally the noise died away. Khaled risked a glance out through the door, then opened it wide. Night had arrived. The ground outside was in shadow. The sky glowed dark blue behind the stark outlines of the containers. Everybody started to leave, hesitating in the doorway before stepping out.

I noticed an envelope on the floor and picked it up. It was folded in half with pencilled figures on it that looked like phone numbers and Arabic writing covering every bit of the rest of the space. There was cash inside.

I handed it to Amalia. 'Is it yours?'

She shook her head but took it from me and went to ask Paulina.

'Marwa,' I called and went to the door. 'Someone has dropped an envelope of money. Could you ask if it belongs to anyone?'

Khaled heard me first and spoke in rapid Arabic to the others. They all shook their heads.

Paulina came up behind me, holding the envelope.

'Are they sure?' she asked. Then broke into Arabic herself and addressed the refugees. Once more everyone shook their heads.

I watched them go. One of them had to have dropped the envelope, which meant someone was lying, but I couldn't for the life of me see why. I was equally sure Sarah knew something. A shot of panic flared across her passive face when I'd first mentioned money.

Paulina pulled the money out. About fifty euros – not a large amount but enough to care about, especially if you had very little. The envelope was grubby and worn and looked as though it had once contained a bigger wad of cash.

'Give it to me,' Amalia said. 'I'll keep it safe until someone claims it.'

She put the money in a drawer and locked it as Paulina watched. Not easy to see in the dim light of the clinic, but I thought she'd redone her lips in a deeper colour.

'Can we go before anything else happens?' Paulina said. She clattered down the steps and I realised she'd changed into shoes with heels. Surely she wasn't going to work in them?

'Is she for real?' I whispered to Ma.

'She's a good nurse,' Ma muttered back.

Amalia showed Rania how to bolt the clinic door from the inside and then drove us out of the camp, dropping Paulina at a bus stop once we'd left the industrial wasteland around the clinic. The heat of the day had dropped since the sun went and we drove with the windows open, welcoming the faint chill in the air.

'I don't like leaving them,' Ma said. 'But Paulina seemed sure Nahla would be better soon.'

'Morwenna,' Amalia said. 'You do understand that Nahla can only stay in the clinic tonight. I know it's dreadful in the containers and I'd like to get all the women out of them but it simply isn't possible.' Her voice trailed away as she sighed.

'I'll have somewhere else for them to stay tomorrow,' Ma said. 'That's why I have to go. So I can get it organised.'

'Don't get your hopes up too much. Or theirs. It's almost impossible to find accommodation. I know of several families who have overrun their allotted time in the camp and are sleeping rough. It's especially hard now, with the holiday season starting.'

'I know. I'm going to ask Peter to take them in until we find something more permanent.'

'You think he'll agree?'

'Yes.'

A little smile curled Ma's lips. She'd always been good at persuading people to do things for her and I guessed the mysterious Peter was another poor sod caught up in her threads. There'd been a succession of them after Pa had left. Men wanting to look after her mainly. Allowed to stay around and be useful until they did something she disliked.

'And before you say it, I know we can't help them all,' she said. 'But I can help Nahla.'

'No one can help them all.'

'I know but that's no reason for me not to help Nahla.'

She was right.

'There he is,' she called as we stopped outside the office. A charcoal grey Passat flashed its lights at us and Ma got out of Amalia's car.

'Ma,' I shouted. 'Don't just disappear. I need to talk to you.'

'Come to lunch tomorrow,' she said. 'I'm staying at Peter's. He'd love to meet you.'

'But Ma,' I shouted after her as she disappeared into Peter's car. 'I...'

The Passat drove off.

'I'm not chasing after them,' Amalia said.

'There's no point. It'll have to wait. Except I don't even know where this Peter lives.'

'Give me your mobile number. I'll send you the address when I get home. You do have a mobile? You're not like Morwenna?'

'I'm not a bit like my mother,' I said.

Eleven

Marsaxlokk was lively this evening. People walked along the quay or sprawled around tables outside the bars and restaurants, sipping wine and laughing. Waiters ran between them, holding trays high above heads and flicking crumbs off tablecloths watched by the darting eyes of the pigeons. Streams of coloured lights lit the restaurants' stone walls and, through their open doors, softer lighting glowed while talk and laughter spilled into the streets.

I wandered among them for a time trying to shake off the weight of the misery I'd seen today but none of the light and colour and cheer around me felt real. It was like walking through a virtual reality experience knowing that as soon as I removed my headset I'd be in an empty warehouse.

But still I walked until I realised I was only doing it to avoid phoning Pa.

I chose a bench on the quay away from the main hub of cafés and bars. A place I'd never have to come back to.

It had been a day of confusing and tangled emotions and the phone call would be no better. I was too tired to even begin to unpick the mess of sticky feelings I had around Pa. All I could do was face up to the fact they were there.

'Pa,' I said when he answered, but I'd gone straight to voice mail.

'Charlie Shaw here.'

The familiarity of his voice shocked me although I didn't know why. Of course I'd recognise it. He was my father.

'You know what to do,' the recording went on.

But I didn't.

What sort of message can you leave your father to stop him from hurting your mother deeply? Especially when you suspect that's what he wants to do.

'Pa, it's Jen here. Please call me.' And after a pause. 'It's urgent.'

It only took him a few seconds. The screen flashed his number. A number but no name. He'd never been in my contacts.

'Hello, Pa.'

'Hello, Jen.'

Pause.

I will not ask him how he is.

'How are you, Jen?'

I will not say fine.

'Fine. And you?'

'Fine too.'

Pause.

'So to what do I owe –'

'Please don't sell Tregonna.'

'Pardon?'

'You heard me.'

'I did.'

Silence. All the reasons why he shouldn't sell Tregonna rose to my lips but I didn't voice them. What was the point? He knew them. Kit had already said them all.

Nevertheless he asked.

'Why not?'

'Because... You know why not.'

Another silence.

'Maybe I think it's time you all had lives that weren't bound up in that hulk of a house.'

I will not say that he may be right.

'That's not really for you to decide.'

'But it is, Jen. It is. It's my house.'

'But it's our home.'

We were playing with words, throwing them at each other like two children batting a ball back and forth.

'Please,' I said. 'Please don't sell Tregonna. It would…'

But I couldn't say it. I couldn't bring Ma into this conversation. It would be a betrayal.

'Please, Pa.'

And forcing the words through a clenched jaw. 'For Kit's sake. And for mine.'

The reflections on the water broke into streaks and the boats bobbed furiously as a sudden gust of wind rolled over the bay. I pressed the phone tight to my ear, waiting to hear what he'd say.

'I'll put a hold on it.'

'What does that mean?'

'It means that I'll pause the whole process. I'll tell the buyers I need more time.'

He still hadn't answered my question. Pause it? But for how long and to what end?

'And?'

'And we can discuss it. Kit and me and you. Together. I'll be in London in a couple of weeks with…'

I waited.

'With Issy. I'd like you to meet her.'

Who the fuck is Issy?

'And she'd love to meet you.'

Something told me Kit knew who she was but he hadn't thought to tell me. Or hadn't wanted to.

'How about it, Jen? A little family get-together?'

I got it. This was the price for stopping the sale of Tregonna. Not exactly couched in those terms but that was the deal.

'Of course,' I said. 'That'll be fun.'

I prayed that my tone of voice hadn't given me away.

'Text me when and where,' I said. 'I'll be there.'

A couple of weeks, I thought as I finished the call. I'd bought us a couple of weeks. That was time enough to prod Ma into action.

Who is Issy? I texted Kit.

Pa's latest squeeze.

Bit more than that? No?

Yes.

Thanks for warning me btw.

How did you get on?

Sale on pause.

Until?

Until we have a jolly family get-together.

No response for a few minutes.

He just called me. Sale definitely on hold.

OK.

And then because I couldn't bring myself to tap the words out, I called Kit and told him to check. To make sure that Pa did what he'd said he would. Because I wasn't planning to keep my side of the deal and, sure as hell, I didn't trust Pa to keep his.

I came to in the dark. Half awake. My brain thick with the threads of dreams binding it.

What was the noise? My alarm? But it was the middle of the night and I wasn't due anywhere for work. I was in Malta. In my hotel room. My phone was ringing.

I answered it without thinking.

'Jen,' a voice I didn't recognise said. 'Thank God. Where are you?'

'In bed. Who is this?'

'Is Morwenna with you?'

'Ma? No. But why –'

'Do you know where she is?'

'Who is this?'

'Amalia.'

I took the phone away from my ear. It was three twenty-two. Why was Amalia calling me at three twenty-two in the morning?

'What's happened?'

'It's all kicked off at the camp. The men who the guards threw out returned en masse and started making trouble. Now it's chaos. They're smashing things up, torching cars. They've overrun the guards' complex and –'

'Why are you telling me this?'

'Morwenna went back to take Nahla food and she's not returned. Peter called me. I've rung everybody I can to find out what's happening. I called you on the off chance you might know…'

'No,' I said slowly as the weight of what she was saying sunk in. 'I haven't seen Ma since you dropped us off.'

I kicked off the sheets and forced myself upright. Shit, shit, shit. Tiredness lay like a coating of lead on my body.

'Not even Ma would go into the camp if there was a riot happening.'

'She could have got in before the trouble began. It was quiet for quite a while.' Her voice echoed the anxiety I was starting to feel.

'Shit.'

'Quite.'

'I'm going down there.'

'No, Jen.'

But as soon as the words left my mouth I knew I had no choice.

'I've rung a couple of clients in the camp with mobile phones. They say it's terrifying. Running battles between rioters and police.' Amalia's voice was flat with despair. 'It's been going to happen for weeks. Overcrowded. Under-resourced. Full of people with little or no hope. We warned the authorities.'

I was sure she was right but I was barely listening as I tried to decide the best thing to do.

'There's no point going there. We won't get near the camp,' Amalia said. 'They've locked the whole area down.'

I'd find a way. I would. I had to know Ma was safe.

'So stay put,' Amalia went on relentlessly. 'I'll let you know the moment I have any news.'

I scoured my brain for memories of the camp layout. The front with its steel gate and its wall ran alongside a smallish road leading to a roundabout at the corner of the camp. The wall would be easy to climb if I could get to it.

'Jen.'

'Yes.'

'We'll go down together as soon as it's safe.'

'Yes.'

'I'll call you and arrange a place to meet.'

'Sure.'

'Are you listening to me?'

I wasn't. I wrenched my mind away from the camp and promised Amalia I'd wait by the phone.

And then, rather than heading out immediately, I forced myself to prepare. I put on the darkest clothes I had and grabbed anything that might be useful from the room, checked the camp on Google Earth and the roads leading to it. I thought about what I might find when I got there and thanked the gods and goddesses Ma believes in that I'd spent so much time parkouring while I was in Cornwall.

For a fraction of a second a few doubts slithered through my mind.

Was I sure?

Yes, I was.

Had I got everything I needed?

No idea. But who knew what I'd find when I got there.

And then I tiptoed down the hotel staircase and went out into the dark.

I didn't drive straight to the camp. Instead I took the main road to the airport, figuring there'd be no roadblocks stopping people from getting there, parked and went on foot. Police cars and fire engines blaring sirens into the night passed me from time to time but otherwise the roads were deserted.

The glow of the fire, filthy orange on the heavy smoke spreading over the ground south of the airport, told me which way to go. I came across a roadblock early on but it was a half-hearted affair. Two policemen stopping lorries and redirecting them to the main port. They weren't expecting pedestrians and all their attention was on the road. Nevertheless I kept out of sight. I slipped up the fire escape of an adjacent building, pulled myself onto the roof and over it, climbing down some ducting on the far side.

I was careful after that, dodging into the rough bushes or jumping behind the low walls lining the road when I heard cars coming. I didn't meet another roadblock until the roundabout where the road to the camp split off from the main road. This was serious though with heavy metal barriers manned by police with guns.

Shit.

There was no way of getting to the front of the camp and its easy-to-climb wall, full of holds where rendering had crumbled and bricks come away. The access road was crammed with police and soldiers. Fire engines flashed blue light and the air was full of the crackle of walkie-talkies.

I looked around. The front of the camp was out of reach but the main road continued on over the roundabout and passed along the back of the camp, although a swathe of gravel separated it from the camp's high fence.

Could I get in that way?

The rolls of barbed wire at the top of the fence would be problematic but otherwise it would be easy, especially as the camp was quiet at this side. The tiers of shipping containers could have been stacked peacefully in a storage yard. Only the faint noise of shouting, of banging, of distant explosions, along with the blooms of orange and black smoke hovering above, showed the rioting elsewhere.

But as I watched and calculated my moves, two minibuses drove onto the land by the fence. Policemen with dogs emerged and started patrolling the fence while others set up mobile lighting towers I knew would eliminate any convenient shadows for me to hide in.

I wasn't going to get in that way.

Only the far side of the camp, which ran through an industrial supplier's yard, was unwatched. But I'd have to get into the yard first and that meant leaping over its fence which ran along a deserted but brightly lit section of main road beyond the roundabout. It would only take a casual glance for the police and soldiers to see me.

I crawled away from the roundabout and called Amalia.

'Any news,' I hissed.

'No.'

'Shit. So she's not back?'

'No.'

'Maybe she's been stopped at a roadblock. It would be just like her to stay and argue. Maybe they've arrested her.'

'Peter's out there looking. She's not on any of the roads leading to the camp and there's no sign of her at any of the blocks.'

Shit.

A police car sped past, sirens blaring.

'Where are you, Jen?'

'Just outside the camp.'

A sudden gasp on the end of the phone, then a short silence.

'How did you get there?' she asked. 'Peter can't get near.'

'I'm on foot. Listen, what kind of car is Ma driving?'

'She'll be in Peter's old mini.'

'Colour?'

'Sort of blue. In between the rust.'

I rang off.

I'd have to get in and find Ma. Or at least check she was safe.

As soon as the police at the roadblock were occupied dragging the barriers open for a truck of soldiers, I slithered past on the ground, half-hidden by the low wall and thanking the gods I'd thought to wear black. I darted down the empty main road between pockets of darkness until I was outside the industrial yard. Everyone's attention was fixed on the camp. No one noticed me. Maybe I could do this.

The fence between the road and the yard was only a run of spiked steel uprights a couple of metres high. Anyone could get over it. After all, who would want to break in and steal from the piles of used tyres, rusting oil drums and broken slabs of concrete inside? I dodged across the road in a dark patch between street lights and chucked the things I'd grabbed from the hotel room over the fence. No one shouted.

My head buzzed with the moves I was going to make as I ran to the far side of the road; my muscles twitched; adrenalin spiked along my nerves and, almost without thinking, I threw myself into a quick handspring and front flip, arcing my body up and up and over in the air, then landed precisely on the kerb. A quick warm up. A moment of reassurance that I could do this. Basic moves, I knew, but my muscles responded instinctively and if anyone had been watching they would have been impressed.

Shouts came from the roundabout.

Shit.

Someone *had* been watching.

Answering yells from nearby, and a dog barked.

It was now or never.

I raced to the fence, letting excitement and fear bite into my blood, launched myself into the air, seized the horizontal bar and used the momentum to lift and kick my legs above my head in a wide flip over the spikes. I landed with a roll on the tarmac the other side of the fence.

Success!

In the distance, car doors slammed and an engine started up. It was time to disappear and I was in a hider's paradise. I snatched my stuff and sprinted behind a pile of tyres then round the back of a stack of rusting tanks. The police car squealed to a stop outside and I bent double as I raced to a mountain of huge concrete pipes, flinging myself inside the first and crawling into its middle.

My heart beat loudly and my breathing was ragged. Through my legs I saw torchlight break the dark and run over the concrete slabs heaped up nearby. I kept very still as it played over the ground then withdrew. Car doors slammed again and they drove away.

I became aware of other sounds: the background murmur of people shouting and feet running; a relentless hissing and crackling; the occasional thud of an explosion; and sometimes a scream. In the distance, the ever-present song of sirens and the sound of shattering glass rose in a discordant duet.

I crawled down the pipe towards the smell of burning and acrid smoke. Only a couple of metres separated the pipe's end from the fence between the yard and the camp.

On the other side, a sudden eruption of shouting broke through the billowing black smoke that clouded everything and figures came into view, racing along the containers' roofs with blazing torches whose flames streamed behind them. Others tore past on the ground, slowing only to smash the windows of parked cars and hurl burning rags inside.

And then they were gone and the only things moving were the flames flickering inside the cars. A burst of fire shot out from underneath one as a sudden explosion crashed into the night. The car shuddered and sank as its tyres burst. A second one fired up and ignited the rubbish from bins kicked over in the stampede.

I knew where I was.

The bins and cars orientated me. In my dash to hide from the police I'd come further than I thought. I'd hidden in the concrete pipes behind the clinic. In front of me was the area used for storage and the place where guards and visitors parked their cars. The building to my left was the Musaeada clinic with Nahla and her daughters holed up inside.

And Ma.

I hoped. Shit, I more than hoped. The camp was no place for anyone to be wandering round alone.

Was her car there? If it was, it meant she was probably safe inside the clinic.

None of the burning cars close to the fence had the low boxy profile of a Mini. I scrambled backwards down the pipe and out. I'd get a much better view from the top.

As I clambered up, I realised I was not alone. Sleeping bags and tattered blankets lay inside the pipes. In one a child's face stared back at me. People slept here. I remembered Amalia saying she knew of families who'd outstayed their time at the camp and were living rough. These must be some of them.

None of them were sleeping though. Most were at the far ends and looking into the inferno beyond the fence and, when I reached the top, a handful of men had gathered there too. They moved aside as I headed to the edge and looked over. One of them was Mohammed, the taxi driver, but he didn't see me. Like the others his face was grim and fixed on the camp below. I wondered what he was doing here then forgot about him as I surveyed the waste ground around the clinic. It was a flickering scene of devastation. Full of cars at different stages of incineration. Some were already burnt out, maybe caught in a previous storm of fire-raising, the greyed and black metal of their bodies distorted and battered. But most had settled to a steady blaze, interrupted only by the occasional crack of a window breaking into fragments or by gobs of melted tyre and plastic launching themselves into the air and landing yards away, hissing.

Was Ma's car here? My eyes hovered over the square frame of a Jeep Renegade, dismissed it, and then I caught sight of the familiar shape of a Mini. She'd made it here. I sagged with relief.

And jumped as two tyres exploded in quick succession. A couple of men let out cries of fright and then we all laughed and looked around at each other in the moment of recognition that follows a shock. They turned to look back at the scene but not before I recognised Khaled from the clinic earlier. His broken nose and lopsided face were unmistakeable.

He saw me and came over with another man who I recognised from the clinic too – Marwa's nephew, or, at least, the husband of her pregnant niece, Zubaida. Try as I might, I couldn't remember his name.

'It is Jen, isn't it?' Khaled said.

'Yes.'

'What are you doing here? It isn't safe for a woman.'

'It isn't safe for anybody.' I shot back. 'Ma – Morwenna, my mother. She came here tonight to the clinic and I wanted to check she was safe inside.'

I'd have liked to know for sure. What if she'd arrived as the violence broke out and hadn't made it into the clinic?

'She is,' Khaled said simply. 'I saw her earlier. It was quiet then. She'd brought food and she offered us some of it.'

Ma was inside the clinic. We just needed to wait until the police took control of the site again and, judging by the numbers assembling outside, that wouldn't be too long. I'd wait here and watch it out, then see her home.

'I am locked out,' Khaled went on. 'With Yousef.' He nodded towards the other man.

Yousef. That was his name. I looked at him more closely, wondering what had happened that had made fleeing Libya with a pregnant woman and two children preferable to staying put.

'His wife, Zubaida, has gone to hospital. Marwa and I went with them while Sarah looked after the children.'

'Is she having the baby?'

'He hopes not because it is too early.'

'He didn't stay with her?'

A sudden flare from one of the burning cars lit up Khaled's face and I felt its heat on my own skin.

'Only one person allowed. Neither Yousef nor Zubaida speak good English, so it was better Marwa, her aunt, stayed.'

I nodded.

'Mohammed brought us back. He knew this place. He thought we might be able to get over the fence and into the camp from up here. I am worried about Sarah, and Yousef wants to get back to his children.'

I looked down. He'd have failed if he'd tried. Coils of barbed wire topped the fence and overhung the camp. It was heavy-duty stuff with razor-sharp blades designed to slice flesh and do serious damage.

A sudden movement in the narrow gap between the fence and

the clinic's back wall caught my eye. The maelstrom of flames elsewhere cast it into profound darkness so I wasn't sure what I'd seen. I peered down. Something moved again. It was more of a flickering in the dark than anything else, as though something had stirred the blackness.

Was someone hiding there?

Ma? Please not Ma. Please don't let it be her, tempted outside by the departure of the rioters. Because they were still around. Yells and crashes still echoed in the distance. Puffs of flame and smoke still shot into the night sky.

I cast a glance at the men up here with me, their sober faces orange and gold in the reflected light. Had they seen it? But all were staring into the distance. Except Mohammed whose face was turned to me, his mouth slack with surprise.

I looked back down. A flash of white broke the dark, followed by a crack and maybe the sound of shattering glass. It was hard to tell against the backdrop of noise but this had sounded nearer and more immediate.

Mohammed shouted and pointed at the tops of the distant containers. Khaled said something to me. I couldn't make his words out, but it didn't matter because I heard it too. The rioting men were coming back. Another stampede of them burst into view and streamed past, some clutching metal bars, some still brandishing sticks tied with flaming cloth. All screaming defiance.

They tore through and went, leaving a sudden and curious peace behind them.

The sound of a mobile phone broke it. It was Mohammed's. He answered it, pacing along the edges of the tubes as he spoke in short bursts. He shouted a few words once he'd finished.

'He says the police are coming in,' Khaled said. 'There will be fighting but the police will win. It is nearly over. *Alhamdulillah*.'

Yousef muttered something in Arabic.

'Yousef is angry because afterwards things will be worse. He says there is no point to all this. He is right.'

I looked down to the back of the clinic again but the blackness was solid now. Nothing moved. Whoever had been there was gone. Then something else split the dark. A flash of gold. No, orange. Then another. They became a steady square of shimmering fire stabbing the night.

I stared at it, wondering why it was a square and how the edges could be so sharp and distinct. So black. Long seconds passed as understanding rose through my brain and hit me with a punch, slamming the breath out of my body.

Fire. It was fire. Inside the clinic. Fire inside the washroom at the back of the waiting room. Fire framed by its little window.

No time to think. I had to get there.

I grabbed the stuff I'd brought from the hotel. My fingers fumbled as I undid the clumsy knots of curtain tieback fastened round a rug. Thank God I'd taken the minutes to seize these things.

And as my fingers worked, thoughts spun through my head.

How long had I got?

Bits of fire regulations and protocols I remembered from work burst into knowledge as I chose my bit of fence. Away from the window, burning brighter and brighter, but near the clinic. The clinic made of wood. Of wood already warmed and dried by the day.

How long had I got? No, not me. How long had they got?

Minutes at most. Less probably. The fire had caught and would spread at speed.

I fixed the rug tight to my body with the tiebacks and raced towards the fence, forcing myself to breathe, forcing my muscles to prepare to explode. And as I leapt over the gap, I sent a plea arrowing towards the clinic.

Please, Ma. Get out of there. You've got seconds. Get the door open and leave. The door. Open the door.

The door was their only hope. There were no windows apart from the little one at the back, the one that had been broken by the fire-raiser and was already letting oxygen through to feed the flames.

My body slammed into the fence. Fingers and toes scrabbled for holds then kicked and seized the wire and pushed me up to the top, holding me for long enough to grab the rug from my back, shake it open and fling it over the barbed wire.

Would it be thick enough?

No time to think. Stop thinking.

I thrust my hands onto the rug, kicked my legs up and vaulted over and out and onto the far end of the clinic's gently sloping roof where I wobbled for a few seconds as the force of the jump juddered out of my muscles.

Heat licked my skin. And panic.

I've made it. Now what?

I scrambled along the roof to the front of the clinic, almost tripping over the cracked and peeling felt, hoping I'd look down and see the door open and swinging, see Ma and the others standing outside.

They weren't. The door was shut. They were still inside.

Shit, shit, shit.

Blasts of hot air swirled into my face like dragon's breath. The hut with its old, dry wood would go up any minute.

I felt rather than heard the thumping beneath my feet. Someone was banging against the ceiling below. Yes! Someone had heard me leap and land, then run across the roof. I stamped back.

My brain raced as I hunted for ideas.

Could I get down and force the door?

Bang, bang, bang.

The noise came from directly below. They were in the surgery.

A new smell shot through the choking air.

Bang.

It was tar.

Bang.

The stench grew stronger until it overwhelmed the sharp bitterness of the smoke.

Bang.

Tar? How could it be tar?

Bang, bang, bang.

The roofing felt was impregnated with tar. On the far side of the ridge above the waiting room, dark glistening pools spread over its dull green surface.

Bang, bang, bang.

I touched the roof and snatched my hand away as the heat seared my fingertips.

Another bang from below.

They were trapped in the surgery by the fire in the waiting room, so fierce its heat was melting the tar in the roofing felt above. It dripped over the edges and sizzled in the dust and ashes below. Any minute the molten pools would reach the apex and start seeping towards me. Forcing the front door would only send more oxygen in to feed what must already be an inferno.

I seized a crack in the felt at the edge of the roof, where it was still cool enough to touch and yanked until it tore away, popping tacks out as it lifted slowly, so, so slowly, off the roof below. I screamed my rage.

Another thud, but this time close by. Khaled landed beside me. He wasted no time but grabbed the felt and pulled too. Together we heaved it away and hurled it over the far side. Smoke poured through the cracks in the exposed timber roofing. A wave of heat smacked my face.

The hut must be nearing flashover. The point at which the walls and roof would spontaneously ignite.

Khaled started to jump. Great kicking leaps that smashed his feet into the boards. It juddered and creaked under his weight but held. I skidded over to join him, timing my desperate leaps to land with his. Shouts from above distracted us for a second. Yousef climbed over the fence where the rug lay over the barbed wire. He held on with one hand, while the other gripped a bundle of loose fencing uprights, their points glittering in the fiery dark. More men swarmed up the fence after him.

We went back to jumping. The boards caved and splintered. Yousef joined us and together we kicked a hole through and tore the insulation beneath away. And then there was hardboard. Hardboard and hope. Because I was sure it was the last layer. The last barrier between us and them. Yousef seized a piece of spiked fence and forced it through. Khaled took another and joined him.

The fire's roar was everywhere now. A great beast. A tiger, crouched and ready to spring.

Smoke poured out of the hole as Khaled screamed down. A head shot through. It was Aya, pushed up from below. The men grasped her and passed her straight to me. She was rigid with terror but there was no time to comfort her. I had to get her off the roof. And, as I looked over the side wondering if I could drop her gently to the ground, the hands of the men who'd climbed after us reached up to take her.

Rania came out next, coughing and screaming something about her mother. I handed her down to the waiting arms of the men and crawled back to the hole. Thick smoke snatched my breath away but through it I saw Ma kneeling on a chair. Her arms clutched an unconscious Nahla, trying to lift the dead weight of her body towards us.

'Ma!'

Yousef, Khaled and I reached down and hauled Nahla up and out. Yousef dragged her to the side and into the waiting arms below.

Down in the surgery, Ma was bent double, coughing violently. Smoke billowed in and hid her. I screamed her name.

Nothing.

Except the noise of the fire and the sound of sirens coming. Too late. They were too late.

I pushed my feet through the hole and prepared to leap down. Khaled's thrust his face into mine.

'No,' he shouted. 'No.'

But before I could shove him away, Ma's hand seized my feet from below and pulled.

'Help her,' I screamed at Khaled.

He saw and plunged his arms down to help her heave herself out.

As she emerged, the hut ignited with a gentle whoosh. A sudden wind whipped the hair off my face as the hungry fire sucked at the air. Flames burst through the roof. People below screamed and fled. We ran to the edge and hurled ourselves off, feet pedalling in a great leap to get as far from the inferno as we could.

And landed with a thud that ground stones and grit into my skin and knocked the breath out of me. Before I could stand, arms seized me and dragged me away.

Blue flashing lights were everywhere. Help had arrived.

Breath poured back into my shocked and empty lungs and raked their smoke-inflamed tissue. I coughed in heaving spasms as though someone was tightening and releasing a thick rubber band round my ribs. I gasped for breath. Someone fixed a mask over my head and I felt the sharp sting of an injection. Cool oxygen streamed through my nostrils and into my shaking body. The tightness and pain faded.

For a while I sat and did nothing but enjoy breathing. The muscles in my diaphragm and between my ribs drew the sweet air into my lungs, waited a blissful second then pushed it out again.

Around me bursts of action broke the night but I felt strangely detached. Firemen pointed jets of foam onto cars, smothering the blaze and leaving dark grey metal skeletons dripping behind. Vans screeched to a halt and disgorged teams of black-clad police carrying riot shields who disappeared into the camp.

The car park filled up with refugees, herded out of their containers at gunpoint and forced to sit, hands on their heads, on the rough and filthy ground.

I was sitting on the ground too with my back against a yellow and green chequered ambulance. Ma was standing beside me. Like me she had an oxygen mask on her face with a tube leading to a white cylinder beside her. Like me she clutched a blanket round her shoulders.

I touched her leg but she ignored me. Her eyes were fixed elsewhere. I struggled to my feet to see what she was staring at.

Bright lights shone from the back of the ambulance onto a quiet drama nearby. A figure lay on the ground with two paramedics kneeling over it. One of them, with arms straight, pumped its chest while the other held its wrist.

It was Nahla.

A group of silent figures watched. I searched among them and found her daughters. Aya clutching Rania. Both of them staring at their mother, their eyes wide and white against the soot covering their faces, their bodies shaken by great gasps for breath.

They shouldn't be watching this but as I tried to move, tall Yasmiin from Ma's yoga class, her face full of anguish rather than fury, stepped forward into the light. She put her arms round the two of them, drawing them to her, while Sarah, Khaled's sister, moved in between them and the dreadful scene playing out on the ground.

131

Another paramedic came out of the ambulance, knelt and spoke to the two beside Nahla. They stopped CPR and shook their heads. Then slowly got to their feet.

It was over.

Nahla was dead.

Ma huddled her face in the blanket. Nahla's daughters were hidden by Yasmiin and Sarah's encircling arms and bodies. Yousef and Khaled were there too. Their faces sombre and exhausted by the night's horrors.

Yousef turned to speak to a man in the shadows behind them. He moved forward and the ambulance light caught him. Everything else blurred and dimmed as my eyes locked onto his face.

A myriad of details detonated little explosions in my head.

In the weeks since I'd seen him, his black hair had grown long enough to pull the curl to an uneven straggle.

The designer stubble had become a drooping moustache and short beard.

His face was still unreadable beneath the thick eyebrows casting shadows over his eyes.

Nick.

Blood drained from my head and black dots ate at the edge of my vision.

Nick was here.

His eyes flicked away from Yousef. He saw me. I was sure he did. Because he froze and his tight mouth slipped open on a quick inward gasp.

Then all around us sprang into life. Paramedics bundled Ma and me into the ambulance, both too dazed to protest, and when I looked out through the doors Nick had gone. Only the women still holding Rania and Aya were there, lowering themselves onto the ground as police with megaphones shouted at them to sit.

The ambulance doors slammed shut and we drove off.

'What about the children?' Ma's voice splintered with the effort of speaking.

'Keep the mask on. Best not to talk,' the paramedic said.

'But there were children with me in the fire. They need help too.'

'Children?' A look of concern crossed his face.

'The daughters of the woman who died.' Ma gasped the words out.

'Ah. Refugees, then. Put your mask back on.'

Ma's mouth fell open and her eyes blinked rapidly. The paramedic took advantage of her momentary confusion to push her onto the other bed and tie the mask over her mouth. There was an unnecessary edge of force in his actions.

I pulled myself together. We couldn't leave now. Rania and Aya needed to be checked over, along with Khaled and Yousef.

And Nick? Had I seen Nick?

'Let us out.'

But there was no point asking the paramedic. Threads of anger ticked beneath his skin and showed themselves in the ridged veins running down his forehead. I banged the side of the ambulance.

'Stop that,' he said.

I didn't reply but carried on – anything to make them let me out.

He reached over to grab my hand.

I pulled the mask aside. 'Don't you dare touch me.'

He faltered, then reached out again. Ma banged against the other side. The driver pulled the connecting window open and called something through in Maltese. They argued while Ma and I banged and banged and banged.

The ambulance came to a halt. The back doors swung open and the driver stared in. I ripped the mask off and pushed my way out.

We were in the road outside the camp entrance. The open gate lay behind us filled with rows of armed soldiers standing ready. It was eerily quiet apart from the crackle of walkie-talkies and impending aggression.

Someone shouted my name and Amalia ran down the road towards us. After her strode a man in an impossibly white and crisp shirt. For a moment I thought it was Pa. He had the same tall and rangy body, the same close-cut hair and the same manner of always being in control. But as he came nearer I recognised him for a stranger.

A wave of dizziness blurred my vision and made my knees crumple. I blurted out to Amalia that Nahla was dead and her daughters needed help as the man leapt into the ambulance and enfolded Ma in his arms, muttering her name over and over again. And when she pulled back to grab the oxygen mask he'd knocked away, the last thing I noticed before I passed out was the huge sooty mark her face had left on his shirt.

Twelve

The clanking of a hospital trolley pulled me out of a deep sleep. I looked at my watch. Ten thirty in the morning. Quite late by hospital standards but I guessed they'd left me to rest since I'd briefly lost consciousness due to exhaustion. We'd only been admitted at five, finally allowing the ambulance to take us once Amalia had promised she wouldn't leave the camp until Rania and Aya were checked over along with Khaled and Yousef.

I felt OK. Tired and only half awake. A bit frayed around the edges. My breathing was easy even without the oxygen mask that had been removed while I slept, and my chest didn't hurt any more. They'd checked me over for burns last night before settling me in this white and sterile room that felt like paradise after the noise and mess at the camp. They'd found a few on my hands and arms but nothing much. I'd been lucky. The fire had had no serious consequences.

Except that Nahla was dead.

I woke up completely.

And Ma and Rania and Aya barely escaped in time.

Memories flooded back and for a few minutes they submerged me. Flames crackled in my ears and heat seared my skin. I gripped the stiff white sheet and forced myself to focus on the here and now.

It was over. And Ma was alive. Kit walked into my thoughts. Thank God I wasn't having to call him with the news she was dead.

I got out of bed and rinsed my face with cold water.

One memory still nagged at me. The dark figure I'd seen round the back of the clinic. The beginning of the nightmare. The fire hadn't been ignited by one of the burning cars although that was what everyone would think. Someone had broken the back window, lit a rag and thrown it in and it hadn't been the angry actions of a rioter. No. This had felt calculated. Targeted. But I couldn't for the life of me think why anyone would want to burn down the Musaeada clinic. I should tell Amalia, though. Whatever the reason for burning the clinic down, she needed to know.

I found my clothes inside the locker by the bed. They were filthy and full of holes where hot sparks had burned through the cotton, and I abandoned the idea of putting them on. My trainers were destroyed as well. Spatters of tar had landed on the tops and the heat on the roof had melted bits of the soles.

Ma opened the door.

'We need to get out of this place before it makes us ill,' she said, sitting down with a thump on my bed and coughing. 'They keep trying to pump me full of poison. I told them I'd got chamomile eyewash at home and I'd take some Euphorbium for my lungs. Or maybe some Kali-bi.'

She went through a few other homeopathic remedies at great speed, counting them off on her fingers as she spoke. I realised she was barely holding herself together.

'I stink,' she added.

She was right. Despite the clean clothes she was wearing, the bitter smell of smoke and tar and chemical clung to her. I sniffed my hair and skin. It clung to me too under the sickly scent of the antiseptic they'd covered me in last night. God, I wanted a shower.

'Are you all right,' I asked.

It was a stupid question. None of us were all right. Nahla was dead.

She wrapped her arms round herself in a tight hug and rocked back and forth.

'Not really. Just need to get out of this place. Peter brought us some clothes.' She handed me a bag. 'He's coming back in half an hour to get us.'

'Peter. Tell me about Peter. Who is he?'

Some of her twitchiness subsided as she told me how Amalia had contacted her to tell her Nahla was in Malta. She'd left immediately of course, taking a coach to the tip of Italy and then a ferry. At first, she'd stayed in a hostel, sharing a room with five other women, but even that had become too expensive for her once she'd realised how long the whole process of helping Nahla was going to take.

'I met Peter at Musaeada,' she went on. 'And he offered me a room. He gives English lessons to the refugees but, at heart, he's a nomad like me.' She stood up and started waving her arms around in a way I guessed was supposed to show how free the two of them were, but the effort was too much. She coughed and sat down again. 'We're both sailing the currents of change and following our destiny wherever it takes us. Both of us on the same path. Both free spirits.' She waffled on a bit more about things falling into place and the universe aligning itself. And I gathered she was trying to tell me that she and Peter were having some sort of relationship.

'So are you sleeping with the poor man?'

She smiled for the first time since she'd come in and sidestepped the question but clearly she was. And even more clearly she was happy about it. Fair enough. I was glad someone was looking out for her. She rattled on for a while and I listened with half an ear as I sorted through the clothes. Being Ma's they were all frilly and wafty but at least they smelled clean and fresh. I chose a vaguely denim-coloured dress with the minimum of flounces and lace. The underwear was plain and white. No shoes though.

I learned that Peter, although from Manchester, had lived in Malta for years and was teaching at one of the language schools in Valletta at the moment, although he had private pupils too, and he donated some of his time free to Musaeada.

He sounded quite together, unlike the other saps who'd hung around Ma before, all of them bewitched by her and trying to look after her, never realising that deep down she was as tough and uncatchable as the bats who lived in the trees around Tregonna.

'Ma,' I said, cutting her off in full flow – something about ridding yourself of the ties that drained your emotional energy. 'What exactly happened last night?'

The smile on her face faded.

'It was dreadful. Oh, Nahla. My poor Nahla.'

'I know.'

'We'd had such a lovely evening until the fire. I went back to the clinic with food for them, real food, not the dreadful meals they get in the camp. And I'd spoken to Peter and he was happy for them to come and stay with us.'

She broke off, went to the window and forced the catch so it opened.

'I should have taken them to Peter's straightaway but Nahla had her drip and I thought it would be better to wait until the morning so they could pack up once and for all. But she was happy. The delirium was gone and I saw glimpses of the woman I used to know. I'd brought a pack of cards and we played a game Nahla's parents used to play with the girls. Rania taught me how. It was such fun and we all laughed, and Rania and Nahla chatted. I don't think Nahla had had any time for Rania for a while; dealing with Aya took up so much of her energy and emotions. Even Aya was more relaxed. She's getting used to me. And I knew I was doing the right thing. They all just needed somewhere peaceful where they could live without fearing the next blow.'

She turned round to face me.

'And then the rioting began,' she said quietly. 'We'd been sitting in the waiting room with the window in the little washroom open, enjoying the cool night air, when it started. The shouting, the explosions. They terrified Aya. So I shut the window and we went into the surgery. It was quieter in there. The noise came in waves. A terrible din for a while and then long periods when it was far away.'

'And you didn't go out at all? To see what was going on?'

'Of course not. I realised I was stuck for the night and, anyway, I couldn't have left them.'

'And you didn't hear anything or anyone?' Even as I asked this I knew what a stupid question it was. 'I mean, no one creeping around.'

'No. I heard the rioters yelling and some banging quite close by. It was terrifying.'

Ma's eyes darkened as she looked back to the night before.

'I thought we'd be safe in the clinic. Until Rania saw the smoke slipping through the door. I opened it, you know. But the waiting room was blazing already.'

She stopped and took a deep breath.

'Nahla pulled her drip out and made a dash for the front door, before I could stop her. I've never seen anything like it. One minute she was fine, the next, her clothing burst into flames. She staggered back into the surgery and passed out. We smothered the fire with blankets. But the smell. I'll never forget it. It was like she'd been cooked.'

She ran her fingers up and down the edge of the curtain for a few seconds.

'I've never felt as terrified as I did then. Rania and I stuffed everything we could round the door but the smoke poured through all the same. Rania was crying and begging her mother to wake up. Then I heard footsteps on the roof. It was you, wasn't it?'

'Yes.'

'I knew it was. I knew you'd come to rescue us.'

We were both silent. Both lost in the memory of last night and the mad panic to get them all out before the clinic ignited.

Should I tell Ma that I thought the clinic had been torched on purpose? Maybe not. She was already barely holding it together.

'Here's Peter,' Ma said from the window. 'Get dressed. We need to get to the camp.'

'To the camp?'

'Peter's going to help Amalia and I need to fetch the girls. If they hadn't forced us to go to hospital last night, I'd have taken them then. I can't leave them there on their own, can I, Jenifry?'

She was right. Of course the girls couldn't be left in the camp on their own. I hoped very much that Yasmiin and Sarah had stayed with them last night. If Amalia was there, I could tell her my suspicions about the fire last night.

'Two seconds,' I said. 'Go down and ask him to wait.'

Another memory gnawed at my thoughts as I dressed.

Nick.

Nick's face in the shadows watching the paramedics try to resuscitate Nahla.

Had it been him? Was he here rather than in some shabby and run-down area of England? Or had my eyes been playing tricks? It had been a dark night shot through with flames and panic and my memories of the moment I'd caught sight of him already seemed unreal, more like a dream you can't shake off when you wake than something that had actually happened. I'd been in shock and suffering from smoke inhalation and oxygen deprivation while the adrenalin that had driven me drained out of my brain. It was probably a hallucination.

Best forgotten.

I hunted round the room, with a vague hope of finding

something like the slippers in my hotel bedroom but there was nothing so I slipped my feet into my ruined trainers, stuffed my burnt and smelly clothes in a bag and went out to meet Peter.

Thirteen

Ma and Peter waited on the hospital steps overlooking the car park. In the light of day, Peter didn't look like Pa. He was older for a start. Although, of course, Pa would have aged during the years I'd managed to avoid seeing him. But besides that, his mouth was softer and his body, although lean, lacked the toughness Pa's had. His head had that curious boniness English men often seemed to develop in later life but the planes of his face were slightly asymmetrical, giving him an unfinished look. He looked at Ma in a way Pa never had. With a wide but uncertain smile on his face and a look of confusion in his eyes. He'd got it bad.

Ma gave the tinkly laugh she reserved for awkward occasions although its edges were hoarse with the smoke's after-effects. Someday, I thought, someday I am going to tell her how irritating that laugh is.

'Peter,' she said holding out her arms to us both. 'You haven't met my daughter properly yet. My lovely Jenifry. Always appearing when you least expect her and saving the day.'

I cut her off before she could say any more.

'Pleased to meet you.'

'The pleasure is all mine.' He shook my hand in an unduly vigorous way, reawakening the soreness in my singed fingers. 'Thank God you were there last night. I shouldn't have let Morwenna go back to the camp on her own. I'll never be able to thank you enough for what you did.'

I pasted a smile on my face and tried not to let his assumption of responsibility for Ma rile me. Of course I saved her. She was my mother. And as far preventing her from going back to the camp, I certainly didn't think he should be stopping her doing what she wanted to. Not that he'd ever succeed; I'd given up a long time ago.

Once we were in the car, he asked me for the full story of the night before and I told him most of it, sparing him none of the details and watching his reactions in the rear-view mirror. Not that I needed to look hard. He was one of those irritating people who interject little noises and facial expressions to show they're listening. Maybe it was a trick he used to encourage his students but after a while it made me want to grind my teeth.

'Khaled and Yousef?' Ma said when I finished. 'Those were the two on the roof with you who dragged me out?'

'We should find them and thank them,' Peter said. 'Don't you think, Jenifry?'

'Call me Jen. Only Ma calls me Jenifry. It's a bit of a mouthful.'

'It's a delightful name. Correct me if I'm wrong but I think you're named after a Celtic saint who was decapitated by her lover when she decided to become a nun rather than marry him. Is that right, Morwenna?'

This silenced even Ma.

'Well, Ma? Did you name me after a decapitated saint who wanted to be a nun?'

'It all ended happily, though,' Peter said. 'Her head was rejoined to her body and I rather think a healing spring poured from the spot where it had fallen.'

'That's good,' I said brightly.

'Of course, I can't be sure it's the same saint. I'm basing this on some distant memory of the name Jenifry being a derivation of Gwenfrewi. Maybe you know, Morwenna?'

But we never discovered whether Ma knew or not because we turned into the approach road to the camp and fell silent.

The gate was shut and the entrance bristled with armed police but the roadblocks had gone and most of the fire engines and army trucks. The smell of last night's riots hung in the air. It was sour with old smoke and the heavy odour of damp ash. The same sourness brooded on the face of the guards.

They stared at us while examining Peter's Musaeada pass with unsmiling faces and opening the gate to let us through.

Shona waited by the entrance to the guardroom on the other side, glancing at her watch from time to time. I noticed that she'd left off her clinking jewellery and wondered if, unlike Ma's, it was worth something, although she was still wearing a flouncy dress and had taken the time to plait beads into her hair.

We parked the car and Ma dashed over. Shona flung her arms round her. I was struck again by how alike they looked, hair and dresses flying around as they swayed together. They could be mother and daughter. I suspected Ma would have loved me to be a bit more like Shona.

'Morwenna,' Shona almost cooed. 'You are so brave to come here. You must be traumatised after last night.'

'I had to come. For Rania and Aya.'

'Of course. Of course.'

She clutched Ma's hands as though trying to convey some unspoken depth of empathy. Ma looked vaguely surprised but pleased.

'How are things?' I asked, trying not to sound irritated.

'I'm trying to persuade the guards to let these women attend their hospital antenatal appointments.' Shona gestured to three women with her, all in different stages of pregnancy. 'There should be more but everyone has been locked down since last night and they've only just started letting the women and children out.'

'Where's Amalia?' Peter asked.

'Over at the clinic. We're picking through the ashes to see what can be salvaged. And then we'll rebuild and it will be better than before.'

'That won't be easy,' I couldn't stop myself muttering.

But Ma clapped her hands and nodded.

A guard came out and waved at us to move on and clear the way for a series of police buses that were leaving. They drove past, sending clouds of half-burnt debris and ash powder into the air as Ma and Shona finished their wittering. Men with sullen faces stared blankly out or buried their heads in their arms.

'That's the last of the rioters,' Peter said. 'I heard they'd already arrested more than a hundred.'

None of us asked what would happen to them.

As we drove towards the clinic, it was clear Shona had been right about the refugees being allowed out. Groups of women were emerging from the containers. A queue waited outside the shower room and alongside a low building Ma told me was the communal kitchen. But the presence of armed police, helmeted and bulked out by bullet-proof vests, kept everyone silent and there were no groups sitting knitting and chatting like yesterday.

A couple of policemen were stationed at either end of the stony ground where the Musaeada clinic had been. The flaming violence of last night was long gone. Nothing but quiet devastation remained. The clinic was a pile of charred timbers and cinders, sodden with water from last night's hoses and exuding an acrid odour that caught in my chest.

Amalia, still dressed in the jeans and blouse she'd worn yesterday, now filthy and creased, had found a couple of rakes and she and Yasmiin were dragging the scorched remains apart. From time to time they bent to pick something up and throw it into a tall bin. When we got out of the car, I saw the traces of tears in the grime on her face. She wasn't crying now, though. Her expression was set and grim.

She held out a warning hand when she saw us. 'Be careful where you tread. There's broken glass all over the place. I've ordered protective gloves and boots but they won't arrive until tomorrow.'

'Is there stuff in here?' I asked. 'I mean, worth salvaging.'

The bin beside her contained some metal bowls and a few implements, all discoloured by the heat and bent out of shape. I couldn't imagine them ever being used again.

'Amalia,' Ma said gently. 'Stop. You need to stop.' She took the rake away from her.

Amalia let her.

'You're probably right,' she said.

'Leave it. Walk away. Get some sleep.'

'And then,' I interrupted Ma, 'ring all your rich lawyer friends and guilt them into paying for the clinic to be rebuilt. Take photos and send an impassioned plea out to them. I'll do it and send them to you.'

A slight smile broke through Amalia's weariness.

'Morwenna,' she said. 'I'm so sorry about Nahla. After all she's been through for it to end this way. You must be devastated.'

Ma shook her head slightly. 'I can't think about it now. There'll be time to mourn her later. I've come for Rania and Aya.'

Yasmiin leaned on her rake and watched us.

'They're not here,' Amalia said. 'They're in the migrant facility at Mater Dei Hospital. They were taken there last night for treatment after I insisted. I don't think the smoke had affected them too much but I wanted to be sure. They're obviously very distressed… But that's a different matter.'

'I'll go there now.' Ma turned to speak to Peter but he'd gone over to Yasmiin and was chatting to her quietly.

'They may not be letting visitors in,' Amalia said.

'I'm not going to visit but to take them back to Peter's.'

'Morwenna.' Amalia's voice was patient although she massaged the bridge of her nose as she spoke. 'I don't think they'll let you do that.'

'Why not?'

'Because...' She took a deep breath. 'Because they have a responsibility to protect minors. Youngsters disappear regularly here. They can't let them go off with anyone.'

'I'm not just anyone. I'm Nahla's friend. Nahla would have wanted them to live with me.'

Live with Ma? Permanently? I shot her a quick glance but nothing in her determined face and stance revealed that this might be a sudden decision.

'Live with you?' Amalia was as surprised as I was. 'Do you mean that, Morwenna?'

'Of course I do.'

I opened my mouth to ask her if she'd thought this through. And shut it. What was the point? I knew she hadn't. But I also knew nothing would dissuade her.

'Well, it might not be very easy. Do you have anything to show that was what Nahla wanted? Anything written down? A will? A letter even?'

Of course she didn't. She shook her head and dismissed Amalia's words with a wave of her hand.

'I'll tell them it's what Nahla would have wanted.'

Then she whirled away and joined Peter, who was listening to Yasmiin and producing plenty of encouraging facial expressions and nods. I wondered how he would feel about Ma's plans to have the girls live with them permanently.

'Is she serious?' Amalia asked.

'Oh yes.'

She thought for a few minutes while I watched Peter's face slip into blankness for once as Ma spoke to him.

'It's not altogether a bad idea,' Amalia said.

Her words surprised me.

'Honestly, Jen, if Morwenna is serious, it might be for the best. There's nothing for the girls here.' She gestured round at the desolate scene. 'They'll be kept safe but not much else.'

She was right. Anything would be better than growing up here. Well, almost anything.

Amalia pulled out her phone. 'I'll call Shona. Get her to speak to the authorities. She works a lot with the unaccompanied minors so she'll know the right people to contact.'

'You think they'll let Ma take the girls?'

She shrugged.

'Despite all her hippy nonsense, she would look after them, you know.'

And I realised how true this was. For all her failings, Ma saw things through.

I went and joined her as she finished explaining to Peter why they had to go to the hospital now.

'I won't come,' I said. 'I'll ask Amalia to drop me at the airport so I can pick up my car.'

I wanted to talk to Amalia about the figure I'd seen torching the clinic last night.

'Come over later,' Ma said.

'I need a shower and some sleep first.'

'Come for dinner then. Call Peter when you wake up.'

Peter scribbled his number and his address on a piece of paper and I stuffed it into my pocket.

Yasmiin came over and joined me as they left, letting the rake fall to the ground with a crash. It broke through the damp top layer of ash and sent flakes swirling into the air. I coughed but it was a reflex —

a woken memory of smoke choking my lungs rather than the ash.

'Morwenna has gone to get Rania and Aya?' she asked.

'Yes. Well, to try anyway.'

'Good.'

She kicked at a piece of exploded rubber and sent it hurtling into the fence. There was a tension in her I didn't remember from before. A sense that she was clamping down on some turbulent emotion rather than letting it rip.

'Khaled and Yousef who helped me last night. Do you know them?' I said.

'A little. I know Khaled's sister, Sarah.'

'How are they? If they hadn't been there last night, I wouldn't have got Ma and the others out.'

'They were fine last night. Just angry at being locked down. They have things to do. We all have things to do.'

A ghost of her previous fierceness broke across her face.

'Right.' Amalia had finished her call and joined us. 'I don't have much time. I need to go to the hospital myself because Shona says they're offering us some help while we're out of action here. I asked her about Rania and Aya. They're both recovering well from the fire. However, the Maltese authorities have taken the first steps towards working out what to do with the girls, so an initial interview with Rania has taken place. And here's the problem. She's told them she wants to go back to Libya.'

She headed towards her car.

'But... but Rania is a child,' Yasmiin burst out as we both strode after her. 'She doesn't understand what she's going back to. You cannot let this happen.'

'Yasmiin,' Amalia got into her car. 'The girls have family there apparently. Grandparents who love them both. Who, according to Rania, they often stayed with and who offered to look after them when Nahla went into hiding.'

Yasmiin gazed at her as though she didn't understand. I thought I saw tears start in her eyes. Amalia turned to me.

'It's a question of law. The grandparents are undoubtedly their next of kin. And Rania wants to go to them. Although she's underage she's old enough to have her wishes listened to.'

'But Libya is a terrible place.' Fury propelled Yasmiin's words. 'You know my story. You know what happened to me there. You know every woman, every child who passes through that country has the same story.'

Amalia reached out a hand and took Yasmiin's for a brief second.

'I know, Yasmiin. But it's not the same for Rania. She's a Libyan national. She comes from an educated and privileged family who live in the best part of Tripoli. I know the situation is unstable there and residents can be caught in the fighting between militias, but it won't be a legal argument to force Rania to stay in Malta against her wishes. Besides, it was her mother who was in danger, not her. And I think you of all people, Yasmiin, would agree that Malta is not always kind to refugees. For what it's worth I think returning home might be the best thing for them. They'll be happier in familiar surroundings and with their family, who clearly love them.'

'Can they do that? Send her back?' I interrupted, while Amalia took a breath and rummaged in her bag for her car keys.

'The EU sends millions of dollars to Libya to prevent migrants leaving in the first place. Of course they can send Rania back. Especially if she says she wants to go.'

She got into the car and prepared to drive away, then stopped and sighed. 'I suppose I should tell Morwenna before she gets to the hospital. Let me give Peter a call.'

Yasmiin pulled me away from the car as Amalia made her phone call.

'You tell Morwenna she must do everything she can to get Rania and Aya away. She must fight for them with every breath in her body. They must never go back to the hellhole of Libya.'

She turned to leave, then hesitated before finally speaking in a low, urgent voice.

'If Morwenna will not do it, I will. I will take them with me when I leave.'

'Leave?'

'Yes. I am going. And soon. There are ways, if you have money, and now they have refused my asylum I will not stay here. Rania and Aya will be better with me than back in Libya.' And before I could ask her how she planned to get away, she strode off.

I hoped she was wrong. I hoped her own experiences in Libya had clouded her judgement. Loving grandparents sounded like exactly what Rania and Aya needed.

I trudged back to Amalia. The rough edges of my burnt trainers were starting to rub holes in my feet and the gaze of the ever-present guards disturbed me. The thought of a shower and sleep became ever more enticing.

Amalia had finished the call.

'Could you drop me at the airport? Or give me Mohammed's number?'

'I'll do both. Mohammed's always useful. Get in.'

We drove away at speed.

'How did Ma take the news?'

'I only spoke to Peter. I left him to explain to her.'

I loosened my trainers and ran a cautious finger round my ankle and heel. The skin felt intact.

'Peter seems nice,' I said.

Amalia clearly knew I was fishing because she laughed.

'You've nothing to worry about. He'll never set the world on fire but he's a kind man and he loves helping people. I wish he

151

didn't because sometimes he promises things we can't deliver. It's a sort of point of honour, I think.'

She swung off the main road.

'Airport, you said?'

'My car's there.'

'I've met Peter's type before. Typical expat. Found a little niche here and enjoys it.'

'Big fish in a small pond.'

'Yes, but well-meaning. His wife left him last year, so I hope Morwenna won't break his heart all over again.'

I couldn't promise that so I kept my mouth shut and wondered how to broach the subject of the clinic fire. I was too tired to be subtle.

'Look,' I said as we neared the airport. 'I think someone torched the clinic last night.'

'Very probably. I don't suppose the rioters stopped to consider what they were doing.'

'No, I don't mean a rioter. I think I saw someone creep behind the clinic, break a window and throw a burning rag inside. But not in a rage. Quietly and deliberately.'

Amalia blinked rapidly as she took in what I said. I realised there were dark shadows under her bloodshot eyes. She'd probably had less sleep than me.

'Someone took advantage of the riot to burn the clinic down,' I went on. 'I don't see what else it could have been.'

I explained how the fire would never have started the way it did if the flames from the burning cars had set it alight but she cut me off halfway through.

'I believe you,' she said. 'We're not popular with everybody. Lots of Maltese don't like the refugees and they see us as encouraging them to come here. Our office in town has had its windows broken a few times and a couple of outbreaks of unpleasant graffiti. We've had to install cameras. But I never thought the clinic was in danger. Unless it was one of the guards. Some of them share the negative attitudes towards refugees.'

'What will you do?'

'It's pointless telling the police. They did nothing about the vandalism at the office and they'll do less about the clinic. Even if they believed your story.'

She smacked her hand against the steering wheel.

'What is the point of all this? It's one step forward and a hundred steps back. Every last bit of it is a battle. Against the Maltese authorities. Against the European authorities. Against the residents. Against the refugees who crack when they lose hope and behave like they did last night. Read the papers this morning. They're full of hate. And the people who are normally sympathetic to my requests are unavailable or very quiet. The refugee-haters must be laughing into their morning coffees.'

I thought she might be weeping, but her eyes were dry.

'I wondered if the fire was something to do with the envelope.'

She looked confused.

'The one I found on the floor of the clinic. With money in it. The one you put in a drawer.'

'You can't think someone would burn the clinic down for that.'

'I suppose not.'

We drove in silence for a while.

'Remind me what was in the envelope,' she said.

I realised her brain had been picking over my words.

'Money inside. And a list of what looked like phone numbers and some other writing but it was in Arabic.'

More silence.

'What are you thinking?'

'Wondering if it's connected with smuggling.'

'People-smuggling?'

'Yes. It goes on. It's unavoidable. So many of the refugees want to get to mainland Europe. It used to be a casual thing, done on the side by some of the fishermen and yacht captains, but it's become big business and the people who run it are ruthless. I only glanced at the envelope, but now I think back, there were names on it that could belong to boats as well as some mention of small ports in Italy. I don't suppose we'll ever know.'

The airport came into sight. 'Can I drop you here?'

'Sure.'

Her phone rang as she pulled over to the side of the road.

'Wait,' she said. 'If this is Morwenna, you can speak to her; I simply don't have the time or the energy.'

It wasn't Ma but whoever it was told her something that took her words away and left her slumped in the seat and staring out through the windscreen when they rang off.

'Amalia?'

'Oh, God,' she said. 'Paulina. I can't believe it.'

I waited while Amalia made a conscious effort to breathe in and out calmly.

'That was Shona again. Terrible news. Dreadful. Paulina's dead. You know, our nurse. Shona told me. She's at the hospital with the women who have antenatal appointments. Paulina worked there too, as well as for us, I mean. I'm sorry, I know I'm not making much sense.'

She sounded completely unlike her articulate self and when she buried her head in her hands I could barely hear her.

'Outside the hospital. Dead. They found her this morning. With her throat cut.'

'What!'

She removed her hands and looked at me.

'It doesn't bear thinking about. How could that happen here? But you know what the worst thing is? When Shona told me, for a few seconds all I could think was that, on top of everything else, I was going to have to find a new nurse.'

Back at the hotel, I took the coward's way out and slipped past reception without stopping to explain why the rug and curtain tiebacks were missing from my room. The shower was bliss. The clean sheets beckoned me but a faint stink of smoke still hung about.

I threw the clothes I'd been wearing the night before into the bath and filled it with hot water and all the little bottles of shampoo and shower gel but the smell lingered. I tracked it down to the dress Ma had lent me, impregnated by the smell from my body, and I hung it from the outside window handle so its smell could dissipate into the afternoon heat. Then I crawled into bed.

Fourteen

The day was slipping into dusk when I woke. I'd slept longer than I meant. My alarm hadn't gone off because my phone was out of battery and, when I plugged it in, a host of missed calls flashed up on screen. A couple from London, offering me work, which was reassuring. Amalia had sent me Mohammed's number as promised. The rest were from the same number as the one on the scribbled piece of paper Peter had given me. A couple of messages in his courteous voice asking me to get in touch asap as Morwenna needed to see me urgently confirmed my guess that Ma hadn't taken the news about Rania and Aya returning to Libya well. I thought about calling her but didn't. It would be easier to discuss it face to face.

Which brought me to my next problem.

What was I going to wear to Peter's? My only decent jeans were riddled with holes from the fire and soaking in the bath. Apart from that I had a couple of pairs of shorts that were clean enough but not really suitable evening wear, a pair of elderly jeans with rips in the wrong places to be fashionable and a massive coffee stain on one knee, and an assortment of T-shirts. I hadn't expected to be having dinner with Ma and her boyfriend when I packed. There was nothing for it. I'd have to wear Ma's dress. At least its exposure to the afternoon sun had banished the last vestiges of smoke from its folds.

Peter's house was in Mdina, an ancient citadel in the midst of the island and hauntingly beautiful according to the guidebook. Not great for people in cars, though. I had to leave mine in a car park outside the ramparts. It also wasn't great for people trying to find an address. I walked up and down the little alleyways, lined with houses whose stone was warmed by a myriad of lights. Here and there plants tumbled from balconies and roofs like green waterfalls. It was pretty magical and for a while I was happy to wander through its quiet squares until I realised I was getting more and more lost.

I found Peter's house in the end by showing the address to a tired-looking woman in a small shop selling ice-cream and postcards. She stopped her embroidery and marked the house on a tourist map of the city. When I found it, standing at one end of a square with a balcony on the first floor, I thought I'd already walked past it a couple of times. It was massive and imposing and not a bit what I expected.

Ma flung the heavy and ornate doors open when I rang the bell.

'At last,' she said as she seized my hand and dragged me down a long, high corridor with ancient black and white tiles on the floor and stone walls lined with heavy brass-framed mirrors and dark pictures. Her hair was tangled and red rims circled her eyes. I didn't think she'd slept or even rested since I saw her this morning.

'It's big, isn't it?' I said as we passed the entrance to yet another opulent room, crammed with dark but polished furniture all upholstered in startling colours. And hideous, I thought.

'Very big,' she said. 'And hideous. And oppressive. I told Peter he needed to throw the furniture out but it's his ex-wife's and until she arranges to get it shipped to the UK, he's stuck with it.'

She led me through a kitchen – modern, gleaming and bristling with devices. Then opened some large French windows – everything was enormous – and we went into the courtyard at the back.

This was lovely, an oasis nestling among high walls of warm-coloured stone. Lights gleamed and reflected in the small pool and fountain to one side, casting rippling shadows over plants shooting up towards the light. In one corner, a table was set with an array of salads, bread and cheese. Opposite, a tall outdoor stove took the chill off the night air. Ma sat herself down on the stone shelf that ran along the wall beside it.

'Thank God you're here. The hospital wouldn't let us in to see Rania and Aya and then Amalia told Peter the terrible news about the girls going back to Libya.'

She started to rant on about the awfulness of everything and how wrong it all was. I knew she'd take it badly.

The smell of the food on the table nearby reached my nose. *God, I was hungry.* I hadn't eaten since last night. I wondered where Peter was. There were three places laid at the table.

'Jen, you're not listening.' There was real anguish in Ma's voice.

'Sorry. I am listening, Ma. But is the news really that terrible? It might be best for the girls to be with their family.'

'You don't understand. They don't have a family. Their grandparents are dead.'

She had all my attention now.

'Listen. Just listen,' she said as I tried to interrupt her. 'Let me tell you the whole story. When Nahla went into hiding, she hoped the people who killed Ibrahim might forget about her if she went quiet. She stopped writing, shut down all the internet things she did and waited. She begged her parents to lie low too. Ibrahim's parents died some time ago, so they were the only family she had left.'

As she spoke, Ma started to wring her hands. Gently at first but then more and more vigorously the further she got into her story. They'd been blistered in the fire last night and she now rubbed the skin loose, leaving damp red patches behind. I put my hands over hers.

'Stop, Ma. You'll hurt yourself.'

'But, of course, the people who killed Ibrahim didn't forget about her. They kept on hunting. A couple of her friends disappeared and she didn't know if they'd been taken or gone into hiding themselves. Finally they abducted her parents. They tortured them, wanting to know where Nahla was. Then they killed them both. Nahla left Libya straightaway then. She knew the people helping her might be in danger and…'

Ma ground to a halt and started to wring her hands again. I held them to stop her.

'But why does Rania think…?' I asked. And then I understood. 'Nahla didn't tell Rania they were dead.'

Ma nodded.

A quiet fury took me by surprise. Part of me understood why Nahla hadn't. It was difficult to tell children such terrible things. Nevertheless she should have. No matter how hard it was. Somewhere along the line Nahla had checked out.

'Nahla told *me*, though. The first evening she was out of detention. As soon as the girls were sleeping.'

Peter came into the courtyard garden through the French windows, a little out of breath. He smiled when he saw me.

'Jenifry. You've arrived. My apologies for not being here to welcome you. I had a lesson booked. A student I couldn't cancel. I'm so pleased you've been here with Morwenna. I hated having to leave her.'

He put his arm round Ma, gazing down at the top of her head with an expression on his face rather like a dog watching his food being spooned into a dish.

'It will be all right, Ma,' I said. 'We just need to tell the authorities.'

I wasn't sure who the authorities were but Amalia would know. Ma shook her head and tried to speak but her voice had

159

disappeared, either from last night's smoke or because of her emotion.

'We've already told them,' Peter said. 'At the hospital. But they didn't want to listen. Apparently the Libyan embassy has already said the girls are welcome and their grandparents will meet them at the airport.'

It made no sense.

Ma found her voice. 'They accused me of lying.'

Peter gave her an uneasy look. 'Morwenna was very angry. They'd already told her she couldn't go in and see the girls.'

I could imagine it. Ma, still exhausted and shocked by last night, had probably made a scene.

'You are sure, aren't you, Ma? Sure that the grandparents are dead. You didn't misunderstand?'

Ma's voice cracked alarmingly as she spoke. 'Do you want me to describe what had been done to them before they died? Nahla told me. Every last detail of it. And I had to sit and listen to it all because she hadn't been able to talk of it to anyone else.'

'No,' I said. 'I'm sorry.'

'It was dreadful. Two gentle and elderly people tortured and… Nahla's friends should never have told her but they wanted her to see how important it was that she left.'

'But I don't understand,' I said. 'Why would the Libyan authorities lie?'

'Morwenna,' Peter said. 'Your mother thinks they want to use the girls to discourage other journalists or writers. Most of them will risk themselves but not their families and not their children.'

'They? But it's the Libyan authorities we're talking about.'

'The government is in turmoil. Half the country is fighting the other half and that's an oversimplification. It's chaos over there. All we know is that someone leapt at the chance of getting those girls back. Think how quickly it's happened. And that makes me very suspicious.'

'The name Nahla Shebani still means something,' Ma interrupted him. 'They'll make an example of the girls. They'll marry them both off to some minor warlord in a publicised ceremony. Or worse. We can't let that happen.'

She scrubbed her face dry and blew her nose.

'We can't let it happen,' she said again.

Of course we couldn't.

The ferocity of my inner response startled me but I contented myself with giving Ma a quick nod of agreement.

Peter looked as though he'd have like to say something but instead he went to the table and poured three glasses of wine from a bottle whose exterior was dewed with moisture. It smelled wonderful – grassy and sharp. I took one sip and then put it down.

'Don't you like it?'

'I don't really drink and I haven't eaten since yesterday.'

'Then let's start.'

We sat down but I no longer felt particularly hungry. I forced myself to eat some bread and cheese. Ma took a couple of gulps of wine and spoke.

'Will you help us with Rania and Aya?' she asked.

'Yes.'

'I knew you would.'

Maybe I should have been a bit more cautious.

'What does Amalia think we should do? Who do we need to speak to?'

They were both silent for a few minutes.

'Have you asked Amalia?'

'I don't think speaking will do any good.' Ma grabbed a piece of bread and started tearing it into small pieces. 'They don't want to believe me.'

'We need a lawyer then. If Amalia can't do it, surely she can recommend someone. I'll pay.'

Ma started to shake her head as another idea came to me.

'We need proof the grandparents are dead. Can you get in touch with her friends or the university and get them to send you statements? Was there anything in the papers about it?'

Some of my appetite returned and I reached for a plate of stuffed vine leaves gleaming in the soft light.

'You don't understand,' Ma almost shouted. 'We don't have time for any of this. You explain, Peter.'

He grasped her hand.

'Morwenna's right. It's going to happen quickly. They won't have to go through any deportation or legal procedures. As far as the Maltese authorities are concerned, Rania and Aya are Libyan nationals, underage and orphaned, with family back in Libya. They have a duty to repatriate as soon as possible.'

'Rania is desperate to go home, apparently.' Ma added. 'She was very close to her grandparents. Both children were.'

She had the sense for once to give me time to let what they'd said sink in.

'There are regular flights between Malta and Libya,' Peter said after a while.

It would be so easy, I thought. Sending two willing youngsters to their grandparents was the perfect solution to one of the Maltese authorities' many problems. The riots had created a huge amount of extra work for them and, if Amalia was right, feelings against the refugees were running high. Somewhere, in the middle of all this, Rania and Aya and what was best for them might get lost.

'I see,' I said.

'We've got a plan.' Ma leaned forward and tapped the table.

She flicked her hands at Peter and he took up the thread.

'We have to get the children out of Malta,' Peter said. 'Hiding them here will be impossible.'

'Hiding? Hang on a second. You mean running away with them?'

'Of course,' Ma said. 'You must see we have no choice. Shona said –'

She broke off.

I trusted Amalia's opinion far more than anything fluttery Shona might have said to Ma, although under her wifty-wafty exterior there must be some steel. She ran Musaeada and Amalia had said she worked with youngsters who had no families.

'What did Shona say?'

But Peter spoke first. 'I have a contact for someone with a boat,' he said. 'Someone who'll take us to Italy. There are plenty of places we can slip ashore where no one will see.'

Of course. Cornwall, Malta, Calais, Libya. It was always the same. Wherever there was a coast and people who wanted to escape, there were men with boats prepared to smuggle them for money.

Every instinct screamed at me that running was a bad idea. We'd be effectively kidnapping Rania and Aya. Surely Ma could see how wrong that was. But as I looked at her face screwed up with hope and eagerness, I realised she didn't have a clue.

'And then what do you plan to do?'

'We'll get them up to the north coast of France – it's easy because of – what's it called?' Ma turned to Peter.

'Schengen.'

'Yes. I didn't have to show a passport at all once the coach I came on got to France.'

I suspected that it might be more problematic than Ma thought but I let it lie. It would be better to know the full extent of what she planned before I picked holes in it.

'And then?'

'Then? Then, I don't know. But I'll work something out. Steal a boat maybe, like you suggested.'

'I never –'

'But first things first.'

She pushed the uneaten dishes of food to one side and spread some photos of a building on the table.

'What's this?'

'Mater Dei Hospital.'

'The hospital?'

She gave me a look like I was stupid.

'It's where Rania and Aya are being held.'

'Held. Don't you mean looked after.'

'You know what I mean.' Ma snapped at me. 'They might as well be in prison,' she went on. 'Peter says there's a wing for refugees. It's guarded and Rania and Aya will be in that.'

'It's not like a prison,' Peter added. 'Once you're inside it's just like any other part of the hospital.'

'OK. But why am I looking at this?'

Ma sighed. 'If we're going to get the girls off the island, we've got to get hold of them first. You said you could climb any building. But I wanted you to be sure before we went there.'

I didn't recall ever saying those exact words to Ma but I wasn't going to quibble. I realised with a sinking heart that Ma intended to put her plan into action now. I wasn't going to get time to talk to Amalia. I cut straight to the chase.

'I'm not breaking into the hospital.'

'But you said you could.'

'I could but I won't.'

'But it's the only way to get them out.'

Her voice rose a couple of octaves and filled the confined space.

'Listen, Ma,' I said, trying not to sound impatient with her. We were both tired and fraught. 'You haven't thought it through.'

God, I sounded like Kit!

'I can climb this building. Architecturally it's a mess, with roofs at different levels and pipes and window frames placed handily everywhere. I could probably even get in if there's a window left open somewhere and no one sees me.'

Ma looked happier but I was about to disappoint her again.

'But say I do get in, what then? Are Rania and Aya supposed to follow me back out? Two girls with no experience of climbing. One of whom is terrified of strangers and probably sedated. And the other who wants nothing more than to be sent back to her grandparents so wouldn't come with me anyway.'

They stared at me. I saw the glimmer of an idea break across Ma's face and transform her despair into hope.

'And before you ask,' I said quickly. 'I'm not going to climb in, appear in their room and tell Rania that her grandparents are dead. It needs to be done properly. And anyway, even if she wanted to be rescued, it would be impossible to get them out.'

They were both silent. Peter cleared his throat a couple of times like you do before speaking but my argument was unassailable.

'Ma,' I said. 'I'm sorry.'

She was crying again. She got up and went over to the pond with the little fountain and stood there with her back to me. I wished I'd been gentler when telling her how impossible her plan was. I wasn't at my best and she was exhausted, wrung out with worry about the girls and her grief over the loss of Nahla.

'Look. Let's talk about it tomorrow.'

Tomorrow, I thought, once I'd had a chance to talk to Amalia and got a clearer picture of the situation. Surely there were other options than running.

'Will you stay?' Peter asked me. 'I have to go out again soon. Another student. And –'

Ma interrupted him. 'I'd like to be alone, Peter. Let Jenifry go.'

She went over to the pool, sat on the stone rim and stared into the water. I hoped she could see the reflection of the stars.

'Don't worry,' Peter said to me. 'We got carried away. You're quite right. It was never going to work.'

And I liked him a little better.

He went to join her, sitting close and wrapping his arms around her. She leant back into his embrace and lifted her head to the night sky. The moon caught them both with its white glow and I felt a bit weird. Memories of being with Nick and staring at the night sky flooded my thoughts. Shit.

I let myself out. Giving them both a little wave as I went. I didn't think they noticed.

Fifteen

I headed back to the car. I wasn't tired. The long afternoon siesta had put paid to that. Part of my brain was already searching for ways to get the girls out. The same part of me that had leaped at the thought of scaling the hospital walls before I forced myself to think it through. I was seized with a desire for fresh air and a view. Mdina was beautiful but like the courtyard at Peter's it felt enclosed with its narrow passageways and small squares hemmed in by the tall houses.

I walked rapidly towards Mdina Gate. There was no one much about now. A few tourists wandered back to their hotels or apartments, but mainly people were indoors. Lights gleamed round the edges of shutters and brief echoes of music or laughter broke the quiet as a window or door opened and shut.

I came out into yet another square and realised I was by the city walls – huge ramparts of stone built to protect the hilltop city from whichever marauding force was fighting to take control of Malta at the time. A set of steps ran up to the top where the view was everything I'd longed for. A haze of clouds with only the moon gleaming through and a breeze with a hint of chill pouring onto my face. From here, the hills rolled down to the sea, broken by ramshackle walls and the occasional house casting shadows over moon-silvered fields.

Some of the stress from the last twenty-four hours drained away and I leaned against the walls and breathed in the earthy smell of the stone.

Footsteps clattered up the steps behind me and disturbed the peace. I turned around automatically.

Time slowed.

Nick stood there.

Unmistakeably Nick. Despite the longer hair, the straggling moustache, the darkened skin. Nick.

A wave of happiness broke over me – taking me by surprise. I was simply pleased to see him. I held out my arms and took a few steps towards him.

'Nick.'

'Be quiet!'

His voice, hard and urgent as a steel dart, burst the moment. Too late I realised that whatever he was doing here, he wasn't doing it as Nick.

'Why are you here?'

I'd never heard that tone before.

'Why have you come to Malta, Jen?'

Everything about him: his stance; his hands; his mouth and eyes. All rigid and sharp as stalagmite. I stepped back and felt the stone wall behind me.

'I came to find Ma. She's here, you know.'

'Yes.' Some of the tightness left his torso and he no longer reminded me of the Nick with the knife I'd seen outside his house in Alájar. 'I know she's here.'

A middle-aged couple, hand in hand, appeared at the top of the steps, chatting. We'd been so intent on each other neither of us had heard them. Nick spun round, then forced himself to relax, but they barely glanced our way before continuing along the ramparts.

'Christ,' Nick muttered when they'd passed. 'I really shouldn't be here with you.'

The breath that carried his words quivered. The moon's cold light picked out a faint gleam of damp on his forehead and made dark crevices of his frown. His hands twitched. The hard urgency with which he'd greeted me had been a shell hiding fear.

'Then go,' I said. 'I won't give you away. And if you're worried Ma might say something, I'll tell her not to.'

He shook his head slowly at me and waited until the couple were out of earshot.

'Listen to me. And don't interrupt. Just hear me out. You've got to get your mother away from Malta.'

'You can trust her, Nick. Like you can trust me. Surely you know that.'

The words came out louder than I meant and I clamped my hand over my mouth as he shot a look back down the steps the couple had just climbed. When he turned back to me, his face had softened into the Nick I thought I knew. The one I liked. Although he still seemed grimmer and darker than before.

'It's nothing to do with trust, Jenifry. Your mother's in danger.'

'Ma?'

'Yes.'

'But how? Why?'

He leant back against the wall and its shadow engulfed him.

'Why? Why is Ma in danger?'

'You won't just take my word for it and get her off Malta, will you?'

I tried to think. What kind of trouble could Ma have got herself into? Lots, now I considered it. This was exactly what I'd been worried about when I decided to come to Malta and find her.

'Never mind.' Nick interrupted my thoughts. I could barely make out his face in the dark but I thought I heard the ghost of a laugh in his voice. 'I knew you wouldn't just go but it was worth a try.'

'Tell me,' I said. 'You trusted me once.'

'I still do. How could you think I don't? But it's better you don't know too much. People give things away without meaning to.'

He was right. He'd trusted me in Cornwall and I'd nearly got him killed.

'Listen, though.' He came and stood by me with his back to the wall too. 'If anyone comes. Like that couple. Don't wait to see who they are, just leave. Do you understand?'

I nodded.

'I mean it, Jen. Walk away and keep walking. If anyone comes after you, run.'

'OK.'

He walked to where he could see the steps without turning.

'I'm part of a counter-terrorism operation,' he said quietly.

'Terrorists.'

Whatever I'd been expecting it wasn't this.

'I thought your work was with migrants and refugees. With the groups who abuse them. Traffickers and –'

'This operation *is* about refugees. Traffickers aren't the only people who take advantage of them. Refugees and migrants cross borders illegally to slip into Europe. They're excellent cover for anyone wanting to do the same. Like terrorists.'

Of course. Thousands of people were on the move. The sheer numbers made it impossible to keep track of them. Impossible to check all their stories. And so a tiny, tiny fraction of terrorists slipped in too. Yet another group of people making use of the refugees but, as Amalia had said, the dirt stuck to them all. Everybody suspected they were terrorists anyway. All the officials checking their stories for evidence of radicalism. The press baying for blood after the Paris and Brussels bombings.

'The fuckers,' I muttered.

'What?'

'Nothing. Tell me the rest.'

'Ever since the Manchester bombing and the bomber's links to Libya we've been on high alert for threats originating there. It's no secret that the current anarchy allows Islamic State to operate easily. We've been expecting IS agents to reach Europe via the migrant routes through Malta or Italy for some time. So we weren't surprised when there were rumours a lot of money was being offered for an absolutely safe passage from Libya to the UK.'

He spoke with the professional's lack of emotion. Someone so familiar with his work that the horror of it didn't colour his tone.

'But they were nothing more than rumours. Nothing concrete. Until we got word someone looking for a passage to Malta was asking a lot of questions. They were asking about routes in Europe. About transport. They wanted information before they paid. And they had money. Moreover they were Syrian, unlike the bulk of migrants from Libya, who are African. Naturally we flagged them as worth watching.'

I suspected Nick wasn't telling me the whole truth. A lot of other intelligence would have led to this operation but his habits of secrecy weren't going to let him even hint at them.

He shot me a look as though to make sure I was following. I nodded and the little breeze, which had been so welcome earlier, now ran chilled fingers over my skin.

'They wanted me to come to Malta then, you know. That's why I was called back to London. Straight after we went…'

He broke off.

Stargazing, I thought. After we went stargazing and everything else. It felt like a lifetime ago. It felt like it had happened to two different people.

'I said no.'

It took a few seconds for the meaning of his words to sink in. He was talking about his last trip away. When I went into the mountains and climbed and felt our relationship was going nowhere and Nick's secrecy was getting in the way. But he'd refused to take the job.

'And then the man in Libya who passed the information to us was killed. His throat was cut and he bled out in a backstreet.'

'An undercover agent?'

'Not really. He worked for people smugglers and he gave us information from time to time that we paid him for. Just another person trying to make a living out there. We don't worry about their ethics. Not if the information is good. And his normally was. So his death worried us even more. Had he been killed because someone realised he was watching them? All we knew was a group of Syrians were looking for a passage to Malta and our suspect was one of them. And that was when my boss – the man you saw at my house – came to Alájar to talk to me.'

We stared bleakly at each other.

'They needed me here fast to infiltrate the boatload of migrants as soon as they arrived. I've been here before, you see. A child trafficking operation a year or so ago. I speak good Arabic. I've got an accent but there are so many regional variations of the language anyway, it's not remarkable.'

Nick spoke Arabic, as well as Spanish and maybe other languages. There was so much I didn't know about him.

'If we can,' he said, 'we always leave an identity functioning. You never know when you might need to pick it up again. Here in Malta, I was a migrant from Morocco, working casually on the docks and not averse to bending a few laws – nothing unusual in that – putting refugees in touch with boats going to mainland Europe. For a price. And when the op was terminated, I left on one of them, saying I'd had enough of Malta.'

He'd never spoken so openly before. People's experiences shape them and I didn't have the first idea what Nick had seen or lived through. I didn't have the first idea who he was.

'I had to take this job, Jen. I tried to explain but –'

'You didn't have the time.'

A quick bark of a laugh.

'No. They needed someone on Malta immediately and I was the only person with an identity ready to step back into.'

A flicker of movement broke the edges of my vision. I flinched.

'A bat,' Nick said. 'Just a bat. You're very nervy.'

'Are you surprised?'

He didn't answer but went on with his story. His job was to ensure he travelled from Malta to Europe with the group in which the suspected IS agent was hiding. To try to find out who the agent was so they'd have a chance, this time, to find out what they were up to and prevent another tragedy like Manchester. His voice and face tightened as he spoke of the bombing.

'And have you succeeded?' I asked.

'Partly. I'm in with the group. I'm travelling with them and I think I know the identity of the IS agent but it's difficult to be sure. They hide in the shadows and use others to do the dangerous work for them. But I have –'

The middle-aged couple wandered back and Nick and I turned as one and leaned over the wall looking out at the view.

Below us stretched a fantastic spider's web of lights tracing the routes of roads and forming pools to show where villages and towns were. Behind us, the many lanterns of Mdina cast multiple shadows of our figures, like two fans overlapping, onto the honey-toned stone we leant on. At the darkest point, a tiny light glowed weakly. It came from a little creature that looked like a caterpillar.

'Maltese glow-worm,' Nick said when I pointed to it.

'You're kidding me.'

'Google it if you don't believe me.'

'I will.'

173

'It lights up to attract a mate but it doesn't stand much chance of being seen among the brightness here.'

He nudged it to the edge where it obligingly crawled down towards the dark ground metres below. He turned to me with a smile and for a few brief seconds he was the Nick I'd known in Alájar but then the couple disappeared down the steps and we were alone again.

He glanced at his watch and swore.

'So, yes, I think I know who the IS agent is. But the problem is, I'm not the only one who knows.'

I realised we'd arrived at the heart of the story.

'Your mother's friend. The one who died,' he said.

'Nahla.'

'Yes. She recognised them.'

'What?'

'She was at the clinic yesterday, wasn't she?'

'Yes.'

'So were some of the group I'm travelling with. They spoke about her afterwards. She was off her head. Couldn't stop talking.'

I remembered Nahla's delirious ramblings at the clinic.

'She was ill with dehydration and stress.'

'It doesn't matter. She said she recognised someone. Someone who wouldn't say hello. Someone who told her to keep quiet. Apparently she went on and on about it.'

'You think she recognised the IS agent? But how? Nahla wasn't involved with terrorism. She was a journalist and –'

'No, but she and her husband were quite radical. The overthrow of Gaddafi brought a lot of disparate groups together. Some, like Nahla, wanted a Western-style democracy but others saw Libya as a future Islamic state. It's complicated but for a time everyone was united in wanting to get rid of Gaddafi.'

There was no mistaking the sombreness in his tone. I waited for him to go on, suddenly wanting to make this time last as long as possible. The two of us sharing our thoughts. He might have felt the same because his next words came from a reflective place, untouched by the dangers that kept him focussed on his mission and staying alive.

'Terrorism. It's a grim word. It conjures up an image of great evil. Malevolent and bitter. But it's more complicated than that. I've seen it in the refugee camps. When people have no hope, when their families have been killed, when they know they've brought children into a world that will give them nothing but misery and starvation and filth and cold... radicalisation breeds.'

He stopped.

I wanted to ask him how he could do his job while he felt like that but I thought I knew the answer. Because nothing he could do would make an iota of difference.

He stretched his fingers out over the top of the wall, trying, I thought, to let its warm and rough surface anchor him. His splayed hand was near to mine. A fraction of an inch closer and our little fingers would have touched.

'Anyway,' he said, taking his hand off the wall. 'It's what happened afterwards that makes me think Nahla recognised the terrorist.'

I gathered my longings together and shut them away.

'Because shortly afterwards she was dead.'

I heard Nick's words. I heard my breaths, rapid but still quiet. And underneath them, I heard the fire cracking and hissing from last night. I smelled the smoke and felt it sting my eyes. And I saw the figure again, creeping round the back of the Musaeada clinic while Ma and Nahla and the girls took refuge inside.

'The fire. It wasn't an accident,' I said.

'There are rumours it was deliberate.'

'I know it was.'

I told him quickly what I'd seen.

'The rumours were right then,' he said. 'Someone saw an easy way to get rid of Nahla. Someone who needed to shut her up.'

'But they could have killed them all,' I said. 'Rania, Aya and Ma.'

'Maybe that was what they meant to happen.'

I waited for the explanation I knew would come, although my brain leaped ahead sparking half-ideas like little electric shocks running along my nerves.

'The nurse who treated Nahla. She was killed last night too,' he said.

'Paulina,' I said, remembering the phone call Amalia had received as she dropped me at the airport. 'You think her death is something to do with this?'

'I don't know. Maybe it's a coincidence. But Nahla spent time with her. Maybe someone's trying to eliminate anyone who Nahla might have revealed their identity to. These agents are trained to strike fast and hard. Your mother escaped the fire, thanks to you, but I think she may be in danger.'

There were shadows of fear in his voice. Was Ma in danger? There was no way of knowing. But it was a risk I couldn't afford to take.

'OK,' I said.

'OK?' He looked startled.

'I'll get Ma away.' Not that I had a clue how I was going to persuade her. 'I'm not stupid. Not that I think Ma knows anything. They're wrong there.'

'It doesn't need to be permanent. We're leaving soon and then I think you'll be safe. We're here for a meeting with the man who's getting us off Malta.'

'We?'

I peered past him as though the darkness might be hiding someone.

'I came early. It's no secret that your mother lives here and I was going to warn her. Then I saw you arrive and hung around. But I have to go, Jen.'

'OK.'

'You'll leave Malta?' he said. 'As soon as possible?'

'I said I'll try.' I thought of Ma, desperate to rescue Rania and Aya. It might be difficult. 'If I can't get Ma to leave, I'll make her stay in the house and not let anyone in. I might have to tell her why.'

He clenched and unclenched his hands as he thought.

'If you must. But no one else. And be careful. Don't go out unless you have to. Keep well away from the camp. I'll try and send word when we've left.'

'I'll be careful. I'll stick to places where there are lots of people.'

'Nowhere is safe. Even in a crowd. It's easy to kill quickly and quietly with a knife and walk away before anyone realises what's happened.'

I didn't want to think how he knew this.

He took a pace towards the steps then hesitated.

'And keep away from Musaeada,' he said, turning back.

'Why?'

'You know what Musaeada means?'

'Help, doesn't it?'

'Yes. But word is you can get a lot of different forms of help there. Not just medical care and assistance with asylum applications.'

'What do you mean? You can't think anyone at Musaeada is involved with terrorism?'

'No, but within the organisation there are people who help migrants get off Malta. Migrants with enough money. They're tangled up in people smuggling and it's not good. Loyalties get confused.'

I thought of Amalia, tired and dispirited as she raked through the ashes of the clinic. Surely not.

177

'Who? Who in Musaeada is tangled up in it?'

'I don't know, Jen. I only know our contact to get off the island came through them.'

'And are you meeting this contact tonight?'

'Yes.'

'And that would be you and who? The IS agent?'

He didn't answer.

I'd reached some sort of limit. A line drawn in the sand he wouldn't step over. He was caught up in a storm of loyalties. Even if he trusted me, every instinct he'd acquired over his years working undercover told him to keep quiet. For my own sake as well as his.

I was on my own with this. He'd done what he could and I was grateful, especially as it was far more than he should have, but now he needed to disappear back into his other life.

'Go,' I said.

He hesitated.

I said the words he needed to hear. 'I'll get Ma away. I'll go away myself.'

He went without another word.

I counted to ten, took my shoes off and slipped down the steps after him. If he wouldn't tell me, I'd find out myself.

He was walking towards Mdina Gate. Would he see me if I followed him? Probably. I was wearing Ma's stupid dress. With its light colour and voluminous folds, it wasn't very suitable for hiding in dark corners. I thought rapidly. I wanted to see who he met. More than anything I wanted to know who had torched the clinic and wanted to kill Ma. Mdina Gate. It was the obvious place to arrange to meet. I hurtled back up the steps praying the path along the top of the ramparts would take me there.

The stone, smoothed by centuries of feet, was warm beneath my bare soles. No point putting my battered trainers back on. I ran as fast as I could, hoping no one would look up and see me fly past with my dress streaming behind me. Mdina Gate came into sight.

Yes!

I slowed to a walk and then to a silent glide until I reached the vast arch that framed the gate and jutted out above the ramparts, then I flattened myself behind its sculpted façade and peered down.

I'd made the right decision. Nick was already there, waiting. A white car drew up. An old white car with the long body and pointed wings of a Ford Zephyr. A car exactly like Mohammed's, the taxi driver from Musaeada. Two passengers got out and then the driver, a shortish, rotund man. I was sure it was Mohammed.

He waited by the car while Nick and the two passengers walked over the bridge to Mdina Gate. Two passengers, one man and one woman.

They disappeared beneath the arch and I darted to the other side. My dress caught on a protruding piece of stone carving. I stumbled and let out a sharp cry. And when I raised my head over the wall, the man stared up in my direction, his face caught by the lights. I dived back down but not before his features had imprinted themselves on my brain.

It was Khaled.

Unmistakeably Khaled with his broken nose.

Was Khaled the terrorist?

Had he seen me? I didn't think so. He was in the light and I was in the shadows. I risked another glance but he'd turned and the three of them were walking away into the city.

I ran along the wall until I found some steps down, but they'd long gone by the time I made it back through the quiet streets to Mdina Gate.

The taxi still waited outside. There was no traffic at this time of night and the driver hadn't bothered to go to the car park. I couldn't get close enough to check it was Mohammed. Instead I ducked back under the arch and called his number, thanking Amalia silently for sending it to me. Sure enough, a phone rang in the taxi and I cut the call before Mohammed answered. Then froze when he got out of the car and looked around. His hand slipped into the pocket of the loose jacket he wore and I thought I saw the dull glint of something metallic in his hand. I shrank back.

A group of teenagers on mopeds erupted into the square and tore through the arch. Mohammed took one look at them and jumped back into his car, slamming the door after him and winding the windows shut before he drove to the car park. The noise of the moped engines faded into the night.

I thought back over everything Nick had told me. Mohammed couldn't be the IS agent. He'd been on Malta too long. But someone at Musaeada was involved in smuggling migrants off the island. Was it Mohammed? I was sure he'd had a gun in his hand. Surely it wasn't normal for taxi drivers to carry guns.

I drove back to the hotel with my brain on fire trying to make sense of it all. Khaled had been at the clinic when Nahla had recognised the agent. Khaled had known Nahla was sleeping there. He'd known Ma was there too because he'd told me when I spoke to him on the top of the concrete tubes.

But he couldn't be the figure I'd seen torching the clinic in the dark. He'd been standing right beside me when I'd seen them. Maybe he'd got someone else to do it. Nick had said the IS agents were good at using others to do the dangerous work for them. Maybe Khaled was there to watch and to make sure it happened.

I couldn't work out why he'd followed me over the fence and helped me rescue everybody. It made no sense at all.

Except...

It had been clear that Nahla was badly injured if not already dead when we'd pulled her out. What might he have done if she hadn't been? Because when Ma was struggling inside, Khaled had hesitated. I'd put it down to fear the building was about to burst into flames. But maybe he hadn't wanted Ma to get out at all. At least, not alive.

Or maybe the IS agent wasn't Khaled. I mustn't forget the woman who'd been with him and Nick. Sarah? Khaled's sister. She was the obvious choice, except I thought the woman had moved with a suppleness Sarah lacked.

With Nick's words about being careful ringing in my head, I parked close to the hotel and raced through the empty lobby to my room. I locked the door behind me and leaned a chair against it too.

The hotel staff had been here despite my leaving the *Do Not Disturb* sign on the door. The bed had been made. There was even a chocolate on the pillow. And I had a new rug along with a new pair of curtain tiebacks. I'd have to explain in the morning.

It took me a long time to fall asleep but when I did my last thoughts were of Yasmiin. Fierce Yasmiin, angry at the way life had treated her. Yasmiin who'd told me she was getting off the island soon. I liked her but I couldn't stop myself wondering if she'd been the woman with Khaled and Nick. And if she'd been the dark figure throwing a flaming rag into the clinic.

Sixteen

I woke early, uneasy and unhappy but knowing I had to do something, just not sure what. Whatever was going on and whoever the terrorist was, Nick thought Ma was in danger and that was enough. I'd head over to Mdina and tell her everything. The problem was Rania and Aya. She wouldn't want to leave them. And neither did I.

I stitched up the worst of the rip in her dress with the sewing kit from the hotel bathroom and put it back on with a pair of leggings underneath and my battered and broken trainers on my feet. Then I pulled the plug on the clothes in the bath and left them to drain, whizzing past the staff in reception. I'd explain about the missing rug and curtain tiebacks later.

Mdina looked different in the day. The streets were filled with tourists oohing and aahing and pointing cameras. Everywhere you looked there was a stunning shot waiting to be taken. A mass of purple bougainvillea framed a green door. A narrow alley, lined with shuttered windows and shrubs, curved out of sight. A glimpse of blue sky and a courtyard garden through an open door. People brushed up against me in the narrow streets and every inadvertent touch, every nudge brought Nick's words about being stabbed in a crowd back to me. At the very least I'd have to persuade Ma to stay at Peter's.

But when I reached the house no one answered. I pressed the bell over and over again and then hammered on the door several times, even though I'd heard the strident ring through the thick wood.

I phoned Peter.

'Where's Ma? I've come to see her. I'm outside your house.'

Please say you've both nipped round the corner for a coffee or she's gone to get bread.

'I'm sorry, Jenifry. We're out. I've got a meeting and Morwenna has gone to the camp.'

'To the camp?'

Despite the warmth of the sun, I felt cold.

'Amalia phoned. Rania and Aya were discharged from hospital this morning. Your mother's gone to the camp to see them and I'm meeting someone in case we need a passage off Malta.'

Ma had gone to the camp. The one place above all she needed to keep away from.

'I didn't have time to take her before my meeting. She said she'd catch the bus and walk the last part. There's no rush because the girls won't arrive until mid-morning.'

Bus. The bus was probably safe. But walking from the bus stop to the camp?

I hurried out through the square and back to my car, the phone pressed to my ear.

'Didn't she call you?' Peter said. 'She was going to.'

'No.'

'I expect she ran out of time.'

I started running, ignoring the looks on the tourists' faces as I barged through them.

'Where is the bus stop? I'll pick her up.'

The thought of Ma wandering blithely through the drab and deserted roads around the camp wasn't great.

He explained and told me when the bus would arrive. I did a swift calculation. I had time.

'Thank you,' I said, slowing to a walk as I reached the car park.

I made a quick detour via the shopping centre in Rabat and bought her a mobile phone – the same model as my own so I could set it up easily – with a pay-as-you-go subscription that I could put money onto myself. If she wouldn't use it to call people, at least she could send and receive messages. I was sick of not being able to get in touch with her. I winced at the cost and thanked God for the large limit on my credit card.

As I quickly set it up for her, I thought about Peter's other news. Rania and Aya were in the camp. I'd never get Ma off Malta while she thought she could stop them being returned to Libya. Maybe the only way out of this mess was to abscond with them. If Peter could arrange a boat… If Ma could tell Rania the truth about her grandparents… There'd be an almighty fallout to deal with but it would get all three out of immediate danger.

I was sure Ma'd be safe on the bus but even so I was relieved when it arrived and she climbed down, saw me and waved.

'Amalia phoned you too!' she said once she reached the car. 'It's good news, isn't it? We can tell Rania and –'

'Get in the car, Ma.'

I locked the doors behind her. But before I could talk to her, my phone rang. It was Amalia. She didn't wait for me to speak.

'Peter said Morwenna might be with you. Is she?'

'Yes.'

'I need to speak to her.'

'You're on loudspeaker, Amalia, so she can hear you.'

'Morwenna, when are you going to get here?'

Ma looked at me.

'About ten minutes.'

'You need to be quick.'

'Go,' Ma said to me. 'You can drive and talk, can't you? I mean it's allowed, isn't it?'

184

Any faint hope I had of persuading her to stay away from the camp faded.

'I misunderstood,' Amalia said. 'I thought Rania and Aya were coming back to the camp permanently but they're here to pick up their belongings because they're on a flight tonight.'

Ma started to talk but Amalia's voice overrode her.

'I told the authorities we weren't convinced the grandparents were alive, but Rania spoke to them yesterday. A brief phone call. Is it possible you're wrong, Morwenna?'

Ma was silent for once, clearly as shocked by this as I was. What was going on? I shot her a look as soon as I'd overtaken a dawdling van. She shook her head slowly, deep in thought, and when she spoke, she sounded calm.

'Maybe. Maybe I misunderstood.'

'It does look as though you might have.' Amalia sounded relieved.

I made a *what-are-you-doing-face?* at Ma. She put her finger to her lips.

'It's probably the best thing for the girls. Reuniting families is always the goal,' Amalia went on. 'But you'll come and say goodbye?'

'Of course.'

'We'll be with you soon,' I said and ended the call.

Ma waited a couple of seconds. 'Has she gone?'

'Yes.'

'She can't hear us?'

'No. What is going on, Ma?'

'I don't know. Rania's wrong. I don't know who she spoke to but it wasn't her grandparents. I promise you, Jen. Nahla couldn't have been clearer.'

'I believe you.'

'I need to talk to Rania. We're going to have to get the girls out. You do see that, don't you, Jenifry?'

Right at that moment I couldn't see any other solution. Was I going to help Ma? Shit. Of course I was.

'It's better if Amalia doesn't know,' Ma went on. 'She can't break the law if she wants to keep on operating here, so she'll stop us if I tell her.'

I nodded.

'We'll have to think of something.'

I nodded again.

Neither of us asked the other what that something might be.

Amalia was pacing up and down by her car outside the camp when we arrived. A queue of people, some clutching papers, waited inside the barrier while those at the front argued with the guards. Police with guns were searching a van with a builder's logo.

'They're checking everyone since the riots,' Amalia said tersely, leaning in through our window.

My forlorn hope that we might be able to simply drive out with the girls disappeared.

Amalia waved at one of the harassed guards and he gave her a thumbs-up sign, went into the gatehouse and opened the barrier.

'Get in my car,' she said.

'We'll go in my car,' I said. 'I can't walk far. Burns on my feet.'

'In fact,' Ma said, 'why don't you leave us to it? I know you've got a million things to do.'

Amalia looked doubtful, then nodded. 'If that's all right. Shona has found a nurse to replace Paulina and I want to go and meet her.'

'Of course,' I said.

'I was very sorry to hear about Paulina,' Ma added. 'Terrible. Nowhere is safe.'

'It looks as though it wasn't a random attack,' Amalia said. 'Apparently she owed money. Lots of money. She gambled, you see. Some sort of addiction, really. I don't understand it.'

Her face creased in puzzlement. Clearly Amalia had never felt the thrill of risking everything on a throw of the dice.

The guard beckoned us through so I drove straight in as Ma waved gaily at him and Amalia left.

'Good,' Ma said. 'Amalia's gone and we've got the car in.'

'They'll check it when we leave,' I said.

'At least the gate's open. We could ram the barrier, couldn't we?'

All the reasons why it wouldn't work ran through my mind but I contented myself a short 'No'.

'Oh well, we'll think of something,' she said again.

There were very few people about. Maybe due to the armed police patrolling in pairs. At least their presence meant Ma would be safer.

'Here we are,' Ma said.

A policewoman waited outside the container where Nahla and the girls had lived. Rania must be inside, packing up their possessions, but Aya stood beside the policewoman, staring at the ground and ignoring her.

Ma got out of the car and ran over to her.

The little girl wasn't motionless. Waves of trembling rippled through her body and her closed lips twitched convulsively. Ma knelt down in the grit and dirt and ashes in front of her, yet not so close as to crowd the child. She didn't try to touch Aya, but simply said her name softly and repeatedly with a voice empty of emotion, empty of everything except calmness.

It took time for Aya to hear her. A long time. But Ma never stopped. Until, still quivering, Aya looked up. I kept back, remembering Aya's fear of strangers. Ma held out her arms but stayed kneeling. The child's eyes blinked rapidly and Ma said her name again. More blinking and then she lifted her own arms. Ma waited until Aya moved towards her, stumbling a little at first, and then she embraced her tightly and they rocked together on the filthy ground. Ma lifted her head and jerked her eyes upward to the container and I understood it had fallen to me to talk to Rania.

Shit. I didn't want to tell Rania her grandparents were dead. I'd rather pull my eyes out than do it. I'd assumed the job would fall to Ma.

I had no choice, though. None at all.

The container was quiet. I supposed the other women and children had given Rania some space to pack on her own or had been asked to leave. The smell was still bad and overlaid with a tang of smoke from the riots. I pushed through the thin cloths demarcating the different families' spaces and found Rania sitting on the bed at the end, staring at a small pile of clothes in front of her.

'Hello, Rania.'

She looked older and thinner, if that were possible. Some of the childishness had left her face and her bones showed their positions under her skin. But she was wearing clean and, I thought, new clothes. Her hair was freshly plaited and she greeted me with a smile.

'Hello. Amalia said you might come to say goodbye and I am pleased. I wouldn't have wanted to leave without seeing you and Morwenna.'

The unexpected maturity of her words made me grit my teeth.

'Ma is talking to Aya, she wants to see you too.'

'I'm glad. Aya is… not good but I know she'll get better once she's home.' She took a deep breath and her skinny ribs showed beneath her T-shirt. 'Thank you for rescuing us.'

'I'm so sorry I was too late for your mother.' I tried to match her curiously formal tone, judging that was how she needed to be, but I wanted to hug her.

She gestured towards the bed.

'I'm not sure what to take with us. Most of it is so horrible I never want to see it again. I'm sure my grandmother will throw it all away.'

I cast a quick glance at the heap of old clothes on the bed. She was right, they were disgusting. I opened my mouth to tell her to leave it all behind, then shut it. This was getting us nowhere. There'd never be a right time for what I had to say so it might as well be now.

'Rania, I have something to tell you. I'm really, really sorry but you need to know your grandparents are dead.'

She picked up a T-shirt and folded it.

'Your grandparents are dead. They died just before you came here.'

No reaction.

She reached for a grey pleated skirt with dirt ingrained in the folds but her hand faltered.

'I'm sorry, Rania. It must be terrible news for you. On top of your father and your mother.'

I wanted to leave. I wanted to run down the steps, get in my car and drive as far away as possible. Anything rather than witness her world smash even more than it already had.

'But I spoke to them? It can't be true?'

Her voice was full of anguish but also doubts. I wondered about the phone call. How sure was Rania she'd spoken to her grandparents?

'Rania. It couldn't have been them. Could you hear clearly?'

She folded the skirt, carefully pressing each pleat into place.

'Rania, I'm so sorry but they're dead.'

'You're wrong.'

'Your mother told my mother.'

'Mama?'

I reached out a hand and covered hers, stopping the fingers squeezing each pleat.

'They died before you left Libya.'

A tremor ran through her bones. I held her hands tight in mine and wished she'd look at me.

'I'm so sorry, Rania. It's dreadful news for you, I know.'

She dragged her hands out of my grasp and, finally, met my eyes.

'You're wrong. They can't be dead. Of course they can't be. Mama would have said.'

'I'm not wrong. I promise you. Your mother didn't tell you because she knew how much it would upset you. I know how awful this must be but you have to accept it.'

I should be giving her unending time for the news to sink in, but I didn't have it. I only had minutes, maybe seconds, until the watchful policewoman downstairs came up to see how we were doing.

'How did they die?' She was angry now. 'Tell me that.'

Should I lie to her? Tell her it had been an accident? Or a sudden illness? No. Look where secrets and lies had got us.

'I don't know the details.'

Thank God I don't know the details.

'You know there were people who wanted to hurt your mother?'

She nodded.

'I'm afraid they killed your grandparents.'

She stopped dead. Every part of her frozen except her eyes, which fluttered and darted. I wasn't surprised. It was too big a truth to take in all at once.

'I don't believe you. Mama would have told me.'

They were the same words as before, but now they lacked conviction. They were a last tug on the cords of hope anchoring her to a past where her grandparents were alive and waiting for her in Tripoli. Soon they'd snap. She was coming round.

But we didn't have time.

An idea came to me.

'Why don't you phone them again? Your grandparents, I mean.' I held out my phone. 'I'm guessing the last time it wasn't very clear.'

She shook her head. 'It was very short and crackly. Their voices came and went. They didn't sound like… But I never –'

And you heard what you wanted to hear, I thought.

'Go on. Call them now.'

She gazed at my phone as though it was a grenade I was pushing towards her.

'They might be out.'

I thrust the phone into her hand.

'Try. Call them.'

I hated myself. I hated the insistent, nagging edge in my voice.

She pulled her own phone out of her pocket and scrolled through to find their number, gave me a quick and hostile glance and sat with her back to me on the bed.

I went to the window and looked out. The policewoman looked up at me. I smiled and gave her a thumbs-up sign. She wandered back to Ma and Aya, still sitting on the earth. Ma was curled round Aya and whispering words into her hair.

Behind me Rania's breath made little fluttery noises like a panicky bird flying at a predator nearing her nest. After a moment, she cut the call and redialled. And then again.

'They keep on telling me the number is disconnected. How can that be?' Her face was flushed although the temperature in the container today was bearable.

'Can you call someone who knows them?'

'Uncle Eso. I'll call him.'

'Uncle?'

'He's not my uncle. He's a friend. We stayed with him before we came here.'

This time I watched her as she dialled his number. It took her three goes to connect and sweat ran down her forehead. I heard the entire conversation but understood nothing because she spoke in Arabic. The music of her voice changed though, moving from hesitant legato to a fierce staccato, as if she were arguing furiously, and then to silence as she listened while Uncle Eso's voice rang tinnily in the enclosed space. From time to time she wiped her damp forehead and hands on the grey skirt.

I glanced outside. The policewoman still chatted to Ma and then to two of the armed policemen who patrolled from one end of the alley to the other and back again. A lone figure strode past them and towards Ma. A wash of fear prickled over my skin. It was Yasmiin.

Ma was quite safe. The policewoman was there. Not that I was at all sure the woman I'd seen last night with Nick and Khaled was Yasmiin. Nevertheless I kept my eyes fixed on her as she went over and spoke to Ma.

Uncle Eso's voice stopped. I counted to ten and turned round. The phone call was over.

'He says we must never return. Never.'

The slightly formal and mature half-adult who had welcomed me was gone, leaving a terrified child in their place.

'What am I going to do?'

Her eyes begged me to help. Begged me for an answer. I didn't have one.

Well done, Jen. You've succeeded in your mission. Rania knows her grandparents are dead. What are you going to do now?

'I said I'd tell the police they were dead but he told me not to. He told me to run,' Rania went on. 'To take Aya and run and hide. But he doesn't understand what it is like here. He doesn't understand what Aya is like.'

She crumbled before my eyes, panting in sharp, rapid jerks as though the air had emptied of oxygen. I tried to put my arms round her but she shook me off.

Uncle Eso was right. The authorities might not believe Rania if she started saying her grandparents were dead. They certainly wouldn't want to. The decision had been made to send the girls back and it was one that worked for everybody. Plus they'd watch her more carefully if they knew she was going back against her will. No, Uncle Eso was definitely right. Keep quiet and run at the first opportunity.

Footsteps clanged on the metal staircase outside. Another glance out of the window told me the policewoman was no longer with Ma. Shit. She'd come to see how we were doing. I grabbed an armful of clothes from the bed and thrust them into a bag.

'Could you take these down?' I asked her as I nipped out of the door and onto the top of the stairs.

I pushed the clothes into her arms. Below, Yasmiin was deep in conversation with Ma, who clutched Aya to her.

'Hi, Yasmiin,' I yelled and waved frantically, wanting to be sure she knew someone was watching.

Rania's panicked breathing was audible even here.

'Looking at her mother's belongings is very difficult,' I said. 'How much longer do we have?'

'Half an hour and then we must go to the airport.'

'I thought they weren't flying until this evening.'

'Neither child has a passport so there is paperwork to complete there.'

My mind raced. It might be easier to slip them out from the airport. Out from the big halls full of tourists and travellers. Certainly it would be easier than trying to get them out of here.

'Can we come with them to the airport?'

She looked doubtful.

'Aya is comfortable with my mother. It might be better,' I said.

'I will make a call,' she said and went back down the stairs.

'Rania,' I said quickly shoving possessions into bags and hating myself. 'I need you to listen. Please. I know how difficult it is. But for Aya's sake.'

She dragged herself together. Her chest still heaved with broken breaths but she had enough control to speak.

'She should have told me. Mama should have told me.'

She was right.

'I know, but now we have to concentrate on getting you out of here.'

'Can you do that?'

I had no idea but I had to give her something.

'We'll get you out at the airport.'

Another idea came to me.

'Listen – I'll give you a phone. I've got one in the car. Keep it hidden and if they won't let us come with you, text us where you are. Send us pictures and we'll come and find you and get you out.'

I wasn't at all sure any of this was possible but I had to give her some hope amid the fear showing itself in her glassy eyes and her bony fingers clenching the folds of her mother's old skirt.

'Here's a biro. Write my number on your wrist. I'll text the phone with it but just in case.'

I picked up the bags and headed down the stairs. Rania followed with another, although she still clutched the grey pleated skirt. She hesitated at the exit to the container and plunged her face into its material. I wondered if it retained some lingering trace of Nahla. Then she pasted a smile on her face and walked down the steps before me. There was steel in her veins despite the wobble in her gait. I couldn't let her down. Somehow we had to get her out of this.

The two policemen walked slowly past on their never-ending patrol, guns slung on straps over their shoulders and held tight in arms whose muscles bulged where they disappeared into short-sleeved black shirts. Ma, her dress coated with dust and dried dirt, waited for us at the bottom of the stairs, with Aya clinging to her leg. Yasmiin was gone and so was the policewoman.

'Where is she?'

'Gone to the guardhouse. Said she had to make a call but I think she wanted to pee.'

'Rania,' I said quietly, one eye on the policemen trudging towards us. 'Let me give you the phone now. While she's not here.'

'I told her,' I muttered to Ma as I reached for the phone I'd bought earlier and flung onto the back seat. It only had a small charge but it was the same model as mine. Easy enough to swap over the batteries.

'Why don't we take them now?' Ma said, leaning over me.

'With those two policemen watching us?'

'They wouldn't shoot us.' Ma's breath was hot on my cheek.

'They might. They'd shoot the tyres anyway. Or run after us and shout. We'd never get out.'

'Maybe they'll leave.' Ma looked hopeful.

I snapped my charged battery into Rania's phone and pressed the power button. All systems go.

'Charger and earphones,' I said and gave them to Rania. 'Put it all somewhere safe.'

A sudden burst of screams and the sound of breaking glass from somewhere behind us. A scurry of chatter on the policemen's radios and shouts away to our left. They moved away, starting to run as the shouting grew louder and disappeared as they cut through the containers to the other side of the camp.

'I think that's Yasmiin,' Ma said.

We gazed at each other. This was our chance. We both knew it. But a chance to do what? *Drive away?* We'd be searched at the gate. *Climb out?* I took one look at Rania and Ma. Impossible. Even without the added problem of Aya, still clinging to Ma's leg. *Hide somewhere in the camp?* At least for long enough to miss the flight. What would be the point? They'd find us eventually and increase the security round Rania and Aya.

But as I stared at Ma, Aya sighed, let go of Ma and slipped into the back seat of the car, then slithered down out of view into the footwell behind the front seats.

Rania peered in after her and dropped the skirt she'd been clutching over the little girl, then swept the packaging debris from the phone on top of it.

'I don't think there's room for both of us,' she said. 'Uncle Eso's car was bigger and he'd removed some of the seat.'

With the skirt on top of her, light grey like the upholstery, Aya wasn't visible at a cursory glance. Would the guards look hard? Probably not. They were after the men who'd started the riots. We were two white women. They knew Ma. But still I hesitated. I could be messing things up for Rania and Aya. Waving goodbye to the chance of getting them out at the airport. Shit, shit, shit.

'Shall I get in the boot?' Rania asked.

'No. They're bound to check that.'

I couldn't make up my mind. What had happened to me?

Rania misinterpreted my silence.

'You can't take me, then?' she said. Her mouth trembled. 'That is fine. It will be good to get Aya out. Maybe I can persuade them to let me stay.'

I pulled myself together.

'Rania, get on the floor in front of the passenger seat and curl up as tight as you can. Get your legs under the seat.'

I pulled the largest and darkest article of clothing, a baggy cardigan, out of a bag and ran round. Ma understood, though. She climbed in after Rania and stretched her legs and loose dress over the girl below her, then took the cardigan and tucked it round the bits of Rania's body still visible.

'Rania. You must keep absolutely still. No matter what happens. Can you tell Aya too?'

196

'I will but I don't think she will move. She is very good at keeping still. Now anyway.'

Ma's eyes met mine.

'Smile,' I said and drove off.

Seventeen

The barrier was open because a truck was parked bang in the middle of the way out, unloading a digger that trundled down two ramps.

Ma leaned out of the window and waved at the guards. One of them detached himself from the group watching the digger driver manoeuvre and came over. He stuck his head through the window and both Ma and I flinched.

'Won't be long,' he said. 'Could you move the car out of the way?'

I nodded and pulled over to the far side of the entrance.

'Did you hear that, Rania?' I said. 'A few seconds' wait. You can answer quietly. They can't hear us.'

'Yes.'

'Will Aya –'

'She won't move until I tell her.'

Ma raised her hands in an intricate arrangement of fingers and closed her eyes. I remembered enough yoga to recognise a mudra. A positioning of the hands with some meaning but here my memory deserted me. Probably protection from negative energy. Hopefully it might stop the police from searching the car. I had my doubts and I thought Ma had a few as well because she moistened her lips with her tongue and swallowed.

A van drove past outside the camp. The road was so close. I itched to be on it and speeding away.

The digger lumbered onto the ground, then turned and hoisted the first of the ramps into the back of the truck. But slowly. So slowly. As soon as he'd finished, as soon as the truck left, I'd nip out after it. There'd be room for the car by the side of the digger. I slipped the handbrake off, my foot poised to stab the accelerator.

Ma inhaled sharply. Through the window of the guardhouse, the policewoman came into view. She stood with her back to us, talking to another policeman.

The guard watching the digger beckoned us over. I obeyed.

'He's going to search us.' Ma's voice was panicky.

I smiled at him as I pulled the lever that opened the boot, got out of the car as though I had all the time in the world and raised the lid. He glanced in. It was empty. He then shot a quick look over the back seat. I prayed. If there'd been a mudra for stopping guards from opening the back door of a car, I'd have done it. But I thought it was going to be OK. I thought he was going through the motions for the sake of the hard-faced soldiers watching us.

And just as he was straightening up, ready to wave us through, Aya coughed. And the torn phone packaging shifted. She coughed once more. I didn't think he'd seen the movement but he'd heard the cough through the open windows.

He hesitated.

Ma coughed. A couple of times. As lightly and discreetly as Aya's. And then she let it develop into a series of hacking barks.

'Allergy,' I said. 'Lot of it about.'

I strolled round and got back into the car, while he walked to its front to gaze in at Ma.

Behind him the truck drove slowly away. The way was clear. As soon as he moved, I'd go. At the edge of my vision I saw the policewoman step out of the guardroom.

Shit.

'Shit,' Ma muttered.

The guard nodded and waved us on. I drove decorously and discreetly out, and headed away from the camp, gripping the steering wheel to stop it slipping out of my sweaty grasp.

'That was close.'

I glanced in the mirror. The policewoman stood in the middle of the road outside the camp staring after us.

'It's not over yet. She's seen us.'

'Shit.' Ma said again.

'She'll think it's odd we've left but she'll have to go back to the container to see if the girls are there. We've got ten minutes at least to get as far away as possible.'

And then what? Hide?

Ma's voice echoed my thoughts. 'Go to Peter's. We'll hide there.'

'No. We're going to have police after us in thirty minutes, tops. The first thing they'll do is call Amalia. The guards know you're part of Musaeada, don't they?'

'Yes.'

'If we're lucky, she won't give us away immediately. But in the end she'll have to give them Peter's address and tell you're staying there. We've got to get right away. Call Peter and tell him we have to get on a boat at once.'

She hesitated.

'Ma. We haven't got time for you to fuss about the radiation or whatever it is that bothers you. Do you know how to make a call?'

'Yes, of course I do. It's not that different from a normal phone.'

She struggled, though. I barked instructions at her as I drove as fast as I could in any direction away from the camp, seizing the slightest opportunity to overtake. She still couldn't make it work.

I realised what was wrong. It had no battery. I hadn't had time to put the flat one from Rania's phone in it, let alone think about charging it up.

'Use Rania's phone.'

A hand reached up and passed it to her.

'Can we let them sit up?'

I shook my head. 'Better not.'

Ma didn't give Peter a chance to get a word in edgeways. She and the girls needed to leave now. She knew he could sort it. Ma's fixity of purpose had infuriated me in the past, many times. Many, many times. But now I was glad she was impossible to shift. Poor Peter didn't stand a chance.

In between listening to her I spent the time thinking.

Ma finished the call.

'He's going to sort it,' she said. 'He'll call us back.'

'Slight change of plan,' I said. 'Nothing major.'

She waited.

'I'm going to have to go with you and the girls. I'll never get off the island otherwise.'

'I'll call Peter back and tell him five of us.'

'Is he sure about all this?'

'What do you mean?'

She didn't realise how much trouble lay ahead for us even if we succeeded in getting the girls off the island, then through Italy and France and finally somehow into the UK. Words like *kidnapping* and *international arrest warrant* ran through my head. We might even be accused of child trafficking.

'Don't you think you should give Peter a chance to back out? He could claim he knew nothing about it.'

She thought for a few minutes, and then called Peter back.

In the distance, I heard a police siren. Probably nothing to do with us. We'd only had twenty of our thirty minutes. It would be better to keep off the main roads now. Maybe find somewhere out of the way and park up. If only the island weren't so small. A thirty-minute start anywhere else would have been time to get clear away.

I slowed right down. A speeding car stuck out on the back

roads. Away from the traffic, a quiet, solid with tension, crept through the car. There'd been no noise from Aya since the cough and Rania lay absolutely still under Ma's legs. Ma listened to Peter and said little. Only interjecting the occasional 'yes' or 'uh-huh'.

'It's on for tonight,' Ma said after she'd finished the conversation with Peter. 'The boat was going out anyway. Peter won't come with us. He'll take the ferry to Sicily and pick us up the other side. The police aren't looking for him and that way we'll have a car in Italy.'

It was a great idea. Having our own car would solve a myriad of problems.

'It's all working out,' Ma said but she chewed the side of her mouth as she spoke. 'I knew it would.'

Was she having doubts? I hoped not. Because the thought of Ma being uncertain was surprisingly tough to contemplate.

'And Peter knows what he's letting himself in for?' I asked.

'Yes. He doesn't care.'

Her tone changed. She was smiling to herself now.

'He said he'd always thought it would be better if he took the ferry but he didn't want me to be on my own on the boat. In case I was scared. He said the crossing can be quite rough.'

We both laughed.

Ma, I was sure, because the idea of her being scared by a quite-rough sea was absurd, but my laugh was tinged with some emotion I couldn't quite identify. Fear? No. Anxiety? Perhaps. But also relief. More than anything, I wanted to get off this tiny island rammed full of people. I wanted to get away from its strange, claustrophobic mix of tourists and refugees whose meeting points sparked frustration and rage. I was quite looking forward to fleeing across Europe. It crossed my mind that I might not feel quite so exuberant if I had no money, no car and no friends to call on but I pushed the thought away.

'Where's the boat picking us up?' I asked.

Eighteen

Someone called Stephan was going to pick us up on the island's southern coast, not far from where Ma held her yoga classes. Working back round to the south while avoiding the main roads was tricky. Neither Ma nor I knew the little roads and Ma was crap with Google Maps. We ditched the car at the end of a track near the meeting point. I would have liked to dump it in a car park, where it might stay unnoticed for a few hours but the nearest one was miles away.

We were on the narrow strip of barren land between the cliff-edged coast and the stony fields inland. A lone prickly pear, bent by the sea winds, marked the path down and the sooner we were off the cliff and out of view of the path the better. Already two walkers were heading our way. I hissed at Ma to stay in the car until they'd passed and keep the girls quiet. Not that I needed to. They'd not moved an inch. Not even when I'd stopped the car and got out.

I smiled cheerfully when the walkers strolled past. We were as conspicuous as hell anyway.

'Afternoon,' they said.

'Afternoon. Lovely day.'

'Not for long. Rain on its way.' One of them pointed to the horizon where a roll of grey clouds blurred the line between sea and sky. They ambled off and, when they'd gone, I told Ma and Rania to get out of the car.

Rania uncurled herself as soon as Ma was out and crawled onto the ground where she rubbed and stretched her limbs in every direction. Aya didn't move until Ma went round, lifted the skirt off her and helped her out.

She crumpled as soon as her feet touched the ground. Rania came over and massaged her legs and murmured to her.

'We get cramp if we can't move,' she told us.

Smears of snot and tears covered Aya's face although I hadn't heard a whisper of noise from her since the cough. Rania didn't need telling we needed to be quick. She shot glances all around in between cajoling and scolding Aya to start moving.

'She's so like her father,' Ma muttered to me. 'I see Ibrahim in every move she makes.'

In the distance more walkers headed our way.

'We need to get off the path.'

We needed to get off the island. A sick feeling crawled into the bottom of my stomach and settled there, only fading a little once we reached the tiny shingle beach caught between two rocky promontories and tucked ourselves under the cliffs, out of view of any passers-by.

I looked at Rania's phone; we had hours to wait. Rania's eyes fell on it and she held out her hand.

'Where's yours?'

'I left it behind. I didn't want them to see I had two phones.'

The skin round her mouth and jaw twitched.

'Music?' I said.

She nodded and I logged her into my Spotify account.

She put the earphones in and turned her back on us. Aya settled herself in Ma's arms and lap and fell asleep.

'It's what they do,' Ma said, seeing my questioning look and brushing a stray wisp of hair off the little girl's forehead. 'There's a lot of waiting when you're a refugee. Waiting in awful places. The children learn to shut off. Aya sleeps and Rania listens to music. It's all too big and terrifying to deal with.'

It was one of the most intelligent comments Ma had ever made.

I couldn't wait patiently, though. Fear nudged me into restlessness. I glanced up at the cliff overhanging the beach. Coastal scree. A mixture of limestone and clay. It would be a nightmare to climb, slippery and crumbly. Still I wouldn't have minded having a go. It would release some of the tension crackling through my body. My fingers started to crimp and curl.

Think of something else.

'Ma.'

She opened her eyes.

'Sorry, I didn't realise you were meditating.'

'It doesn't matter. What did you want to say?'

'Yasmiin. Did you think she caused the disturbance that took the police away at the camp?'

'Yes. I told her we needed to rescue the girls and she said she'd help.'

Maybe Yasmiin hadn't been the woman with Khaled and Nick at Mdina.

I checked Rania was still listening to music.

'Did Nahla say anything to you about seeing someone she knew here? Someone she'd known in Libya?'

'Here, in Malta?'

'At the clinic, probably.'

'No.'

'Are you sure?'

Ma eyed me curiously.

'You're sure,' I repeated, 'she didn't say anything? When you were together before the fire started.'

'Nahla and I didn't talk about anything serious that evening,' Ma said. 'The drip and the drugs had worked and she was feeling better – especially when I told her about coming with me in the morning.' Her eyes glazed over briefly. 'She and Rania chatted but in Arabic and I was happy to leave them to it. I think they discussed Aya for a while. I heard them mention her name a few times. I think they were starting to talk about the future…' Ma's voice drifted into silence.

Ma knew nothing. They were after her for nothing.

They? Who was the agent, the terrorist? Everything pointed to Khaled. He'd been at the clinic and with his broken face he was easily recognisable. He'd also been at Mdina. And although he couldn't have torched the clinic because he'd been with me, he could have got someone else to do it for him.

My thoughts raced on, because there was also Paulina to consider. Was her death a random thing? Or linked to her gambling debts? Or had she been murdered because someone feared Nahla had said too much to her?

Khaled could have killed her. He'd been up at the hospital with Yousef before the riots broke out. If only I knew the time of her death, but now was not the moment to ring Amalia and ask her if she knew.

I didn't want it to be Khaled. That was the problem. Not after he'd helped me rescue Ma and the girls. I liked him. There was an air of positivity about him. Of hope. And it was very attractive.

I'd have preferred it to be Mohammed. Mohammed who carried a gun and who switched off his veneer of bouncy cheer at the drop of a hat. But he'd been on Malta for some time and Nick had implied the terrorist had arrived recently.

'I knew Nahla was dead before you rescued us,' Ma said suddenly. 'I checked her pulse just before you smashed through the ceiling.'

There was no sign of a yacht out to sea but on the horizon a small black speck appeared.

'I wanted Rania and Aya to have a body to bury. It's important to have an ending.'

The black speck resolved itself in an inflatable boat, a RIB.

I stood and waved. A man in an orange T-shirt waved back and headed for a flattish part of the rock. I poked Rania's shoulder but the engine noise woke Aya. She saw the boat, opened her mouth and screamed. And screamed. Then stood and ran towards the path we'd come down.

Her six-year-old legs were no match for mine. I grabbed her but she fought back, yanking at my hair and sinking her teeth into my shoulder. I tried to encircle her with my arms but it was like holding a strong and wriggling octopus with claws on the end of its tentacles. I didn't dare carry her to the boat while she was like this. I was already struggling to stay upright and if I fell on the rocks we'd both end up in the sea.

A harsh voice shouted. The man leapt out and headed towards us, his hand raised to slap her. Ma was there in an instant.

'Don't you dare!' She stood between him and us. For a minute I thought he might hit her instead but he lowered his arm.

'Get on board.' He strode back to the boat.

Between us, Ma and I carried the screaming and struggling Aya. Ma climbed in first and sat herself next to Rania, holding her arms up for Aya. The little girl's cries grew more frantic. I gripped her harder and bent over but the man scooped her out of my arms and placed her next to Ma where her yells became even more hysterical.

'Quick as you like,' he said to me. 'We've already gathered quite a crowd.'

On the cliff above, half a dozen people stared down at us.

I seized his arm and stumbled into the boat.

So much for slipping off Malta quietly. How long would it take for one of the onlookers to hear about refugee children abducted by a couple of women and put two and two together?

We tore away from the little beach, smashing into the top of each wave. Each jolt sent a mini shock through my bones and when we smacked into a particularly large wave I thought the force of it might knock me overboard despite my grip on the handles round the edge. Aya was a damp and quivering lump, shrieking with each jerk and threshing her arms and legs.

Ma made no effort to keep her quiet. Instead she muttered words of encouragement each time the little girl made a noise.

'That's it,' she said. 'Scream. Loud. Go on, Aya. Louder.'

And she matched Aya's noise, so their voices rose in an urgent crescendo over the crashes of the boat's passage until Aya lifted her head into the wind and gave a series of piercing howls that shook me more than the boat itself.

She burst into proper tears then. Not a quiet trickle of tears but gasping sobs that racked her chest. She buried her head in Ma's lap and cried her heart out.

'Could we slow down?' I yelled in between splashes of spray that stung my face. 'It's Stephan, isn't it?'

'Sit on the bottom. Like her.' He jerked his head at Ma.

I did as I was told.

He was a nasty git. The blonde bristle on his chin was deeply unattractive as was his crinkly fair hair, coarse and unwashed so the curls looked like the plastic ones on a cheap doll. With his roughened red skin and faded orange T-shirt revealing a tuft of darker hair on his chest, I didn't like him one bit but I'd have to put up with him until we got to Italy.

Stephan shouted something but the wind tore the words out of his mouth. A white yacht gleamed a short way from us.

'Is that it?' I shouted.

He nodded and wheeled the boat round to the yacht's back end where a lower and flatter space with a ladder made it easy to climb aboard. Up close the boat wasn't quite so gleaming. Faint yellow stains discoloured the white hull and barnacles clung to its surface. As Stephan climbed the ladder, the yacht swung, revealing white salt marks mottling the darker paint below the waterline.

'Down below,' Stephan said once we'd clambered aboard. 'And I don't want to see any of you on deck until we get to Italy.'

'How long?' I asked.

'Depends on the weather. The marine forecast isn't good for tonight and I was going to wait until tomorrow but, thanks to the little girl and the attention she attracted, we need to go now.'

We followed him down. Me, Rania, and then Ma with Aya. The steps had seen better days. The wood was dented and patches of paler wood showed where the varnish was worn. A smell of coffee wafted up through the space not blocked by Stephan's shoulders. And the noise of people chatting quietly.

We weren't alone then.

Stephan stepped into the cabin and to the front end, leaving the way clear for me to see. The steps ended in the centre of a saloon, with a table in the right-hand corner encircled by a banquette and another banquette along the left. A small kitchenette ran behind me and into the back of the boat.

The saloon was full of people.

Most of whom we knew.

Their voices died away as they saw us.

Khaled and Yousef sat at the table with Sarah.

My thoughts whirled.

Marwa and her niece, Zubaida, occupied the banquette opposite with Zubaida's two children.

To my left, Yasmiin leaned against the sink in the little galley, a smile breaking across her face.

Ma nudged me from behind, not understanding why I'd stopped. I stepped down and turned right to give Ma space to get down.

Nick stood in front of me. For a brief moment his eyes opened into black pools of horror and then his face shut down and he walked away and into a cabin in the back of the boat.

PART THREE

The Mediterranean

Nineteen

The quiet in the cabin lasted until Ma, weighed down by Aya in her arms, saw everybody and laughed. At the same time a wave hit the boat making it lurch and sending Rania sprawling onto the floor. I helped her up as the rocking subsided.

'Just another boat going by,' I said as she gripped onto me.

'Too fast,' Ma said.

'In here.'

Stephan's voice interrupted my raging thoughts and he opened a door at the front end revealing a vaguely triangular cabin with a small double bed tucked into the apex.

'Peter insisted you had a cabin. You'll have to make do with mine. There's a shower in here.' He flung a door open, revealing a tiny bathroom as we crowded in after him. 'Wash that kid before you put her anywhere near my bed.' He gestured to Aya who'd wet herself with terror. 'In fact, you could all do with a bit of a clean-up.' And he went out.

'And sod you too,' I said after he'd closed the door behind him. I sat on the bed, putting my burnt and grubby trainers on his bedding for good measure. 'What a... an unpleasant man.'

'Typical captain. He's a good sailor, though,' Ma said as she carried Aya into the minute bathroom and sat her on the loo.

'How can you possibly tell that?' I said, although my mind was on the refugees the other side of the thin walls.

Thank God Peter had got us a cabin.

213

'Look at the yacht.' Ma undressed Aya. 'She could sail at a moment's notice. The main looks neatly stowed. Sheets and halyards all properly coiled and hitched to the right cleats –'

'Enough. I believe you.' I might not know much about sailing but I understood the importance of keeping ropes in order and using the right knots.

What should I do?

'Did you see?' Rania took her earphones out. 'Yasmiin and Sarah and the others?'

'Yes,' Ma said. 'Open the door, Rania. I don't see why we have to be shut in here.'

'No, wait a minute. There are a lot of people in a very small space out there. Give Aya a chance to settle.'

And me a chance to think.

'Aya's fine,' Ma said rinsing her off in the shower. 'She's going to sleep now. Aren't you, sweetheart? Look, she can hardly stand.'

Ma was right. Aya was already half asleep. She would have fallen if Ma hadn't been holding her up.

'Will you dry her, Rania, while I find her something to wear?'

'Is she all right?' Rania wrapped the towel round the little girl and sat on the bed with her. There wasn't much room to stand with Ma opening and closing every locker.

'Not yet,' Ma said as rifled through the drawers. 'But she's taken a step in the right direction.' She found a clean T-shirt – Stephan's I presumed – and dressed Aya in it. Aya rolled into the covers and shut her eyes. A soft thudding noise started up, making the walls vibrate.

'Engine?'

'Yes,' Ma said. 'A great shame on a boat like this.'

That meant we were leaving. Should I try to get us off?

'Are we safe now?' Rania asked me.

Her eyes begged me to say yes and I opened my mouth to reassure her then thought better of it. No more hiding the truth.

Ma gave me a curious look and I knew she was waiting to hear my answer.

We couldn't go back to Malta. Whatever lay ahead, there was nothing for us there.

'It's good we're on the boat,' I said. 'And it's good we're leaving. But we've got a long way to go.'

I wouldn't lie to her, whatever she asked. But if she had questions she didn't voice them.

'Can I go out and see Yasmiin?' she asked.

'Of course,' Ma said.

'Wait,' I said.

They both looked at me.

I thought rapidly.

There was no danger for any of us really, not while we were all crammed into a tiny space on the boat. No one could kill Ma without someone seeing. But the closeness meant she couldn't fail to see Nick. I needed to talk to her alone.

'Of course, go and see Yasmiin. If you're not too tired, that is.'

She shook her head and left. I made sure the door was firmly closed and kept my voice down.

'Ma. Did you see Nick? Nick Crawford? From home?'

I wondered again what Nick's real name was.

'Nick Crawford?'

Ma rubbed the bridge of her nose. She was another one who looked like they needed time out.

'He rented a cottage near the lighthouse last year and he's on this boat.'

'Is he? I didn't see him.'

'Well, when you do see him, you mustn't let on you know who he is. Not at all. Not even a hint.'

I tried to think where to start in order to explain how desperate it was.

215

'Alright,' she said and when I gaped at her, she repeated it. 'Alright, I won't say a word.'

'I can explain.'

'If you want to, but not now.' She massaged her temples and leaned against the plastic wall of the cabin, then pushed herself away. 'Doesn't it bother you?'

'What?'

'The dreadful noise.'

I listened. Apart from the underlying *putt-putt* of the engine taking us steadily away from Malta and the sleeping Aya's snuffly breathing, I could only hear the smothered murmur of people talking in the main cabin and the slosh of the sea against the hull.

'I can smell it too.'

I realised she was talking about the engine.

'All those fumes. Poisoning the air. Poisoning the sea. Slowly suffocating the lungs of the planet.'

I had a feeling the Amazon rainforest was normally referred to as the lungs of the planet but I got her point.

'It's choking me. I need air,' she said and flung open the door, marched through the crowded saloon to the steps and up onto deck, opening and shutting the hatch as she went.

I checked the cabin quickly.

Sitting at the table to my left, Khaled read an English book on engineering while Yousef stared at chess pieces on a board. Marwa and her pregnant niece, Zubaida, played cat's cradle with Zubaida's children on the banquette to my right, nestled down in a heap of rugs and cushions – all faded but clean. On one side of the steps Sarah made tea in the tiny kitchen while Yasmiin and Rania sat on the floor on the other side. Beyond them a door opened into the rear cabin, smaller than ours and filled with a bed on which I could only make out a pair of feet.

No sign of Nick. Was he in the cabin with the owner of the feet?

Ma was safe enough on deck because all my suspects were here. I relaxed a little.

Sarah came over and put cups of tea on the table, then slipped in beside Khaled. He lifted his head out of his book as she sat beside him and caught my gaze. He smiled revealing the jagged edges of broken teeth. I suspected he'd got them at the same time his nose was broken. There was nothing strange in his injury. Many of the refugees were marked. Yousef had scars down his arms and I'd noticed Zubaida had lost the end of one finger.

Khaled looked as though he might talk to me but I couldn't face chatting to him. I painted a smile onto my face and headed for the galley. I'd make myself tea.

There wasn't much choice. Bog standard supermarket or something with seaweed in it. I chose the bog standard, refilled the pan with water and put it on the gas stove.

Someone came up behind me. Familiar hands placed two dirty mugs on the counter. Nick's hands.

'Will there be enough water for two more?'

His voice shocked me. It was deeper and thicker, with the soft consonants and rolled 'r' of the Arabic accent.

'I think so.' And then because I couldn't think of anything else to say. 'Shall I rinse the mugs out?'

'Please.'

I glanced round the cabin as I washed them. No one watched us. The rhythmic hum of the engine and the general buzz of conversation in such a confined space crammed with people created a kind of privacy. The engine noise was at its loudest here. I guessed it was housed under the steps.

'What are you doing here?' he said as he took the sugar out of a locker without changing the bland expression on his face.

'You told us to get off the island.' I kept my eyes fixed on the pan of water as I muttered. 'This was the only way with Rania and Aya.'

'It's a disaster.'

I darted a look at him but his face showed nothing.

'You never said you were leaving so soon,' I said as I dried the mugs.

'I didn't know.'

'Did you know we'd be on this boat?'

'Jesus, no. We were told we were waiting for someone but not who it was.'

My breath came out in a wobbly sigh. I hadn't realised I'd been holding onto it.

'Bit of a coincidence, though? Are you sure?'

'There aren't that many boats smuggling refugees off the island. Not ones that are safe. Not ones that are organised through Musaeada. I guess that's how you arranged your trip?' He said this in a light and chatty tone leaning against the counter and facing the cabin.

There was every chance he was right and Peter's contact came through Musaeada.

I gave a little laugh. 'Ma doesn't know anything, by the way.' I plastered a pleasant smile on my face. 'Nahla told her nothing.'

We could have been two strangers exchanging polite pleasantries.

The hatch at the top of the steps beside us was thrown back and Stephan clumped down with Ma following him. Both of them deep in conversation about asymmetric spinnakers. He opened an overhead locker and tossed her a yellow oilskin, then stomped back upstairs, while she looked into our cabin.

'Aya's fast asleep,' she said to me as she headed back for the deck. 'Call me if she wakes.' She nodded to Nick and the shadow of a smile passed across her face.

Shit. She was enjoying this.

'Is anyone up there with you?' I asked quickly. 'Apart from Stephan?'

She shook her head and darted up the steps. We heard her call out to Stephan cheerfully before the hatch thudded back into place.

'Ma won't say anything about you.'

'I hope you're right.'

I hoped I was right too. I hoped she'd taken the seriousness of what I'd said to heart and not been too distracted by her hatred of the engine and its noise.

The water boiled and I poured it into the three mugs, amazed at how steady my hand was despite the stress and the motion of the boat.

'She needs to be very careful,' Nick said, so quietly I almost couldn't catch his words. 'Best to stay in your cabin.'

'I'll try,' I murmured back.

He said nothing but carried on squeezing out the teabags.

A man came out of the small rear cabin and walked past us. It was Mohammed.

'What's he doing here?' I muttered.

Before Nick could answer a scream broke the hum of quiet chat and engine throb. It came from our cabin. Aya had woken up. Rania shot to her feet. Ma appeared at the hatch above.

'It's Aya,' I said.

'I'm coming,' she called and slid down the steps before I could move. The little girl's jagged sobs and shouts rose as Ma went into the cabin. Her voice, telling Aya this was a safe boat, filled the occasional gaps as Aya paused to take a ragged gasp of air.

Everyone stared towards the cabin and Nick moved close to me and spoke rapidly into my ear.

'Mohammed works with the people smugglers. Putting refugees with money in touch with the right people.'

So that was what lay behind the smiley persona he projected when I'd first met him with Amalia. That was why he'd been at Mdina.

'I came across him when I was on Malta before,' Nick went on. 'So we know each other. But he's a nasty creature. I always suspected he was on the outskirts of the child trafficking operation I infiltrated but we could never pin anything on him.'

'Why is he on this boat?'

'He's being paid a lot of money to act as an escort. To make sure someone reaches their destination.'

'The —'

'Shh. I don't know. He didn't say who but it would make sense. I can't ask too many questions.'

The hatch above us slammed shut and Nick sprang away from me as everyone turned round. Aya's piercing shrieks had reached the deck and Stephan had clearly had enough. Once everyone's gaze moved away, Nick spoke again.

'Whatever they're planning, it must be big. So big they need to ensure a safe passage. So big they don't want to leave anyone who might suspect them alive. Big, Jen. Really big.'

I took a step back and looked at his face but his eyes were focussed on the distance and I wondered if he too was seeing images of the injured and bloody figures shown on the news after each bombing atrocity.

Aya's staccato cries settled into a continuous sobbing. Ma came out of the cabin, carrying the little girl, limp and unresisting, in her arms.

'I'm taking her on deck,' she said.

'Really?'

But she disappeared up the steps before I could suggest Stephan might not like it. The gentle buzz of chatter and engine hum took over the cabin again.

'Be very careful,' Nick said as he picked up the mugs of tea. 'Both of you need to be very careful.'

I nodded, wordless, as he went towards the rear cabin, emerging a few seconds later minus one of the mugs and joined Khaled, Yousef and Mohammed round the table. He pointed to the chess game and said something that made them all laugh.

Too late, I wished I'd asked him if he knew now who the terrorist was.

He flopped back into his seat and nudged Yousef cheerfully. No one would have guessed he was living on the extreme edge of danger, alert at every second to anything that might betray him – whether it was something around him or an action or word of his own. How could he smile at Yousef's riposte and sip his tea while on deck Ma – unreliable and unpredictable Ma – held his life in her hands?

Twenty

I went back to our cabin and sipped at my tea while watching everyone through the open door. Yasmiin sat on the floor with an arm round Rania, muttering to her from time to time. I didn't like it one bit.

I still had no idea who the woman with Nick and Khaled in Mdina was. Sarah seemed the most likely choice. She was, after all, Khaled's sister. But something about the swiftness of the figure walking with Nick and Khaled hadn't seemed like the hesitant Sarah to me. It had spoken of confidence and determination, qualities Yasmiin had in abundance. Maybe I was all wrong about Khaled. Maybe he was the person being used as cover by the IS agent. And maybe the agent was Yasmiin.

Because she could have torched the clinic. She'd been inside the camp when it happened. And then I remembered. Yasmiin hadn't been in the clinic that afternoon. Whoever Nahla had recognised it hadn't been Yasmiin.

If only I'd asked Nick what he knew. It was so tough trying to keep Ma away from everybody.

Marwa put her head round the door.

'How is Aya?' she asked. 'Rania told us she hates boats.'

'I'll go and see in a moment but I think Ma would have brought her down by now if she wasn't OK.'

Of all the refugees, Marwa was the one I felt most comfortable with. Yasmiin and Sarah were too close to my own age. When I was with them, I felt conscious of the differences in our lives and that made me feel awkward.

Yet I should be careful. Marwa could have been the woman with Khaled and Nick. She'd certainly been there when Nahla had recognised the IS agent and she'd been sufficiently interested to ask me about the family afterwards. Another person to add to my list of suspects.

Marwa smiled and hesitated by the door, looking as though she wanted to say more. I smiled back at her. Why not talk to her? See if she gave anything away.

'Your niece,' I said. 'Zubaida. How is she coping?'

'She is fine. Happy to be away from the camp.'

'Yousef told me she'd been in hospital.'

'Yes. What do you say? A false alarm. Which is good because we would have missed this boat if the baby had come. We stayed in hospital until the following morning, so we also missed the rioting, which was good too.'

Of course, neither Zubaida nor Marwa could have torched the clinic because they'd been in hospital all night, which left Yasmiin who hadn't been in the clinic… or Sarah.

Another thought came to me. What if the woman in Mdina with Nick and Khaled hadn't been a woman? It could have been a man. A man disguised in women's clothing.

Marwa took a step into the room.

'Zubaida and I,' she said quietly. 'We are so happy that Rania and Aya are with you. Yasmiin told us that they might be sent back to Libya. Whatever you have to do, the girls must not go back to Libya.'

Libya, I thought. Libya was where this all started. Libya was where Nahla had met the terrorist she'd recognised, although Nick had said they travelling with a group of Syrians. But did that mean they were Syrian themselves?

'Is anyone here from Libya?' I asked.

'No one here is Libyan, except Rania and her sister, of course. Yousef, Zubaida and I are all from Syria but we spent a long time in Libya. So did Khaled and Sarah. They are also from Syria though. Why?'

'I just wondered.'

None of this was at all helpful and Marwa was looking at me with a small frown.

'The others?' I asked. 'Where are they from?'

'Yasmiin is from Somalia.' She looked back into the main cabin. 'Brahim is from Morocco.'

I realised she meant Nick.

'And Mohammed and his daughter – they come from Syria too.'

'I don't think I've met Mohammed's daughter?'

'Leila. She is sleeping in the cabin.'

I nodded as I tried to think what else I could ask.

'So Syria,' I said. 'You mainly come from Syria.'

'Raqqa,' Marwa said. 'I come from Raqqa.' She took pity on my blank face. 'It is a city. It *was* a city in eastern Syria. But all the people fighting over Syria, my country, between them, they have destroyed it. It lies in ruins now. No matter, we will never go back.'

A flash of emotion lit up her normally still face and she turned away as though seeking a moment of privacy. The light caught the scarring down the side of her face. Faint but unmistakeable.

'The fighting and the bombing,' she went on, 'it killed so many people doing nothing but trying to exist. Queuing for bread. Walking home from work. Children going to school. My husband and I, we talked about leaving but it was difficult. My parents were old. Travel was impossible for them.'

She paused.

'But you did leave?' I said and smiled encouragingly.

If I could get her to talk to me about how she'd got to Malta, she might reveal something helpful.

'Yes. We left. Eventually there was nothing to stay for. I have told this story so many times. My story. Marwa's story. Sometimes it no longer seems very real. But the words are all I have left of my old life. One night our entire neighbourhood was bombed. I wasn't there. I was working nights and so was my husband, but my parents were at home. And when I returned, everything had been destroyed. There was nothing except rubble and dust and dead bodies. That's what I remember most. The bodies lying everywhere. People were sleeping on the balconies, you see, because of the heat, so they were blown clear by the blast. Many looked as if they were still asleep, apart from the dust and the grime covering them. There were many though who weren't untouched. I found our dog first. He was still alive. One of the other searchers helped me put him out of his pain. Then I found my parents' bodies. I was lucky. Many families didn't find anything. And many, many dead had no one left to look for them.'

She darted me a quick look. 'But maybe you don't want to hear? We all have stories like this and we get used to telling them. To each other. To the people who help us. To the authorities who want to know if we count as refugees.'

'I do want to hear.'

I felt distinctly uneasy, though, about encouraging Marwa to relive such hideous memories.

'In any case, our stories are all the same. All of us have had the same experience. We were all forced from our countries and came to Libya. My husband and I came with Yousef and Zubaida. Yousef had friends already there who helped us settle in the east of the country. We lived comfortably for a long time but the civil war changed everything. My husband died.' She paused briefly. 'Yousef and Zubaida looked after me but Yousef lost his job and life became impossible for foreigners. So we decided to leave. Again.'

She smoothed a crease in the sheet.

Rania came into the cabin and went into the toilet. She looked exhausted although a hint of curiosity washed across her face when she saw Marwa sitting on the bed.

'My son,' Marwa said when Rania had shut the door behind her. 'Rania reminds me so much of him.'

There was a hint of tension in her hands as she spoke. Subtle but present. I'm not good at reading faces but hands and bodies are easy. She'd not mentioned a son until now. And she was travelling without him. Did that mean he was dead too? I waited to see if she would talk about him but she stayed quiet.

'Can I make you a tea?' It was all I could think to say.

'No, thank you. I will go and help Zubaida with the children.' She left.

I knew I should have asked about meeting the others but I couldn't. I didn't particularly like what I'd just done anyway. In fact, I hated it. Encouraging her to tell her life story while my brain pulled it apart and looked for clues. I'd thought it was bad last year when I wasn't sure who was trying to kill me and I'd looked at every friend and every member of my family with eyes clouded by suspicion. But this was worse. A gulf separated my rich and privileged life – my white rich and privileged life – from theirs and I was staring over the gulf like a superior Sherlock Holmes.

They were just people. People who'd been dealt an utterly shit hand. And something about the randomness of it terrified me.

Time to go on deck and talk to Ma about Nick because, whether right or wrong, I was finished playing detective. I'd concentrate on keeping Ma safe from everyone and as soon as we met up with Peter we'd get as far away from them all as quickly as we could.

I headed for the steps as a young woman emerged from the rear cabin. She was tall, as tall as Yasmiin but awkward with it, and I realised, despite the headscarf and long dress, she was young, barely out of her teens. This must be Mohammed's daughter.

'Leila,' he said and beckoned her over to join them at the table.

She passed me but stumbled as the boat gave a sudden lurch, grabbed the steps to steady herself and muttered some Arab expletive, before going over to the table and sitting next to Nick.

She gave him a half-smile and lowered her eyes as he moved over to give her some space. A typical shy youngster, cast in the same mould as Sarah. They both wore scarves tied tight around their faces. They shared the same stillness. And the same wariness. Both sat with hands on their laps. Sarah's were hidden by the table but Leila was sitting at the end. Her hands weren't still. She pinched the end of each finger hard between the thumb and index finger of the opposing hand. As soon as she'd finished each circuit, she began again.

The engine spluttered into a different rhythm and I realised I was staring like an idiot. Then it stopped. The yacht jerked from side to side and water slapped against the hull. The hatch above opened and Stephan stomped down the steps. As soon as he'd pushed past me, I hurried up and went out on deck. The wind hit me straightaway. A wind full of salt and freshness. I staggered and clutched the handrail.

Fuck.

My brain cleared and the realisation that had been tapping at my thoughts broke through. *Fuck*. Leila had muttered *Fuck*. When she'd stumbled down below deck. Not some Arab exclamation but *Fuck*. Definitely *Fuck*. No doubt about it. And with an unmistakeably Scottish accent.

Wind blew my hair into my face. I brushed it away. Ma and Aya sat in the cockpit, both wrapped in the same oilskin. Ma bent over the little girl, pointing at the masts and speaking. Aya was silent and listening, although her eyes were watchful.

'Bit rough,' I said, eyeing the turbulent grey water sloshing against the hull and rocking the boat from side to side.

'This! Not at all. Glorious sailing weather.' Ma looked up at the empty masts with a wistful smile.

I gripped a handhold. I'd forgotten how much I hated the feeling of being on shifting ground.

'Why have we stopped?'

'Engine cut out. Stephan's gone to check…'

The wind blew away the rest of her words. She pointed towards the opening I'd just come up. I staggered back and peered down.

The steps were gone.

Ma saw the confusion in my face.

'The engine is under the steps,' she said, leaning forward so I could hear.

Sure enough, in the black hole where the steps had been, I saw the glint of metal tanks and dials and tubes. Stephan, wearing a head torch, bent over, his hands busy unscrewing a bolt. Khaled moved into view and Stephan barked a few words. Khaled retreated.

Another wave half hit, half lifted the yacht and it landed with a thump the other side. Aya yelped and Ma bent over her.

'Like a seesaw,' she said, wrapping her arm round Aya and swaying them both from side to side.

'Shit,' I said. 'I suppose we can't go back down while he's working on it.'

Ma shook her head.

And no one could come up, I realised.

Another wave hit us.

'Shouldn't you turn the boat round so the waves hit the front?'

'The bow?'

'You know what I mean.'

'You need to be moving to steer. Under engine or sail power.'

'So we're stuck with the waves smashing into us.'

'Yes. Isn't it fun?'

I wasn't so sure.

Ma leaned her head back and shut her eyes. She did look like she was enjoying herself. I sat down.

'Listen. About Nick Crawford. You know you absolutely mustn't say anything to anybody.'

'I know, Jenifry. Stop fretting about it.'

I wished I could trust her not to forget in the spur of the moment.

'Not even to Stephan.'

'I wouldn't say anything to him.'

'I thought the two of you were best buddies. Up here comparing sailing stories.'

She laughed. 'He's tolerating me because Peter told him to look after us. I don't like to think how much he's paid him.'

A series of bigger waves tossed the boat around. I thought of the water beneath us. Thousands of metres of unstable sea. Moody and sullen at the moment but capable of breaking out into a rage at any time. I'd have much rather been clinging to a rock above thousands of metres of fresh air.

'Shouldn't we be wearing life jackets?'

'Probably.' She laughed again. 'They'll be under a seat.'

I rummaged round and pulled two out, giving one to her. There was nothing Aya's size. The sooner this part of the journey was over, the better. In every way.

'What happens when we land? What have you arranged with Peter?'

'He'll pick us up and we'll head for France.'

'Does he know where we're landing?' I had another thought. 'Do you know where we're landing?'

'Sicily, I think.'

'Ma, that's quite a big place. I mean massively bigger than Malta.'

'Stop worrying. It will all work out.'

A sizeable wave hit the yacht and sent a plume of spray arching onto the deck. It splattered us both and Ma flung her hands up in pleasure. Aya watched her and lifted up her hand too. She didn't smile but didn't look distressed.

I didn't smile either.

It was alright for Ma and Aya. The water ran off the voluminous oilskin they were wrapped in. I was soaked.

'Stop being so negative, my darling, darling daughter. I expect Stephan will ring Peter and tell him where and when to pick us up.'

She was probably right. And I had Peter's number anyway. The worst that would happen was a bit of a wait while he located us. I remembered that the battery for my phone was in Rania's and the new one from hers was uncharged. Was there somewhere to charge a phone on board the yacht?

Another lurch snatched the words out of my mouth as I went to ask Ma. No matter. She wouldn't know anyway.

'Isn't this wonderful?' she said, stretching her arms up into the air and dislodging a shower of drips onto me. Her face was alive and alight with happiness and a brief echo of the same emotion flashed across Aya's. I wasn't sure I'd ever seen Ma quite like this. I never went sailing with her as a child. Kit did a couple of times. I remembered him coming back and spending hours with pencil and paper drawing diagrams of sails and arrows for wind direction, trying to understand how a boat could sail into the wind, and questioning Ma. Not that she was any good at explaining. She just knew how to make the wind and the sea and the sails all work together to produce motion.

The noise of slamming from below reached us. Stephan's head appeared at the top of the steps.

'Get back below,' he shouted.

After sitting in the gusty wind on deck, the cabin felt even fustier and more confined. It rocked around now and everyone except Stephan sat on a bench or the floor, watching him in silence. Stephan, clearly in a foul mood, washed his oily hands in the tiny sink.

'What's wrong?' Ma asked. Everyone's eyes turned to her. I guessed they thought addressing Stephan directly was a mistake. Ma didn't care. Stephan pursed his lips as he dried his hands but when he spoke he was terse but polite.

'Fuel filter's clogged. In these conditions it'll take me an hour or so to sort it and… Well, let's just say that's too long to stay this close to Malta. Not after your very noticeable departure. So we'll have to sail.'

He surveyed the seated refugees.

'You and you.' He pointed to Khaled and Nick. 'Do you speak English?'

'Yes,' Khaled replied.

'You come and help me. The rest of you, keep out of the way down here.'

'Maybe I could –' Khaled started to speak.

But Stephan disappeared up on deck. Nick and Khaled followed him. Above, Stephan's voice barked orders and the sound of footsteps mingled with the squeal of ropes passing through blocks. I sensed when they raised the sail. The yacht ceased its slapping around and came to attention like a racehorse guided into the starting blocks. A quiver juddered through the cabin and I felt her move off, unbalancing me in her eagerness so I had to grab the counter. She settled smoothly into motion, cutting through the waves so their sound became only a soothing swish against the hull. Ma nodded happily and in that moment I understood why she loved sailing so much.

'Well,' she announced to everybody. 'That's us sorted. Shall we make some supper? Aya and I are starving. Aren't we, Aya?'

Aya nodded.

231

Twenty-One

Ma woke me in the middle of the night, shaking my shoulder.

'Jenifry,' she whispered.

I looked blearily up at her then sat bolt upright as I remembered where we were. Aya lay wrapped in the duvet on the tiny bench seat and Rania on the floor under a spare rug from the pile in the main cabin.

'What is it?'

The door to our cabin was still closed with the little bolt drawn across. I breathed again. The bolt would break at the first shove but at least the noise would wake us.

'Have we arrived?'

I was freezing. I'd followed Ma's example and nicked one of Stephan's T-shirts to sleep in while the dress I seemed to be fated to wear forever hung to dry in the shower, but the T-shirt and the sheet weren't enough without the warmth of Ma lying near me. I noticed Ma had appropriated a large jumper, which hung baggily over the leggings she was wearing.

'Hey. You've nicked my leggings.'

'They were dry. I'm going on deck but you made me promise to wake you if I wanted to leave the cabin.'

'What is it?'

'There's something wrong. Can't you feel it?'

'Feel what?'

'The yacht.'

I realised the motion had changed. The boat no longer raced through the sea, rising and falling as it shouldered the water aside. Instead it was buffeted by waves and slopped around like it had when the engine failed.

'The sails are flapping,' Ma said.

'Is that the smacking noise?'

'Yes.'

'I guess they're not supposed to do that?'

'We've weathercocked.'

'Ma, speak English.'

'The boat's turned into the wind. We're not sailing anymore.'

I wasn't much wiser except that not sailing meant we weren't getting any closer to Italy. Someone stumbled in the main cabin. We weren't the only people awake.

'I'm going up top.'

'No, wait.'

The sharpness of my tone roused Aya, who sat up and said something in Arabic. It was the first time I'd heard her voice, surprisingly piercing and sweet.

'Shhh. Don't wake the girls. They're both exhausted.'

Ma stroked Aya's hand, murmuring gentle words as the little girl slipped back into sleep. I watched Rania anxiously but she slept on. Her emotions had caught up with her last night and she'd spent much of the evening weeping and shaking, only calming a little after Ma had chatted to her for a while, but she'd struggled to get to sleep and I'd heard her muttering to herself throughout the night.

A sudden sideways lurch. My stomach churned. Last night's supper, a strange mixture of tinned beans, cheese and tomatoes concocted by Ma, sat in it uneasily.

What was happening?

I couldn't let Ma go out on deck alone. Not in the middle of the night with the yacht jolted by waves. Too easy for an accident to happen.

'Wait for me. I'll come with you.'

My underwear had dried but the dress was still damp. I took a leaf out of Ma's book and rummaged through Stephan's lockers until I found a T-shirt and some shorts with a belt to hold them up. I was beyond caring if he objected.

'Don't wake the others,' I whispered as Ma opened the door.

I did a quick check.

Marwa and Leila were fast asleep on the seats on our left while Yasmiin and Sarah shared the bench on my right.

Mohammed, who'd been very sick last night after Ma's meal, lay, wrapped in a blanket despite the cabin's stuffiness, on the floor. Yousef slept nearby.

Zubaida and her children had taken the back cabin. The door was closed, leaving me no way to be sure who was inside.

Khaled sat on a rug on the kitchen floor, still in harness and life jacket. His eyes were open and he looked at us.

My heart jumped and blood pumped in my head. I felt curiously breathless.

Ma saw Khaled too. 'What's happening?'

'I don't know.'

'Why aren't you on deck?'

'Stephan told Brahim and me to get some sleep. A couple of hours ago. He sent us away.'

He meant Nick. I looked around for him but he wasn't there.

'Stephan said to come back around three. I just woke and heard someone moving around and I thought maybe it was Brahim getting ready to go on deck.'

I looked at my watch. It was quarter to three.

'Stephan was sailing on his own?' Ma sounded startled.

'He didn't need us.' Khaled's voice was tense. 'We'd turned

round, you see. We're going back to Malta. He said it would be calm for most of the way.'

'Well, it isn't calm any more,' Ma said.

Khaled's words sank into my brain.

'We're going back to Malta?'

'We're not going anywhere at the moment,' Ma said. 'The boat isn't sailing. That's what woke me up.'

'How long ago did we turn? How long have we been heading back to Malta?'

'A couple of hours. Stephan looked at the forecast. There are high winds on the way. Worse than he thought.'

Shit. We were in deep shit. All of us in deep shit. None of us could go back to Malta. The refugees would be detained. The girls would be returned to Libya. Ma and I would be arrested. I saw from Ma's face the same thoughts were running through her mind.

'You should have woken us.' Ma's whisper was fierce. She glanced round at the rest of the sleeping refugees. 'Do they know?'

Khaled shook his head. 'What was the point? We couldn't do anything. Best to let them sleep.'

'Let me talk to him!' Ma cut off the rest of Khaled's explanations and shot up the steps. I followed her with my head whirling. Ma was right. Khaled should have woken us. Told us all. Given us a chance to persuade Stephan to keep going.

On deck, the night was full of confusion. Wind whipped the hair off my head and glued the T-shirt to my skin. The mainsail cracked and flapped and the rigging jangled. Lights gleamed here and there. Some glowed from instruments, others lit the deck. The cockpit was empty. Ma darted to the wheel and stared at the screen fixed into the deck in front of it, then looked up at the sails.

'Stephan,' she shouted into the dark, her head whipping round as she tried to peer through the thrashing sail. 'Jenifry. Get

Stephan. He's in the bows.' She pointed to the front of the boat. 'But hold on. Hold on tight.'

The spray tore tears from my eyes but, through them and between the flailing sails, I made out a figure. He was on his knees, hands clinging to the rail and staring down into the sea while the foresail buffeted his head. I struggled towards him, clutching the rail myself, glad of the additional grip from my bare feet on the deck despite the chill.

But it wasn't Stephan. As soon as I got closer, I realised the figure with its head half blotted out by a head torch was Nick.

'Where's Stephan?' I shouted.

He jerked his head towards the sea. Horror blanked my mind.

'Overboard,' he added in case I hadn't understood.

A larger wave hit the hull and I staggered, fell and slid over the deck towards the sea. The yacht heeled. For one giddying moment there was nothing between me and the grey waves rearing up to seize me. I snatched at a lifeline stanchion and missed. Shit. Nick grabbed me and dragged me back.

'Jesus, that was close,' he shouted into my ear. His arms dug into my ribs, painful and breath-constricting, like a rope that breaks a fall.

'Get yourself clipped on. You nearly went overboard.' His words were angry but, when the deck tilted and we slipped towards the sea again, he held me tight.

We struggled to our feet with the light from Nick's head torch jerking over the water streaming off us. It was pink with a darker streak of red where Nick's arm, in its dark sweater, still held me tight.

Blood. I was sure it was blood. Was he hurt?

I tried to wriggle out of his grasp so I could see his face but he wouldn't release me.

'What are you doing?' There was real panic in his voice now. 'This is dangerous.'

'What happened?'

236

'Not now. Get back to the cockpit.' He shoved me round.

Someone stood with Ma by the wheel. Khaled. He'd followed us on deck. I pulled myself out of Nick's arms and reeled to the cockpit, the impetus of fear keeping me upright. Khaled reached out a hand to steady me. I dodged it.

'Careful,' he said.

His face showed only concern.

'Where's Stephan? We need Stephan.' Ma's voice rang out above the wind beating the sail.

'I don't know.'

Nick spoke with his thick accent again. The sudden transformation into a man I didn't know felt like a slap to my face.

'He told us to sleep for a couple of hours and then come back,' Nick went on. 'But when I came back, there was no sign of him.'

He was lying. The way he'd said *Overboard* when I'd asked where Stephan was had been an answer not a question.

'Is he below deck?' Nick asked. He didn't look at me.

'Could be. We're on autohelm.' Ma pointed to the screen. We clustered round.

'In the toilet, perhaps.' This was Khaled. 'I heard someone coming down to the cabin. It's what woke me.'

'Or overboard?' I said. It was my turn not to look at Nick. 'Maybe he's fallen overboard.'

It was a reasonable suggestion after all.

'No,' Ma said. 'He'd have been clipped on. Sailing at night.'

'And in a storm,' I said.

'This isn't a storm,' Ma said. 'It is quite lively, though. He must be below.'

She disappeared down the steps.

Khaled, Nick and I stared at each other.

'Why have we stopped?' Nick asked.

And I didn't know if it was a genuine question or if he was asking because he and Khaled needed to pretend to be innocent refugees in front of me. I peeled away the layers of possibilities in my head and was left with a slippery mass that squirmed out of my grasp.

'I don't know.' Khaled shook his head. 'But we need to get moving. Morwenna might not think this is a storm but Stephan said there was one coming.'

The two men looked out at the sea. Grey-topped waves raced by and slapped water into the yacht.

Khaled took the wheel and turned it to his left. The mainsail flapped wildly and the boom creaked. The boat smacked into an oncoming wave.

Ma stuck her head out of the cabin. 'What are you doing?' she screamed at Khaled and without waiting for his reply. 'Leave the helm alone.' She wore a harness and flung one at me along with an oilskin. 'Put them on. And you two, stay clipped on at all times.'

Khaled hesitated but Nick obeyed.

'Do as she says.' I had to yell over the wind. 'She knows what she's doing.'

Ma seized the wheel from Khaled, clipped her karabiner to the rail and barked orders.

Nick and Khaled did their best but finding their way around the boat in the dark with the deck continually rolling and the sails knocking into them made everything very slow. The noise submerged Ma's yelled instructions and they were both reluctant to pull or release any of the ropes without her confirming it was the right one.

In the end, she made me take the wheel. 'Just don't turn it until I tell you,' she said fiercely before she fought her way around the boat, pointing and shouting at Nick and Khaled as she clipped and unclipped herself.

Gradually the canvas stopped flapping. The boom ceased swinging. The sails tightened until they were almost dead in line with the boat. The wind stretched and filled them and the yacht surged forward. Ma was everywhere. Staring at the sails then loosening a rope here and tightening one there, making gestures at me to turn the wheel a little to my left or right. Bit by bit, the boat settled. The din calmed a little. Waves still smashed into us but the boat rode them. I couldn't help but be impressed. I saw the same admiration on Khaled's face.

Nick's was unreadable.

Eventually she came and took the wheel from me, made a few adjustments, shouted a final instruction to Khaled and then beckoned them both over.

'We're set a bit looser than I'd like but it's more comfortable for everyone down below.'

I nodded. I didn't know what she meant but it didn't matter. Despite the dark and the turbulent sea and the wind, she thought we were OK.

Mohammed and Yousef appeared at the hatch. Nick went over and the three of them had a loud and vehement conversation in Arabic, but they finally nodded and went back down.

'The noise woke them,' Nick yelled over the wind. 'I told them everything was alright and to stay below.'

This sounded like a remarkably brief account of their conversation.

'Aya is very distressed,' he said to Ma.

She took a step towards the hatch and stopped, looked around her at the boat.

'You can't go down, Ma. We need you here.'

'We need Stephan,' Ma shouted.

The four of us formed a little huddle. It was the only way to hear each other without yelling all the time, but prickles of adrenalin ran across my skin every time Khaled leaned close to Ma.

'He wasn't here when I came on deck,' Nick said. 'He must have fallen into the sea.'

'Maybe the pole at the bottom of the sail hit him.'

'The boom, you mean,' Ma said to Khaled. 'Not possible. He was an experienced sailor. I don't understand how but he must have gone overboard.'

'Did you see anything in the water?' I asked Nick. 'Stephan had a bright yellow oilskin on, didn't he? And a life jacket.'

'Nothing,' Nick said.

Was he lying? I wanted to grab him and shake the truth out. Except I couldn't. Not while Khaled watched us.

It was all too complicated.

'We need to look for him,' I said to Ma.

She was staring at the screen that told her where the yacht was.

'Ma, shouldn't we go back? To look for Stephan. He must be nearby.'

More than anything, I wanted Stephan to have been knocked into the sea by the boom. But my thoughts kept on returning to the blood staining the water that had run from Nick's hand and jumper. His arm now rested lightly on his knee. If I squeezed the sleeve, would it ooze red again?

Ma shook her head. 'He could have gone overboard ages ago. The boat was on autohelm. It was sailing itself. I expect Stephan set the course and the sails right after he turned the boat back to Malta. When was that?'

'A couple of hours ago,' Khaled replied. 'And then he sent us away.'

'Well, he could have gone overboard at any time in the last two hours. We'll never find him.'

She glanced up at the sails and twitched the wheel to her right.

'The wind has changed. It was from the west last night when I turned in. It's from the southeast now. The Sirocco, I'd say, coming over from the Sahara. Her sails were set for a beam reach when I came up, exactly as I'd expect with the wind as it was. It was the wind changing that woke us because Stephan wasn't there to deal with it. I still don't understand how he could have fallen overboard, though.'

'Accidents can happen,' I said. 'Even when things are running smoothly. A top climber falls on an easy face. I've seen it happen time and time again.'

I heard the desperation in my voice. It had to have been an accident because, if it wasn't, Nick had certainly been involved.

'But that's the whole point.' Ma spoke as though she was talking to herself. 'This isn't easy sailing. The sea's heavy. The wind is high. It's night. Stephan would have been careful.'

What she said made sense. But no one in their right minds would have killed Stephan. We needed him to sail the boat.

'So,' Ma said. 'What are we going to do? We're on a course for Malta.'

Nick and Khaled looked at each other. Their faces grim. Khaled, once again, spoke first. 'We should go somewhere else. Anywhere else.'

'Can you get us to Italy?' Nick asked.

Ma looked at him for a long time. It had all been such a panic before, this was probably the first moment she'd had time to think about who he was. He met her gaze with Brahim's wary face.

And my line of reasoning crumbled into dust. Stephan hadn't been taking us to Italy. His usefulness had disappeared as soon as he headed back to Malta. But Ma, she could sail. And Nick had spent months in Craighston, the Cornish village I come from, where everybody knows Ma. Everybody knows she sails.

'I don't know,' Ma said. 'Stephan thought it was too dangerous. I need to know the forecast. Jen, can you go below. The radio is —'

'I don't know how it works.'

I wasn't leaving Ma alone with Khaled. Nor Brahim — it was easier to think of Nick as Brahim — less complicated. Brahim was a nasty piece of work. I was beginning to suspect Nick as Brahim was capable of things Nick as himself would never do and it was breaking my heart as well as sending shivers of fear to ice my flesh. There was no one I could trust.

'Morwenna is right,' Khaled said. 'Maybe the weather isn't as bad as we think. Stephan wasn't as motivated as we are to get away from Malta.'

I wouldn't have caught his quiet words over the wind if we hadn't been clustered so closely together.

'But he'd have been in serious trouble with the Maltese authorities if we'd been caught,' Ma said.

'No, Stephan wouldn't have been in trouble,' Nick said in his Brahim voice. 'He never planned to be caught with us in his boat. He was going to put us in the RIB as soon as Malta was near.'

'All in the RIB?' Ma pushed her windswept hair off her face. 'All of us? But it's far too small.'

'We wouldn't have had a choice. Or, at least, not much of one. Stephan had a gun, you see.' Khaled's face was tense in the bluish light from the screen. 'The choice would have been between a sure death or a tiny hope of escape in the RIB.'

Ma looked sombre but whatever she thought, she merely handed the wheel to Khaled with strict instructions to do nothing except hold it tight. She and Nick went below to listen to the marine forecast. I ignored Khaled, huddling into the hood of my oilskin as I tried to think.

Stephan's death hadn't been an accident; someone had killed him. I was sure of that. As soon as he'd said he was taking us back to Malta, his life was over. Someone had killed him silently and without a second thought. Khaled? I thought so. If I was right about him. But it could have been Nick. Or Nick could have helped.

The memory of the blood oozing out of Nick's sleeve when I'd fallen on deck chilled me. Had he cut Stephan's throat? Was he so deep in with Khaled, or whoever the IS agent was, that he'd kill if they asked? To protect them? To protect his mission? Nick was a chameleon. I knew that. I'd always known that. But I'd thought he'd stop short of murder even if the part he was playing demanded it. Now I wasn't sure.

We only had their word Stephan had sent them off to sleep. Ma had thought it strange Stephan wanted to sail alone. Maybe he hadn't. Maybe he'd kept them on deck with him. Nick and Khaled watching for an opportunity? A moment when Stephan was distracted. Easily overpowered. Throat cut from behind, then unclipped and shoved overboard. Was that how it had played out?

I didn't want to think how adept Nick was with a knife because every time I did my stomach roiled like the sea around us.

And while Nick got rid of the body, Khaled went below. Maybe planning to wake Ma and get her to take control of the boat. Except he'd heard us and, knowing she was awake already, he'd waited for her to emerge from the cabin.

Ma and Nick came back onto deck. She'd removed the rings that crowded her fingers so clearly she meant business. What had she decided? She was only safe as long as she was useful to Khaled. Not that she'd want to go back to Malta unless there were absolutely no other option.

'Right.' Ma planted her feet firmly on the deck and lifted herself to her tallest. 'We're going to set course for Italy. The weather's bad but not impossible.'

Relief tore through my body leaving it trembling.

'Aya is terrified,' she added. 'But I can't do anything. I told her it would be fine. I promised her.'

Her eyes fixed on me.

Please, please don't ask me to go and look after her. I have to stay with you.

'You are sure we can do this?' This was Khaled.

'What other choice do we have?' Ma's eyes blazed and her body, with Stephan's huge jumper dangling down beneath her harness, was taut with determination. She could do this. I knew she could. And I felt an answering thrill surge through my veins. Fuck it. We'd do it.

'Besides,' she added. 'I promised Aya. And I won't break that.'

And at least, while we were sailing, Ma was safe. I'd think about what came next once we were on our way. Except I couldn't stop wondering about the gun. Stephan's gun. Had it gone overboard with him or did one of the men still have it?

Twenty-Two

We changed course to head for Italy. Nick, Khaled and I worked better as a team supporting Ma now. The men were beginning to understand which rope did what and how to operate the winches smoothly. I could feel the changes in the yacht's motion that meant I needed to turn the wheel. Not that I ever did unless Ma told me to but the understanding made the pounding of waves on the hull and the smacking of canvas less frightening. Windspray bit my cheeks. Winch handles whirred. Ma shouted a warning and Nick and Khaled ducked as the boom smacked over their heads, then they scurried around wrapping and tying ropes while Ma grasped the wheel.

'Done,' she yelled at me. The yacht pulled away, faster now, driven by the strength of the wind behind her, and I turned to look into the darkness behind. Malta was there, crouching below the horizon's curve, ready to seize us if we got too close. It felt good to be moving away again.

Except it wasn't altogether dark out there.

A light had appeared on the horizon. Not Malta. It was too small and too bright. I grabbed a pair of binoculars. It was another boat. A big one, not a sailboat like us, but cutting through the water on powerful engines as it ran from west to east. Not a pleasure boat either, I realised between snatched glances, as the endless motion of the sea jerked the binoculars around. Angular and predatory

245

in shape, its colour was steel grey pierced by tiny black portholes, with a stubby tower of comms devices. Something official then? Navy or coastguard?

As I watched, it slowed and turned in a great arc, its lights painting curves on the water, until its bow pointed in our direction. Then it sped towards us.

Shit.

I shook Ma's shoulder.

'Don't,' she screamed in my ear, her eyes fixed on the sails. 'We're running downwind.'

'Can't we go any faster?'

'Faster!'

'There's a boat chasing us.'

She snatched a quick glance behind her, then grabbed the binoculars from me.

'They turned round as soon as they saw us,' I said.

'We need to speed up. You!' Ma banged her fist into Nick's arm. 'Take the wheel and hold it tight. Jen, you keep watching.'

I lifted the binoculars again as she moved around the deck, hauling a rope in a couple of inches here and releasing one there, stopping only to gaze at the results of her tweaks.

The ship came nearer. Its bow raised two arcs of white-topped water as it sliced through the sea. They were fast and there was no doubt in my mind they were after us. Someone, somewhere had finally put two and two together. Two children abducted from the camp. Two children seen carried screaming onto a small RIB. A boat that left shortly after.

The yacht pulled a little harder and Ma raced back to the wheel and took it from Nick.

'That's it,' she said. 'That's as much as I can get out of her.'

We stared back at the boat following us. We'd achieved little. The lights still crept closer to us. Maybe we'd put off the moment when they pounced and clamped their jaws tight round us by a few seconds but that was all.

An idea grabbed me.

'We need to disappear.' I yelled at them all. 'Lights. Turn off the lights.'

Nick's eyes met mine but nothing sparkled. I hoped he might remember the chase across the moors in Cornwall when we'd played the same trick with my car but, if he did, nothing showed. We'd been on the same side then. I wished I could be sure we were now.

I turned to Ma. 'Can you turn off the lights?'

She looked shocked. 'The navigation lights but –' And then she understood. She reached down and flicked switches, plunging the deck into darkness. Light still poured out through the cabin hatch. Khaled tore down the steps and in a few moments all went dark below.

'Now,' I said. 'We need to change direction.'

I heard Ma's intake of breath. Even through the wind and waves.

'And fast,' I added.

Although the moon and stars were cloaked by thick cloud, there was still a faint light from the clouds. Skyglow, I thought. The scattered reflections of light elsewhere, held in the molecules of dust and gas above us. Land was not that far away. Not in this part of the Mediterranean where Africa and Europe stretched out arms to try to touch each other.

Khaled pounded back up on deck.

Ma explained in terse words what had to happen. Pleasure no longer danced behind her fear. Instead she looked tired and worn. We'd turn west, she told us, for a little while, at least. It was the easiest manoeuvre. She ran through the sequence of things Nick and Khaled would have to do and the instructions she would shout.

'And me,' I said when she'd finished. 'What can I do?'

'Watch,' she said. 'Watch for anything. We're running blind without the instruments. And nothing can see us. This is a busy stretch of water and the weather is worsening.'

The sea was a writhing mass of ink, sucking up what little light there was. It threw buckets of water at me that lashed my face and froze my hands gripping the rail, then tugged at my sodden feet as it drained away. I could see little even when the pause between waves gave me time to dash the water off my eyes. And I could hear nothing except the restless growling and gunshot-like cracks of the wind on the canvas.

I knew when we'd changed course because the spray from the waves hit me from the side. The yacht's motion was worse now, like a theme park ride jolting and jerking, then rising high and dropping.

Khaled lurched to my side. I shrank back in a moment of terror. Another wave sloshed onto the deck and dragged at my feet. He wiped the water from his face.

'I think we have lost them.' His voice was soft in my ear and his breath warm. Warmed by his blood. I leaned away and suppressed a shudder.

'Yes.'

'I would like to get the engine going.'

'Can you?'

'An engine is an engine and I am an engineer. The oil filter was blocked. Stephan changed it but he didn't have time to bleed it afterwards. I can do that.'

'Go for it.'

'Once the patrol boat is out of range and we can put the lights on, I will.'

We both gripped the rail tighter as another wave lifted and dumped the yacht.

'It is good it is rough.'

'How so?'

'Their radar will be confused.'

Shit. I hadn't thought of radar.

It was a long and uncomfortable wait, broken only by the pitching and rolling of the deck and the thunderous claps as it hit the sea on the far side of waves. My teeth felt jolted. My bones felt as though their joints had been shaken apart. And I'd long since stopped worrying about how wet I was.

The patrol boat never turned to follow us but stayed on its old course until finally it disappeared. Ma waited until it was long gone, then switched the lights and the screens back on. We changed course yet again, this time for Italy and, to my relief, Khaled disappeared below deck to try to get the engine working.

The wind became stronger. Ma hung grimly onto the wheel, her face strained and bleak, her eyes flicking in a continuous circuit between the sails, the sea and the screens. I huddled on the floor of the cockpit for a time, shivering but sheltered a little from the blasting wind, letting my mind grow numb and only vaguely aware of Nick and Ma working again on the sails.

Nick's voice broke my torpor. He and Ma stood at the wheel.

'We should keep a watch.' He still spoke with Brahim's voice and his hands moved with Brahim's gestures, even though Khaled had left.

The hatch and door leading down to the cabin were open. So Khaled might have heard him. I got that. But Khaled couldn't see him. Nick could have smiled instead of burying every vestige of himself beneath Brahim.

'You can stop pretending,' I said to him in a voice no one would hear but us.

But he turned without a word and carefully made his way to the bow. If that was what he wanted, it was fine. He was Brahim to me now. So be it.

I hauled myself up from the floor and sat next to Ma.

The bottom of the mainsail had been folded over, making it smaller. I pointed to it. Ma nodded.

'Reefed,' she half mouthed, half shouted and when I looked blank, 'too much wind. Too much sail. Reduced it.'

'How far to go?' I asked and before she could start to talk in nautical miles, 'how long will it take?'

'A few hours.'

Was she up to it? She looked exhausted.

'We haven't seen the worst of the weather,' she said. 'Not yet. It will pass quickly when it comes but it will be rough…'

She didn't need to say anymore.

'We'll manage. You've done great, Ma. We'd have been stuffed without you.'

My words didn't cheer her. And, as I stared out into the dark looking for the giveaway lights that would signal the presence of another boat, I wondered how much danger we were in.

Coastguard searching for us, with the risk of being caught more and more likely as we got close to the Italian coast. Worse weather on its way. And even if we survived the storm, the biggest threat would remain.

I picked up one of the winch handles and put it next to me. I could inflict some damage with it if I had to. Whatever happened now, I would stick to Ma's side, because if we made it through the storm and if Khaled got the engine working, she wouldn't be needed and there was no one I could trust to keep her alive except me.

Twenty-Three

Time passed. The wind blew harder until it became one relentless blast. I almost became used to the rise and terrifying smack of the yacht as she breasted the waves. The ever-present salt water lashed my body and stung tears from my eyes. I let them run down my face. My hands were so wet it was pointless wiping them away. My eyes were starting to play tricks on me anyway, seeing sparks of light that glinted for a few seconds on the horizon then disappeared and never returned.

Every time I glanced round at Ma she stood at the wheel, her hands white with the force of her grip and her face tilted upwards to her sails. She never sat. She never relaxed. This was the storm. I hoped this was the storm. We wouldn't survive anything worse.

Ma bent and tried to wind a winch with one hand while the other gripped the wheel. I went to help her and together we dragged the handle round with brute force until she signalled me to stop. I looked forward. We'd reduced the foresail by half.

'Wind still too strong,' Ma screamed in my ear. 'We need less sail.'

I started to shriek questions over the noise, but a blast of wind picked off the top of a wave and hurled it at us. The mainsail flapped and the yacht heeled over. For one moment I thought we were going all the way into the sea but the boat righted herself with an angry jerk.

'We… need… to… lower… mainsail.' Ma's words were bitten

off by the howl of the wind. 'Get… him.' She jerked her head at Nick.

I gave her a thumbs-up and fought my way through to Nick in the bows as the deck see-sawed and jumped under my feet.

'Nick. Got to lower the mainsail,' I shouted. 'Ma needs you.'

He turned as I said his name. His hair had become a drenched and dripping mass, the weight of the water pulling the curls into rats' tails.

If he speaks to me with his Brahim voice, I thought, *I'll punch him*. Like Kit showed me when he was twelve and started boxing lessons. He tried to teach me but I ended up breaking his nose and he gave the lessons up.

But Nick merely nodded and pushed past me.

I struggled after him. Ma shouted instructions and gestured with her hands and by the time I reached them, he was pulling the mainsail down. Ma waved me to help. Inch by inch, we forced the great sail down the mast while the wind battered it, sending great ripples through the looser canvas. Ma made rapid and anguished circles with her hands to tell us to hurry up. The sail slithered down a couple more feet and stopped. We yanked on it but it wouldn't budge. Harder. Still nothing.

'Take the wheel,' she screamed at me as she stared up to the top of the mainsail.

I unclipped and clipped my way over to her and grabbed it.

I don't know what I'm doing. I don't know what I'm doing.

The words hammered my head over and over again as I gripped the wheel. Ma rushed to the mast. She staggered and stumbled like the rest of us but her footing was much surer, her body instinctively compensating for the boat's roll and thrash.

Nick and Ma screamed at each other for a few minutes and then she came back to the cockpit.

'The main halyard's jammed,' she shouted and knelt on the

floor at my feet, lifting a section of floor to reveal a storage compartment. She seized something that looked like a harness with additional padding round the bum.

'Bosun's chair,' she yelled. 'I'll have to go up and fix it.'

Her eyes fell on my hands glued to the wheel. Worry deepened the dark shadows round her eyes.

'The life raft is under the starboard locker. If you need it.' She tapped it with her foot to make sure I understood then leant over the navigation screen and ran her fingers over it.

'Right. We're on autohelm. You need to help winch me up.'

I chased after her to the mast putting my feet where she did and trying to keep my balance. She grabbed the shackle spliced on to a rope that Nick held out to her and attached it to the harness.

'You can't go up in this,' I screamed at her. The boat rolled and bounced with each wave whipping the mast from side to side. 'You can't.'

'No choice. Got to release it.'

'Well, at least use a knot.' I yanked the harness out of her hands and attached it to the rope with a bowline. 'Never trust someone else's shackle. Not when you can tie a knot.'

She reached out her hands for the harness. I snatched it away.

'I'll do it.'

'No.'

'Yes.'

She grabbed at the harness again and I nearly fell as she tried to wrench it out of my hands.

'You don't know anything about sails,' she shouted.

'The halyard is a rope. I know about ropes and I can climb.'

She hesitated.

I leapt in.

'Ma, we need you to sail. Please.'

'If only we had a knife,' she said. 'Stephan must have one somewhere but I haven't got time to look for it.'

'A knife?' Nick and I spoke at once and I couldn't tell whose voice he used.

'Yes, a knife. Then Jen could just cut the halyard.'

Nick reached under his oilskin and fumbled briefly. His hand came back carrying a black-holstered knife. He unsheathed it. It was neat and unadorned and utterly vicious, designed to cut effectively and nothing else.

'Will this do?'

Ma cast a quick glance. 'Perfect.'

He waited until I'd strapped myself into the harness then held the knife out to me. I didn't want to take it. Didn't want to touch it. Not when I suspected the last time it had been used was to cut Stephan's throat. Not when I thought its black handle might hide the deep, deep red of shed blood.

Ma saw me hesitate.

'If you're not sure, I'll go up.'

A wave rolled under us and the wind caught and filled the loose mainsail. The yacht heeled over again. We clung onto the mast until it passed and the boat righted herself.

No more time left. The next wave might plunge us into the sea. I reached out for the knife but Nick held it tight.

'Are you sure?' he shouted and this time it was Nick's voice that came out of his mouth. Fear flared from his eyes and drowned his face. 'Jen, are you sure you can do this?'

'Yes.'

He held on for a couple more seconds as he searched my face for the truth. I glared back. He shook his head and released the knife. I clipped it to the side of the harness, then lunged at the mast while it was still upright. It was cold and slippery and vibrated beneath my hands. I grasped one of the ropes that ran its length and pulled myself up. Ma and Nick turned the handle of the winch and I felt the harness take my weight as I half climbed and was half hauled up the first couple of metres.

It was nothing like any climbing I'd ever done. The boat rolled and swayed and each jerk smashed me into the mast and then tore me away. It was like climbing a rock face that shook beneath the force of an earthquake, where every hold, every crack, every ledge broke off in your hands and someone above jerked the rope you were hanging from. I was as helpless as a sack of flesh and bones.

Fear bit its way into my head. *Shit.* I might get hurt doing this. Any minute something might smack a hole in my skull or rip my finger off. I grabbed at a wire cable. It slipped through my fingers and I flung my arms round the mast and held tight. The yank of the harness tried to drag me loose. Nick and Ma were still hauling me up. But I couldn't let go. I opened my mouth to yell at them to let me come down and a horde of panicked faces screamed at me from my memories. All the people I'd seen get hurt because their fear crowded everything else out and stopped them thinking.

I wouldn't give up.

I pulled my mind out of the panic and things became clearer.

I couldn't climb this. No one could climb this. So stop trying.

Nick and Ma would have to do the heavy lifting. I released my grip on the mast and let them take my weight. Instead of climbing, I focussed on not getting hurt, on using anything within reach – odd bits of metal that protruded from the mast and the endless jumble of ropes – to guide my ascent and stop my legs and arms and head being beaten and thrashed to pieces.

Bit by bit, I edged upwards.

From time to time the yacht's swinging tore me away from the mast and flung me high in the air, and then I'd catch sight of Ma and Nick staring up, never taking their eyes off me for a moment and adjusting their speed to help me. The sight was oddly comforting.

Giddy, dazed and hurting all over, it took a moment to clock when they stopped winching me up. I only knew something was different. Then I saw I'd reached the top of the sail. I clamped my arms and legs round the mast and for a few seconds rested my cheek against its chilly metal and became part of the boat, swaying with it. It was almost a pleasure.

A metal shackle held the head of the sail to a rope, pulled tight by the sail's weight. The jam was somewhere above me. Thank God Ma had thought of the knife. A few slashes and this would be over.

But as soon as I let go of the mast to cut, despite my legs gripping tight, my body jerked all over the place. I hacked at the rope, sometimes connecting, sometimes missing and scratching the mast. Once, the blade ricocheted off the metal and missed my face by millimetres. But finally I sliced through the last strands of rope and the sail tumbled to the deck.

Job done.

The boat swung and the blade sliced across the knuckles of my other hand. I didn't feel a thing except the sudden warmth of blood and a massive relief it was over.

As Nick winched me down, lights on the forward horizon caught my eye, appearing and disappearing as the yacht rose and fell.

Another boat? No. Lights on boats didn't flash steadily like that. It was a lighthouse. Two lighthouses. The one on the left with two steady glints and the one on the right with three.

They vanished over the horizon as Nick lowered me to the deck. My legs gave way beneath me and I crawled over to Ma in the cockpit, turning the winch that controlled the front sail and shifting the yacht's direction a little. Her face, though white, was calm and, in my shaky state, it made me think of the moon. She flung her arms round me and I sank into her embrace for a few seconds.

'Lighthouses. I saw lighthouses.' I pointed in the rough direction. 'Maybe showing rocks?'

'No. You saw Sicily,' she said. 'The lighthouses. They're guiding us to land.'

God. Land. I wanted so much to feel it beneath my feet.

'How long?'

'A few more hours, maybe longer. We're not going fast.'

There was blood on the front of her oilskin. I lifted my hand. It dripped. Ma seized it and summoned Nick from tidying away the sail and ropes.

'First aid kit. Probably in the bench locker,' she said as she probed my hand.

'It's nothing, Ma. It doesn't even hurt.'

'You should go below deck and clean it.' This was Nick. Or rather this was Brahim speaking, his voice soft and guttural. My doubts about him returned.

'I'm staying up here. With Ma.' I heard the sadness in my voice. The knife nestled in my pocket underneath my oilskin. I wished I trusted him enough to give it back.

Khaled's voice called up from below. Nick handed me the first aid kit, then turned without a word and leant through to tell the others what was going on before returning to the bows and staring out to sea again.

I sat as close to Ma as I could get and we sailed on through the night. The boat still whipped around but less since we'd lowered the mainsail and after a while, exactly as Ma had said it would, the wind eased and the motion softened. A chill sank into my bones. I huddled against Ma. Not that she gave off any heat but it felt better. She no longer stared rigidly at the sail, winching it in and out, but relaxed a little and once I heard her hum a snatch of a tune.

Speed, bonny boat? No it wasn't that. It was something I didn't know. But the tune of the song I'd learned at school sang itself through my head.

Twenty-Four

I woke with a start. Shit, I'd been deeply asleep. What sort of bodyguard was I? I checked quickly. Ma sat beside me. Nick was walking back to the bows and there was no sign of Khaled.

'How long have I been asleep?'

'Not long. Maybe an hour. Weather's calmed.'

It had too. Although the boat still bounced up and down, the waves no longer pounded against the hull and the howl of the wind had subsided to a bluster.

'I feel like shit,' I said. 'And I'm freezing.'

'Ask them for some coffee down below,' Ma said. 'It's calm enough for them to make it. One for me as well.'

Ma never drank coffee but even in the dim light, purple shadows were visible beneath her eyes and her lips were tight with the effort of keeping awake.

I called down for coffee. Khaled raised his face and gave me a thumbs-up.

'Tell Morwenna, not long now. I've nearly finished. Tell her too that Aya is asleep.'

I relayed the information to Ma and handed her the first coffee in an insulated cup with a lid on. It smelled wonderful when Ma unscrewed it but she grimaced as she sipped it.

'Too hot?' I asked.

'Too sweet.'

'Not a bad thing, really, Ma.'

Khaled's hands, grimy with oil, appeared at the hatch with two more cups. I took them, shouted to Nick to come and get his and wedged it under a strap.

'Go to the bow and talk to him,' Ma said. 'I'm fine and no one will hear you. I'll give you a shout if anyone comes on deck.'

I wondered what Ma thought was going on. I hadn't told her anything about why Nick was here. Nor about how we were travelling with a terrorist, who had killed Nahla and who, very likely, wanted to get rid of her. And although I wasn't sure I wanted to speak to Nick, I did want to know their identity.

Maybe I was finally getting my sea legs because I walked to the bow without staggering. Nick's face was turned to the sea and he didn't acknowledge me as I came to stand beside him.

I sipped my coffee, feeling its heat roll down into my stomach and sneaking a hand into the deep pocket of Stephan's baggy shorts to check the knife was still there. I'd neither the time nor the energy to lead up to the subject. Either he'd tell me or he wouldn't.

'Do you know who the IS agent is?'

No answer. Only a faint tightening of his mouth.

'You must, surely?'

'It's obvious, isn't it?' His voice caught in his throat, as ragged and tired as his expression.

'Khaled?'

'Who else?'

'Anyone could have come up while the two of you were asleep below deck... unless you were lying about leaving Stephan alone?'

'I wasn't. I've lied about one thing but not that. Khaled and I went down to the cabin but something woke me. I thought I heard someone moving about. I went on deck and Stephan's body was lying there. That's the only thing I've lied about. Someone had cut his throat and unclipped his body but the

259

harness had caught and wedged in a winch. I freed it and pushed him overboard.'

'Why?'

'He was dead, Jen. I needed to protect the person who did it. They're my way into whatever is being planned.'

He gulped at his coffee and shivered like a dog, shaking himself all over. The rat's tails of his hair flicked water into my face.

'Khaled?' I said again.

He nodded with a movement so small that anyone not staring at him would have missed it. He begrudged me this truth.

'You're sure?'

'I am.'

'Why?'

'Because he was the only other person who knew Stephan was taking us back to Malta. Because he knew he could get the engine working again. For him, Stephan was expendable.'

It made sense. Only Khaled had the right knowledge. Unless…

'What about you?'

The question was out of my mouth before I could stop it.

'What do you mean?'

I'd never noticed how dark his eyes were. Not brown but almost black. Unless it was a trick of the night.

'You knew all these things too and you knew Ma could sail,' I said.

There was a long silence. My accusation lay between us. Finally Nick hurled his coffee cup into the sea.

'I did not kill Stephan,' he said. 'That's all I can say. Either you believe me or you don't. I've done some questionable things for my job but never that. Now, I'd like you to leave me. I need some time to dress myself in Brahim's life again. So he can become friends with Khaled. Because that's his job. His job, Jenifry, and it's important he succeeds. Khaled is heading for the UK and

Brahim needs to go with him. To find out where he is going and who he meets. So we can stop whatever they plan to do.'

I walked away and back to Ma.

'That was quick,' she said.

'We didn't have a great deal to say to each other after all.'

Maybe I should tell her everything? Except looking at her tired face, now was definitely not the right time.

From the deck Sicily still wasn't visible but the sky glowed faintly where the island must be. Soon the lighthouse beams would appear, like arms stretching out over the sea to carry us to land. It made me think of home. Of the lighthouse up the road from Tregonna where I'd spent most of my childhood and I was seized with a longing to be there. To be running along the cliffs on a spring day with the long, reedy grass whipping my shins and the sweet but salty winds mussing my hair.

I hadn't felt homesick like this for years. Not since Pa went when I was a teenager and left a big hole behind him. Now, memories of the early years of my childhood, the golden times, reached out to me as bright as the lighthouse beams and it was the silence and loneliness of the time afterwards that seemed unreal.

'Ma,' I said, 'why did Pa leave without a word?'

She almost laughed. 'You do pick the strangest times to ask questions like that.'

'Please don't be slippery.'

'Slippery?'

'Not answering a straight question. You always do that.'

'Is it that important to you?'

'You see what I mean. A question answered with a question…'

For once I thought she did. She shot me a glance as though I'd surprised her.

'Here's another question,' I continued. 'Why did you never tell me you'd separated?'

261

'That's easy to answer. I did… when I realised myself. But it took me a long time.'

She paused, staring out to sea, and I thought she was seeing into the past.

'He went to South America. Another expedition… I can't remember which mountain it was. There were so many. And after that, he stayed on for another. He wanted us to come out and join him. But it was impossible. What with you and Kit and schools and the house… well, no matter. I said no. And then…'

I waited for her to carry on.

'Well, we never heard from him very much when he was away, as you know. To be fair, communication was difficult in the places he went to. At least it was then. So, at first, I thought nothing of it. Then I bumped into one of his friends who'd obviously been in touch with him, so I guessed he was maybe a little angry because I'd refused to come out. I was probably very stupid but it took me a long time to understand that he wasn't coming back. I tried to get hold of him then. And once I knew…' Ancient anger made Ma's voice tremble or maybe it was just fatigue. 'Afterwards, I wasn't in a good place. For quite a while I couldn't see beyond my own misery. So I probably failed you, Jenifry.'

It was the closest Ma had ever come to admitting that her life could be as shit as everybody else's rather than some wondrous adventure provided she kept herself aligned to nature's positive forces. I squeezed her hand with my undamaged one.

'Ma. About Tregonna.'

'Yes, I know. You tried to tell me something before.'

'Pa is trying to sell it. We – Kit and I – think you can stop him. But you need to call your solicitor.'

'Is that what you want?'

I bit back my instant 'Yes', aware the question had layers of meaning, aware too that I was answering for Kit.

'Yes,' I said in the end. 'I think you should decide what happens to Tregonna.'

Khaled appeared from below. I stuck my hand into my pocket to curl it round the knife.

'The engine should be fine now,' he said. 'Can I try it?'

Ma nodded. Khaled pressed a couple of switches on the control panel and wiggled the lever. The engine jolted and then thudded into life.

Ma wound the foresail completely round the spar.

'She's all yours,' she said to him and stumbled as she stood. 'Wake me when we get close and I'll guide us in.'

I followed her down the steps and into the main cabin. Everyone was asleep, slumped on seats and the floor. A faint smell of vomit lingered despite the open hatch. They'd had a broken night as well. Rania was curled up near Yasmiin on one of the benches and through the open door into our cabin I could see Aya asleep on the bed. We went in and I locked the door firmly behind us.

Ma didn't ask me why. She flopped onto the bed and closed her eyes. Tears seeped out from beneath her eyelids.

'Ma!'

She wiped the tears away with a corner of the sheet.

'I'm just tired.'

'You were magnificent. We'd all be crammed in the lifeboat if it wasn't for you. That's if we'd known where to look for it in the first place.'

'I know,' she said and the tears started once more. 'This is stupid. Get me some toilet roll, please, Jen.'

I tore off a great wodge and passed it over. She wiped her face again and blew her nose.

'It was the responsibility, I think. The fact that you were all depending on me.' She laughed her stupid, tinkling, irritating laugh. It didn't bother me one bit. 'I'm going to sleep.' And she took off her outer layer of damp clothes and lay down. 'I will call Mr Penrose, though.'

'Mr Penrose?'

'My solicitor.'

Then she rolled over and didn't move.

I wrapped myself in a blanket on the floor and thought about doing the same but I couldn't stop thinking about Ma. She loved sailing. She and the boat and the sea and the wind had been as one. Something I'd never realised came to the surface; we were very alike in some ways.

Twenty-Five

The first thing I noticed when I woke was the light pouring through the overhead hatch. The second was that the engine had stopped and the third was the absolute quiet apart from the lapping of water against the hull.

I grabbed my phone. What time was it? No way of telling. The battery was flat now. I'd forgotten to plug it in.

The door to our cabin was wide open. But Ma still lay beside me, fast asleep. I relaxed. Aya looked at me from the seat by the door. She was eating a chocolate bar with great concentration and swinging her feet.

'Did you get hungry?' I asked.

Her eyes flashed worry.

'It's fine, Aya. Is it nice? Your chocolate bar?'

She stared at me for a few seconds and then applied herself to removing the rest of the wrapping. She must have woken, hungry, got up and opened the door.

Careful not to disturb Ma, I slipped off the bed and stuck my head into the main cabin, my hand tight round the knife I'd slept with.

No one was there. The doors to the tiny bathroom and the back cabin were open, revealing their emptiness. Aya followed me out of our cabin as I noticed that all the baggage had gone too.

'Stay here,' I said. 'I'm going on deck.' And I tried to usher her back to our cabin. She stood firm and pointed a chocolatey finger at a cupboard above the sink whose open door revealed a stack of bars like the one she'd been eating. She must have climbed up to get it. I tried to remember the last time we'd fed her. Poor kid. She must be starving. I reached for one and unwrapped it.

'Do you want this?'

She hesitated, her eyes fixed on the chocolate and then slowly nodded.

'Good girl,' I said and gave it to her.

I noticed again how quiet it was. It wasn't only the absence of stormy winds and seas, there was no noise at all. I went up the steps cautiously and peered out. The deck was empty. In fact, the yacht was empty, bobbing on a light sea with its anchor down. And a few hundred metres away, some part of Italy glimmered in the morning sun. Everyone had gone. There were no refugees. No Nick. No one was left.

No one?

Shit, shit, shit.

I tore back down the steps and shook Ma awake.

'They've gone. All of them. While we were asleep. They've taken the RIB. And, Ma, they've taken Rania.'

Ma gazed at me with eyes still lost in her dreams, then snapped into life. She rushed round the cabin then raced on deck. I followed her.

'Why?' she said as she gazed around the empty deck. 'I understand they might leave without us. We were never travelling together. But why take Rania?'

I wished I knew.

Had Khaled taken her? Planning to use her to keep Ma quiet?

'Listen,' I said. 'There are a few things you need to know.'

I told her about Nick's mission. The strange meeting with him in Mdina and everything he said to me. How Nahla had recognised the IS agent travelling with the refugees. And how they'd burnt down the clinic to get rid of her.

Up until then, Ma had listened without interrupting, but now she put up a hand to stop me.

'Give me a second to take it in.'

'We don't have a second. We need to think what to do.'

'The fire was deliberate?'

'Yes, Ma.'

'But how? Are you sure?'

'I saw them do it. While I was watching from the other side of the fence, someone smashed the back window and threw a lighted rag in.'

She shook her head slowly as the meaning of what I'd said sank in. Above us the rigging twanged cheerfully in the light breeze.

'And afterwards,' I said. 'The nurse who Nahla saw – Paulina – she was killed. Nick thought they were getting rid of anyone Nahla might have told. He warned me you were in great danger.'

'But who is it? This terrorist?'

'I don't know for sure but I think it's Khaled.'

'That doesn't make sense. Give me a minute to think.'

She paced around the tiny cockpit. Her hair was spiky with sleep and stiff with salt. Her clothes much the same. She looked as though she'd been at sea for weeks. I guessed I looked the same.

'How could you have kept quiet about it? My life was in danger.'

In some sense she was right but it hadn't been as straightforward as she implied.

'I did ask you about Nahla recognising someone but you knew nothing.' I gave up trying to defend myself. We didn't have time to argue. 'Maybe I should have told you.'

'There's no maybe about it.' Ma was closer than I'd ever seen to losing it with an edge to her voice like a cracked bell.

'Ma, we need to concentrate on Rania. I'm wondering if they've taken her to make you keep your mouth shut.'

'No, Jenifry, they haven't taken Rania to keep *me* quiet, they've taken her to keep *her* quiet. Because she's the one Nahla told. Nahla told Rania. When we were together in the clinic – before the fire.'

Ma was shaking with anger. It woke an answering emotion in my bones. Had Rania been the one in danger all along?

'Why didn't you tell me?' I shouted at Ma. 'I asked you while we were waiting for Stephan to pick us up. I asked you if Nahla had mentioned recognising someone.'

'Because I didn't know then.' She didn't bother to hide her fury. 'I only found out yesterday evening before the storm. You know how Rania was. Grief for her mother was overwhelming her. We talked and I reminded her about the time before the fire, when she and her mother had been chatting and happy. She needs to remember the good times. Rania told me Nahla had recognised one of the refugees at the clinic that afternoon. A friend from her past. But not Khaled. A woman.'

Shit! Yasmiin?

Since we'd been on the boat, Rania had spent so much time huddled with Yasmiin. Had she given herself away?

'Did Rania tell you who it was?'

'Marwa.'

My thoughts refused to connect.

'Marwa,' I repeated.

It was all wrong. Marwa was all wrong. Too old. Too gentle. Too thoughtful.

'Are you sure?'

'Of course I am.'

That was the whole point, wasn't it? You didn't send someone suspicious to sneak through Europe's porous borders. You sent someone unthreatening like Marwa.

'We need to get ashore and go after them,' Ma said abruptly.

'They've taken the RIB.'

'Where's your phone? I want to call Peter.'

I ran down to the cabin and plugged it into a wall socket I should have noticed before. And remembered something.

'Ma,' I said when she came in. 'If Rania has kept her phone turned on. If she's left it logged onto my Spotify account, I should be able to track her. I had to log her into my Google account to...'

But there was no point explaining.

The phone woke up after a few seconds and I put in my code. It searched for a signal. Aya appeared at the door to the cabin and tugged at Ma's hand.

'She wants a chocolate bar. Locker above the sink.'

Ma went without a word.

'I've got no signal.' I shouted at her. 'We'll have to get closer to land.'

I heard her go on deck and the sound of the anchor being raised. The engine started up but I stayed below, waiting for the little icon showing it had found a service provider to appear, while the blood pumped against my skull.

When it finally burst into life, an endless stream of messages from Vodafone Italy welcomed me. I ignored them all and with fumbling fingers went onto Find My Device.

Rania's phone was still logged on. It was on the outskirts of Messina, a town at the point where the island of Sicily met mainland Italy. I prayed that it was still in Rania's jeans pocket.

How could I find out? Text her? Too dangerous. I didn't want to draw attention to the fact she had a working phone. Before I could think of a solution, a new message flashed up.

From Rania.

She was alive.

You pinged me.

Of course. Shit. I'd forgotten her phone would get a notification when I looked for it. With trembling fingers I started to text a reply and stopped. What should I say? I needed to be careful. Thoughts raced so fast through my head, my vision blurred.

Rania was alive. And she didn't seem to know anything was wrong. She'd have texted me before if she was worried. I needed to reply without alarming her. I steadied my thoughts and typed.

Mistake. Sorry.

Her reply came quick as a flash. Typical teenager.

OK. Was Aya alright in little boat?

She didn't know we'd been left behind. It would have taken several trips in the RIB to get everyone ashore safely and there wouldn't have been room for all of them in one vehicle. If she'd set off first, she'd think we were following. After all we'd never told her any of our plans.

Where were they going? That was the most important thing. Did she know where they were going? The UK? I thought so. That's what Nick had implied. Which probably meant going through France to Calais.

Aya fine. See you in France. XXX

OK

I wasn't sure if the 'OK' meant she knew they were going to France or not. At least she hadn't contradicted me. I needed to stop her texting before someone noticed, though.

Don't text anymore. Battery low. Jen

It was a stupid excuse but it was all I could think of. I followed her progress on the phone for a few minutes and then I looked up Messina. It was over 200km from the southern coast of Sicily and a 2hr 15min drive away. Shit. We were hours behind them.

Aya appeared at the door to the cabin. She'd wet herself again. Not surprising, really. I cleaned her up automatically and found another of Stephan's T-shirts while I thought about her. And about Ma and Peter.

And I knew what I had to do.

PART FOUR

From Italy to France

Twenty-Six

Ma wasn't happy about me going on my own but travelling solo meant I could fly which would be impossible for Ma with the passportless Aya in tow. It meant I could get to somewhere I'd be sure of meeting up with them. Like Calais. We'd never catch them up in Peter's car.

'Just get Rania quickly,' she said in the end.

The unspoken *before* hovered between us... Before Marwa killed her... If she hadn't already.

'I think she's safe while they're travelling together. Marwa still needs the other refugees as cover. She can't kill Rania in front of them.'

'I'll get you as close to land as I can but you'll have to swim a little. There's a waterproof belt in one of Stephan's lockers.'

I went below and found the belt and a plastic bag for my clothes, then took up my barely charged phone. She called Peter.

'Is Aya alright?' Ma asked once she'd finished.

'She's asleep again now she's eaten.'

The little girl had curled herself under the covers when the boat began to move, seeking to lose herself again in sleep.

'Peter and I will catch up with you as quickly as we can.'

I wondered if she'd realised how difficult travelling with Aya was going to be.

'Be careful, won't you?' she said without looking at me.

'Of course.'

I lied. I had no intention of being careful. And I didn't think she had either. Her fingers trembled as she rested them on the wheel but it was the remnants of her rage that shook them as well as fear.

'The terrorist...'

'Marwa.'

'Marwa,' she said. 'Yes, Marwa is dangerous. But people like her, they're good at making others do things for them. Be careful of everybody.'

Nick had said something similar.

The land seemed close enough now. I stood up, desperate to get going.

'Here?' I asked.

'Not yet. There should be a beach round the point. It'll be the easiest place for you to get ashore.'

'Can we go any faster?'

'No.'

The boat edged round the coast and a sandy beach came into view.

'Wait a little. I'll get you as close as I can.'

She slowed the engine even more and the boat crawled towards the shore. I opened my mouth to ask her if she could go any slower and managed to stop myself.

'Nick,' she said. 'Will he...?'

'Help?'

'Yes. Will he help?'

I wasn't sure. He wouldn't kill Rania. I knew that. I'd known since our conversation on the boat about Stephan's death and Nick's anger when he'd realised I suspected him. But would he step in to save her? His job as Brahim was to infiltrate a group of people who intended to kill and maim. It would fail if he stepped out of character and rescued Rania. Would he weigh the potential loss of more life in the future against the loss of Rania's life now? Rania's life against hundreds of others?

'I don't know, Ma.'

She cut the engine and told me to lower myself over the seaward side of the boat in case anyone on land was watching. I felt nothing but relief that the waiting was over.

The water was freezing, despite the sun. I struck out for the shore as the boat moved away and, once my feet felt sand beneath them, I stopped and surveyed the beach.

It was a sunny day. A few children played at the sea's edge, darting in and out of waves. A couple of serious swimmers in wet suits braved the early summer water. Further up, groups of youngsters played volleyball or sunbathed. I tore the taped-up plastic bag from my waist and, clutching it, staggered to the shore in my mismatched underwear, trying to look casual.

This should be Pozzallo. A small town on the Sicilian coast. Nothing very important about it except it had a train station and a direct service to Catania Airport where I was going to take a plane to Paris.

If I could.

If the Maltese police hadn't put out an alert for me.

No one paid me much attention and I flopped onto the sand and shivered a bit. The waterproof belt, containing my passport, wallet and phone, had lived up to its name. The plastic bag hadn't survived the immersion in water, though, and the dress and towel were drenched. I wrung them out and laid them on the beach, hiding the knife underneath. They were going to take hours to dry.

I couldn't wait so I put my squelching trainers on, watched until a young woman about my size and shape ran off towards the sea with her boyfriend, sauntered over to where she'd been sitting and picked up her towels and clothes, walking swiftly away.

White shorts and a striped Breton top wouldn't have been my top choice of attire for what lay ahead but it was better than Ma's dress which I left on the beach without a single regret. The knife I put in the pocket of the shorts. As soon as I'd run far enough away from the beach to be out of range of an angry swimmer returning to find her clothes stolen, I slowed to a walk, went down a few side streets until I found a little café with a dark interior, sat down and ordered hot chocolate.

The heat and the sweetness banished the last of the shivers and I ordered another, drank it more slowly and checked my phone. It was working although it still didn't have much charge. No messages from Ma, which meant Peter hadn't picked her up yet. He'd told her he'd borrow a friend's boat and come out to meet her. She'd promised she'd let me know via his phone as soon as they were on their way in his car.

I headed for the station but the next train to the airport wasn't for three hours and would take more than four to get there. However, the taxi outside was more than willing to take me when I waved a large amount of cash, courtesy of a stop at the cashpoint, in front of him. An hour and a half, he told me, and a hundred and fifty euros.

No problem.

I checked Rania's progress despite the perilous state of my battery. She was moving up Italy, now around three hours south of Naples. Still heading to France. I risked my battery and googled flights from Catania. There was one to Paris direct at 18.05. The taxi would get to the airport with loads of time to spare. If I was right and Calais was their destination, I'd be way ahead of them. My spirits rose a touch.

They rose even more when I discovered Catania Airport wasn't as tiny as I'd expected. It had shops and I had time. Two pairs of jeans, some canvas shoes, several T-shirts, underwear and toiletries later I felt better prepared. I bought a bag and a coat and picked up a power bank for my phone plus a small rucksack and a pair of binoculars.

I shovelled down a burger and chips, then thought a bit more. I went back to the shop where I'd found the rucksack and bought a larger bag, shut myself away in the disabled toilet and packed it with the knife wrapped in the clothes, then checked it in.

No problem.

I made it through passport control without any problems too – clearly if the Maltese authorities had issued an international request for me to be apprehended, it hadn't reached Catania… yet.

The departure lounge was grey and institutional with rows of metal seats bolted to the ground, a hangover from the days when airports weren't seen as retail opportunities. The burger and chips had been a good idea because the only concession to hunger here was a vending machine selling crisps and sweets. I found a corner where the tinny reverberation of voices was less harsh, plugged my phone into a socket and watched its charge creep back up to a reasonable level.

No word from Ma. I texted Peter asking what was happening. It didn't show as being read so I hoped that meant he was on the yacht with Ma and therefore out of range. Rania's phone was still on the move, not far from Naples now. Twenty hours from Calais according to my Maps app.

I'd be way ahead of them.

My phone rang as I reached the head of the boarding queue. Peter? I stepped back and let the person behind me go first.

It was Peter.

I rejected the call and sent him a quick text.

Can't talk. Boarding for Paris. All OK?

No reply. That probably meant it was Ma calling on Peter's

phone rather than him. Which also meant the two of them had met up. One less thing to worry about.

'You need to board, madam.' The attendant held out his hand for my card.

I waited until the last moment before putting my phone into flight mode, but no text arrived.

The flight was full and my last-minute booking meant I was in a middle seat, between a businessman in a sharp suit who flipped open his briefcase as soon as we took off and a youngish guy snorting quietly with laughter over a book he was reading. I had nothing but my thoughts to keep me company during the two-hour flight. Listening to music made me think of Rania and reading was equally impossible.

I thought of Marwa.

I still found it hard to accept she was the IS agent. I hadn't liked the idea of Khaled being one. Nor Yasmiin. In fact, the more time I'd spent with any of the refugees, the more impossible it had seemed that any of them could be agents of terror. They were just people. People doing their best to get lives that weren't full of war and death and abuse and…

But Marwa?

I'd liked her.

But making herself liked and trusted was part of her job and she was very good at it. Like Nick. Like him, she could clothe herself in another identity until the real person disappeared.

When I turned my phone on again in Paris, I had a couple of missed calls and a text.

OK. On our way too. Keep in touch. Peter.

Where to now?

Calais? Or stay in Paris? A quick check on Rania showed her still moving north through Italy and now on the outskirts of Rome. I'd stay at the airport until I was sure they were coming to France. Calais was only two or three hours away so I'd have plenty of time to beat them to the north coast and, if they headed elsewhere, I could pick up another flight.

I rented a car, a Mercedes A-Class in case I needed a bit of speed, parked it and went back into the airport where I found a secluded corner with a power point, plugged my phone in and the power bank and watched the little blob that was Rania's phone move north through Rome, then a host of places whose names were only vaguely familiar: Civitavecchia, Grosseto and Piombino. As she approached Livorno and Pisa, the airport emptied. I bought a sandwich and a coffee and found a more comfortable chair. The announcements became less frequent. The hum of chatter died away. Rania went through La Spezia and towards Genoa as a scattering of passengers scurried past me and checked in for the last flights. I wasn't alone in the airport. When I went to the toilets, I noticed a few other people huddled down on chairs and trying to sleep. Had they missed their flights or were they simply homeless people taking advantage of the airport's comfort? Not that it was very warm. In the last couple of hours, the heating had been turned down and there was a definite chill in the air. I wrapped myself in my coat and went back to watching the dot that was Rania on my phone.

The cleaners woke me, hoovering around my chair. I seized my phone. It was nearly six o'clock in the morning. Rania was still travelling. They'd crossed from Italy into France during the night. I guessed they'd probably come via the Alps where the roads weren't watched all the time. Maybe even walked over the border and picked up another vehicle the other side. I was sure they were heading to Calais. Time to go there myself.

I thought about calling Peter to speak to Ma but in the end, hoping they were asleep, sent them a quick text telling them what I was doing.

The roads skirting the airport were busy with early morning commuters but I overtook and undertook, ignoring the irate horns as I zigzagged through the traffic until I hit the autoroute heading north. Then, as I sped along, I had time and space to think about what I was going to do when I met up with them. I hoped I'd be able to remove Rania without any confrontation. Maybe text or even call her and make up some story about why she needed to slip away.

Like what?

I could tell her the truth?

Except it was so complicated. It would take too long.

Panic fluttered in the base of my stomach. How was I going to do this? Maybe I should simply wait until they were all together and walk up to them, take advantage of Marwa's surprise at seeing me and of her reluctance to do anything to give herself away to the other refugees. Then run with Rania.

I pulled into the next service area to check where Rania was and to grab a coffee.

North of Lyon now, but her phone had stopped moving. I zoomed in and my panic subsided a little. They'd stopped in a service station. They'd taken a brief break.

I went into the little café and shop, drank a couple of small bitter coffees that turned to acid in my stomach, stocked up on chocolate bars and, realising I might have a long wait ahead of me, bought a thermos. I ordered another three coffees and two hot chocolates and, to the horror of the man behind the counter, poured them all into the thermos.

Back in the car, my phone rang.

It was Rania.

'Where are you?' She sounded unsure. Wary even. 'Where's Aya?'

'Following.'

'But you're not on the other minibus. We've been waiting for it and it's just arrived.'

'Where are you now?' I asked.

'I don't know the name of the place.'

'I mean, are you with the others?'

'No, I'm in the toilet.'

I breathed again and forced my brain into order.

'Yasmiin said you were in another car further behind. But –'

Yasmiin?

'But Leila told me just now you'd stayed on the yacht. She said she and her father were the last ones off and no one went back for you.'

I remembered Leila, Mohammed's daughter, the young woman I was sure had sworn in English and with a distinctly Scottish accent. How did she fit into this?

'I won't be any trouble, you know.' Rania's voice was thin with fear. 'Please don't take Aya away from me.'

Oh, God. She thought we'd abandoned her.

'I'm coming for you. I promise I am. But –'

What should I tell her?

'Leila told me to stay quiet. To say nothing. What is going on?'

I sent a silent prayer of thanks to the mysterious Leila.

'It's complicated, Rania. But we haven't deserted you. I'm trying to find you. But you mustn't tell anyone. No one at all. Do you know where you're going to?'

'Calais. They keep on saying we're going to Calais.'

'It's a big place. Did they say anything else?'

'They talked about a…'

She stopped.

'A what, Rania?'

She said a word in Arabic.

'What?'

'Menara.'

I repeated it as best I could.

'*Menara*. What is that?'

'I don't know the word in English. It's a *menara*. Like a tower, you know. I think its name is *greenie*. But don't you know where we're going? I don't understand. How are you going to meet us?'

Fear infused her voice and it rose several notches in tone and volume like a guitar string tightened to breaking point.

'Rania!' A voice barked her name and followed it swiftly with a stream of Arabic. Then there was silence.

'End the call.' I whispered. 'Hide the phone. And say you were talking to yourself.'

Short blasts of her breath sounded in my ear. They seemed like thunderclaps.

The voice called her name again.

'Answer, Rania,' I hissed.

A slight whimper punctuated Rania's breathing, followed by the sound of doors being kicked open and finally a banging on the door that I guessed was the one to the cubicle where she was. The phone went dead.

I stared at it helplessly. What was happening? Was Rania alright? I flicked back onto the map that showed her location.

The dot was still there. Motionless for a few minutes and then it disappeared.

I forced the app to update.

Nothing.

And again, although I knew there would still be nothing. Had Rania turned it off? Or had she been discovered with it? I waited 15 minutes, hoping it would reappear, but it didn't. Whatever had happened, it was no longer functioning as a guide. I'd be driving blind from now on. Unless I could work out what she'd meant by *menara greenie*.

Twenty-Seven

*M*enara was an Arab word meaning 'minaret', the tower in a mosque from where the muezzin called the faithful to prayer, according to an online dictionary. But I couldn't find anything in the dictionary for *greenie* nor *greeny* and not even *green*. Maybe it was the name of the minaret?

Back to Google.

There were seventeen mosques in the Calais region. None of them had a name remotely like *greenie* and only two had minarets – both in a city called Arras, an hour and a half further along the road to Calais.

This must be where they were going. Where they would meet the next link in the chain taking them to Britain.

Arras was magnificent, even through the grey drizzle that had arrived as I drove north. I passed by its vast cathedral and through two huge squares lined with ornate buildings without a second glance and found the two mosques in a dour part of the town, dominated by high-rise blocks of flats. It was grim, especially as the day was growing greyer by the minute.

The two mosques were recent, their minarets barely taller than the low-rise shops around them. But still minarets. Nothing on the notice boards outside them suggested either might have a name resembling *greenie*.

Shit.

What else could I do but wait and hope? I worked out the

refugees should arrive around half past one but I couldn't be sure. It was just after twelve now. I called Ma. She answered immediately and told me they were heading into the Italian Alps because Peter knew a way over the border there.

I interrupted her.

'I've lost Rania. Her phone's off. But she said they were going to a *menara*. She didn't know the English word. She said it was a sort of tower. I looked it up and the dictionary said "minaret". Is that what it means?'

'I think so. *Menara* is minaret.'

'And *greenie*? What does that mean?'

'*Greenie*?'

'Yes. I thought it might be the name of the minaret.'

'I don't recognise the word.'

'Well, could you try and find out. I'm outside the only two mosques with minarets in Northern France and I need to watch both of them. I can't find things out while I'm driving.'

'Yes,' she said and rang off without asking me any stupid questions or huffing because I'd spoken to her a bit abruptly. Ma was good like that.

I circled, cursing Arras for having two mosques with minarets, and as the time grew nearer I felt sicker and sicker. One thirty came and went. At two thirty I stopped in front of the red brick mosque. They should be here by now. I'd got it wrong. I'd trusted the words of a teenager and a quick glance through an online dictionary too much.

Ma called.

'Yes,' I said.

'*Greenie* means nothing,' she said, 'but *Menara* isn't just a minaret. It can mean any sort of tower. Or it can mean a beacon or a source of light.'

'That's not very helpful.'

'A lighthouse maybe?'

She hurled questions at me but I wasn't listening. Lighthouse. Of course. That's where they were going. A lighthouse on the coast. How much more likely than a minaret over an hour inland.

'I'll call you back.'

I cut her off and searched for lighthouses.

There was one in Calais, but before I raced off, I made myself check again. I'd got it wrong once already and wasted hours so they were undoubtedly ahead of me now. I had to get it right this time. I expanded the map and found another lighthouse. Twenty miles along the coast from Calais. At a place called Cap Gris-Nez. The Gris-Nez lighthouse. Even with my limited French I recognised the words. They meant *grey-nose* but to someone who'd never learnt French, like Rania, the two words would sound exactly like *greenie*.

It took me three hours to reach Cap Gris-Nez. An accident outside Calais added more than an hour on the time. The crawl through traffic drove splinters into my hope and broke it apart.

I wished I'd had time to tell Rania to stay with the group. To keep away from Marwa. To keep away from Yasmiin. I was increasingly sure she was involved. I remembered her telling me she'd take Rania and Aya with her if Ma wouldn't. I'd thought that was so kind. I'd thought the girls' plight had distressed her deeply. Now I thought she was working with Marwa. How could I rescue Rania if she was glued to Yasmiin's side?

Sweat coated my skin although I felt chilled to the core by the time I arrived at Cap Gris-Nez. I pulled into the car park by the path leading down to the lighthouse and the cliffs. The evening was creeping towards night and low rays of sun bounced off the windows of the cars scattered over its gravelled surface but I only had eyes for two small minibuses, side by side in the far corner. Rania had talked about minibuses. I parked away from them and put my coat on and the hood up to hide my face. They looked deserted. The breeze felt heavy with damp against my bare legs. I wished I'd thought to change out of the shorts I was still wearing but it was too late.

Two cars pulled up beside the minibuses as I walked over and a large family group got out, the kids moaning and saying they were hungry. I passed them quickly and looked inside the first bus.

It was empty except for litter over the floor. Biscuit wrappers, sandwich cartons and a couple of empty cans of an orange drink called *Aranciata*. I'd seen it at Catania airport. It was an Italian drink. I'd caught up with them.

A shadow blocked the sun's reflection in the car window and a hand smothered the cry as it rose to my lips. Even as fright vibrated through my body, my brain told me it was Nick. I knew the hand squashing my lips against my teeth, remembered the smell of its skin and the feel of the shoulders my head was pressed against.

He released me, sliding a hand down my arm and grabbing my hand.

'Come on,' he said. 'We don't have much time.'

He strode into the reed-covered dunes surrounding the car park, releasing my hand as I followed him. At the top, the sand sloped into a hollow. He squatted down and patted the sand beside him. I sat. We were out of sight.

'Rania,' he said. 'What happened? Why is she here?'

He looked stained and grubby. The sort of person I'd swerve to avoid in the street.

'Where is she?' I asked.

'On the beach, a few hundred metres west of here. Waiting for the transport with others. Many others. We don't have this boat to ourselves.'

She was alive. A faint wobble of relief shook me.

'And Marwa?' I said quickly.

'Marwa?'

'You were wrong. Khaled isn't the IS agent. It's Marwa. And Rania knows.'

I told him everything Ma had told me.

'You've been making friends with the wrong person. Time to drop Khaled and cosy up to Marwa,' I added, unable to keep the bitterness out of my voice.

I hated Nick's job. I hated his ability to submerge himself in another person's skin. It spoke of a looseness at the heart of him.

'Marwa,' he said again.

He ran his hands through the sand, picked up a handful and let it trickle out of his fist.

'Was she the woman with Khaled?' I asked. 'That night in Mdina?'

'You saw?'

'I followed you.'

He laughed.

'Was it her?' I asked again.

'Yes.'

'But you never suspected –'

'Of course I did. I suspect everybody. It's safer that way.'

Children's voices penetrated our hiding place. They were climbing the sand dune towards us but an adult called them down and the sound of their chatter faded away.

'I hate this,' I muttered.

'You think I don't?'

He kicked at the sand. I didn't think I'd ever seen him so wired.

'I don't even know if you'll help me rescue Rania.'

His face, dark in the fading light, was unreadable.

'See,' I said. 'You don't know either.'

'Of course I'll help you,' he said. 'I feel like we've missed something though. There's something off about this whole operation.'

'Then get out. We'll run to the beach, take them by surprise, grab Rania and disappear into the dark.'

For a brief second, fire flashed in his eyes and I thought he might join me. Then the weight of his responsibilities smothered it. His bloody, bloody job. I knew it was important. I knew he'd been given a chance to prevent something terrible happening. I knew all that but still I wished he'd run with me.

'They'll never catch us. Not if we're quick enough.'

He shook his head and a sudden rage seized me. I grabbed the front of his jumper and tried to shake him but he was as unmoveable as granite.

'Listen to me,' he said. 'Your plan won't work. You won't take them by surprise. I was waiting for you in the car park. Waiting because I knew you were coming. Mohammed told me to keep an eye out for Morwenna's daughter. He said you knew we were leaving from Cap Gris-Nez.'

How could Mohammed know? Had Rania somehow given me away? And herself?

'Someone called him and told him,' Nick went on. 'So he's edgy and watchful. Very watchful.'

Someone called him. It wasn't Rania who'd given me away then.

'Who called him?'

'He didn't tell me. He only said to watch for you. He knows me from before but that doesn't mean he trusts me enough to tell me everything.'

He unhooked my hands from his sweater.

'He's got a gun, Jen. As do all the smugglers waiting to see us onto the boat. Your plan won't work. We'd be shot before we got ten metres away.'

Men. Guns. Mohammed watching for me. Shit.

'I don't care.' I yanked at a clump of reedy grass but it wouldn't budge. 'I have to try. I'll think of something.' I used the grass to haul myself to my feet, sending sand skittering in all directions. 'Go and do your job and I'll do what I have to do.'

I turned to walk away but his hand grabbed my ankle.

'Sit down. I said I'll help. I just want you to know what we're up against.'

He gave my foot a tug and I sat again.

'When the boat arrives, there'll be confusion and chaos. Everybody will rush into the sea and the smugglers will be occupied loading them on. That'll be the moment when Rania can slip away without anyone noticing. That's our best chance.'

'But Marwa will be watching her. And, I think, Yasmiin.'

'I can deal with Marwa and Yasmiin. In the dark. In the rush. It'll be easy to distract them. And Marwa needs to get on that boat.'

I didn't like his plan. It seemed fraught with potential failure, relying on everything falling into place at that one minute.

'I don't think Marwa will let Rania disappear.'

'I'll deal with her if I have to. I promise you.'

'But how?'

He picked up a handful of sand and watched it trickle between his fingers.

'I don't think you really want to know. Although I hope I won't have to because it would mean the end of the operation.'

I watched the sand too.

This, I thought, was the answer to my doubts about him. Because I understood exactly what he meant.

'Trust me,' he said. 'I am quite capable of dealing with Marwa.'

'OK,' I said.

'The path down to the beach will be watched.' He drew lines in the sand to show me. 'It's west of the place where the boat comes in. I'll tell Rania to run east. Towards the lighthouse. Can you find another way down and come along the beach to meet her?'

'I'll climb down if I have to.'

A smile flickered over his mouth.

'Of course you will. If I tell her you're waiting for her, will she do what I say?'

'I think so. She knows I'm coming to get her.'

He stood. 'We'll do that then. Now, I need your phone.'

I hesitated. I'd need it myself.

'I need it, Jen. I have to make a call on a safe phone.'

I nodded and he reached out both hands as I told him the code. One took my phone but the other wound its fingers through mine.

'Go,' he said.

'I can't while you're holding my hand.'

'If I told you to be careful, would you take it the wrong way?'

'Yes.'

I pulled at my hand but he held tight.

'So don't be careful,' he said and I heard an echo of laughter in his voice. 'Run headlong into danger if that's what you want, but make sure you stay alive.'

He lifted my hand and kissed it, released it and walked away.

I gave him a couple of minutes then went back to the car park. It was empty apart from a couple heading towards the path to the lighthouse. I sped up and joined them. Safety lay in being surrounded by people. Once I got to the lighthouse, I'd find the coastal path and a way down onto the beach.

The path led to a decked and fenced area in front of the lighthouse with a spectacular view over the Channel. If the couple thought it was odd I stuck so close to them, they were too polite to say. The deck was full of people, however, all staring at the sky slowly flushing red with the early stages of sunset. A thin and jagged line of luminous pink broke the horizon. I understood. I was looking at England. At the famous white cliffs, tinted rose by the reflected light from the sky.

Home.

So close.

To the west, the horizon bit the bottom part of the sun away. Night was coming and I had no time to be admiring the view. A set of steps led off the deck to the cliffs' edge. I took them and looked down at the rock face. It was sandstone for sure and probably some chalk although its colour was grey rather than the white of its Dover sister over the Channel. The grey was clay. Slippery clay. Almost unclimbable. Especially with the damp surface made even wetter by the recent drizzle. But I could slither down. I was sure I could. The gradient was only steep in parts with bushes and outcrops of stable rock to cling onto here and there.

I looked back at the deck. The light was fading quickly now. Would anyone notice if I disappeared over the edge? The last thing I wanted was to attract any attention, but most people had left. Only a young woman with a rucksack and an older man with a cloud of puffy white hair rippling in the breeze remained. The woman hoisted her rucksack onto her back and walked back towards the car park. I lowered myself as though going to sit on the ground and slowly lay down until I was out of sight in a shallow hollow. I peered back through the reedy grass to see if anyone was watching me.

The older man with the strangely luxuriant white hair was still there but he was no longer alone. A familiar figure leaned over the fence that encircled the platform next to him.

It was Mohammed.

The two of them were staring out at the horizon and the dying light. They hadn't seen me in the dark ground.

They talked without looking at each other until the man reached into his jacket pocket and, turning, handed an envelope to Mohammed, who opened it and counted the money inside. I couldn't see how much there was but enough to take a while to count. The man watched him. A large and bony nose dominated his face while his jawline and cheeks sagged with soft, loose flesh. Bulky but shapeless, with white skin and white hair and dressed in a crumpled linen shirt and grey jacket, he loomed over Mohammed like a ghost. Mohamed nodded and put the envelope into his pocket. The man touched two fingers to his forehead in a mockery of a salute then came down the steps towards me.

I ducked but he turned left onto the cliff path and when I risked a glance through the grass again, he was a distant figure striding into the deepening dusk. Mohammed, now at the bottom of the steps, watched him too.

And then turned sharply in my direction. I froze. Had he seen me? Maybe the wind had blown the grass aside for a brief second. Who knew? He'd seen something. Something that made his body stiffen and his hand slip into his pocket and emerge wrapped round a dark metallic object. I shoved my head back down.

Shit. Nick had said he had a gun.

'Get up,' he shouted.

I didn't.

I couldn't. My body had frozen.

A sharp crack broke the air above my head and hissed past me over the sea. Life slowed as understanding reached my brain.

Mohammed had fired at me.

'Get up,' he said again.

His voice was nearer now. I looked up. He stood over me, the gun trained on my head.

I had no choice. I staggered to my feet, my thoughts casting around for some way of escape. I should have rolled over the cliff as soon as he saw me. Too late. Too fucking late.

'You,' he said. 'What are you doing here?'

Behind him, a figure appeared from round the side of the deck. It sped towards him, black and insubstantial, as though a piece of dark had detached itself from the night. And, as he tightened his grip on the gun, readying himself to shoot me, a hand emerged from black cloths, snaked an arm round his neck then retracted it with a swift jerk. Shock wiped Mohammed's face clean of emotion. He reached his hands to his neck as blood spurted out and splattered his shirt. His head dropped and he swayed and crumpled onto the grass. Blood pumped out of the gash in his throat, then slowed to an ooze.

The figure and I looked up at the same time.

It was Marwa. A Marwa I barely recognised. Her patient smile and kind eyes had disappeared. This Marwa's face was all hard lines and her eyes crackled with a cold anger, dark and edged with steel. The only colour was the red that stained the knife's blade and her arms. Blood dripped from her hands, gleaming in the setting sun's last light.

Fear was acid in my mouth. The gun. Mohammed's gun. Mohammed had a gun. I needed the gun.

It had dropped from his hand as he fell and lay on the ground in a shallow pool of blood. I grabbed it. Wiped it on my top and held it tight despite its stickiness, pointing it at her.

'You don't need that,' Marwa said. 'I would never hurt you.'

I couldn't help myself. I laughed. A ragged whimper of a laugh.

'I saved you,' she said as she pulled a handful of clean grass up and wiped her knife.

I kept the gun trained on her.

'Mohammed was going to shoot you.'

It was true. And it was true she'd saved me. And, for the life of me, I couldn't see why. Why save me? Why kill Mohammed? If Nick was right, Mohammed was being paid to see her safe to the UK. None of this made sense.

I should shoot her. To be safe. Maybe only wound her. Disable her. And do it now. The longer I waited the harder this was going to be. But I couldn't pull the trigger. Not like this. Not with her standing quietly watching me while the harsh anger on her face drained away, revealing the quiet woman I knew behind.

The blood was drying and leaving a gritty residue on my hands and on the gun. I wondered briefly if the blood leaking out of Mohammed's throat was doing the same – one last desperate attempt of his body to save itself. But I didn't dare look down.

'I know what you are,' I said. But even to me my voice sounded as thin and dry as the reeds whipping my bare legs in the breeze.

'A killer,' Marwa said. 'I understand you're shocked. I never thought that's what I'd become. But I have.' She broke off, pulled a leather sheath out of a pocket of her black dress, slipped the knife in it and put it back. 'But I'm not going to kill you. Why would I kill you?'

She was so calm. Almost gentle. I forced myself to remember Nick's warning. And Ma's. People like Marwa were expert manipulators. But still I couldn't shoot. A kind of misery descended on me. I didn't know what to do.

'Why would I kill you?' she repeated.

'Because you're a terrorist.' I was sick of the lies.

Her eyes fluttered and I thought a rasping gasp lifted her chest but the air was so full of sea and wind it was hard to tell.

'How can you think that?' she said in the end.

'Because Nahla recognised you and you killed her. Because she told Rania and you took her. Because you killed Stephan when he threatened your plans and you killed Mohammed.'

She stared at me without moving for a few seconds, then blinked rapidly and took the sheathed knife back out of her pocket. I tensed but she held it out to me.

'Take it,' she said. And when I didn't move, she pushed it towards me. 'Take it and listen to me. We don't have much time before the boat arrives.'

I snatched it from her, telling myself to be careful. She might have another.

'You are right. I killed Stephan and, of course, I killed Mohammed. And I have killed others.'

Night was settling around us like a black mist rolling in off the sea.

'I killed them because they were scum. Scavengers feeding off the helpless. But I didn't kill Nahla. Nahla was a friend. Not a close one but a woman I respected. I knew her father from the university and Nahla and I worked together in Tripoli with other women, trying to make our country into a place fit to live in.'

The intensity of her voice reached me. I knew I'd have to listen. I couldn't pull the trigger while there was a chance I was wrong about her.

'And I don't understand how Nahla could think I was a terrorist. Did she tell you why?'

Nahla had never spoken to me – I had no idea what Nahla thought of Marwa – so I had no answer to this.

'I will tell you why I have killed,' she said when I didn't reply. 'But first, we need to get rid of the body. In case someone comes along. Throw it over the cliff. It will be high tide soon and the sea will take it away.'

'You do it,' I said and watched as she rolled and kicked Mohammed over the edge. His corpse fell onto the beach below, battered by ridges and knobs of rock as it went. It came to rest with its head on a small patch of sand and its legs half hidden by a mass of seaweed. Afterwards she sat herself carefully on the grass, a couple of metres from me, and continued.

'I have a son,' she said. 'But I told you that before. And my story is about him. Or, maybe, I had a son. He could be dead. I don't know. And I don't know which is best. His name is Sa'id. My Sa'id. A little older than Rania. And like her, he was bright and young for his age. Thin as a reed and ran around all day, laughing and curious.'

She pulled something out of her pocket and handed it to me. A photo of a boy in a garden somewhere. A photo capturing the moment when you call someone's name to tell them you're there. They look up and, for a second, pleasure at seeing you lights up their face.

'That is Sa'id,' she said. 'He arrived after we'd thought, my husband and I, that we were not going to be blessed with children so he was doubly precious. And even more so after my husband was killed in the endless fighting. Life has been dangerous in Libya for so long. Especially if you tried to stand up for people's rights. And like Nahla and Ibrahim, there were people who wanted rid of me and I knew we were in danger. A few months ago, a family I knew well were leaving and they suggested we went with them. But the cost was enormous. I couldn't get the money for both of us but I scraped enough together for Sa'id to go.'

She crossed her arms and disappeared into her thoughts.

'What happened?' I asked.

'Things went wrong,' she continued. 'They were separated although Sa'id made it to Malta. And I was so happy. I thought he'd be safe there until I could join him.'

'But he wasn't.'

'No. He'd send me messages on other people's phones when he could. He hated Malta. He was lonely and unhappy. You have to understand, I was trying to join him but I didn't have the money. I was selling everything I could. But it took time. Then he told me someone was going to help him. Help him get off Malta and help him get into school. He told me that was what they did. That their name meant *help*. They helped people like him. I thought that was good news.'

She broke off and fixed me with her eyes.

'But he disappeared and I never heard from him again.'

I remembered Nick talking about a child trafficking operation he'd closed down and Amalia telling Rania not to go out alone on any account. What chance had a youngster, all on his own, stood?

'And after that,' she said, 'I asked around. I learned all the things I should have learned before. I thought the smugglers, demanding huge sums of money from desperate people and sending them to sea in deadly craft, were scum, but there are worse. There are people who prey on the weakest of those fleeing, who pick them off and sell them on for...'

'I know,' I said.

'Sex,' she said.

'I know.'

'With vile men.'

'I know.'

'I didn't. I sold everything then, for any price. Things my parents had given me that I hoped to keep. None of it mattered. I went to one of the smugglers who'd transported Sa'id and asked about a crossing, but I had too many questions for him. I couldn't help myself. And he didn't like my questions. He didn't like me. And a few days later I realised he was following me. And I was frightened. So I hid and waited for him. Then I...' She swallowed. 'I never thought I could kill someone but when it came to it, that first time, fear made it easy.'

She was silent for a long time, staring into space.

I was sure this was the truth. It chimed too closely with what Nick had told me about the sudden death of their informer in Libya.

'I slept well the night after I killed the first man.' Marwa's voice interrupted my thoughts. 'The first time since Sa'id went missing. Strange, isn't it? But I think it was because I'd finally done something.'

She told me how she'd come to Malta with Zubaida and Yousef. They weren't related but she'd been a close friend of their aunt who had died recently. They were also desperate to leave Libya. Marwa took the aunt's place and her passport. The story she'd told me on the boat was mainly the aunt's with little bits of truth. On Malta she'd realised quite soon that the people whose name Sa'id had said meant *help* must come from Musaeada.

'I took Zubaida to the clinic,' she said. 'And I asked the nurse, Paulina, if she could help me get off the island. I offered her money and I knew straightaway I'd come to the right place and the right person. Her eyes lit up like jackals' as they circle a weakening animal. I gave her money, a lot of money, and she made some calls. And I watched and memorised the numbers and listened to her conversations. She didn't know I spoke English and understood every word she said. And then I made a mistake. I asked her about Sa'id. I asked her if she'd met him. If she knew who had taken him. She shut right down and hustled us out of the surgery. I knew I'd gone too far. Given myself away. And when we went back into the waiting room, Nahla was there. She recognised me as quickly as I recognised her. Even said my name.'

'Your name?'

'My name is Aya. Marwa is Zubaida's aunt's name.'

I remembered Nahla suddenly standing in the clinic when Marwa and Zubaida had come through from the surgery. Aya, her daughter, had fallen from her lap and she'd called out the name. We'd all thought she meant her daughter.

'I made a sign to keep quiet. I didn't want Paulina to know I was travelling under a false name. But I would never have hurt Nahla, although her death was all my fault.'

I waited for her to explain.

'As soon as Paulina went back into the surgery with Nahla and your mother, I wrote everything I could remember from Paulina's calls, all the names and numbers, the boats and the people, down on the envelope of money I'd brought. But I was in a bad way that afternoon. I'd asked Paulina too many questions and Nahla had recognised me. I knew she would never give me away deliberately but she was delirious and saying things without meaning to. I must have dropped the envelope in the rush to leave after the fighting and I panicked when you asked whose it was. And even more when Paulina looked at it. She recognised what I'd written and it wouldn't have taken her long to work out who it belonged to. She looked straight at me when she asked us whose it was and I knew I was on borrowed time.'

Her voice faltered briefly.

'I killed her later when I was at the hospital with Zubaida. I knew she worked there. The first time, the smuggler in Libya, it was a panicky and desperate thing. Not with Paulina though. I will do anything to get to Sa'id. Anything. Do you understand?'

'Yes.'

'So before I killed her, I made her speak. I held the knife to her throat and let her think she might live if she spoke. She told me Sa'id had left on Stephan's boat. Mohammed had organised it. He often sent children to Europe, where there were people who pay for them.'

The damp in the air had turned to drizzle, a fine rain, which woke the smell of Mohammed's blood on my clothes and Marwa's hands.

'I was careful after that. I got Yousef and Khaled to organise a passage on Stephan's boat and I waited until everyone was asleep and Stephan was alone. I asked him about Sa'id but he said he saw many children travelling alone and he couldn't remember any of them. They were all the same to him. And all the time he was talking to me about my son and about all the refugee children who'd sailed on his boat, all the time, his eyes were elsewhere. They glanced at the sails and the sea and the navigation screen. He never once looked at me. I was nothing. Sa'id was nothing. Just cargo.'

So you killed him too, I thought. And, afterwards, you went back below and Nick woke up. Not that it mattered. I didn't much care about Stephan. He must have guessed what would happen to the youngsters he was transporting.

'And Nahla?' I said. 'You said her death was your fault too?'

'That was Paulina, because of the envelope. Amalia took it and locked it in a drawer but Paulina knew as soon as she or anyone who could read Arabic looked at it, they'd realise its significance. And if Amalia knew people in Musaeada were smuggling she wouldn't have taken breath until they were all arrested. So Paulina told Mohammed. He wanted someone to break in and take it but when he realised it was going to be impossible, he told them to burn the clinic down.'

I remembered Mohammed watching from the top of the concrete tubes next door, his face grim in the reflection of the bursts of flames.

'How do you know this?' I asked.

'Because Yasmiin told me.'

'Yasmiin burned the clinic.' I wasn't asking a question.

'Yes. But she had no idea Nahla and the others were in there.'

Her hands moved restlessly in her lap, plucking at the thin black cloth of the skirt she wore. They were patched with dried bloodstains like mine.

'She has no money and Mohammed offered her a free passage off Malta if she would do this small thing for him. She was devastated when she learned Nahla had been inside.'

The sun had long gone now and the clouds swallowed up the rosy-orange glow it left behind.

'I think Sa'id is dead. Mainly I pray he is dead. Because there is no hope for him now. Not after what he will have seen and felt. But until I know for sure he is dead, I must look for him.'

With the coming of the dark, a damp that tasted of salt and the harsh, clean tang of seaweed had filled the air.

'And I will kill the scum who did this to him.'

I believed her now. There was a horrid inevitability about what had happened to Sa'id that rang true. This wasn't about international terrorism. How could Nick and his colleagues have got it so wrong?

I handed her the photo back.

'And Rania. Why did you take Rania?'

She avoided my eyes as she spoke, focussing on the photo instead.

'I didn't. She got on the little boat without thinking. Mohammed told her you would be following on.'

'You didn't stop her, though.'

'No.'

I waited.

'Bait,' she said.

'Bait?'

'For the people who buy and sell children. I saw the way Mohammed looked at her. Paulina had told me he was involved. So I watched him and tried to find out where he took the children. And I was lucky. Sometimes help comes from strange places. I found out he was meeting the buyer here to get his money – you saw them both – and afterwards he would have handed Rania over on the beach.'

'You were going to let him do that?'

'Of course not. But I needed to know who was going to buy her. And now I will hide at the top of the path to the beach and after the boat has left, I will follow the rich white man who buys children and find out who he is. Rania is safe now Mohammed is dead. Yasmiin will make sure she gets on the boat. She let Rania slip away once. At one of the places where we stopped on the motorway. One minute Rania was there and the next she'd gone. I thought Mohammed had taken her. We panicked until we found her in the toilets. I told Yasmiin everything then. And gave her Stephan's gun.'

She was wrong.

Nick's words rang in my ears. *I can deal with Marwa and Yasmiin.* And I was sure he was right. He'd fix Yasmiin so Rania could slip away into the night. Slip away into the child-traffickers' waiting hands. Between us we'd given them the perfect opportunity to pick Rania off.

'Marwa, I have no time to explain. I've believed you and now you must trust me. When the boat comes in, Rania is going to flee to find me and someone is going to stop Yasmiin from staying with her. The traffickers will take her then. I have to go.'

Marwa didn't hesitate. She rose in a fluid movement.

'Give me the gun,' she said. 'I will stop them.'

I only waited a minute before I handed it over. I didn't think I could use it and I had to trust her.

'I'm going down to the beach here,' I said. 'No one will expect me to come from this direction.'

She glanced over the edge and nodded.

'I'll go along the cliff,' she said. 'And come down to the beach by the path. It's the way everybody will use and I will kill as many of them as I can.'

She turned to run.

For a moment I thought there should be something else. Some kind of farewell. Some kind of acknowledgement of what had passed between us. But there was no time. She ran into the dark and I pushed myself over the cliff.

Twenty-Eight

I half fell, half slithered down the cliff. It was too dark to see so none of my climbing skills were any use apart from the strength of my hands that grabbed at cracks and knobs, at tufts of grass and clumps of sea plants and dug themselves into patches of clay to slow my descent. Although every time my downward tumble felt safe, fear for Rania drove me to push myself down faster.

And towards the end, it wasn't safe. The slope steepened. Gravity snatched me and for a second there was nothing but air whistling around me as I fell. I stretched out flailing arms, kicked feet in every direction, spiralled in space like a crazed and high dancer jerking to the last song of the night, then bounced against the cliff and tumbled onto a gentler slope of clay whose stickiness slowed me enough to break my fall and let me roll the last few feet onto the beach.

No time to catch my breath.

West, Nick had said. If I went west, I'd meet Rania coming towards me. I headed west and away from the lighthouse as fast as I could, dodging round the biggest boulders and avoiding the places where seaweed disguised the surface underneath, hunting out the light patches that meant sand and stability and the possibility of running flat out for a few yards. Occasionally I glanced out to sea. The boat coming in to pick up the refugees would be silent and dark but still I hoped for the quick flash of an uncovered torch to show me how far I had to go.

I dreaded bursting upon the refugees and the smugglers unawares. Of hearing startled cries and sharp intakes of breath. Of feeling the sharp explosion of a bullet hitting my body and tumbling me into the ground to lie as broken as Mohammed. But I forced myself to run fast.

And then I began to worry I'd passed them. That I'd missed the small movements a group of humans clustered together in the dark might make. That eyes had watched me stagger past but kept still and silent. My feet began to splash through water and the sandy patches disappeared under the waves. The tide was rolling in and judging by the seaweed on the cliff, high tide met the land far above my head.

Were they behind me or still in front?

Or had Marwa been lying? Had it all been some final trick? My gut believed her story but my head whirled with doubts and suspicions.

The dark, full of rain and sea mutterings, was broken only by the white frill of waves splashing onto the rocky shore and the Gris-Nez lighthouse beam above. But suddenly I heard shouts together with the faint noise of an engine. A slow-moving patch of black floated on the dark grey of the water. On the beach ahead torchlights flashed and, caught in their broken rays, people plunged into the sea and pushed through the incoming waves. Far more of them than I'd expected and I remembered Nick saying many other people were travelling. The sea was full of heads and arms while bodies waded through the shallows.

Was I too late?

As if in answer to my question, the dull crack of bullets echoed through the dark.

A brief staccato salvo of shots and screams.

Then silence.

I prayed the shots had come from the gun I'd handed to Marwa.

Beams of torchlight swung round in my direction and lit a figure running past me in the dark. Breathing in fast, hard jerks, its feet slapping the sand and the rocks. Short and skinny. Rania? But as I turned to chase after her, I slipped and fell into a pool where the rock-filled beach met the cliff.

And before I could stagger to my feet, someone raced past me shining a torch on Rania's fleeing back. I heard their gun fire and saw its smoky flash. Rania stumbled and fell. And stayed down. They'd shot her. The figure ran to the rocks where she'd dropped and stared down at her. Another dark figure tore past me and joined the first. I saw the gun flash again and heard the shots. Two of them. Fired from too close to where Rania had fallen to miss.

'Dead,' the first one shouted. 'She is dead.'

It was a woman's voice. Not Marwa's. Not Yasmiin's.

Answering shouts came from the beach but I had eyes only for the two figures now trudging past me and back to the others.

The first was Leila, gun and torch in hand, her face lit by its reflection in the water covering the beach. Nick picked his way over the rocks by her side. They talked fast and intensely to each other.

They didn't see me in the pool where I had fallen with the water drenching my clothes and stinging the grazes and cuts on my legs.

I was cold. Icy cold.

Nick had stood there and watched as Leila fired two bullets into Rania's fallen body. Maybe he'd thought she was dead already. Maybe she had been. Maybe he'd realised it wasn't worth giving himself away when she was already dead.

I hated him. I hated him for having a brain cold enough to work that out.

More shots rang out on the beach but I couldn't see what was going on. Then there was nothing but the noise of the sea and the occasional cry. I counted to thirty, dragged myself out of the pool and crawled further into the shadows.

Along the beach, people still waded into the waves, all heading for the boat. Gradually the sea emptied as they clambered aboard. Their faint cries were replaced by the whirr of an engine. Now only a few people remained on the beach. The smugglers, I supposed, although my brain was chilled and slow. Most turned and walked away but two of them dragged something heavy down to the water's edge and swung it into the waves. And again they trudged down the beach with another load and dumped it where the tide would take it away.

Bodies.

Then they too turned and left and I watched until their torches disappeared.

I don't know what to do.

Close by my head, the pungent seaweed smelled of my childhood. Of fishing in rock pools and the salt making my hair sticky and puckering the skin of my limbs. The water was always cold then.

Cold.

A wave broke over me. Instinct kicked in. I sat up, coughed and brushed the water from my eyes. Apart from the sea, it was quiet. The tide was coming in fast now. It ate away at the land with an insistent liquid growl.

I should get off the beach.

But not quite yet. I was going to look for Rania. I was going to find her body and get it off the beach too. I couldn't bear her to be yet another soul cut adrift from her life and her family and lost in the sea.

The moon had risen and its dim glow lightened the clouds but even so I cursed Nick for taking my phone because it was hard to see a body among the shadows and the rocks. The tide washed ever higher and submerged my ankles, then my shins. I tripped and bashed my knees for the millionth time. Surely I should have found her by now. I screamed her name, pointless as it was. Soon I'd have to get off the beach myself.

The cliffs soared vertically along this stretch of coast. Sandstone and chalk, friable and damp. And slippery clay and mud. The occasional bush clung but higher up, above the high water mark. Below it were only clumps of greasy seaweed. It wouldn't be an easy climb, but I wouldn't leave yet. Not until I had no choice. I thought I must have missed her body so I turned and went back the way I'd come, muttering angry words as I stumbled on. No one would hear me anyway.

But over my mumbling and the relentless swoosh of the sea, I heard a faint call, like the noise a solitary gull makes when it wheels for the last time in the dark before settling into its perch on the cliffs. It came again and I knew it was my name. Someone was calling me.

I looked up ahead to where a small figure stood on a rock beneath the cliff face, waving. A small, thin figure calling my name over the sea rushing to fill the gap between us.

Rania.

I waded towards her, scrambled up the rock and hugged her as she threw herself into my arms. Despite the wet, despite the mud all over me. Despite the blood.

'You're here,' I said.

'Brahim told me you would come.'

For half a second everything was right with the world, then a wave splashed over the rock and over us both.

'Tell me later. We need to get out of here.' I looked quickly up and down the beach and felt the beginnings of panic. The tide was racing in and the previously lapping waves had become breakers that crashed around and over the rock we were standing on.

The only way off the beach now was the cliff. Wet through from the rain and sea, it was no easy climb, not even for an experienced climber.

I ran my fingers over the face as Rania watched me. A rounded edge crumbled as I tested it with my weight.

Shit.

A large wave swept over my legs and retreated, sucking and pulling at my feet. I grabbed onto Rania as it knocked her over.

I knew how to climb this cliff. It would have to be done lightly and fast, never staying still long enough for the stone to flake under the pressure of feet and hands. Always ready to shift my weight if the hold started to break. The knowledge was waiting in my bones and my muscles.

But not in Rania's.

She'd never climbed. She didn't have years of practice shaping her muscles, honing her technique to the point where moves became instinctive.

Another wave broke against the cliff in a rippling crash from west to east. It bounced us against the stone and I gripped Rania again to stop her disappearing.

The next big wave would wash her away.

'Listen,' I said. 'We're going to climb.'

Her eyes flicked up over the dark cliff.

'It's not as big as it looks and we only need to get beyond high tide level.'

This was true. The tide had hollowed out the face immediately above us so it was near vertical but afterwards the cliff sloped gently and the climb would be an easy scramble.

Afterwards. Could I get us to the afterwards bit?

'OK,' she said.

I'd been ready to cajole her, to calm her fears, even bully her. Her agreement took all my words away. She was frightened, though. Seismic shivers ran through her body. Nevertheless she nodded and reached her hands up the stone to show me she was ready.

'Not like that,' I said. 'Use your feet to push you up and your hands to steady you. We're going to climb together and I'm going to tell you exactly what to do.'

But how? How am I going to compress years of climbing into a few sentences?

I stood directly behind her and pointed to a ledge a couple of feet above us. She started to lift her right foot. Thank God she had plimsolls on her feet. Old and battered but soft and supple.

'Wait two seconds, Rania. Once we start, we have to climb quickly. No waiting. No resting. No stopping. Everything keeps moving all the time. Imagine you have a rope round you pulling you upwards. And do exactly what I say.'

What am I going to say?

The sea round my legs drained away with a guttural rattle, sucked out by the pull of a big wave preparing to lash the coast. No time to wait. Time to go. Time to let the doubts drain away like the sea and launch ourselves at the cliff before the pursuing breaker smashed us against it.

'Go,' I screamed at her. And then more calmly in case I'd frightened her. 'Now, Rania.'

We climbed together, my body on the outside, half pushing her up the first few feet, her hands seizing the holds as mine left them and reached above for the next. I shouted at her where to put her feet at first but the sandstone here was eroded in horizontal ripples and she quickly started feeling for the next one herself.

Momentum carried us up the first part but as the slope curved into the overhang gravity started to pull us away from the rock. I peered through the rain and dark, looking for a way round.

Above me to the left was an open dihedral – a place where two planes of rock met at almost right angles to form a corner leading up the face. Easily climbable if you had the technique. If you knew how to stem. How to use the forces of opposition.

I'd seen youngsters get it quickly but they'd been in the gym, after careful explanation from an instructor, and even then they'd fallen the first couple of times and been saved by the rope. I'd never seen anyone grasp the concept at night, with rain and wind whipping their sodden hair against their face and sending shivers of cold and fright to stiffen their limbs, while climbing stone that dissolved into sand if you rubbed against it for too long. It was our only chance, though.

'Rania,' I shouted as I directed her towards the dihedral. She hesitated and her foot slipped a few millimetres then held. 'Keep moving. And do exactly what I say. No matter how weird it sounds. You have to trust me. OK?'

'OK.'

We edged along a slippery ledge, our fingers gripping a narrow horizontal crack. So far, so good. At the bottom of the dihedral, I dug my feet into the opposing planes of rock and steadied myself. The miracle of two conflicting thrusts giving stability. A resting position for me. Not that my muscles were tired. Adrenalin and fear drove them. But this was as solid as I could possibly be. Enough, I hoped, to catch Rania if she fell, when she fell, because I was sure she'd fall.

I grabbed her back through her sodden T-shirt and guided her inside the dihedral.

'Right. Push your feet into the stone,' I shouted above the grumbling roar of the sea as I positioned her feet against the corner's opposite sides. 'As hard as you can.' I gripped her ankles and thrust them into the rock, feeling her leg muscles tighten and strengthen as they took the weight of her body.

'That's it.'

She felt the moment when her feet, each placed on an opposing wall, each pushing into the rock and against each other, took her weight. And then she lost her trust in it and with it her force. Her feet slipped over the crumbly surface. She panicked, lost her centre and clung on with her fingers. She was going to fall.

'Ram your feet into the rock again,' I yelled and wrapped an arm round her to hold her up. I dug my feet hard against the rock but her weight and the slippery surface were too much. The thick, black sea roiled and crashed beneath me as we slid towards it.

'Rania,' I shouted. 'You must trust me. Push your feet into the stone.'

And she tried. Her feet thrust out. Her legs locked and straightened. Her core gripped and held while her hands rested against the rock for balance.

She'd got it. Wonderful, fabulous girl!

'Now,' I said, my mouth close to her ear. 'Feel the strength of your legs and the rock holding you up like a steel rod running from foot to foot. The harder you push into the rock, the stronger you are. Got it?'

I felt her nod.

'Now you're going to take your right hand and push it in turn into the rock and against your left foot. Not too far up. And when that same force runs between right hand and left foot. When the steel rod snaps into place. You're going to release your right foot and move it up.'

She took her time. Rainwater ran down the cliff loosening the sandstone and coating it with fine mud as she transferred the strain from feet to hand and foot, then back again. Every bit of my consciousness was focussed on her. I spoke to her all the time, encouraging, directing and congratulating. I'd never helped someone climb like this but the words came out of my mouth as though they'd been inside me waiting for the right time and I realised they were Pa's. The words he'd said on those long-ago days when we climbed the cliffs and quarries and rocks near Tregonna.

The distance between us and the point where the gradient flattened grew less. Inch by inch it came closer and when we finally hauled ourselves onto it, I saw the rest of the cliff was a gentle slope. It would be a simple scramble on all fours to the top.

'We've done it,' I said and put my arm round Rania. 'Well done, partner. You were magnificent.'

She said nothing but stared down at the way we'd come. Her hands rubbed the wet stone and I wondered if she felt the loosened grains of sand and understood how treacherous it had been.

'The rest is easy,' I said.

She nodded but, although her face was sharp and tense, her body seemed to wilt.

'We'll rest for a few minutes,' I told her.

I understood. This was the moment after a great effort when your energy fails. When doing the slightest thing feels impossible. I knew because I felt the same. The thought of clambering up to the top, then walking back to the car. Of deciding what to do next. Of finding Ma. Then getting the girls into the UK. It all felt impossible.

Shut up, I told myself. *One step at a time. We've got this far. We'll do the rest.*

But as the rain drizzled down through my hair and into my eyes, as my wet clothes leached the warmth out of my body and my energy seeped away, I felt like curling up on the cliff and doing nothing. It had all been too much.

I realised Rania was weeping. 'Mama,' she said. 'Mama.'

Grief had caught up with her again. So on the top of the face with my feet sticking out into space, rain falling all around us and the wind rushing salt spray into my face, I hugged her tight and let her cry. There were no words that would help her.

*

At the top we walked along the road towards the car park.

'We'll clean ourselves up a bit,' I said. 'Then find a hotel. No one will take us in looking like this.'

Rania was wet through and dripping, still streaked with mud. I was worse, for where the rain had washed the mud off my clothes the dark remnants of Mohammed's blood stained my top.

The signs for the car park appeared.

Shit. My car keys? Did I still have them?

I did. Deep in the bottom of the waterproof belt Ma had given me. I wondered where she was and felt for my phone, then remembered I'd given it to Nick.

He must be on the boat heading across the channel. Was he looking back at the French cliffs and hoping I was safe? Had he managed to work out what was going on?

I remembered him with Leila as she fired her gun at Rania. Except clearly she hadn't. No one could have missed at that range.

'What happened?' I asked Rania as we trudged along the road. 'On the beach?'

'Brahim whispered to me that you were here. And I was so relieved. I was frightened you wouldn't find me. He told me you'd come to get me but I needed to be careful. He said to wait until the boat arrived and everyone started wading into the water, to slip away into the dark then and head towards the lighthouse. He said if anyone saw me to run as fast as I could and not to stop until I met you.'

She paused and wiped the rain trickling down her forehead. My battered trainers slapped against the wet tarmac.

'So I sat at the edge of the group as we waited for the boat and I kept very quiet. No one spoke much anyway. Yasmiin was close by me but Brahim started talking to her, asking her to help Zubaida and Yousef with the children when the boat came because Marwa was missing.'

313

I wondered what Nick had thought was going on with both Marwa and Mohammed missing.

'And he was right,' Rania continued. 'When the boat came close, there was a big rush and I slipped away. But a man seized me from behind and plunged his hand over my face. I couldn't shout so I tried to kick him, tried to struggle. Anything to make a noise. But everybody was running to the water's edge and calling to each other. And then I think I heard guns firing. I saw Yasmiin stop and turn round to look for me. She put the child she was carrying down and started to walk back up the beach.'

'And then?'

'I don't know. Someone howled my name and the man dropped me. Marwa was clinging to his back and stabbing him with a knife. She screamed at me to run and I did.'

I guessed Marwa hadn't dared use the gun on the man holding Rania so tightly in his arms.

'And then there was a lot of shouting and gunshots. Something hit the rock beside me and sent bits into the air. I tripped over and I was too frightened to get up.'

Rania's face shone clear in the white glow of a streetlamp. The rain had washed it clean of mud but not of the horror darkening her eyes.

'I wasn't very brave,' Rania went on, wrapping her arms around herself. 'I knew I should get up and run but I couldn't. It was like my legs belonged to someone else. Someone who was so frightened they couldn't stop shaking. I heard them coming for me. I heard someone splashing through the sea and then stop when they saw me. And when I looked round, it was Leila. She had a gun too. And I thought –'

She quivered like the string of a bow when the arrow had left. I held my arms out but she just grasped my hands.

'Brahim came running up too. But Leila... She lifted the gun

314

high and then she fired it. Twice I think. It hit the sand a long way ahead and then she shouted back that I was dead.' She swallowed. 'And then I don't know what happened. It was like I went away for a little while.'

'You didn't hear me looking for you?'

She shook her head. 'After a while, I knew I had to get up because the water was covering me and I crawled onto the rock and then I heard you. You were swearing.' She laughed. 'You were saying *shit, shit, shit*.'

'Quite probably.'

'Leila saved me, didn't she?'

'Leila and Marwa and Yasmiin,' I replied. 'And you saved yourself too.'

It was nothing but the truth. I might have helped her up the cliff but I couldn't have done it without her determination and courage. And without her own efforts and those of the other women, she'd be another dead body on this beach… or worse.

Leila. Leila was a mystery. How involved was she in her father's business? Why had she saved Rania? I had no idea but Marwa had said something I didn't understand. Something about finding help in strange places. I wondered if that help had come from Leila. As Mohammed's daughter, no one was better placed to give Marwa information than her.

'Come on,' I said. 'It's not far now.'

But she lingered.

'Why did the man grab me?'

I owed her the truth.

'There are evil men who will pay a lot of money to have sex with young girls like you. I think that is what this is all about.'

She was silent and I wondered if she'd understood. Maybe she was remembering Amalia telling her the same thing in the car in Malta.

'Is that why Marwa fought him?'

'Yes.'

'Is she…'

'Dead?'

Rania nodded.

'I think she might be.' I remembered the second body being thrown into the sea. 'And possibly Yasmiin too.'

'They were very brave.'

'Yes.' I wondered if we'd ever know. Nick would be able to tell me if I ever saw him again.

We reached the entrance to the car park, dark away from the street lights, but as we headed for the car, a sudden glare of torches blinded me. Voices shouted.

I shaded my eyes. It was the police. French police. Gendarmes. Lean, tough-faced men with guns holstered at the waist and torches.

What did they want? Had someone reported the refugees on the beach? Had someone seen two wet and filthy people on the road?

I'm too tired for this.

One of them barked something at me. I didn't speak French. I knew how to order a coffee and a beer but I didn't think that was going to help. And then I realised he was saying my name and speaking English. Heavily accented but, nevertheless, English.

'Madame Jenifry Shaw. You are Madame Shaw?'

They know who I am. How can they know who I am?

'Yes.'

Something told me there was no point lying.

'Please come with us.' He pointed to a police car. 'And the girl, please.'

Despite the 'pleases', refusing clearly wasn't an option.

I put my arm round Rania, wondering if I was about to be

arrested for child abduction, and forced my brain to whir into some semblance of life.

'Say nothing,' I muttered to her as we got into their car. 'Nothing at all.'

Twenty-Nine

They separated us at the gendarmerie although I begged them not to. It was too much for Rania. Her courage failed her and they had to peel her arms from round my neck and carry her, kicking, away.

I felt like doing the same myself.

'I want a lawyer,' I said

They ignored me and we marched along a grey gloss-painted corridor.

I tried a different tack. 'I want to make a phone call.'

I'd call Miranda. She worked in the camps at Calais. She must know a French lawyer.

They flung open one of the many doors lining the corridor.

'I have the right to make a phone call.'

Surely I did? The law couldn't be that different in France?

'Go in, please.'

It was a cell. Grey like the corridor and with a raised concrete area along one side that served as a bed. The mattress on top was thin. Nothing else apart from a toilet half hidden behind a waist-high concrete wall. No basin. A high and barred window would let some light in when morning came.

They started to shut the door behind me. All thoughts of lawyers and phones left me. They were going to lock me up.

'Please,' I asked and gestured towards my filthy wet shorts and top. 'Please could I have some clothes? Clean ones. And something to wash with.'

The door slammed shut and they went.

Bastards.

I sat down on the so-called bed. It was as hard as it looked. And tried to make sense of what had happened.

I guessed Malta had finally put out an international arrest warrant for me. The police had known who I was so it wasn't a chance pick-up. With a flight from Italy booked in my real name, I'd have been easy to track to France. Then I'd rented a car in Paris, again in my real name. Didn't rental cars have tracking devices these days? Probably. The police had arrested me in the car park after all.

I paced up and down the tiny cell, trying not to think about what might lie ahead. Trying not to think about what might be happening to Rania. Exhaustion and cold made me huddle on the bed but images of Rania being dragged onto a plane chased my thoughts down dark passageways and it was a long, long time before I fell asleep.

The noise of the door opening dragged me out of a restless doze. Light filtered in through the window. A woman in an overall, with a gendarme standing behind her, put a tray down on the floor. The smell of coffee filled the room.

'Ten minutes,' the gendarme said.

He shut and locked the door behind them before I could ask him what he meant. Ten minutes, and then what?

Ten minutes was enough to drink the orange juice (watered down from concentrate but wet and sweet), stuff the bread, butter and apricot jam down my throat and drink the coffee (sour but drinkable with four lumps of sugar in it).

They were as good as their word. In ten minutes, the door opened again. I stalked out with as much dignity as anyone could when they were dressed in shorts and a stripy top ingrained with mud and blood, with stiff hair flattened onto their head, and arms and legs covered with bruises and grazes.

They took me up several flights of stairs to a larger room, empty apart from a table and two chairs, ignoring my demands to see Rania, and locked me in.

The small panes of the only window were made opaque by a vinyl overlay stuck over the glass. One piece of vinyl was peeling off and I helped it along, peering down to a black tarmacked courtyard below. As I watched, the gates swung open to let a car through. A man stepped out. White shirt. Short hair. Very short hair. I could only see the top of his head from my peephole high above. Someone important, judging from the waiting reception of gendarmes on the station steps. Some shook hands. Some saluted. One pointed up towards the room I was waiting in.

The man looked up. His bony face, sharp with angles, gleamed in the morning sun. He had a moustache. Nothing more than a smudge above his lip. A stupid affectation. But along with the immobility of his features it made him seem more like a sketch of a person than a living, breathing human.

I knew him. I just couldn't remember from where. So it wasn't a surprise when steps outside the door and the murmur of voices announced his arrival.

No one followed him into the room and he took great care to shut the door behind him. He didn't look at me or speak but put his briefcase on the table and turned his attention to the walls and ceiling, scanning them from top to bottom and running his fingers over uneven patches in the painted plaster. He snapped the briefcase open and removed a device about the size of a phone with a stubby mast like a walkie-talkie. He walked slowly round the room waving it up and down and staring at its screen. I moved out of the way as he approached the window.

A smell of spray starch came off his crisp white shirt and the hands that guided the device were small with neatly trimmed nails. I shoved my own in my shorts pockets and sat down.

I guessed he was checking the room for listening devices and my stress levels ratcheted up another notch. What was going on? I was sick, sick, sick of all the secrecy and double-dealing.

'Bonjour,' I started and then my French deserted me. 'Who are you?'

He put a finger to his lips, placed his machine in the briefcase and removed a small bluetooth speaker, putting it on the floor in the centre of the room. He took out his phone.

'Anarchy in the UK' blared out of the speaker.

I wondered if I was still asleep and dreaming as he sat down opposite me.

'I've checked the room thoroughly but you can never be sure.' He leaned forward as he spoke. 'This is a small police station in a quiet town, so we'll keep our fingers crossed.'

He was English through and through with the easy, cultured tones of someone who'd been to the best schools.

'And if I'm wrong, hopefully Johnny Rotten and co will prevent any of our friends from listening in.'

Underneath the smell of starch, a faint hint of cologne mingled with the antiseptic scent of mouthwash. I leaned forward to reply. I hoped I stank.

'Where is Rania?'

'She's quite safe.'

'Where is she?'

'Somewhere in this police station.'

'I want to see her.'

'You will.'

'And I want a lawyer. Lawyers for both of us.'

He sat back in the chair and gazed at me thoughtfully. 'You don't know what this is about, do you?'

I kept my face still as Johnny Rotten shouted that anarchy was the only way to be.

'We have met,' he went on, 'but I think you've forgotten. You were angry then too, as I recall. Stormed off.' His voice was amused but his face was deadly serious.

And I remembered.

'You're the man who –'

He cut me off with a sharp scissoring of his hands echoing the strident chords of Steve Jones' guitar.

I'd got him now. And I wasn't surprised it had taken me so long to remember. I'd only seen him twice. Both times for a few seconds. In Alájar. He was Nick's boss who'd turned up at his home on that last day. Out of the blue. And taken Nick away with him.

He saw that I'd remembered. 'We have a mutual friend, yes. And neither of us is going to say their name. Not here. Not ever. You understand?'

The table's wooden top felt rough and splintery on my fingertips. It reminded me of the loose and tricky surface of the sandstone last night. I needed to be very careful.

I nodded to show I understood not to mention Nick.

'Why are you here?' I asked.

The Sex Pistols came to a halt and the room filled with silence. He waited until the music started again. It was 'Anarchy in the UK' once more. He must have it on loop.

'Why am I here?' he repeated my words. 'Good question, Ms Shaw. Let me answer it. I'm here because our mutual friend broke all protocol to tell me to get you out of the situation. To rescue you, if you like.'

Nick was behind all this?

'No contact,' he went on. 'Those were the rules for this operation. No contact until they reached the UK and we could establish a safe channel. But our friend broke every rule and called me on an open phone. Yours, I think?'

He moved his head even closer to mine as he spoke. His tone was light, as though he were discussing a minor breach of a business plan, but underneath I heard the restlessness and strain.

'Where's Rania?' I asked again.

His eyes narrowed.

'Later. You should be thanking me by the way. We're going to help you.'

'Thank you.'

'And I'm hoping,' he continued, 'I'm hoping you may be able to help us a little.'

Here it was. The sting in the tail. The hand reached out to help that turned out to be too greasy to grip.

'I want to see Rania.'

He went to the door and exchanged a few words with the gendarme outside.

'Look out of the window.'

I peeled the vinyl right off a small pane and watched. After a few minutes Rania came out into the courtyard. The woman with her pointed up at the window and she looked at me and waved. Good. I took a few minutes to think before I sat down again.

I was in trouble. Caught with an illegal and underage migrant. Rania and Aya would be sent back to Libya and some sort of court case lay ahead for me. I suspected Nick's boss could get me out of a lot of shit.

'What do you want?' It came out quietly and I wasn't sure he'd heard over the music.

'How did the smugglers know you were coming to Cap Gris-Nez.'

I hadn't expected that. Did it matter?

'Why?'

'Someone knows something they shouldn't. That's a disaster for me. I need to work out what else they know. And fast. So let's start talking.'

His voice was quiet too and I struggled to catch his words.

'You want to talk here? With this noise going on?'

The track had finished and restarted again.

'Does it bother you? I hardly notice it now.'

'Could we go somewhere else?'

Out of the police station, I thought. Me and Rania.

'No time,' he said. 'I need the information now; besides it will take a while to get you out. The French were curious. Looked you up. The Maltese police will be next in line to interview you.'

Shit.

'But you will sort that out.' I waited. 'Won't you.'

It was not a question.

'And make the Malta thing go away. For me and my mother. And get Rania and Aya whatever they need to get into the UK.'

Something told me he could.

'Of course.' His voice was impatient. 'It will take a few hours, maybe a day or so. Now, please, I'm not going to lie to you – the information you have is vital. But I need it quickly, while the boat is still out in the channel.'

I let Johnny Rotten sing a whole verse of 'Anarchy in the UK' as I tried to decide what to do. Once I told him everything, I'd lose my leverage and I wasn't sure I could trust him. Nick did, though. And I realised I did trust Nick.

'OK,' I said.

'Who knew you were on your way to Calais?'

'I think Mohammed could have guessed I'd come after Rania –'

'There was no guessing involved. He was informed you were on the way. Someone told him. So again – who knew what you were doing?'

'No one except my mother and –'

'And who?'

Peter.

Shit.

Peter who gave English lessons to refugees. Peter with links to Musaeada. Peter who'd known how to arrange a covert passage to Italy. Peter with a handy friend on Italy he could borrow a boat from. But even if he were involved with the smugglers, I couldn't quite believe he'd have betrayed me.

'What is it?' Nick's boss saw the confusion pass over my face.

'Peter,' I said. 'Someone she's travelling with. He would know too.'

He listened as I poured out all the coincidences.

'But it might not mean anything,' I said. 'I mean… He's very keen on my mother. I think he just wanted to help.'

He removed an envelope of photos from his briefcase and dealt them like cards on the table. Rapid snaps of people in different places. Taken without their knowledge and with a long lens.

Amalia looked up at me with her uncompromising stare and Shona smiled. Paulina was pictured as well as Mohammed and there were other people I didn't recognise but I understood.

'They're all people associated with Musaeada?'

'Yes. Which one is your mother's friend?'

I picked up Peter's photo. It showed him walking out of the office with a smile on his face, amused by something his companion was saying.

'Might your mother have told this Peter about –?'

The track came to an end and we waited for it to restart.

I knew what he was asking. Might Ma have told Peter about Nick?

Not deliberately. But she would have had to explain why the refugees had snatched Rania and why I was chasing after them like a mad thing. Could she have done it without mentioning Nick?

I wasn't sure. Which meant Nick could be in great danger. The people-traffickers would get rid of him if they suspected he was an undercover policeman.

The opening riff of 'Anarchy' thrashed out again. Johnny Rotten yelled 'Right… now' and laughed.

'Might your mother have said something to this man about our friend?' His voice had a sharp edge.

I answered immediately. There was no point thinking any longer.

'It's possible.'

He left the room without speaking.

For a long time it was just me and the Sex Pistols until I turned the little speaker off.

Between us, there was every chance Ma and I had betrayed Nick. That we'd cracked the thin shell of lies keeping him safe. Shit. He'd been right to keep me out of his life.

I got up and paced round the room, stopping only to peer out of the window. Nick's boss appeared in the courtyard. On the phone. He too paced as he talked. He must be organising a rescue for Nick. Bringing him in from the field.

Unless it was too late.

Memories of the second body the smugglers had dumped in the water plagued me. I was sure the first was Marwa's and I'd thought the other might be Yasmiin or maybe the people trafficker Marwa had attacked. But now I thought it might be Nick. A last volley of shots had rung out when he and Leila rejoined everybody. Had they shot Nick? Had word come through from Peter that someone undercover was travelling with the refugees? Maybe they'd found Mohammed's body. Anyone looking over the cliff could have seen it. If they'd known about Nick, they'd have assumed it was him and that he was too dangerous to leave alive.

There was nothing in the room to distract me from the image

of Nick's body rolling in the tide, the water loosening the black curls of his hair until it floated like fine seaweed round his head.

I wondered where Ma was. Last time I'd heard from her she'd been heading into the Italian Alps but that was nearly twenty-four hours ago. Even if she, Peter and Aya had stopped somewhere to sleep, they should be close.

Thinking of Peter took me straight back to Nick. If he was alive, I'd go to Alájar, sit in Angel's bar and wait for him to come back. I didn't care how long it took. I'd tell him I was sorry and I'd tell him how right he'd been not to trust me.

Once this was all over... If it was ever all over... If it ended well.

A long time later Nick's boss came back.

'Is he safe?' I hissed as soon as he'd put the music back on. 'Our friend,' I added so there was no mistake.

'I hope so. We'll find out as soon as they land. We're tracking them now.'

I wiped my sweating palms on the sleeves of my top. They were filthy when I laid them back on the table but I didn't care.

'And now,' he said, 'I need to know everything. Everything you've done and seen since you went to Malta. Every little detail. The people you met. Everything they said and did. And everything that's happened since.'

'Everything?'

Tiredness blanked my thoughts and we sat and stared at each other for a while. I thought I should probably tell him the end first. About who Marwa really was. So he knew this wasn't all about terrorists and threats to national security but it was too complicated so I told him everything from the beginning. From arriving in Malta to ending up here: meeting the refugees, the clinic fire, the mad night in the boat heading for Italy and chasing everybody to Cap Gris-Nez. I told him the bare facts, skirting around Nick warning me about the danger Ma was in at Mdina and his plan to rescue Rania. Those details weren't important and I suspected his actions had broken even more rules.

His boss made notes on a small laptop while I spoke and from time to time I tried to tell him to wait until he'd heard the whole story but he waved me on. He only stopped when I came to Mohammed's death and the strange conversation with Marwa on the cliffs with the night gradually cloaking us in darkness. He closed his laptop then and walked around the room as I related what I'd seen and what Rania had told me had happened on the beach.

'And then,' I said, 'we climbed up the cliff and walked to the car park where the gendarmes picked us up.'

He carried on pacing round.

'And that's all,' I said and rested my head on my arms.

He turned the Sex Pistols off, went to the door and ordered coffee and food and some wet wipes and while I ate and drank we sat in total silence. I knew I'd never be able to listen to the song again.

And then he turned it back on and made me repeat the whole story again.

Every now and then he'd interrupt with a question or to make me go back over part of it. He only made me stop once and that was when I told him once more how Marwa had attacked the child trafficker. Then he got up and walked around again before telling me to continue. From then on, I thought he'd accepted Marwa's story although he never revealed a whisper of emotion so I couldn't tell if he was disappointed or horrified or relieved. He seemed slightly distracted but I guessed this meant he was no longer listening to me with all of his brain. Some part of it was already planning what to do.

As soon as I'd finished, he went out again, without a word, and this time he didn't appear in the courtyard.

I left the Sex Pistols on. The noise filled the emptiness. I sang along a few times, enjoying the way the words, now imprinted into my memory, rolled off my tongue, and then he came back.

'What happens now?' I asked when he sat down.

'The boat has landed,' he said. 'We've picked them all up. The operation is finished. It's been shut down.'

Waves of relief washed through me, although one thing stung.

'What about the child traffickers?'

'They're a French problem. We'll check your story and pass the information on. It's up to them afterwards.'

The tightly wound urgency at his heart had relaxed. His voice was less clipped and even the creases of his shirt had softened. Faint stirrings of anger tugged at my thoughts. There was something very wrong about his calm lack of interest in the child traffickers.

'How much of your story does our friend know?' he asked.

I shrugged. I had no idea what Nick knew. When I left him, he still thought Marwa was an IS agent. Her attack on the child trafficker must have been a shock.

His phone vibrated once. He glanced at it briefly.

'Let me tell you what I've organised for you.'

'OK.'

'Officials are scurrying through Whitehall as we speak. The international arrest warrant will be rescinded in the next few hours although I'd recommend you spend a day or so in France before trying to cross any borders. The information at the frontiers can be tediously out of date. In any case you'll need to go to the British Embassy in Paris before you travel. I'll have a name for you shortly. They'll give you some sort of paperwork for Rania and her sister.'

He paused.

'Where will you go then?'

Good question, but, strangely enough, the answer came to me straightaway.

'Cornwall,' I said. 'My old family home.'

I wanted to go home. And I wanted Ma to come too. And the girls. Tregonna was quiet and out of the way. And I thought a time of peaceful and dull routine might be exactly what Aya, traumatised by things she should never have even seen, let alone experienced, and Rania, grieving for her mother and her old life, needed.

In the short term anyway.

Afterwards we'd see. I wanted Rania to have some choice.

'Not back to Alájar.'

Maybe. But I wasn't going to tell him.

He cast a quick look at his phone.

'You know.' He gave me a smile that didn't warm his face. 'Our friend – he didn't want to go on this trip. He refused when it first came up.'

He ran his fingers round the corners of his briefcase like someone checking a stack of papers was perfectly aligned.

I knew this. Nick had told me he'd said no when they'd dragged him to London. But why was his boss telling me?

'We tried to persuade him. I made him have another psychiatric evaluation – living a lie for long periods – well, I'm sure you can imagine. But he came through all clear. And then he told me he was resigning. That he needed a change.'

My breath felt curiously light, as though it were passing through my body and leaving nothing behind. I kept my face still. I hadn't known this and I desperately wanted to be alone to think about what it might mean. He glanced at his phone again and I wondered if this story was his way of filling in the time as we waited for word Nick was safe.

'But you tried again. You came to see him.' The words came out of my mouth before I could stop them.

'Unfortunately,' he said, 'it became clear that the operation was a non-starter without our friend's participation. We risked losing the opportunity to infiltrate the heart of a terrorist group in the

UK.' He paused and shook his head. 'Or so we thought. So I came over. Unannounced. To have one more go at persuading him. And I met you.'

He tapped the table and gave me a smile that sat uneasily on his mouth. 'Our friend knew as soon as he saw me why I'd come. He was furious.'

But you persuaded him, I thought.

Five minutes, I remembered. That was how long Nick had had to tell me he was going away. Five hours wouldn't have been long enough given the things he wasn't allowed to say. Given the uncertainty between us. Given how unsure I was.

His phone rang. He listened and said a few quiet words then finished the call, placing the phone carefully on the table, adjusting it until perfectly aligned with the corner.

'They're sending photos. I need you to identify the refugees our friend was travelling with.'

'But –'

'It won't take long.'

He opened his laptop again and tapped for a few minutes then turned the screen so we could both see. The photos were head and shoulder shots, taken against a dirty green wall. Tired and blank faces stared back at me, all wet and cold despite the silver blankets wrapped around their shoulders. As he zoomed in on each one, emotions appeared. Most were frightened but here and there were faces where hints of anger showed. Or despair. At first they were all strangers. So many unknown faces. How had they all fitted on the boat? The first refugee I recognised was Yousef.

Nick's boss made a note.

The others followed in quick succession. Zubaida and her children, then Khaled and Sarah, without her glasses but still with a wary look. I'd misjudged her, I thought. Seeing deceit beneath the wariness. Seeing things that weren't there.

I sped through the final pictures. They were all men. No sign of Marwa. But that wasn't a surprise. I was sure she'd died on the beach. But, also, no sign of Yasmiin. That was hard to take.

'They're not there,' I said, after he'd made me go through them all again. 'Nor is Mohammed's daughter, Leila. At least, I don't think so. I don't know her as well as the others. Why can't you ask N…'

'Our friend?'

'Our friend. Sorry.'

He ignored my question and pulled the Musaeada photos out again, rifling through them until he found the one he wanted.

'Here's the daughter,' he said. 'And you're right, she wasn't on the boat. She must have stayed in France. Maybe looking for her father.'

I picked the photo up. It showed Mohammed with a young woman standing next to him. She was a total stranger. Not Leila. Or, at least, not the woman I'd met on the boat.

I opened my mouth to tell him and then shut it. Whoever she was, she'd saved Rania's life and she deserved something for that.

'You can leave very soon,' he said. 'The French police will drop you wherever you want.'

'And Rania?'

'Of course.'

He pulled a pad of paper out of his briefcase and scribbled a number down.

'Call this. It's the embassy in Paris. They'll fix an appointment for you to come in and pick up Rania and Aya's papers.' And as an afterthought. 'Do you need anything? Money? Somewhere to stay?'

'No. Just drop us back at my car.'

He pulled my phone out of the pocket on the side of his briefcase.

'Our friend left it for you. By your car.'

And to mark it out for you and the police, I thought. Nevertheless Nick had called him. Even though it was forbidden. Nick had asked him to save us.

I picked the phone up and looked into my message folder. Empty! As was the call log.

'We've deleted a few things,' he said.

He tapped the table. 'A few words first, if I may?'

He framed it as a question but we both knew I had no choice.

'You know a great deal more about this affair than you should and you must share it with no one. Not even your mother. No matter what happens. You understand? No matter what.'

I muttered a quick 'yes', impatient to get this over and done with, but he hadn't finished.

'Your reckless behaviour has endangered our friend's life and potentially wrecked a crucial operation. You could have been the cause of many deaths and injuries from terrorist activity in the UK and wasted a huge amount of the money and time invested in protecting the country.'

He stopped and waited for my reply.

I longed to point out that his terrorist operation was a total fiction. That he and his colleagues were a bunch of witless idiots infected by blind paranoia. That they were the ones who'd wasted everybody's time and money. But I didn't. I just wanted to get out.

'I get it,' I said.

He turned the music off and packed everything away, then inspected the room. A reflex action, I thought. To check he'd left no trace of himself behind.

'How long,' I said quickly. 'How long before Nick goes home?'

A crack of anger passed over his face. Because I'd said Nick's name? And spoken into the silence? Probably.

'I couldn't tell you,' he said shortly. 'He wasn't on the boat.'

'You said he was.'

'I don't recall *saying* anything about him. But if he is still alive, more than anything he needs you and your mother to keep your mouths shut.'

And with that he turned and went.

Thirty

Rania's face was puckered with tiredness when the police brought her to join me in the back of the car. Someone had washed her clothes and she looked thinner than ever with knees poking through her torn jeans as sharp and ridged as two camellia buds breaking through the shrub's dark green foliage.

'It's over,' I said to her as the car moved off and we could talk under the engine noise. 'You're safe. No one's going to take you away again.'

The hard stare of the gendarme in the mirror reminded me to be careful nevertheless. I lowered my head onto hers and spoke into her hair. She still smelled faintly of mud and sea and a hint of sweat. I didn't like to think how I smelled and looked.

'We're going to my car and then we're going to find my mother and your sister. We can talk about everything then but for now you just need to know that everything is fine.'

My phone rang.

The screen told me it was Peter and I hesitated. The thought of talking to him now I suspected he'd betrayed me was sickening.

Nick might be dead because of him.

For a few moments, I saw nothing except Nick's body rolling in the sea, curiously relaxed and empty, as though deeply asleep. I'd never seen him asleep. The one night we'd spent together, he'd woken first.

I'd have liked to see him asleep.

I drove the thoughts out of my mind. For now, I needed to focus on Rania and Ma and Aya and the final stages of getting us all home. Wherever that was.

I let the call go to voicemail and when the police dropped us by my car I told Rania to get in, then listened to the message.

It had been left by Ma – not Peter.

A Ma I'd never heard before. Something had unanchored her voice and it quavered and jerked as though tossed on the storm we'd sailed through two nights ago.

Where are you, Jenifry? Why don't you answer? Please call me. Something terrible has – She broke off as a voice addressed her in French, and she stuttered a few *Oui*s and *Non*s in reply. The wail of a siren drowned some of it out and then the message stopped.

I called her straight back.

'Ma. What's wrong?'

'Jenifry. It's you. Thank God.'

'What's happened? Where are you?'

Her breath, unsteady and rasping, broke her words into shards. 'An accident. A car ran him over. Peter. At the hotel.'

'Where are you?'

'I'm in a police car. They're taking me to the hospital. They've taken Peter already. Jenifry, I think he's dead. The paramedics didn't say anything but their faces told me.'

'Where, Ma? What town?'

'Amiens.'

'Amiens.'

Where was Amiens?

'I'll be with you as soon as I can, Ma. The hospital in Amiens. Just hold on until then.'

According to my phone, Amiens was an hour and a half away. I forced myself to concentrate and explained to Rania where we were going.

'There's been an accident. Aya's fine. But someone she and Ma were travelling with is injured.'

Dead. Ma thought Peter was dead. A shudder of new ideas rippled through my brain. It was convenient for me, no doubt about it, but it was also very, very convenient for Nick and, of course, for his boss.

I felt sick.

As soon as I'd told him Peter might be the source of the smugglers' information, Nick's boss had left the room. I'd seen him walking around in the courtyard outside, on the phone, and assumed he was organising Nick's extraction. But at that point he'd still believed he was tracking a terrorist and I wondered if he'd got rid of Peter rather than close his precious operation down. No wonder he'd told me to keep quiet no matter what happened. He must have known I'd suspect he was behind Peter's death.

We found Ma and Aya sitting side by side in a double-height reception area, amidst a sea of people with minor injuries. Ma had her eyes closed and her arms wrapped round Aya but the little girl looked around. She saw us and pushed herself out of Ma's arms as Rania ran towards her. The two of them hugged each other tight.

Ma and I clung to each other too.

'I promised Aya we'd find Rania,' she said. 'I'm so glad I haven't failed.'

'How has she been?'

'She slept a great deal. And I let her. I know it's a defence, a way of shutting the world out, but travelling wasn't the best time to deal with it.'

'Peter?' I asked.

She shook her head. He was dead. They'd broken it to her shortly after she reached the hospital. She told me what had happened. They'd been exhausted and stopped at a motel to grab a few hours of sleep. In the morning, Peter had gone on ahead to the car with his luggage. When Ma had come out, he was lying on the ground by the boot – clearly knocked over by a car that had long gone.

'Let's get out of here,' she said. 'Before they start wondering about us and the girls.'

Some of the pallor had receded from her face since I'd arrived.

'We'll go to a hotel,' I said. 'Wash, eat, sleep. Then decide what to do next.'

'Next?' she said as though the idea there might be a next seemed impossible.

'Yes. Next,' I said. 'Everything's sorted. We're free. The girls are free. I'll tell you the whole story later.'

She seized her hair with both hands and twisted it until it formed a tight ball at the back of her head and then, for want of anything to hold it in place, let it drop and slowly unwind.

'Shall we go to Tregonna?' she asked.

'Where else?' I said. 'But first, a hotel. I want a shower and clean clothes.'

Once we were ensconced in a suite at the nearest hotel (more battering of my credit card), and were washed and fed, Ma and I sat outside on the balcony, wrapped in snowy-white duvets while the girls, stupefied by hot baths and food, dozed. A few streets away Amiens cathedral rose above the nearby roofs.

I told her most of the story. About catching up with everybody at Cap Gris-Nez, meeting Nick, and Mohammed's death. When I recounted Marwa's story, Ma's face settled into stone and she pulled the duvet tight around her. I paused before I came to the part on the beach to see if she wanted to ask anything about Marwa. However, she shook her head and gestured to me to go on. As I reached the moment when I saw the torches of the smugglers ahead of me and heard the gunshots, Rania came out to join us.

'I woke up,' she said. 'And heard you.'

'Jenifry is telling me what happened. Get a duvet or a blanket and come and join us.'

After that Rania and I told the story between us until we reached the climb off the beach when I let Rania take over. Her voice lit up with the enthusiasm of success as she explained how we'd climbed and I wondered if she'd realised how desperate it had been.

'And then we got to the car park and the police arrested us. They took Jen away and I didn't know what was going to happen. That was very scary.' She pulled at a loose thread on her duvet. 'What is going to happen now?'

'A lot of that is up to you,' I said quickly before Ma could launch into a great spiel about the marvels of Tregonna and carry Rania along in a relentless tide of enthusiasm.

'Up to me?'

'We'd like you to come with us to Cornwall, to our home. And that's probably the best idea for now. It's quiet and beautiful and there's lots of space. I think you need time to recover before you decide what you want to do.'

I expected Ma to speak over me at any moment but she was strangely silent so I ploughed on.

'There's a lot to think about. Aya will need professional help. You'll be wanting to go to school. It may be that Cornwall isn't the right place for you.'

A look of worry crept into Rania's face. Shit. Had I gone too far with the independence thing?

'But I'll be with you every step of the way,' Ma said. 'And so will lots of other people. People who knew your mother from the time she spent in London. I think some of her old friends from Libya already live in Europe. We'll visit them and you can ask their advice too.'

She gave me a look halfway between a glare and a frown.

'Jenifry is right. We don't want you to do anything you're not happy with but –'

'We'll come to Cornwall,' Rania said. 'For now,' she added, then stood up, suddenly restless. 'Can I watch television?'

'Yes,' I said before Ma could object.

'I hope you meant that,' I said to Ma as soon as Rania had gone back into the room. 'About letting Rania have some say in her future.'

'Why are you saying this to me? When have I ever stopped you from doing what you wanted?'

To be fair, there was some truth in this.

'And what about all the psychiatric help Aya needs, and Rania probably too. Don't go thinking you can sort it out with crystals and herbs.'

'But –'

'Ma, I mean it.'

'Don't underestimate their power, Jenifry.' She sighed. 'But, of course, I'll make sure the girls get everything they need.' She thought for a moment. 'I expect Sofija will know the best place to start.'

I opened my mouth to speak and thought better of it. Sofija was my brother Kit's wife and Ma had clearly decided to forget all the awful things she'd said about her in the past. I wasn't going to remind her. The two of them would have to make their peace if Ma were going to return to Tregonna. And it looked very much as though she were.

Ma and I were both quiet now. Both staring out over Amiens. I didn't think either of us saw the exquisite façade of Amiens cathedral, though; instead our minds were absorbing what had happened.

'Marwa,' Ma said. 'Do you know what happened to her and Yasmiin?'

'I think they were killed. I saw the smugglers throwing bodies into the sea.'

'Poor, poor women.'

340

There was nothing to add to this.

'I knew you were facing a deep peril,' she said. 'A nexus in your life was upon you.'

'Nexus?'

'A point where the past and the present collide and throw up many paths you could choose to travel along.'

'Like being dead? That would hardly be a choice.'

'Death is always a potential path.'

This was Ma's mystical waffle at its finest.

'I kept on trying to get in touch with you,' she added.

I remembered my empty message and voicemail folders.

'Did you leave me lots of messages?'

'Yes.'

'Did you tell me where you were staying?'

'Of course. I thought, if you'd found Rania, you might come and join us.'

So Nick's boss, with my phone, would have known exactly where they were. The last of my doubts about what he'd done disappeared and the quiet ruthlessness of it sickened me. I wished Nick wasn't part of it. Or hadn't been…

We sat in silence again after that. Beneath the railings of our little balcony, overlooking the hotel entrance, taxis dropped guests off. People returned from tours of Amiens to get ready to sample the city's nightlife.

'What did you do with the boat?'

'We left it to drift,' she said. 'And went ashore in Peter's friend's inflatable.'

'I'm sorry about Peter, Ma.'

'So am I. I thought we might have had a future.' Grief darkened her voice.

I remembered her anger with me on the boat because I'd not told her everything. I was sick of lies and secrets and uncertainty. Sick,

sick, sick of them. I didn't know what had happened on the beach after Rania had fled. I wasn't sure if Marwa and Yasmiin were dead, whether Peter's death was an accident or who Leila really was. And, most importantly, I didn't know what had happened to Nick. Was he dead? Or only missing?

Ma deserved the truth. Besides, I wanted to know if she'd given Nick away.

'Maybe you and Peter had a future,' I said. 'But maybe not.'

'There's always a maybe not.'

'But this time it's a strong one. Someone betrayed me, Ma. Someone told the people smugglers I was on my way to the lighthouse at Cap Gris-Nez. Mohammed knew I was coming.'

'How?'

'Ma, you were the only person who knew. You and Peter.'

'Peter? You think he betrayed you? It's not possible. He would never have done that. I promise you. He would never –'

'Ma, you must have told him.'

'I did. But –'

'There you are.'

'No. There's no *there you are* about it. I told someone else. After you asked me what *menara* meant, I rang Amalia to check.'

Amalia. I couldn't bear to think of Amalia being involved.

'But she wasn't there. So I spoke to Shona.'

Of course she had. I suspected Ma and Shona had been bosom buddies on Malta.

'Shona told me *menara* could mean beacon. I asked her about *greenie* too. And I explained to her that Rania had been taken and *menara greenie* was the only clue we had to her whereabouts. I needed her to understand how important it was.'

So Shona had known as well as Peter and one of them had passed the information on. But which one?

'Besides,' she carried on, 'Shona was the person Peter asked to help organise our boat off the island. He knew she had contacts among people smugglers.'

Probably Shona, then.

'You think Shona is –'

'I don't know, Ma. It has to have been one of them.'

'Shona, then. Definitely Shona.'

I waited for her to say something about Shona's aura always seeming false.

'Amalia's too quick to trust people. Because she's desperate for help.'

She could be right. Not that it mattered unless…

'Ma. You've never breathed a word about Nick to anyone, have you? Not Peter nor Shona? Or suggested that one of the refugees might be something other than he seemed?'

'No,' she said.

I believed her.

'Nick asked me the same question,' she said. 'After the storm, while you were asleep on deck. I told him I'd banished all knowledge of his true self from my consciousness. That I'd forgotten Nick Crawford.'

The cathedral's grey stone sprang into colour as hidden lights came on, bringing the intricate masonry to life and making the sculpted figures seem ready to step out and greet us.

We stopped talking to look.

'I'm off to bed,' Ma said after a while.

The droop of her mouth hollowed the flesh under her cheekbones and there were craters round her eyes. She looked old and tired and full of grief.

'I'm not quite ready.'

She kissed the top of my head and left.

I stared out at the cathedral as the bright colours of its exterior blurred. Where was Nick? Was he alive? Or was he dead? If only

343

I knew. Tomorrow would be better. Tomorrow we'd have slept and we'd be a few more hours away from what had happened. Tomorrow we'd take the next steps to getting to Tregonna.

I already knew I wouldn't stay, though. I'd wait until I was sure the girls were going to be alright. Kit would help. I knew he would. And Sofija would too. The more I thought about it, the more I realised Ma was right. Sofija would know all the right people to see and the right things to do.

I'd thought I might go back to Alájar. My camping car was still at the farm in the hills that surrounded the village and I thought Angel wouldn't be surprised if he looked up from washing glasses one day and I walked in. But I couldn't. Tregonna and Alájar were too full of reminders of Nick. I didn't know if he was alive or dead and until I did I was as unanchored as the boat Ma had left to drift.

Epilogue

A beach in Northern France

The smugglers' torches on the beach glinted through the drizzle and spray long after the boat's pathetic engine had started to chug its passengers towards the English coast.

'What are they doing?' Leila's voice came out of the dark.

'Tidying up,' Nick said. 'Hopefully they won't be much longer.'

'Will you be able to swim all the way back?'

'We've barely made a few yards' progress,' he replied. 'It's going to be a long voyage for you.'

And a pointless one, he thought. He'd given Hendricks, his boss, enough information for them to track the boat. They'd be followed after they landed if not picked up straightaway. In fact, definitely picked up as soon as Hendricks knew there was no undercover IS agent travelling with them and no terrorism threat. He'd hardly believed it himself when Yasmiin and Leila had told him everything they knew as they squashed together on the boat. How could Hendriks and his cronies have got it so wrong?

When Marwa started shooting the smugglers and attacked the one who'd seized Rania, he'd known something was off. He'd raced after Leila as she chased the fleeing youngster, sick with fear about what she would do and too far behind to stop Leila's first shot. But when he reached them, Leila raised the gun, aimed it carefully and shot way above where Rania lay shaking. Then she shouted back that Rania was dead and pointed the gun at his chest.

He'd known since he met her on the boat she wasn't Mohammed's daughter, not unless she'd changed beyond all recognition. Plus he had a feeling he'd seen her face before. A video or a photo, he thought, but in a context so different he couldn't place it. But then, with her arms rigid as they aimed the gun at his chest and a strange look of rage and fear contorting her features, the memory returned, and with it, the understanding that she was the person Mohammed was escorting.

He said her name. Her gasp and look of panic confirmed he was right.

'I won't give you away,' he said urgently. 'But it would be better for you if you didn't shoot me. It would be hard to explain why you'd done it, and you, of all people, need to get on the boat, don't you?'

There'd been no time for anything else until they were rammed on board, him and Leila and Yasmiin, crunched into a tight group, sharing information under cover of the noise of the waves and the wind.

He understood then that getting on the boat had been a bad decision.

He was terrified for Jen and Rania. Terrified they wouldn't get off the beach before the tide overwhelmed them. Terrified they'd go up the path and be snatched by the traffickers.

'I think they've left.' Leila tapped his arm and broke him out of his thoughts. 'I haven't seen any torches for a while.'

She was right. He lifted his legs over the side and prepared to slip into the water.

'Listen,' he said quietly, aware that once again he was breaking every rule in the book. 'Try and get off the boat before it lands. It should be morning by the time you reach England. Leave as soon as you think you can swim ashore.'

He pushed himself off before she could ask him why and swam towards the beach. The incoming tide helped, although the breaking waves tossed him off course from time to time. When he finally reached land, most of it had disappeared beneath the sea. He scrambled onto a rock at the base of the path and looked towards the lighthouse. Rania should have run in its direction. It was the way he'd told Jen to come. He hoped they'd met.

He heard a faint shout that broke the air over the roar of the sea. It could have been his imagination but he thought it was Jen. The call seemed to come from halfway up the cliff. Who else could it be!

He hoped it was Jen because the beach between them was deep under water. He started up the path. He'd walk along the cliff and look over until he found her.

Despite his fear, his mind was easier than it had been for weeks. His time as Brahim was over. The operation was over. And the fiasco of its ending had clarified things for him. He wouldn't be going back to work. At least not undercover. He'd had enough of living a fabricated identity

Now he wanted only to find Jen and to be himself with her. Free to talk without checking every word before it left his mouth. Free to smile and laugh. And, above all, free to run with her next time she suggested it. He hoped she would. He hoped she'd suggest lots of things they could do. He might even go climbing with her.

He was halfway up when he realised his mistake.

There must have been two of them watching the path. One to challenge him with a gun and the other to cosh him. With a sandbag, he thought, as he slipped into unconsciousness, maybe filled with sand from the beach – and for some reason or other he found that funny.

Author's Note

Cut Adrift is a work of fiction, so the mirror it holds up to reality shows a distorted image and nothing I have written should be perceived as factual, whether it deals with the experiences of undercover agents, climbers, refugees or any of the other characters who people this thriller. Nevertheless, I have tried to be as accurate as possible. I am grateful to the many people who have shared their experiences with me and to the following books, which informed and influenced my writing process:

Alone on the Wall: Alex Honnold and the Ultimate Limits of Adventure by Alex Honnold and David Roberts

Undercover by Joe Carter

The Ungrateful Refugee: What Immigrants Never Tell You by Dina Nayeri

Dying to Live: Stories from Refugees on the Road to Freedom by Danielle Vella

The Displaced: Refugee Writers on Refugee Lives edited by Viet Thanh Nguyen.

Acknowledgements

Cut Adrift is the second book in the Jen Shaw series but it's the first book I've written with deadlines, so a huge thank you to Jenna Gordon, my editor at VERVE Books, for her insight as well as her never-ending patience and good humour as many of my deadlines slipped by unmet – and also for letting me make major changes at the point where we thought *Cut Adrift* was finally finished. *Cut Adrift* is a far better book than it would have been without her input.

Thank you to Sarah, Ellie, Hollie and Paru at VERVE Books, and also to the rest of the team. I love working with you, and I'm very proud to see my books rubbing shoulders with all the other fabulous titles you publish.

A special thank you to my beta readers, who play an absolutely vital role in helping me to step back and see what I've actually written rather than what I hope I have written: to my sister, Nikki, who reads my words before anyone else and always manages to be encouraging; to Fiona Erskine for her razor-sharp advice and for inspiring me with her *Chemical Detective* series; and to Lorraine Wilson, whose words of wisdom never fail to shine a light on my writing and whose books (*This Is Our Undoing* and *The Way The Light Bends*) are a joy to read.

I'd like to say a big thank you from the bottom of my heart to all the book bloggers and reviewers out there who devote so much time and enthusiasm to reading and sharing their thoughts with readers. Publicising a book is hard work, and their role is vital. Thank you so much!

Specifically for *Cut Adrift*, thank you to Mike for advice on how cars burn (I don't want to know where you got the knowledge from), to Beth and Henry for reading the climbing parts of the book and correcting them, to Marion for all sorts of advice on every conceivable subject and to Jacques Delbecke and Caroline Kinnen for coming up with Cap Gris-Nez. I am very lucky to have John Schofield as a writing friend. He writes beautiful lyrics and is also an expert sailor. His contribution, advice and suggestions for the sailing elements of *Cut Adrift* were invaluable. Any errors are, of course, entirely mine.

Thank you to my family, Nikki, Steve, Richard, Ruth, Andy, Tara, Rosina, Beth, Olly and Sue for always having my back and for the way you threw yourselves into supporting the launch of *On The Edge*. It means a lot to me. Love you all.

A special thank you to Tamara for sharing her experiences with me, and to Lucy for making me think again.

And, finally, thank you to Alex, my other half in every possible way.

A LETTER FROM JANE

Dear Reader,

Writing a book is a strange experience in many ways, but one of the oddest parts is the huge amount of time I spend thinking about a group of people I may never meet – you, the readers! I'm continually trying to second-guess your reaction. Will you solve this particular plot twist if I drop a hint in here? Have I made this passage clear? Will this make you smile?

So if you have a moment, let me know what you thought of *Cut Adrift*. You can message me via my Facebook page, Jane Jesmond Author, or via my website, www.Jane-Jesmond.com, where you can also sign up to receive my newsletter, which includes book recommendations, author interviews, competitions and special offers.

Thank you for choosing to read *Cut Adrift*. If you enjoyed it, please spread the word and, if you have time, leave a review or rating on Amazon, Goodreads or BookBub. It makes a huge difference.

If you'd like to read more of my novels, *A Quiet Contagion*, an unsettling historical mystery for modern times, will be published by VERVE Books in November 2023. And look out for the third book in the Jen Shaw series in 2024!

Best wishes and thank you,

Jane

vervebooks.co.uk/jane-jesmond

VERVE BOOKS

Launched in 2018, VERVE Books is an independent publisher of page-turning, diverse and original fiction from fresh and impactful voices.

Our books are connected by rich storytelling, vividly imagined settings and unforgettable characters. The list is tightly curated by a small team of passionate booklovers whose hope is that if you love one VERVE book, you'll love them all!

VERVE Books is a separate entity run in parallel with Oldcastle Books, whose imprints include the iconic, award-winning crime fiction list No Exit Press.

WANT TO JOIN THE CONVERSATION AND FIND OUT MORE ABOUT WHAT WE DO?

Catch us on social media or sign up to our newsletter for all the latest news from VERVE HQ.

vervebooks.co.uk/signup

📷 f 🐦 ♪ @VERVE_Books